BY CHARLIE HUSTON

Caught Stealing

Already Dead

No Dominion

The Shotgun Rule

Half the Blood of Brooklyn

Every Last Drop

The Mystic Arts of Erasing All
  Signs of Death

SIX BAD THINGS

SIX
BAD
THINGS

A NOVEL

CHARLIE HUSTON

BALLANTINE BOOKS

New York

A Ballantine Book
Published by The Random House Publishing Group

Copyright © 2005 by Charlie Huston

Published in the United States by Ballantine Books, an imprint of
The Random House Publishing Group, a division of Random
House, Inc., New York, and simultaneously in Canada by
Random House of Canada Limited, Toronto.

Ballantine and colophon are registered trademarks
of Random House, Inc.

www.ballantinebooks.com

Library of Congress Cataloging-in-Publication Data

Huston, Charlie.
Six bad things : a novel / Charlie Huston.—1st ed.
p.   cm.
ISBN 0-345-46479-6
1. Americans—Yucatán Peninsula—Fiction. 2. Russians—Yucatán Peninsula—
Fiction. 3. Yucatán Peninsula—Fiction. 4. Organized crime—Fiction. I. Title.
PS3608.U855S59 2005
813'.6—dc22   2004052778

Text design by JoAnne Metsch

Manufactured in the United States of America

8 9 7

mom and dad

PART ONE

DECEMBER 4–11, 2003

Four Regular Season

Games Remaining

'M SITTING on the porch of a bungalow on the Yucatán Peninsula with lit cigarettes sticking out of both my ears.

I like to go swimming in the mornings. When I first came to Mexico I liked to go drinking in the mornings, but after I got over that I took up swimming and I discovered something. I have unusually narrow ear canals. Go figure. I discovered this while I was trying to sober up, paddling around in the lukewarm morning waters, and found that my ears were clogged. I tilted my head from side to side and banged on my skull, trying to dislodge the water, but no luck. I plugged my nose, clamped my mouth shut, and blew until it felt like my brain might pop out of my ass. No good. I crammed Q-tips up my ears, prodding at the blockage. That's when things got really bad. For a few days I walked around half-deaf, feeling like my entire head was packed with waterlogged cotton. Then I went to a doctor. I have a habit of saving doctors for a last resort.

Dr. Sanchez looked in my ears and informed me of the tragic news: unusually narrow ear canals. The water was trapped deep inside and my irresponsible Q-tip use had sealed it in with earwax. He loaded a syringe the size of a beer can with warm mineral water and injected it into my ears until the pressure dislodged the massive clogs of wax and washed them into the small plastic basins I held just below my ears. He gave me drops. He told me never to stick anything in my ear other than my elbow, and laughed at his own joke. He nodded sagely and told me the solution to my problem was quite simple: When my ears became clogged, I must stick a cigarette into each one and light them. The cigarettes, that is. Then he handed me a pack of Benson &

Hedges, told me they were his preferred brand for the task, and charged me a thousand pesos.

So. I am sitting on the porch of a bungalow on the Yucatán Peninsula with lit cigarettes sticking out of both my ears. The cigarettes burn and create a vacuum in my ears, sucking the moisture into the filters. I have a towel draped over each shoulder to catch the hot ash as it falls. I've been doing this a couple days a week for years and it always works. Of course, I do now smoke two packs of Benson & Hedges a day, but there's a downside to everything in life.

The sun has dipped far in the sky behind my back and the reds of the sunset are reflected in the perfect blue sea before me. A soft breeze is caressing my skin and I adjust my sarong so that it can waft higher on my legs. The heat of the cigarettes has become intense. I reach up and pinch them out of my ears, careful not to squeeze so hard that the waxy fluid trapped in the filters leaks out. I dump them into an ashtray near my feet, slip the towels off my shoulders, stand up, and start walking toward the water. The beach is pretty much abandoned. A ways off to my right I can see a small group of local boys covered head to toe in sand, kicking a soccer ball around on their homemade field. In the opposite direction, the silhouette of a pair of lovers kissing. When my feet hit the wet strip of sand near the water's edge I give my sarong a tug. It falls to the ground, leaving me naked, and I walk down into the gently lapping waves. The beach slopes away so shallowly that I can walk upright in the water for almost fifty yards before it will cover my head. I walk in the water with the sun sinking behind me, hearing the soft slap of the tiny waves quite clearly in my unclogged ears. I'll probably have to do it all over again when I get out, twisting the cigarettes into my ears, lighting them, and waiting patiently while they burn down, but it will be worth it. I want to take one last swim today. I'm going home tomorrow and I don't know if I'll ever be able to come back here.

MACHINE GUNS wake me up in the morning, but they're just in my head. I have my backpack ready by the door, the waterproof money belt draped over it. I go to the bathroom and stand under the showerhead. The water is a gentle warm sprinkle, not the thing to snap you out of a nightmare. Still sleepy, I close my eyes. Pedro explodes past me backwards, his torso stitched open by a cloud of bullets. My eyes snap open. I walk out of the shower and drip water across the bungalow floor to the boom box. I search the CDs for something loud. Led Zeppelin? Something *fast* and loud. The Replacements. I put in *Pleased to Meet Me,* the opening chords of "I.O.U." blare out, and Paul Westerberg starts screaming. I turn it up.

I finish my shower; pull on a pair of cotton fatigue-style pants, grab keys, sunglasses, my papers, and a hefty wad of pesos. I check the money belt, make sure the extra passport and ID are where I can get to them easily, and strap it on. A tank top, short-sleeve linen shirt, a pair of trail sneakers, and I'm dressed. I grab the backpack and sling one strap over my shoulder.

—Come on, cat.

Bud leaps from the comfy chair, walks over to the kitchenette cabinet, and meows.

—Sorry, Buddy, no time. You can eat at Pedro's.

He meows again. I walk over, grab him by the nape of his neck, and put him on top of the pack.

—Fresh fish at Pedro's. Trust me, it'll be worth the wait.

I turn off the box, take a last look around. Did I forget anything? I mean, other than not to fuck up my life again? Nope, all taken care of. Back door bolted, storm shutters padlocked. Good enough. I walk onto the porch and set Bud and the pack down next to the door.

I'm pulling the tarp off the Willys when I see a white Bronco turn off the trail a quarter mile down the beach and come bouncing across the sand toward me. Could be they just have a few more questions, but I don't think cops roll up on you at dawn to ask questions.

I drop the tarp, wave, and point to the bungalow with a big smile on my face. One of the *Federales* in the Bronco waves back. I walk to the bungalow, grab Bud and the pack, step inside, lock the front door, go out the back, and dash across the sand into the jungle that is my backyard. All I have to do is get to Pedro's and I'll be OK. Unless the cops are there too.

THIS IS how things get fucked up again.

Once every three months you walk to the grocery next to the highway and use the pay phone to call a guy in New York. And this one time you call, and he tells you about a story everyone back there is telling.

—Say you're a guy and you're out taking a walk and you get thirsty and it's hot, so what you really want is a beer. Thing is, it's really hot, August hot in the City, with the garbage piled up and stinking, and the people with dogs that they don't pick up the shit after, so you don't want a beer from a deli, not even one of those sixteen ouncers from the bottom of the ice barrel the places put right out on the sidewalk. It's so hot and the street stinks so much from garbage and dog shit and piss, what you want is a cold beer in a cool dark room. So fuck the can from the ice barrel, you're going in this bar right here that you know it's a bar 'cause out front is a neon sign that says BAR.

You tell the guy you get the point and wonder if maybe he can get to the payoff. You hear the gurgling sound of a bong over the long-distance line. Then he starts talking again, in the unmistakable voice of someone trying to hold in a gargantuan lungful of smoke.

—So you go in and it's just what you hoped for, cool from the AC, dark 'cause the window is tinted. There's maybe something good on the juke like Coltrane, "My Favorite Things," but not too loud. And not crowded 'cause it's the middle of the day in the middle of the week; just the bartender and a couple regulars.

There's a huge whoosh over the phone as the guy lets the smoke out, but he doesn't cough. The guy you're talking to hasn't coughed on a hit since he was maybe twelve; he would consider it unprofessional at this point is his life. The thought of smoke knocks against something in your head and you dig in the pocket of your shorts for a cigarette.

—So you sit down and the bartender puts down the paper he's looking at and he comes over and he's never seen you and you've never seen him, but he gives you a little nod and you nod back 'cause you know you're each other's people 'cause he's working in a bar in the middle of the day and you're coming into one at the same time. You tell the guy, *Bottle of Bud,* toss a twenty on the bar, he opens the fridge, grabs your beer, pops the cap, sets it on the bar, takes your twenty off the bar, and walks to the register.

No cigarettes.

—Bartender comes back, drops seventeen bucks in front of you, which, three bucks ain't too bad for a bottle of Bud in New York these days, so you feel pretty good about that. You guys do the nod thing again and he goes back to his paper. You wrap your hand around that bottle and take your first sip. It's cooooooold. Bartender reads his paper, bar hounds over there, one is doing a crossword, one is just chain-smoking and making his Old Crow last. You drink your beer, listen to the music and you're having a pretty good day, figure you'll stick around that place and drink the rest of that twenty.

You know what he's talking about. You've had days like that.

—And that's when the door bangs open, some dingleberry comes in, orders a fucking margarita so now the bartender has to work and he sits down right next to you and starts with the fucking chatter. There goes your mellow, right out the window.

You think about the pack of smokes sitting on the little table on your porch at home. Down the phone lines, the bong rips again, and you know this story isn't getting any shorter.

—This dingleberry, he lives in the place, but you can tell by the way the bartender doesn't give him the nod and the way the boozehounds turn their stools away from him a little that they all wish he would fucking move out. Right now he can't believe his luck, a new fucking face in this place he can chew the ear off of. He starts right in with, *Hey my name's so and so and I do such and such and ain't it hotter than a bitch out there and this bartender he can't make a good margarita to save his life and here's the secret to a good margarita.* And the questions. *What's your name anyway? Ain't seen you here before, you from around here? You never been here before, you don't know about this place? Every-*

body knows about this place, how can you be from around here and not know about the old M Bar, the old Murder Bar?

You stop worrying about the cigarettes.

—Yeah, the dingleberry calls the place the Murder Bar. It's that place, you know the one. They had it closed for a couple years? Well, now it's open again. So he tells this story about the place, how it's not really named the Murder Bar or even the M Bar, that's just what people from the neighborhood, people in the know, call it 'cause they were living here when it happened. He tells you, *Feel around under the ledge of the bar, the wood there, you can feel the holes that are still there from when they shot the place up and killed all those people in here.* And he's right, the holes are there. They sanded them down so you don't get any splinters, but the holes are there, man.

You hear the guy on the phone take a quick drink of something and you know exactly what it is. You can almost smell it, the warm bite of Tullamore Dew.

—Now the dingleberry starts telling you about it, how a guy that used to work in this place, when it was the bar before this one, got in some kind of money trouble or something and came in the place one night to rob his own boss and he went haywire and ended up blowing away everybody in the place, like twenty people in cold blood. How it didn't end there and how you *must* have heard this story, how the guy went on a killing spree all over the city. God knows how many people he killed, including some cops. And then this psycho, this murder machine, this maddog, how he just plain disappeared. FBI put him on the Most Wanted list for awhile, but he got bumped for some bigger names, Middle Eastern names. Cops got bigger fish to fry in the City these days. So, the thing is, no big deal right? It's just a story and people tell stories all the time especially about the kind of shit that went down in that bar, regardless of how this dingleberry may have the facts all fucked up. This ain't the first and it won't be the last time you hear a version of this story. Except now, he gets all intimate with you, leans in close, 'cause he's got the *real skinny,* he says. Tells you, *This guy, who did all this killing, he didn't have money trouble, well he did, but the money trouble he had was how many people would he have to kill to get this big sack of cash that all these people were after.* Tells you, *There was this bag of cash and the killer was looking for it and some black street gang from the Bronx called the Cowboys and a whole precinct of dirty cops and the Tong, and the Russian Mafia and even this semipro professional wrestler called the Samoan Tower.*

You think about things. A gun going off in a Chinese kid's mouth. A big Samoan in the middle of a café, blood gushing out of his left temple. A cop on his back in the rain, waiting for you to finish him. The brothers who beat your woman to death, ripped open by your bullets.

—And the maddog is the one who came out on top, took all that money, like twenty million easy, and slipped off to someplace warm, *south of the border, Mexico way. Out of sight. But that kind of cash?* The guy says, *That kind of cash, that's like treasure and people want to hunt for it. And they do. Like* It's a Mad Mad Mad Mad World, *if Sam Peckinpah directed it. People go hunting for this maddog and his loot. All. The. Time.*

You think about being hunted. What that feels like. You think about going through it again, and curse yourself for forgetting the damn cigarettes.

—Anyway, that bit about the money and Mexico and the treasure hunters is a coda to this particular story that you have never heard before, which is why you are hearing this story right now from me.

And that is how things start to get fucked up again. That and the backpacker with the Russian accent.

THE BUCKET is right on the beach. It's a small place, a thatched palm roof over a bar, no walls. Stools don't work on the beach, so eight rope swings hang from the beams, and sets of white plastic tables and chairs are on the sand. There's no electricity. Pedro hauls bags of ice down here every morning on his tricycle and dumps them into corrugated tubs full of bottles of Sol and Negro Modelo. If you order a cocktail, you get the same ice the beer sits in. If you want to eat, Pedro has a barbeque he made by sawing a fifty-five-gallon drum in half. You can get ribs, chicken, a burger, or whatever the fishermen happen to bring around that day. Every now and then Pedro's wife will come down with her *comal*, make fresh tortillas, and we get tacos.

I'm at The Bucket around nine, after my morning swim. Pedro gets the coffeepot off the barbeque grill, pours me a cup and drops yesterday's *Miami Herald* in front of me. His wife gets the paper every day when she goes in town for the shopping or to pick up the kids from school. Pedro brings it to me here the next day. I glance at the sports page. Dolphins this, Dolphins that.

Pedro has chorizo on the grill and a frying pan heating up. He cracks a couple eggs into the pan, gets a plastic container of salsa from the cooler bag on his tricycle, and stirs some in, scrambling the eggs. He takes a key from his belt, unlocks the enameled steel cabinet beneath the bar, grabs the bottles of booze, and starts to set them out. I walk around to the grill, give the eggs a few more stirs, and dump them onto a plastic plate. The chorizos are blackened, fat spitting from the cracks in their skin. I spear them, stick them on the plate next to the eggs, and sit back down on my swing at the bar. Pedro brings me a folded towel and sets it next to the plate. I open it up and peel off one of the still warm tortillas his wife made at home this morning. I stuff a chorizo into the tortilla, pack some of the eggs around it, fold the thing up, take a bite, and sear the inside of my mouth just like I do every morning. It's worth it.

Pedro is about my age, thirty-five. He looks a little older because he's spent his whole life on the Yucatán. His face is a dark, sun-wrinkled plate. He's short and round, has a little pencil moustache, and wears heavy black plastic glasses like the ones American soldiers get for free.

He tops off my coffee.

—Go fish today?

I look out at the flat, crystal blue water. Up in town the tourists will be loading into the boats, heading for the reef to go diving or to the deep water to fish. The local fishermen here have already gone out and Pedro's boat is the only one still in, anchored to the shore by long yellow ropes tied to lengths of rebar driven into the sand. I could fish, take the boat out by myself or wait for Pedro's brother to show up and go out with him for an evening fish. If he doesn't have a job tonight.

—Not today.

—Nice day for fishing.

—Too nice. I might catch a fish. And then what? Have to bring it in, clean it, cook it.

No, no fishing today.

—Game on later?

—Every Sunday, Pedro. There's a game every Sunday except for the bye week.

—Who today?

—The Patriots.

—New England.

—Right.

—Fucking Pats.

—You're learning.

I MET Pedro up in town a few years back when I first came to Mexico. I came to Mexico hot. Running. I walked out of the Cancun airport, got into a cab, and told the guy I wanted to get out of Cancún, down the coast somewhere. Someplace smaller. He took me about an hour down the road to a little vacation town. Small hotels along a nice strip of beach. It was OK for awhile. The tourists were mostly mainland Mexicans, South Americans, or Europeans. Not many North Americans at all. Then they started building this giant resort community on the south end of town and that was it for me.

I found this spot: driving distance to town, a handful of locals with vacation *palapas,* some expatriates living in bungalows, some backpackers and day-trippers looking for a secluded beach. But no bar. Pedro was working in the place I spent most of my time in. I knew he wanted his own business and he knew I wanted a place to hang out. We made a deal.

I'm a silent partner. I pay my tab like any customer and nobody knows I backed Pedro to open the place. I gave him half the bar for moving here to run it; he's working off the other half. Shit, I could have given him the whole thing outright. I got the money. God knows I got the fucking money.

THE DAY-TRIPPERS are starting to drift onto the beach. They hear about it in town or read about it in *Lonely Planet* and come looking for unspoiled Mexico, but they're usually pretty damn happy they can get a cold beer and a cheeseburger. The expats will come around in the evening when they get back from fishing trips or working in town. The locals mostly show up on Friday and Saturday evening to drink. Me, I drink soda water all day, haven't had a real drink in over two years. It's the healthy life for me now. I take another sip of coffee, light the first cigarette of the day, and get back to the sports page.

The Dolphins have a problem. Their problem is a head coach who happens to be an idiot. I have a problem. My problem is the Miami fucking Dolphins of the National fucking Football League. When I got down here, I found out I couldn't give up sports. I tried to get into *fútbol,* but it just didn't click. A basketball season is like a basketball game, only the last two minutes count. And, unless I was ready to watch bullfights, that left football. Baseball? Yeah, I like baseball. I would have liked to have spent the last three years watching, listening to, and reading about baseball just like I did the thirty-two years before them, but that's one of the things I had to give up. I got into football because I always hated football and nobody looking for me is gonna look for a guy who likes football. It makes it harder for people to find me and kill me.

And you know what? After three years of watching football, I hate it more than ever. But I hate the Dolphins' idiot head coach more than anything else, because I am a sucker who has developed a bad habit of *caring* about the Dolphins.

Fuck me.

A classic warm-climate team, the Fins always start fast and collapse come the winter. All reason and all past history indicate that the Fins should be sliding. But they are not. Their new rookie running back, Miles Taylor, is shattering first-year records left and right and, despite his gutless teammates and inept coach, he has them winning consistently.

I am not deceived. In the AFC West, Oakland, San Diego, and Denver have been playing out of their heads and all look play-off bound. Miami will need to edge past the New York Jets if they want to get to the post season. Right now, despite the teams' identical 9–3 records, the Fins are in first because they beat NY in an early season matchup at Miami. But even if they keep that lead for the next three games, it will be at risk on the last day of the season when Miami travels to New York for the finale.

Even my limited experience has taught me that you can always depend on Miami to do one thing: lose on the road against a division rival in December. Bet on it. So I will enjoy the wins they have now and not count on getting any more. Maybe if they miss the play-offs their coach will finally be fired. One can hope.

By noon there's about twenty people spread along the half mile of beach and three more sitting at the bar with me. Pedro takes the radio from beneath the bar, clicks it on, and twirls the dial till the fuzzy sounds of WQAM Miami come through. He extends the antenna, alligator clips one end of a wire to it, clips the other end to the sheet of chicken wire that covers the palm roof. Suddenly the signal jumps in loud and clear.

I sit at the bar, sip seltzer and smoke, and listen to the game. Some pretty Spanish girls in bikinis stop at the bar to buy some beers. One of them smiles at me and I smile back. She asks me for one of my cigarettes and I slide her the pack. I watch as she and her friends walk off down the beach, and she glances back at me and smiles again. I wave. I like pretty girls.

The game drones on predictably. The Fins jump out early with three unanswered touchdowns, stand around while the Pats cut into their

lead just before the half, and then come out flat for the third quarter.
By the start of the fourth quarter, they're hanging on to a three-point
lead and the coach is calling plays as if they were still up by twenty-
one.

A shaggy backpacker wanders up the beach and over to the bar. He
shrugs out of his pack and takes a seat on the swing next to mine.
Pedro is poking at some ribs on the grill. The guy is sitting backwards
on the swing with his elbows on the bar, looking at the ocean. He
glances over his shoulder at the radio. The Pats have just pinned the
Fins on their own two-yard line. He looks at me and nods his head.
—Football.

Nothing odd about that, a perfectly reasonable observation. Except
that he says it in a Russian accent, which is not something we get a lot
of around here. Me, I take it in stride, just spit-take my seltzer all over
the bar. I'm smooth like that. The guy slaps me on the back while I
choke.
—OK?

I nod and wave my hand.
—Fine. Choke. Fine.

I point at the radio.
—Fucking Dolphins.

He shrugs.
—American football. Too slow.

The Fins try to run up the gut three times, get one yard, and punt
miserably to their own thirty-five. Pedro comes over and the guy orders
a shot of tequila and a Modelo.
—Hockey, very fast, good sport to watch. You like hockey?
—Not really.
—European football, soccer?
—Not really.
—But to play, yes? Americans like to play soccer, but not to watch.
—I guess.

The game comes back on. New England tries a play-action pass
down the sideline. It's complete. The receiver dodges the cornerback

and sprints for the goal line. I hang my head, ready for the inevitable New England game-winning touchdown. The Fins' strong safety hammers the receiver. The ball pops loose into his hands, and he's running upfield. I jump off my swing and pound my fist on the bar.

—Go, go, go, go!

As he runs the ball all the way back for a touchdown.

—Yeah!

The backpacker guy nods his head, smiles like he approves of the play, takes a sip of his beer.

—What about baseball? You like baseball?

JUST AFTER sunset I walk back up to the north end of the beach. I pass the group of Spanish girls. They have a little overnight camp set up about a hundred yards from my bungalow. They've slipped shorts or baggy cotton pants on over their bikini bottoms in deference to the marginally cooler evening air. Two of them are walking in from the tree line that stretches the length of the beach, their arms full of deadwood for a fire. The girl with the nice smile is sitting cross-legged on one of the blankets they have spread on the sand, braiding the hair of the girl in front of her. There are five of them, none can be more than twenty-three. I try to remember what I was doing when I was twenty-three. I was still in college, studying something I never used. Christ, why wasn't I camped out on Mexican beaches with girls like these?

I watch her quick hands weaving hair as I walk past. She looks up at me, smiles again.

—Buenas noches.

In that Spanish Spanish accent.

—Buenas noches.

She tilts her head toward my bungalow.

—Su casa?

—Mi casa.

—Bonito.

—Gracias.

Tossing the strands of hair between her fingers the whole time, slipping a rubber band from her wrist when she gets to the end of the braid, cleverly twisting it into place. The girls with the wood arrive and dump it in a pile next to the blanket. She hops up, starts digging a hollow in the sand for the fire and gives me a little nod as I continue on to the bungalow. Behind me I hear Spanish chattered far too quickly for me to follow. There's a great deal of laughter and I get the distinct feeling I'm being talked about. But it's nice to be talked about by pretty girls, no matter what they might be saying.

THE BUNGALOW really isn't much, but she's right, it's bonito in its way. Wood walls up to about waist level, topped by screen windows that circle the one-room building, with heavy storm shutters. The whole thing is set on pilings that lift it a foot above the sand, and topped with the same palm thatching as The Bucket. I step up on the porch, past the canvas-back chair, small wooden table and hammock, and dig the key from the Velcro side pocket of my shorts. In the normal course of things, if I was just a guy down here living on the beach, I wouldn't really need to lock my door. But I'm not that guy and I do need to lock my door. I have secrets to hide. I open the door and secret number one says hello.
—Meow.

I GOT into some trouble when I lived up in New York. I did a guy a favor and I got into some trouble for doing it. The favor he asked me to do that led to all the trouble, to me being on the run in Mexico, was he asked me to watch his cat. I said yes. And here I am three years later, still watching his cat.

BUD JUMPS down from the bed and limps over to say hi. One of his front legs was pretty badly broken in all that trouble. And some of the fur on his face grows in a weird little tuft because he has a scar from the same encounter that broke his leg. The guys that did the leg-breaking and the scarring are dead. Someone felt bad about that, not Bud. He rubs his face against my calf and I bend down, scoop him off the floor, and drape him over my shoulders.

—Jesus, cat, you're getting fat. You are a fat fucking cat and no two ways about it.

I walk to the low shelf that holds my boom box and CD collection. I rummage around until I come up with Gram Parsons's *Grievous Angel*. Gram and Emmylou's harmonies twang out of the speakers. I open one of the kitchenette cupboards, grab a can of Bud's food, scoop it into his bowl, and he leaps off my shoulders and digs in.

—Enjoy it while it lasts, cat. You're going on a diet.

It's pretty dark now, so I light a few candles. Like The Bucket, my place has no electricity, just batteries for the boom box, and candles and lanterns for light.

I take off my shirt and sit in my comfy chair. My face, arms, and legs are a deep, reddish brown from my years here, but my torso is white. Just like I don't follow baseball or talk about my cat, I don't take my shirt off in front of other people. They would kind of notice the livid scar that starts at my left hipbone, wraps around my side, and stops a couple inches from my spine. I took a bad beating up in New York and my kidney almost ruptured and had to come out. Later, some guys wanted some information from me and got the clever idea that I might be encouraged to tell them what it was if they started ripping out my staples. It was a really good idea because I would have told them anything, except that I didn't know anything. Yet. Anyway, I keep the scar covered around people because if I didn't, and anyone asked them if they knew anyone with a big kidney scar, they could happily say yes and I'd be a step closer to dead.

I leave the music on and walk down to the water. I usually do this naked, but I keep my shorts on tonight because of the girls right over there sitting around their fire. The water is perfect. It's always perfect. I wade out, lean back, let my legs drift up and my arms float out until I am bobbing on the surface of the Caribbean, looking up at the stars.

And for half a second I almost forget the Russian backpacker who set up his tent at the opposite end of the beach. The one who might be here looking for me and the four and a half million dollars that the New York Russian mafia thinks is theirs.

I have that money.

But it's mine.

I killed for it.

BACK THERE at the bar, he sat and waited, the baseball question floating between us while I took another sip of seltzer.

—No, never got into baseball much. Just the football really.

Pedro comes over with some ribs for me. The backpacker is mostly quiet while I listen to the Dolphins actually hold onto a fourth-quarter lead and win the game. Of course, the radio tells me that the Jets have just beaten Buffalo, so we're still locked in a death march to the last game of the season. But hope springs eternal after every win. And next week the Jets have to go to Green Bay, where come December the Packers treat opposing teams the way Napoleon got treated once the Russian winter hit him. Meanwhile, Miami gets to play 2–11 Detroit, at home. So you never know. God, I'm such a sucker.

I light a cigarette. The backpacker points at the pack.

—Benson Hedges.

—Want one?

—No. Don't smoke. You know, only Russian doesn't smoke in whole world.

—Huh.

—Father smoked Benson Hedges.

—Oh.

—Died, lung cancer.

—Yeah, it'll get ya.

—No smoking for me.

—Good call.

It's late afternoon. People are packing up on the beach after baking

all day. Pedro is sitting on the far side of the bar with his guitar, strumming almost silently, whispering a song to himself. No one else is at the bar. I take a paperback from the rear pocket of my shorts, bend it open till the spine cracks a little, and lay it flat on the bar in front of me. The backpacker turns around on his swing to face the ocean again, still sitting right next to me. I read the same sentence a few times. He cranes his neck and tries to see the title of the book printed at the top of the page I'm staring at. I hold up the book, show it to him. *East of Eden*.
—Good book?
—Yeah.

I flatten the book on the bar again and stare at the sentence, waiting.
—Vacation here?

I surrender, flip the book facedown, light another cig, and turn to face him.
—Nope, live here. That's my place up at the end of the beach. What about you, been on the road long? Doing the whole vagabondo thing or just on a quick vacation?

Which is how I end up spending the next hour chatting with Mikhail the Russian backpacker who really likes to be called Mickey.

He's in his early twenties and has a round face and the kind of patchy beard and scraggly hair that all backpackers aspire to. He tells me that his family is originally from Armenia, but was in Russia for five generations, how his father was an importer/exporter of some kind who moved the family to America in '95, which is where the Benson & Hedges caught up with him. He tells me about his four years in Jersey City and the four he spent at NYU in the film department and how he's been on vacation since last May, but he has to be back after New Year's to start graduate work in the second semester. And as he's sucking on his ninth or tenth tequila since he first sat down, I'm thinking that if he really is a Russian gangster hunting me, he has the best cover act ever. Then he leans closer to me, shaking his head.
—I say my father was importer and exporter of goods, but truth is different.

He does another shot of tequila and chases it with *sangrita*.

—Truth, he was "business" man.

He says it so I hear the quotation marks.

—Wanted me in "business" with him. Mother was actress, married him for money. Big fucking deal, you know. Everybody in Russia married for money if they could. Mother was so happy I wanted to be artist like her. Pissed father off, pissed him fucking off. But I go to film school. Make film about dancer marries gangster. He dies before he can see film. Fucking "business" man.

I nod my head.

—Businessman, huh?

He's crying now, big Russian tears.

—Big-shot "business" man.

He slips off the swing, almost hangs himself on the ropes. I steady him and get him standing. He wipes the tears from his eyes.

—Thanks you. Got to put up tent. Sleep.

He stumbles away from the bar.

Pedro comes over.

—Didn't pay his tab.

—Get him tomorrow, he's not going anywhere.

—Russians. Can't drink tequila.

—But don't get in a vodka-drinking contest with one.

"Business" man.

I chew on that for awhile, until Pedro's brother buzzes up in his dune buggy with Rolf. They take fuel cans and fishing gear out of the buggy and start hauling it all down to the waterline. I go over and lend a hand.

—Hola.

Rolf bumps fists with me.

—Que pasa, dude?

—Nothing.

He grabs one end of an ice chest, I grab the other and we lift it out of the buggy. Rolf is an American expat: a dreadlocked, nipple-pierced, surf bum vagabond from San Diego who washed up on the Yucatán about ten years ago. He mostly works up in town as a diving instructor for the tourists. He got into business with Pedro's brother because he likes the action.

They do actually run night-fishing excursions, but I can tell from the amount of fuel I'm now shouldering out to the boat that they won't be catching anything tonight. Pedro's brother, Leo, is up in the boat. He has the same flat face and short round body as his brother, but the roundness covers muscles made hard by hauling fishing nets. He easily one-hands the fifteen-gallon fuel can I've carried to the boat and tucks it away in the stern. Rolf splashes up, pushing a sealed plastic tub that bobs low in the water. I boost up onto the gunwale and help Leo pull it aboard. Through the translucent plastic I can see a GPS rig, a high-power halogen spotlight, battery cells, and the AK-47 they bring along for these trips. Leo nods his thanks as we clunk the tub down in the bottom of the long-hulled, open fishing boat. I jump back into the water and head for shore. Looking back at Leo, I give him a thumbs-up.

—Via con Dios.

—Always, man, always.

Then he's yanking the engine to life. I pass Rolf on his way to the boat with a six-pack, the last of the supplies. I bump fists with him again.

—How many?

—Just two. Supposed to be offshore in a raft. We'll see.

—Luck.

—Fuck that, dude. See you in the morning, you can buy me a beer.

—You got it.

At the bar Pedro and I watch the boat grind off into the surf.

American policy says that any Cuban who can reach U.S. soil legally or illegally will be granted residency, but they're sticklers on that "soil" part. Get stopped in the water a foot from dry land, and forget it. And since 9/11, those Coast Guard gauntlets around Florida have become a bit more intense. The average Cuban peasant will still get in his raft and cross his fingers. But if you have a couple bucks, you can get guys like Leo and Rolf to help you out. They'll shoot out to Cuba, pick you up, and bring you back to Mexico, from where, the thinking goes, it's a lot easier to get to America. And if you fail, it's still a hell of a lot nicer than Cuba. The money usually comes from a relative here or in the States, because, let's face it, nobody in Cuba has a pot to piss in, and if they do, they don't really need to leave.

Pedro watches until the boat disappears from view, shaking his head. Leo is his younger brother and Pedro worries about him. I could tell him they'll be fine, but that's no sure thing. It's around two hundred miles from here to Cuba, a long haul in open water for a boat like that. And they don't bring that AK along just for the sharks. Anyway, nothing I can do about it. I push away from the bar.

—Hasta mañana, Pedro.

—Hasta.

And I head off to take my swim.

I LIFT my arms out of the water in a slow backstroke, then roll myself over and start to swim in earnest. I swim long and hard, making sure to look up at the girls' fire on the beach from time to time so I don't end up bobbing halfway to Cozumel. When I'm good and tired, I swim in to shore. I can see that the girls are passing around a couple bottles of something and I think I can smell a little hash on the breeze.

Back at the bungalow, Gram Parsons is just starting in on "Hickory Wind." I peel off my shorts, drape them over the porch rail, grab the towel I left there, wipe most of the sand from my feet and lower legs. Inside, I pull on a pair of cutoff jeans. The music ends and I throw in some Bill Withers. I grab a bottle of water, my book and a lantern, and go back out on the porch. The smiling Spanish girl is standing there in the sand at the foot of the steps, holding an empty two-liter jug.

It takes a couple minutes to fill the jug from my water tank. Through the open door, I can see her reclining sideways in the hammock, her feet dangling over the edge. I should put on a shirt, I should put on a shirt before I go back out there. But I don't. I bring out the filled jug, set it at her feet on the porch, and sit down on the chair.

—Gracias.

—De nada.

She plays with the jug with her toes, tilting it this way and that, daring it to fall over. I pump up the lantern, light it, and turn it very low. The waves slap lightly and the lantern hisses. Her hair shines black. She's wearing shorts and has a small scarf tied around her chest. No tan lines on her shoulders. The jug falls over. I lean out of my chair and right it before more than a cup can glug out. She giggles, points at one of my many tattoos, the one on the inside of my left forearm. Six thick, black hash marks. She asks something I don't understand.

—No comprende.

She asks again.

—Sorry, my Spanish, not very good.

Turns out her English is great.

—American. We thought you were Costa Rican.

—No.

—Yes, because, the color is right. With the German blood, you know? And also your accent, your Spanish, is somewhat like that, and you do not act American.

—Thank God for that.

—Si, gracias a Dios.

She laughs.

—But we like Americans also, but here they are always so drunk.

—I don't drink.

Her toe grazes the jug.

—Except the water.

—I like the water.

—And you smoke.

—Do you want one?

—No.

She rocks in the hammock.

—Do you want to smoke with us? With me?

She takes a small baggie out of her pocket and shows it to me. I can see papers, a little chunk of hash, a tobacco pouch. I haven't been high in months, but it's not like the booze. There's no rule . . .

—Sure.

She smiles, and wobbles around in the hammock getting herself balanced cross-legged.

—Something flat?

I toss her my book. She looks at the title before putting it in her lap.

—Steinbeck. I read for school, *The Grapes of Wrath,* about American farm laborers and the Great Depression.

—Good book.

—I liked it.

She takes a rolling paper from the bag and sprinkles tobacco into it. I shift uncomfortably on my chair. Watching a pretty girl roll a smoke. Something inside me shakes its head.

—Before, I asked about the tattoo. The lines. What are they for?

The tobacco is spread evenly and she starts to grate hash over it, tiny flecks falling into the European-style joint. There are things I don't like to remember, things I mostly forget.

—They're things I don't want to forget.

—What things?

—Things I did. Bad things.

—You've done only six bad things in your life? You are very good, then.

—These were very bad.

She's rolling the joint between her fingers now, rolling it out smooth, tucking in the edge of the paper, pinching it with her thumbs. She runs her tongue across the glue strip, rolls her thumbs upward, spinning the whole thing into a tight, experienced joint, then pops the whole number in her mouth, covering its length with the thinnest film of her saliva. She holds it out to me, eyes sparkling.

—What kind of very bad things?

On cue, "Ain't No Sunshine" starts to play.

In New York, four years ago, a woman lays spread-eagle on a table, her body covered with bruises. Dead.

—You should go.

—Como?

—I really think you should leave now.

The edge in my voice. She still has her arm extended, the joint offered to me.

—Que pasa? Is there something?

—Go away. I want you to go away.

My body starting to tremble.

—You are sick? Can I?

—Get the fuck out of here. Get the fuck off my porch. Go back to your fucking friends.

Keeping my voice as steady and quiet as possible. Watching her flinch back from the first obscenity. Struggling out of the hammock, all her grace disappeared in the face of my abuse.

—Just get the fuck away from me.

Stumbling off the porch and running away, across the sand to the safety of the fire as I pick up the water jug and fling it into the darkness after her.

I kill the lamp, walk through the door over to the boom box, kick it to the floor, and the song ends. I go around the room, pulling the rods that drop the storm shutters, close and lock both doors. Bud is hiding under the bed.

—That's right, cat! Better fucking hide, know what's good for you. Fucking cat! Fucking cat! Nothing would have happened, nothing without you. You! Stupid! Fucking! Cat!

I'm screaming now. Bud is terrified. I tear the back door open and run. I run across the twenty yards of sand to the tree line where the jungle begins and then I run through the jungle, tripping and falling a dozen times before I huddle in the roots of a tree, shivering and sobbing, hugging the trunk.

Having been reminded of Yvonne who liked to roll her own cigarettes, and who is dead because of me. Having been reminded of the six men I've killed, two by accidents of a sort and four in cold blood. And crouched here all night long, wretched and sobbing, I never once feel sorry for myself. Because I'm a maddog killer and I deserve everything I get.

*   *   *

THE FRIEND'S name was Russ. He gave me the cat to watch and then he disappeared and then guys started showing up and hurting me and killing my friends because Russ had failed to let me in on a key piece of information. He had failed to tell me that there was a key hidden in the bottom of Bud's cage, a key that unlocked a storage unit that contained a bag that contained four-and-a-half million ill-gotten, whistle-clean dollars.

Still, things turned out a fuck of a lot better for me than for Russ. He ended up dead from having his head beat in with a baseball bat. That's a fact I know for certain. I know because I was on the other end of the bat when it happened. I didn't really mean to kill him. My reason was fogged at the time. A barroom full of my friends had just been machine-gunned to death. Anyway, he wasn't the last guy I ever killed.

Or the first.

IN THE morning I go back to the bungalow. I pick up the boom box and the spilled CDs and pop the shutters open. The Spanish girls' camp is gone and the area has the look of having been broken up quickly in the dark. Sorry, girls. So sorry.

This isn't easy. Living isn't easy. But the less I expose myself to life, the easier it is. The less chance there is that something might remind me of who I am. Boozing made it easier, but I don't want to booze anymore. Because it shouldn't be easy. With the things that happened, the things I did, life shouldn't be easy. So last night is a reminder: keep your life small, keep the people in your life few, and keep them in front of you. Because life isn't easy. And you can lose control of it in an instant.

Bud watches me from the bed until I come over and sit down next to him. Then he climbs into my lap, stretches, and rubs the top of his head against my chin.

—Sorry, Buddy. You're a good cat. Not your fault, I know that.

He jumps off the bed and walks over to the cabinet where his food is. I take the hint and get off my ass to feed him.

—Yeah, I know, apologies are like assholes, right? Want to make me feel better, feed me.

I leave him to eat and go into the little bathroom. It's just a tiled chamber with a showerhead at one end and a small commode at the other. A rain tank with a filter unit is on a small tower right outside. That takes care of my washing-water needs, and Leo brings me a few five-gallon jugs of drinking water every week.

Where I really luxuriated when I had this place built was the septic tank. That cost a pretty penny, as does getting it pumped. But, trust me, when you grow up with indoor plumbing, you are simply not prepared for the places most people in the world have to crap.

I wash up and find several cuts on my arms, legs, and feet from my run through the jungle. I sterilize those and take care of them with a few Band-Aids. Then I go for my morning swim, get my ears clogged so that I have to do the cigarette trick, put on shorts and a guayabera shirt, lock up, and walk over to The Bucket, where I find Mickey already sitting on my swing, drinking from my coffee cup, and reading my paper. And I start to remember very clearly just what it feels like when you really *want* to kill a man.

I MADE that call to Tim back in August. I'd been going out to the pay phone by the highway every three months to call him at home. He'd let me know what was up, if the cops were still poking around. And they poked. I mean, in the forty-eight hours I spent running around Manhattan getting chased, the death toll reached fourteen. At the time, it was a pretty impressive number. Then some really fucked-up people rammed a couple airplanes into these tall buildings in New York and I dropped off the radar.

So things had been quiet for awhile. That shit never seems to last. After Tim told me his story about people maybe looking for me in Mexico, we changed our MO. I started calling him every week at a pay phone in Grand Central.

And it didn't take long for Tim to start noticing some things.

—What do you mean, "things"?

—I don't know, man.

—Well that helps, Timmy.

—OK, so people, they like to talk to me, right? Always, on the bus, whatever, I'm the guy people sit next to and like to just start talking to. And, mostly, so, OK, I got ears, use 'em, right? But then, lately? I think I may have noticed something, a trend in the topics of conversation.

It's starting to rain on me; fat, warm drops.

—Timmy?

—Yeah?

—Can you please get to the point?

—Crime, seems like people, all the time, want to talk to *me* about *crime.*

The rain gets heavier and, all at once, is a deluge.

—Want to talk about, *Is it better now than it was before? Is the mayor doing all he can? Seems it was better when Rudy was around. With exceptions, of course. Shit happened even when big bad Rudy was sheriff around these parts.* And then, some guy might chime in, *Yeah, like remember that time?* And guess what time he means?

Water is pouring down my body. I might as well be in the ocean.

—And even one of the guys at work one day pops out with, *Hey, remember that guy went berserk, that guy you knew him? What the hell was that about?*

The dusty ground has already turned to mud.

—So what I'm telling you here is that I think I'm noticing some things. A trend in conversations wherein people, some I know and others I don't, are asking questions of *me* that frequently lead to *you.*

The rain stops and the sun comes out and hits my drenched body. And I tell Tim, fuck it, get your boss to give you a transfer and get the hell out of town. Now.

That's what he did, got his boss to move him to his western operation. I sent money to cover moving expenses and whatnot, because it pays to take care of the only man in America that knows where you are. And that's how Timmy ended up dealing grass in Las Vegas.

And I ended up being on edge every time I heard a Russian accent.

PEDRO SEES me walking up to The Bucket. I gesture at Mickey's back and Pedro shrugs his shoulders. I lean on the bar next to Mickey. He looks up from my paper, smiles. It's a pained smile, the smile of a man in the grips of a savage hangover.

—Good morning.

—Yeah. Look, no offense, man, but that's my cup.

—Cup?

—That cup you're drinking coffee from? I bought it in town, brought it all the way down here because I wanted a really big, heavy cup for my coffee.

He looks confused.

—I'm sorry, it was . . .

—And that's my paper.

—These things, they were, you know, on the bar.

—Yeah, Pedro does that for me, has my stuff waiting for me. Because I live here and I pay him extra for it to be that way.

Pedro has his back turned to us, rotating my chorizo and stirring my eggs. His shoulders are shaking as he tries to keep from laughing. Mickey starts to slide the paper and coffee cup over to me.

—No, Mickey, that's OK, just leave everything there.

Pedro is starting to lose it, little pops of laughter escaping from his mouth.

—You are sure? It is OK?

Puppy dog all over his face, he just wants to make me happy. Just to end the noise of my voice so his head will hurt a little bit less.

—Yeah, just leave it there.

He smiles, relaxes a little.

—Thank you. I am very embarrassed.

—Yeah, just leave it there, 'cause that's also my swing you're on and I'll want my things right there when you get up so I can sit down.

Pedro gives in. Guffaws. Mickey gets tangled in the ropes again and almost falls from the swing. I grab his arm and direct him onto the next swing over.

—I am sorry. I did not know this was for you. I sat and I thought . . .

I sit. Still laughing, Pedro brings my plate, the tortillas, and a cheap plastic cup for Mickey. I stick a chorizo into a tortilla.

—Hangover?

—What? Yes. Hangover.

—Pedro, bring the guy a Modelo.

I finish making the little burrito and hand it to him.

—Eat this and drink that beer. Trust me, I know what to do to a hangover.

HE KEEPS his mouth shut this time and I pass him sections of the paper as I finish them. He eats the food I give him and drinks the beer and then the coffee and then I tell him to drink water for a few hours and he'll be right as rain. He's grateful as hell. He's not really a bad guy, and it turns out he's leaving tomorrow anyway. He's planning to start heading north, but really wants to get over to Chichén Itzá before he moves on.

—And then I must go home.

—School?

—Christmas. My mother must have me home for Christmas.

Christmas. Right. It's December and Christmas is at the end of December. How did I forget that? But I know why I forgot it. Because I wanted to. I always used to go home for Christmas, too. And I don't like to remember what it was like. How nice it was.

Before I know it, I've volunteered to give him a lift to the ruins tomorrow.

He insists on paying for breakfast and I let him. Then he takes his water bottle and walks off to loll in the sand and sweat out the rest of the hangover. Pedro picks up my plate and wipes the bar.

—He was asking about you.

—What?

—Before you got here.

—What?

—How long have you lived here. Where do you come from. Do you work.

Little shit bastard.

—So?

—So?

—So what did you say?

He looks at me and snorts through his nose.

—Cabrón. I kept my mouth shut.

—Sorry, sorry, man.

—I don't talk about you with no pinche tourist.

—Mea culpa, Pedro, it's cool, I know you wouldn't say anything.

I stick out my hand and he takes it.

—Si, si, but you have to watch that shit. I never talk about you.

—Claro.

Shaking his head, he starts scraping the grill. He never scrapes the grill. I light a smoke. The only way I can make up for insulting him will be to stay up late into the night while he gets drunk and we sing songs together and repledge our friendship. No relationship, no number of psycho girlfriends, can prepare you for how easy it is to hurt the feelings of a Mexican man.

I'm worrying about how to make it up to him, along with the prospect of playing "Am I really a Russian gangster?" with Mickey on a three-hundred-mile drive, when the boat pops up on the horizon and Leo drives it right up on the beach so it will be easier to lift out the Cuban with the huge machete gash in his thigh.

IT'S NOT like Mexican immigration has to fight a pitched battle to keep illegals from flooding the country, but what Leo and Rolf are up to is against the law and it would be best to keep a low profile. Mickey is dozing on the sand down by his tent; other than that, no one is on the beach yet. Pedro drove the dune buggy home last night and brought it back this morning, but it's a rocky mile to his place and the Cuban has been bounced around plenty in the boat.

We have him on the bar. The other Cuban is holding tight to the tourniquet they made out of a belt and put at the top of his friend's thigh. The Cuban's foot is ice cold from lack of circulation. Fuck, his whole body is cold and clammy from shock.

—My place.

Pedro stays to get the bar ready for business, and Rolf takes care of the boat while I help Leo and the other Cuban carry the injured guy to my bungalow. Leo was one of the guys that I hired to build the place, but he hasn't been inside since. No one but Pedro has been inside.

Bud runs for cover when we bang through the door.

—The table.

We set him on the table.

—Leo, there's a first aid kit under the bed.

He goes for it. The other Cuban is still clutching the tourniquet, staring at his friend's face. I take hold of his fingers and pry them free. He looks at me. I nod my head.

—Tranquilo, tranquilo.

His eyes are bugging from his head.

—Toallas.

He shakes his head.

—Toallas. Baño.

I tilt my head toward the bathroom.

—Ahí. Muchas toallas. Si?

—Toallas, si.

He goes to the bathroom for the towels. Leo puts the big, green first aid kit on the table.

—How long you been in Mexico?

—Awhile.

—Your Spanish sucks.

—Fuck off, Leo. Hold this.

He takes the tourniquet from me while I open the kit, find some latex gloves and slip them on.

—OK.

I take the tourniquet back and start to loosen it.

—You might want to put on a pair of these. Last time I checked, AIDS was epidemic in the Caribbean.

—Puta madre.

He puts on the gloves. The other Cuban comes back with a stack of towels. I'm prying my fingers under the tourniquet where it's dug into the guy's skin. I pull it loose. Blood gushes onto my table. It's not spraying, so the artery's not severed. Then again, I'm working with a few classes I took about fifteen years ago for an EMT certificate I never got so what do I know? I cram a couple towels against the wound, take the other Cuban's hand, put it on the towels, and press down. He gets the idea and holds the towels in place. I pull off my blood-slicked gloves, roll on a clean pair. Leo is just standing there.

—Massage the guy's foot.

—Say what?

—Massage his foot.

—Por fucking qué?

—I don't know, maybe to get the circulation going so it doesn't die and have to be cut off.

He starts a stream of curses under his breath and rubs the foot. I find the suture set. With my free hand I get the bottle of antiseptic, bite the cap off, pour some on the needle, then hold the bottle over the wound. The other Cuban guy pulls the towel away and I pour antiseptic into the wound. The guy on the table moans a little and his leg jerks. I empty about half the bottle, then use one of the towels to wipe some of the blood away. The gash is long, shallow at the top, cutting deeper as it gets closer to the knee. The blood is just oozing now; that first flood, a reservoir that had been held back by the tourniquet.

—OK, Leo, kind of hold the flesh together here.

His curses pick up in volume, but he puts his fingers on either side of the wound and pinches the edges together. Is this right? There are probably capillaries and shit in there that need to be put back together. Should I leave the wound open for a real doctor?

—So are you going to sew this shit up or what, man?

I sew the shit up.

—Who did it?

—He did.

Leo has his head inclined toward the other Cuban, who is sitting next to the table now, looking pale and ill.

—Why?

—We got out there, man, and find these two cabrónes in a leaky raft with a couple bottles of rum, a sack of coconuts, and a machete. Fucking peons are hacking the tops off the coconuts and pouring in the rum. Drunk like American kids on spring break. *Wild On Cuba* in a sinking raft.

—That satellite TV is gonna ruin you.

—What the fuck, where do you think I learn the English? Maybe you should have watched MTV Latin before you came down here. Learn how to speak the language, man.

—So what happened, they get in a fight?

—We pull alongside and culo there stands up with a coconut and the machete so he can make us a cocktail.

—No.

—He swings at the coconut, misses and hits his buddy in the leg instead. Puta fucking madre. Blood everywhere. Screaming.

—Why didn't you leave them?

Leo looks at me, looks at my hands sewing the leg back together.

—Why are we in your house, man? Su casa is not mi casa, you know. So why are we here?

I tie off another little knot.

—We didn't leave them because the fucker's leg was almost cut off, they were drunk in a leaky raft, blood everywhere, and sharks in the water.

—Got it.

It takes awhile to stitch him up. Rolf shows up when we're about halfway done and comes in. My sanctum sanctorum: Grand fucking Central. I tell him where the plastic garbage bags are and he starts mopping up blood and bagging ruined towels. When I'm done I pour more antiseptic over the wound, gently wipe the leg clean, and feel the foot. It's warm. We pick him up and start to carry him to the bed.

—Do you need help?

I twist my head and see Mickey standing in the doorway that Rolf left wide open when he came in. Bud meows.

—A cat. I did not know you have a cat.

HE SHOWS up early the next morning. I'm already outside getting the Willys ready. Mickey pitches his pack in the back and we're ready to go. I roll us slowly down the beach, stop at The Bucket and tell Mickey to wait for me in the truck. Pedro has a sack for me with a couple water bottles and some tortas his wife made.

—You are taking him to the ruins?

—Yeah.

Pedro shakes his head.

—What?

—You have your secrets. I do not know nothing about them.

—So?

—So I do not know how is the best way to keep them.

—I'm just giving the guy a ride so he doesn't have to take the bus.

—The man who asks the questions, you are giving him a ride.

—Pedro.

—Not my business. I do not know shit.

And he's scraping the grill again.

—Pedro.

—Si.

Great, now I'm getting the Spanish treatment.

—I'll see you tonight.

—Si.

—Maybe we can sing some songs when I get back.

—Si, jefe.

I'm walking away when he shouts.

—The bar needs limes.

—Sure thing.

I get in the truck and pull onto the trail that cuts to the highway. I need to get Mickey out to the jungle. Bodies rot quickly in the jungle.

I TOLD Mickey we didn't need help and Rolf walked him back onto the porch and closed the door. We got the Cuban onto the bed. Leo and me cleaned up while the other Cuban sat with his friend. I lit a smoke.

—Now what?

—I'll go get the buggy and we'll get him the hell out of here.

I pop one of the shutters open. Rolf and Mickey are standing next to the porch, chatting. Ten or fifteen people are dotted over the beach now.

—He can stay till evening.

—Claro?

—Yeah, he needs to stay in one place for at least a couple hours anyway.

—Thanks, man.

—Where you gonna take him?

—Mi casa.

Leo lives in town, about an hour's drive.

—Their cousins are probably there waiting for us. I should drive up and chill them out.

—Call Doc Sanchez while you're there, get him to meet you when you bring this guy back. Fix that mess I made.

Leo points out the window at Mickey.

—Him?

—What about him?

—Is he cool?

—Good fucking question.

Leo grabs Rolf and they take the buggy. I sit on the porch steps with Mickey.

—These guys had some trouble and I'm trying to help them out. You understand?

—Of course.

—It's not the kind of thing that it would be good to talk about. Even when you get back home.

—Yes, I understand. With my father's "business," there were things I could not talk about.

—Right. Good.

I get up and walk to the door and peek back inside.

—But, sometimes, people would, you know, talk anyway. And I would hear things.

—Uh-huh.

Both Cubans are squeezed onto the bed, asleep.

—Stories.

—Yeah.

I should have told Leo to hit a *pharmacia* in town for some antibiotics.

—When we go to Chichén Itzá tomorrow?

—Yeah?

We should be getting them into him now.

—You should bring a million dollars with you.

I turn from the window.

—Otherwise, I will tell my father's "business" partners where you are with their money and your cat.

I look down. There are droplets of blood on my feet, sand stuck to them. I rub my feet together to grind them off.

—We'll have to go to Mérida, to the bank. My safety deposit boxes are there.

HE STILL wants to stop at Chichén Itzá to see the Mayan ruins. Guy's banking on a million at the end of the road and he wants to get some snapshots from the top of Kukulkan. Whatever.

I turn north onto Mexico 307 heading for 180 West, the toll road outside of Cancún. I stop at one of the Pemex stations on the highway and gas up. Mickey's not talking, still waking up. It'll take about an hour to get to Cancún, another two or three to Chichén Itzá.

We swoop onto the 180. There's hardly any traffic. I put the pedal down and open the Willys up a little to clean it out. It's a 1960 Utility Wagon. A previous owner chopped the roof off and installed a ragtop. I bought it when I moved to the beach; had Baja tires put on because the trail floods out at least a couple times every month. I don't really drive it much. I used to not drive, period. Not since the time in high school when I rammed my Mustang into a tree and killed my best friend. Rich. I used to have nightmares about Rich. But that was a long time ago. And I've killed more people since then.

Mickey's waking up and becoming his chatty self.

—This place, I love it, you know.

—Huh.

—The whole peninsula, jungle, all the way to the beaches. It is beautiful. I started in Mexico City, you know, and that was wonderful, but very much like Manhattan, but if it were always hot. And then, I went to Guadalajara and to Puerto Vallarta and around the coast to Acapulco and east to Oaxaca and then into Guatemala and Belize and then up to Quintana Roo and the jungle and the beaches and the Caribbean and it is the most beautiful thing that I have ever found, and also very lucky for me, I think, because that is where I found you.

He wants me to know it's nothing personal.

—And I did not come down here to look for you, you know. I wanted to see Mexico and get drunk on beaches and fuck women, but I had heard the stories.

—Tell me about the stories.

—Oh.

He starts to laugh.

—Oh, are they pissed at you. My father, when he was still alive and in "business," I can remember I was at school and came home to their house for a visit to see my mother. And my father, he was very angry. Stomping, slamming, cursing. And he said your name! And, you know, I had heard your name because this had just happened with all the people being killed and your picture was in the newspapers and on the TV and I was living in Manhattan for school and I was very scared of you. Really. Everyone I knew was scared. And then I go home, out of the city until the killing stops, and I go to my parents and my father is cursing your name. And many people were cursing you, but this was, he was cursing you like he would curse me when he got angry, like you did something to hurt him.

Great.

—But then, I did not know anything until later. When he was sick and his friends would come over to talk "business" at the house where my mother had put in the hospital bed and hired the nurse, and I would come home sometimes on the weekend to visit. But they were not really talking, you know, "business" with him. They drank vodka and told stories and tried to make him laugh, but all of them always ended up crying. But in a way that was good, you know?

The jungle presses right up against the two-lane blacktop. We've passed a tour bus and a couple trucks and an abandoned VW Bug. There will be two toll stops and one gas station between here and Chichén Itzá. After that, nothing until we join the regular road at Kantunil.

—Sometimes I would listen to the stories and always there was the one that they would tell. The story about you and how you killed so many of their men and stole their money and they would curse you and drink to your death and curse you some more. And they would then talk about where you had run to and what they would do when they found you. And, but, you know, they would almost always say something about you in Russian that would mean you were a sly, crafty, tough bastard and that they would have done what you had done if they could have, but that they would kill you anyway.

Every so often there are little dirt trails cutting off the main road and into the jungle. These lead to small rancheros that are, almost without exception, abandoned. People buy these little plots of land hoping to have a place in driving distance to the beach, but the jungle always kicks their ass. Turn your back on it and the jungle is at your back door. Any one of these little roads would do. I could say I needed to pull off and take a leak.

—So of course, you know, when I came to Mexico I knew your story and I had many times heard my father's friends talk about you and that they thought Mexico was a place you could be, and I had seen your picture and a picture of your cat from the TV. But I did not come here to look for you, but I also remembered to look a little, because it would be stupid not to. But not for them. I don't look for them, for my father's friends and their "business." I would not do that to you, tell them where you are so they can kill you, but I am not so stupid that I do not want something, you know, to not tell them. So the million dollars is a good deal for both of us because you will still have so much and it will be so much more than they would give me.

I spot one of the trails up ahead, slow the Willys, and start to pull off.

—What?

—I have to go.

—Me too.

I drive a hundred yards to a partial clearing. Sure enough, there's a cinderblock house, abandoned and being disassembled by the jungle. I shut off the engine, climb out, and undo my fly. But I don't have to go. I hear Mickey get out the other side. A groan as he stretches, a zip and then splashing. I button up, turn, and there's Mickey, his back to me, watering a tree. There's a piece of broken cinderblock right at my feet.

I get back behind the wheel. Mickey gets in next to me. I start the engine.

—Hang on.

I get back out, turn my back, and undo my fly again. Because now that I know I'm not gonna kill this guy, that I can't kill him, I can pee. I get back in the truck. Mickey smiles.

—Missed some?

—It crawled back up.

—I hate that.

—Yep.

I steer the truck back onto the highway, going west. I'll take Mickey to Chichén Itzá. I'll climb the temple steps with him and walk around the ruins. And when it's time to go I'll tell him the truth, that the

money's not in Mérida, it's back at my place. I'll take him home, give
him the million, and send him on his way. Then I'll start looking for a
new place to hide, a new country. I'll do it that way, take the chance,
because I don't want to be a murderer again. I don't want to be a maddog.

A COUPLE hours later we pull off at the exit for Piste, drive a couple
miles of open road and then through the town itself. Every time we
have to slow for a speed bump, kids mob the car with mass-produced
Mayan souvenirs. I ease the truck through them while Mickey laughs.
On the other side of town it's another mile or so to the National Park
where the ruins are. I take a ticket from the parking guy, find a spot,
and turn off the engine, killing a mariachi-rock version of "Twist and
Shout."

The rain is coming down hard and people are coming out of the
park, climbing into their cars and refilling the tour buses. I look at the
sky, look at Mickey.
—Might not stop for awhile.
—I like it, let's go.
He reaches in his pack and pulls out his poncho and rain hat. I do
not have a poncho or a rain hat. We get out of the truck and I am
soaked through before we get halfway to the main building. Once we
are safely under cover the rain slackens to a gentle drizzle. Fucking
Caribbean. I have to buy Mickey his ticket. He tells me he owes me.
We go through the turnstile, past the gift shop, the bookshop, the coffee shop, through another turnstile where they snap on our wristbands,
and then into the park itself. You walk through a little tunnel of trees.
Into a clearing, and there's Kukulkan. And you know, it is pretty cool.

I'm not big on sightseeing, but I've been out here a couple times in
the last few years, enough to pick up some details, and now I play tour
guide for Mickey. He wants to save the climb up the temple steps for
last, so we start with the Ball Court. We stand at one end and look
down the length of the stone stadium. Mickey nods his head.

—Big.

—Two hundred and seventy-two feet by one hundred and ninety-nine.

—Big.

We walk down the court and stand under one of the stone hoops mounted at midpoint on either side of the Court. Mickey leaps and tries to touch the bottom of the rim, but can't get close.

—That is where they put the heads through to score?

—Nah, they used a rubber ball.

—I thought heads?

—No. The Toltecs, when they took over, there's some evidence that they might have sacrificed the losing team.

—And they played like soccer.

—Any part of your body but your hands.

—See, soccer rules. Much better than American football.

I can say it now.

—I don't like football. I like baseball.

—See, you know, I know this about you also. But still, soccer is also better than baseball.

I turn my back and walk toward the rest of the ruins.

WE DO the Temple of Warriors and the Thousand Columns and the smaller features of the main clearing, and then Mickey is ready for the climb. Kukulcan, aka The Temple, aka The Castle, aka The Pyramid, aka El Castillo: it's why people come here. The seventy-nine-foot zig-gurat built over a smaller pyramid that is still housed inside. There's debate over whether it was built by the Mayans or the Toltecs, but they both seem to have used it as a place of worship and sacrifice, and also as a calendar of some kind. There are ninety-one steps on each of the four sides and a small temple on top representing a single giant step. Do the math: three hundred sixty-five steps altogether. Neat. There's more! Kukulcan was a golden serpent god, and on both the spring and autumnal equinoxes, shadows that look like writhing snake bodies play on two of the staircases. No shit. But mostly, mostly, it's a long fucking climb up a stone staircase on something around a forty-degree incline. A climb that will be made in the rain today. Rain that is getting harder.

Mickey trots up, of course. I keep a pretty brisk pace, but, having a stronger sense of my own mortality, I take time to plant each foot firmly on the rain-slick steps, gravity tugging at my back the whole way up. We're climbing the west stairs, which have been restored and even have a handrail running up the center. The north stairs have also been restored, but only have a rope strung from top to bottom. The east and south faces have been allowed to erode so tourists can get a sense of the condition the place was in when it was found. I pass a couple people crawling down backward on all fours, but nobody going up.

Mickey is waiting for me at the top, arms thrust up in a V. He wants me to take a picture of him like that with the jungle in the background. I do. A few people are up here, hiding just inside the temple, waiting for the rain to ease off before they go down. Mickey wants to go inside the temple and see the Jaguar Throne.

—You go ahead.

—No, but you must go with me.

—I've seen it.

—You can show me then.

—Look, it's tiny in there and I don't really like tiny places. Besides, it's smelly.

He steps a little closer to me, still smiling.

—No, but, you know, you really must go with me because I do not want you to be alone.

Jesus H.

—Mickey, can I have a word with you?

We edge around the outside of the temple, away from most of the people, to the east face of the pyramid. Looking out over the endless jungle.

—What is it?

—I'm not going anywhere. What I am going to do is keep our bargain. I'm gonna give you a million dollars to keep your mouth shut because I don't want to die. I'm not looking to ditch you, so just go poke around inside and then we can look at the Observatory if you want and then we'll drive back to the beach and I'll give you your money.

He squints at me.

—We will go to Mérida and you will get me the money.

Sigh.

—The money's not in Mérida, it's at my place.

—You said Mérida.

—I lied.

—Why?

—Because.

His mouth tightening into a straight line.

—You wanted to take me to Mérida, for what? To do something. To do something to me.

—Look.

—No! You cannot fuck with me. I know what this is, what you were trying. My father was in "business," I know about "business." You were thinking to kill me.

And funny as it may be, him saying it fills me with shame.

—Yeah. Yeah, I was.

—Fucking, fuck. I cannot trust you.

—Let's just.

—I will tell you what we will just do. You, you will take me to the money and you will give me two million. No, you will give me *three* million.

He's getting loud and spittle is flying from his lips. I look around to see if we've drawn an audience, but the rain is letting off and the other people are moving to the north and west sides to climb down.

—Mickey.

—Do not call me Mickey. That is for my friends. You now call me Mikhail, like my father named me.

—You need to settle down, and we'll work this out.

—It is worked out, you will give me three million or I will tell where you are.

I can keep my cool here. I know I can.

—You're going to get a lot of money, but I will not give you three million. I can't.

He throws up his arms in disgust.

—You are wanting, you know, to bargain with me? You are selfish. Yes, because this is not just about you.

—What do you mean?

—A selfish shit dog of a man.

—What do you mean, not just about me?

—My father's friends, they are not stupid, they know where your family lives. And you, selfish man, want to bargain with your family's life?

—No, I don't.

And I push Mickey down the rubbled east staircase of the Temple of Kukulcan. The first human sacrifice here in nearly a thousand years.

ON THE way home I stop in town to pick up a few things at the store. I go to the Chedraui, Mexico's version of Costco. I find the tape gun and reinforced packing tape I want, but none of the cardboard boxes they have for sale are big enough. I grab some cat food and a few other things, then go outside and pull around to the loading dock. They have a big pile of discarded boxes and the guys let me take my pick.

It's after ten when I get to The Bucket. There must have been a couple folks hanging out late because Pedro's just locking up the booze. I turn off the Willys and walk over with a huge sack of limes from the Chedraui.

—Sorry I'm late.

He takes the limes and stuffs them into one of the cabinets.

—No problema.

—Everything OK today?

—Si.

He looks at the Willys.

—You dropped off the Russian?

—Yeah. I dropped him off.

*   *   *

IT TOOK over an hour for the Federales to show up.

In the meantime the local police throw a tarp over Mickey and keep me sitting on the steps next to him. They don't shut down the park, just wave curious tourists away from the body, and share their Boots cigarettes with me because I left mine out in the truck.

Over the years the reputation of the Mexican police force has taken a beating. Everybody has heard stories of Mexican traffic cops scamming tourists for *mordida*, planting pot on unsuspecting kids on spring break, and the notorious involvement of the military in the international drug trade. And most of it is just plain true.

These guys get paid next to shit to do shit work and are given shitty equipment with which to do it. What's the worst job in the world? Mexican cop. So I wouldn't be surprised if the Federales who show up to question me turn me upside down and start shaking to see how much cash falls out of my pockets. Instead, they turn out to be honest, hardworking cops just trying to do the job.

Sergeants Morales and Candito are appallingly young, neither can be more than twenty-two, but they seem quite good at what they do. Which may be unfortunate for me. Their English isn't good enough to make up for my Spanish, so we conduct our interview through a translator. One of the tour guides from the park.

We sit in a small room in the park's administration building. Morales and Candito light Marlboros and give me one and the tour guide lights one of his cheap Alitas. The room chokes with smoke and they start asking questions about me and Mickey.

I tell them I just met Mickey a couple days ago and don't really know much about him. I tell them how I offered him a ride on my way to Mérida. They ask me why I was going to Mérida and I tell them I was just going up for a couple days to eat at one of my favorite restaurants and do a little shopping. They ask me what I do for a living and I tell them I'm retired. They observe that I seem youthful to be retired and I tell them I made a certain amount of money on the stock market before the American economy folded. All of which is consistent with my FM2 immigration documents, U.S. passport, and the other ID that Leo supplied me with two years ago. Then they ask me what happened.

I tell them how Mickey wanted to climb the pyramid even though it had started raining, how we went around back to look at the view, how he wanted to stand near the edge while I took his picture, how his foot slipped on the rain-slick stone, and how we reached for each other, our hands colliding rather than grasping, sending him tumbling down the steps. And Sergeant Morales rattles something in Spanish to Sergeant Candito, who looks at something in his notebook and rattles something to the translator, who turns to me and asks me if I could please tell them what that was about, the argument?

—Um, argument?

The translator says something in Spanish and Sergeant Candito answers and the translator turns back to me.

—The sergeants have a statement from a witness that you and your friend were arguing and they would like to know if you can tell them.

—That was nothing. I mean, we were arguing, but it was just about me wanting to get going and him wanting to stay longer. That's all.

The translator translates and Morales looks at Candito and Candito looks at Morales and they both look at the translator, who shrugs his shoulders.

And they let me go.

Of course they let me go. I'm an American citizen of some apparent wealth who has chosen to live and spend that wealth in Mexico.

But they keep my passport.

Which means they don't buy it.

And they don't buy me, either.

I SIT at the bar. Pedro pops the top off a seltzer for me and I tell him that Mickey is dead. I don't tell him the truth. This is not because I don't trust him. I do. I don't tell him the truth for the same reason I've never told him who I am and what I'm running from: to keep him the hell out of trouble.

Pedro finishes cleaning up, opens a beer for himself, and sits on the swing next to mine.

—Dead.

—As a door nail.

—Como?

—A door nail. It's a turn of phrase.

—Sure.

He squeezes a wedge of lime into his beer.

—Nails that are special just for doors?

—I don't know.

—What is so dead about them?

—I don't know.

—Deader than . . . a coffin nail?

—I don't know.

He nods, finishes his beer, crawls up onto the bar, and leans far over so he can pluck another from the nearly empty tub. He wobbles, almost falls, but I grab his belt and pull him back. Pedro slides onto his swing.

—Gracias. So what now?

—Nothing.

—They took your passport.

—It's no big deal. The guy was clumsy, he fell, the cops will investigate, and it will be over.

I drink my seltzer and Pedro drinks his beer.

—But I've been thinking about taking a trip.

—Claro.

—Maybe you could talk to Leo, tell him I might want some help.

—Claro. Cuando?

—Soon.

—American time, si?

—Yeah.

—OK.

I help him dump the water from the ice tub and offer him a ride in the Willys. He declines and pedals off on the tricycle. I drive over to my bungalow. I take my groceries, the tape gun, and the cardboard box inside. Bud is restless and darts around the room when I come in. I can see a little pile of cat poop in the middle of the room. He never does that.

—Not getting enough attention these days, guy?

He looks at me like he doesn't know what I'm talking about, which I suppose is literally true, but he knows, he always fucking knows. I clean up the crap, open a can of cat food, and sit on the floor next to him while he eats.

—Better?

He makes a little rumble in his throat that I interpret as a yes, so I flip on the boom box and put in *Wish You Were Here.* "Shine On You Crazy Diamond" starts playing and I get to work.

Out to the back porch. I open the footlocker and grab the shovel. It's developed a thin sheen of rust, like many of my tools. I should really keep them oiled, but I like the rust. It reminds me of old farm equipment piled in the yards of houses on the outskirts of my hometown.

Home.

I push that thought back down. Soon, but not yet, I can think about home.

I go back in, drop the shutters, and drag the bed into the middle of the room. I put a candle on the floor and feel around for the crack between the tiles.

WE HAD a great time building The Bucket and my bungalow, me and Pedro and Leo and a couple of their cousins. We hung out on the beach, working hard in the morning, taking a nice long siesta, then more work, then kicking a soccer ball around for an hour or two while the sun went down. Then everyone else would head home and I'd camp out to keep an eye on the tools and materials.

The Bucket was a breeze. We dug the holes for the pilings by hand, sank them, buried them, and built the roof frame. Then we built a box frame for the squared horseshoe of the bar, faced it, and anchored it to some four-by-fours we also sank in the sand. And that's about all you want to do for a beach bar because the whole thing is gonna blow away every few years when a hurricane blasts through. The bungalow was a bit more involved. We hired a guy with a Cat to come down and drill our piling holes extra deep, framed the roof and floor, nailed plywood over the floor, and planked the walls. Then the pros came in.

The pros were three brothers, their father and grandfather, and about ten of their little kids. These are the guys who do the palm thatching. They came in, took one look at the roofs we'd framed, tore them apart, and put them back together. Then they spent two days walking around up there, bundling and tying palm fronds together in such a way that a trapeze artist could drop on them from five stories and wouldn't break through. It was cool. The plumbing and sewage guys came during the next week and put in the water tank, toilet, sink, shower, and septic tank. And all that was left was the tiling, which I did myself.

I FIND the crack.

I keep a flat, stainless steel bottle opener on my keychain, but I don't use it for opening bottles. It's there for one purpose only, and this is its first time doing the job. I slip it into the crack, flex it, and pull slowly upward. The edge of a square of tile and plywood lifts away. I wedge my toe against it before it can fall back. I drop the bottle opener, get a fingertip grip on the panel, lift it up, and set it off to the side. Now comes the fun part: standing in a space not quite a yard square and shoveling sand in the dark.

I first dug this hole on one of the nights I spent alone on the beach. We'd staked out the frame for the bungalow, but hadn't started building it yet. I picked the spot where I planned to put the bed, dug a hole, and got a big box from the bed of the Willys. Then I lowered it into the hole and filled it in. After the bungalow was done, I built the secret panel into the floor. Of course, I didn't realize then that when the time came to dig out the box I'd be doubled over with my back in knots, rapping my knuckles on the edge of the hole in the floor with every stroke of the shovel. It takes awhile.

The shovel clunks into the top of the box. It's one of those indestructible packing cases rock bands use to haul their equipment in. I get down on my knees to clear the sand away from the lid and twist and flip the clasps. The top pops off and there's a Hefty bag inside. I squat, grab the top of the bag, heave it out of the box, up through the hole, and into the bungalow. I put the top back on the box and jerk the handle side to side, wiggle it free of the sand, and into the bungalow. Then I push the sand back into the hole, which leaves me with an only slightly smaller hole because the box is no longer in it. I end up slithering around under the bungalow, scooping sand to the hole to fill it in. Once again, it takes awhile.

When I'm done with the sand I put the plug back in the hole in the floor, push the bed into place, and open the Hefty bag. The money belt is on top, prepacked with a hundred grand American. I put that to the side. Underneath is a Ziploc bag. I put that to the side. I'm not ready yet. Beneath that is a huge block of plastic-wrapped money. And seeing it for the first time in around two years, I remember just how confusing dollars can be when there are over four million of them together in one place.

You really do get more for your dollar in Mexico. After I leased my beach property, built my bungalow and The Bucket, and put a nice chunk in a bank up in town, I still have just about four million right here.

My mad money.

And I am mad now, make no mistake, I am mad as hell.

THERE WAS a moment as Mickey fell away from me, arms outstretched, hands grasping, where I might easily have grabbed him and pulled him to safety. But I didn't try. I watched his body twist in the air and his arms flail as he tried to brace himself for the first impact. He crashed against the steps and his head jerked and slapped the stones. He bounced and tumbled all the way down, blood pinwheeling from his body.

And right there, I answered the old question, *What would you do if someone threatened your family?*

I'd kill him.

*   *   *

I PUT the money back into the packing case, cut the cardboard box so that it lies flat on the floor, then place the case on top of it. I wrap the case in cardboard and enough reinforced packing tape that you'd have to saw your way through. That done, I get into the shower and rinse off all the sweat and sand stuck to my body. Finally, when all the cleaning is done and the box is standing near the door and I've tugged a sarong around my body, I take the lantern out onto the porch, light a cigarette, and open the Ziploc.

The first thing I pull out is the police photo of the bruises on Yvonne's dead body. Nowhere to go from there but up.

I haven't looked at the photo for years. I haven't needed to. I can see it whenever I want to, just by closing my eyes. Now, I look at it, study it, close my eyes and see the same pattern of bruises flashed against the inside of my eyelids. I will never look at it again. With my eyes still closed, I tear the photo into eighths. I open my eyes, put the pieces in my ashtray, and set a match to them.

—Sorry, baby.

But I don't really need to apologize. Not to her. Not for this. She would have approved of this gesture, would have done it herself long ago. Yvonne Ann Cross, not one for carrying ghosts around.

Next are three business cards.

First: Detective Lieutenant Roman. Roman, the hero cop gone bad who orchestrated the slaughter at Paul's Bar. A snapshot from my memory: a pile of bodies, my friends, on the floor.

Second: Ed. Brother of Paris. The DuRantes. Bank robbers. Killers. A snatch of brain-movie: In their car, bullets from my gun erasing Ed's face. Paris's last word, his brother's name.

I toss the cards on the tiny fire and look at the third.

Third: A glossy black card with the name Mario embossed in gold gothic script. I smile, remember pot smoke and disco music in the back of his Lincoln as he drove me to the airport and the plane that brought me to Mexico. Nice guy, Mario. I burn him.

I take an envelope from the bag. Inside: the ID and credit cards of John Peter Carlyle, a man who never was. The custom-made identity I came to Mexico with. I won't be able to travel in Mexico as the man I've been for two years, not while the cops are looking into Mickey's death. My real name isn't an option. But I might be able to get away with being Carlyle again. I flip open the passport, look at the photo. I'm twenty pounds heavier now, an even two hundred, bulked up through the shoulders and chest from all the swimming, but with a little roll of rice and beans around the middle. The hair that was buzzed and bleached in this photo is now a sun-lightened brown and collar length. Once clean-shaven, I now have a short beard. And the tattoos. Tattoos scattered across my chest and down my arms, tattoos that were meant to help hide me, but have become a way of marking the passage of time. I don't look anything like this photo. I can cut my hair and shave so I look more like Carlyle, but I will also look more like the man I was, the man wanted for murder. Fuck it, the passport's date of issue is years old, there's no reason I shouldn't look different. I stuff it and the rest of Carlyle back into his envelope and set him aside. There's only one piece of paper left in the Ziploc.

United Flight #84
12/20/00
Depart: New York JFK 8:25 AM
Arrive: Oakland 11:47 AM

A ticket home, old and out of date. It had been meant to get me there for Christmas. I didn't make it that time, maybe this time I will. It burns quickly.

I FILL out the International Airway Bill, stopping for a moment when I get to the boxes where I'm supposed to write in the total value for carriage and customs. If I value this thing at less than two hundred bucks, it may very well zip past customs with nary a look. Then again, in the U.S.A.'s current state of heightened security, some clever boy could notice that a guy in Mexico has paid more to ship this box than the stated value of the contents. And that is an invitation to have this thing ripped open by people wearing yellow biohazard suits. Option two: value it at a couple grand, fill out all the supporting documentation, have it go through customs the old-fashioned way. Of course, this involves someone picking it up at a post office in the destination city to pay the duty fees. A great way to get ambushed by Feds. Tricky. This is why I'm at the Pakmail in Cancún, talking to Mercedes. She is going to help me ship four million dollars to America via FedEx.

I finish the Airway Bill, putting the value at two thousand and listing the contents as books. I take a piece of paper from my wallet. It lists the titles of a number of difficult-to-find to semi-rare Mexican art and history books I've been collecting. The titles, that is, not the books. I write those titles on the Pro Forma Invoice. To make things extra special tidy, I also have a Certificate of Origin that I had notarized earlier when I stopped by my bank to pick up a few things.

I lift the box onto the scale and Mercedes makes a little woof sound when it tips in at over sixty kilos. She makes the sound again when I hand her the Airway Bill and she sees the destination. Like most service workers in Cancún, her English is good. She says everything with a little song. I like it.

—Lotta money.

I sing back at her.

—Lotta money. You got that right.

She giggles, smoothes the various shipping labels onto the box, hands me my copies, and rings me up for something more than two thousand pesos. I pay in dollars. No big deal in Cancún. She takes another look at the invoice.

—Your friend likes to read.

—I don't know, he just bought 'em from me.

—eBay?

—Yeah.

—I love eBay. Bought these on eBay.

She's pointing at her earrings. I bend down to get a closer look.

They're little Miami Dolphins dolphins, leaping through the air, wearing tiny football helmets.

—Fins. Alright. Hell of a year, huh?

—Oh sure, but now . . .

—Yeah, I know, late season, but they look good with Taylor.

—Oh!

She jumps up and down a little.

—Miles! I love him! He's so cute.

She stops jumping.

—But his ankle now.

—What?

—His ankle.

Oh no.

—Please don't tell me.

—On the TV last night. *SportsCenter.* Very bad.

The Pakmail is right in the middle of a giant strip mall, so it only takes a minute or two for me to find a news kiosk with a copy of today's *Miami Herald.* It's on the front page: "Taylor's Ankle Fractured, Docs Say Four Weeks Minimum."

THE FOOTBALL season is a long season. It's not as long as the baseball season and they only play a tenth as many games, but the abuse your average starting football player absorbs in one game is *at least* equivalent to what a baseball player suffers in ten or twenty. Thus, one of the keynotes of prevailing wisdom among NFL coaches: as the season waxes, the practices wane.

—So this moron, this spastic that they actually pay to coach the team, decides the guys weren't hitting hard enough on Sunday when the Pats were making their run. So what's he do? He calls contact drills. Contact drills in fucking December! So the starting defense is out there, running around, knocking the shit out of the scout squad. And you know those poor chumps are hating it. I mean, these guys get paid about minimum wage and now they have to run around and get the crap pounded out of them by a bunch of psychos who're pissed at the feeb who's running the show. Meanwhile, the starting offense is down on the other end of the field, shooting the shit, and running pass drills in their shorts, right where the defensive guys can see them. Now tell me, you ever heard of a guy named Dillon Walker? No, you haven't. The reason is that Walker was a hundredth-round pick defensive back who, until last Sunday, was a scout scrub himself. However, due to a series of injuries that have ravaged the secondary, he has been elevated to backup and even has a slim shot at starting free safety this Sunday should the gods not smile on Terrence Lincoln's severe turf toe. Needless to say, this is a man with something to prove. And he's proving it, flying around the field, hitting anything that moves, trying to show Coach his heart. For example, the scrubs run a little out, and they complete it. This is an *out* mind you, a play within ten yards of the line of scrimmage, a play the free safety should not be anywhere near. And he's not, he's ten yards away when the receiver steps out of bounds. Ten yards away, running full out, helmet down so he can launch himself at the poor scrub *five yards out of bounds*. And standing right on the other side of this scrub, who is standing there? Standing there and, I don't know, talking on his cell to his agent about how he's gonna spend all his bonuses or maybe chatting up a cheerleader, setting up a three-way with her and her fifteen-year-old sister or whatever the fuck twenty-two-year-old millionaires do on the sideline at practice, standing there is Miles Taylor, who is promptly crushed beneath the scrub and Dillon fuckstick Walker.

I pause long enough to light a smoke and inhale half of it.

—Walker bounces right back up and heads for the field, shit-eating grin on his face, ready to huddle up with the D and brag about the massive knock he just put on that pussy scrub. Dumb shit can't figure out why everyone is standing around on the field, their faces white, staring at something behind him. So he turns to take a look and gets steamrolled by the entire starting offensive line, who have just watched him take out their bread and butter, the guy who has been helping them to earn *their* bonuses. And all those D boys, the ones who have been running around hitting in full pads while the offense took it easy, they take serious fucking umbrage. Riot. The O and D go at it; starters, backups, everyone except the scrubs, who wisely clear the field. And in the midst of this melee, as the coaches are screaming and trying to pull everyone apart, Miles Taylor stands up to announce that, hey, he's fine, right before a huge mass of three-hundred-pounders lurches onto him and crushes his ankle.

I inhale the second half of my cigarette.

—I swear to God, I swear to fucking God, if I ever see that fucking retard coach walking down the street, I'm gonna stab him in the neck with a fucking fork. I hate football, I hate it.

—So is that what you called to talk about?

I breath deep and get my shit back together.

—No, Timmy, it's not.

—Oh. So what's up then?

—What's up is I'm sending you a package.

—You're sending me what?

—I'm sending you a *package*.

—What package?

I'm standing at the pay phone in a Pemex near the Cancún airport. From here I can see the billboards for T.G.I. Fridays, Senior Frogs, the Bulldog Café, etc., that line the road to downtown. My pulse is still racing from my rant about Miles Taylor's ankle, so I light another cigarette. 'Cause, hey, that'll calm me down.

—Timmy, I'm sending you the money.

Silence.

—Timmy?

—Are you fucking nuts?

—Look, I've thought about this.

I have thought about it. A lot. And it breaks down like this:

A) Tim is an ex-junkie. He is an alcoholic. He is a deliveryman for a drug dealer. He lives in *Las Vegas*. He is clearly the last man on earth any sane person would send four million dollars to.

B) Tim knows where I am. He knows about the money. He knows

about the several rewards available for information leading to my capture. He knows about the money the Russians would pay for my head. And for the years he has been privy to this information, he has kept his mouth shut.

C) I am going to cross the border into the United States illegally. I cannot be caught with the money. If I am caught with the money all bets are off. If, however, the money is out there, I will have something to bargain with. I will have a tool with which to bargain for the safety of my parents.

D) I. Can. Not. Be. Caught. With. The. Money.

—I DON'T care if you've thought about it, I don't want that shit anywhere near me. This is fucking *Vegas*. Did you know people out here train themselves to smell money? No fucking joke, I mean, I was happy to get outta Gotham and lie low and all, especially seeing as it's on your dime, but I am not planning to spend my life here, because, basically, this town sucks. People are fucked up here. It's all the money floating around, they can see it and play with it, but they can't have it and it just makes 'em want it more. So the minute they smell it on you they come after it. Do not send me that fucking money, because I love you, you know that, but there are fucking limits to what a man can do. OK? Are we cool on this?

—I already sent it.

—What?

—I already.

—Where?

—To your apartment. It should be there the day after tomorrow.

—Man. Man! I cannot believe you fucking. Fine! Fine! It can get here whenever it wants, but I will not be here to receive. You got me? I will not be here. Good-bye.

But he doesn't hang up.

—Did you hear me? I said good-bye.

I take a last drag off my smoke, drop it on the ground, and crush the butt.

—Someone found me, Timmy. He found me and threatened my parents and I killed him. And now I'm coming home.

—Oh, shit.

I EXPLAIN how it will work. How FedEx employs customs brokers who usher their customers' goods through U.S. Customs, pay all duty and taxes, and have the package delivered right to the recipient's door along with a bill for services and fees. I tell him all the paperwork is in more than shipshape, that the only danger is if the package is singled out for a random search. I tell him I don't know the odds against that, but he'd have a better chance hitting the jackpot on one of those million-dollar slots.

—I'm not sure how long it will take me to cross over, but I hope to be in California by early next week. All you have to do.

—Shit, maaaaaaan.

—All you have to do is hang on to the package, just stick it in a closet until I call and then you'll just call FedEx and have them pick it up and bring it to me.

—Maaaaaaaaaaaaaaaaaaaaaaaan!

—I'll . . . *listen*. When you get a page from number code four-four-four followed by a phone number, that'll be me. Just call me at that number and.

—Can't you come get it yourself?

—I need to stay with my folks, Tim. Until I can figure out a way to deal with the Russians, I need to stay and keep an eye on my folks.

—Yeah, OK.

—And, Timmy, listen to me. If someone *does* come for it, I mean the law or the Russians, all I want you to do is give it to them and just sell me out. Nothing is gonna happen, but if it does, do whatever you have to do to stay alive and out of jail. Anything they want. Got it?

—Oh, I got that part, you bet I do.

—OK. So what else, is there anything else?

—Couldn't you come straight here instead and just?

—No. You know I can't.

—Yeah, right. Look, just take care of your folks. I gotta go.

This time he does hang up.

THERE'S THE usual collection of sunbathers spread around the beach, and a few hanging around the bar. Pedro is flipping burgers on the grill. I park the Willys next to The Bucket and get out. Pedro waves his spatula at me.

—Hola.

—Hey.

I go behind the bar, grab myself a seltzer from the tub, and go stand next to him at the grill.

—You get a chance to talk with your brother?

—I called.

He gives the burgers a flip. They look good. I open the cooler, rip off a lump of ground chuck, and start kneading it into a patty.

—What'd he say?

—Nada.

—He can't help?

—He didn't say anything.

I throw my patty on the grill as Pedro crumbles *queso blanco* on top of the ones he's making.

—He didn't say anything?

—Si.

I watch the cheese melting.

—Why didn't he say anything?

—He was not home.

He chortles as he scoops the patties off the grill and onto buns. I grab the spatula from him as he places the burgers on paper plates with a handful of tortilla chips on the side and takes them to the folks at the bar. I poke my burger around the grill while he opens a few beers for his customers. He comes back and takes the spatula from me.

—You have to . . . You move it and . . . aplastar?

—Uh.

—Aplastar. Like this.

He makes little pressing motions with the spatula.

—Squash?

—Yeah! You squash the poor thing. All the juice, the good part, you squash it out. You got to wait. Tranquilo.

So I wait while he lets the burger cook, puts the cheese on it, toasts the bun, and hands it to me when it's all done. And he's right: I do try to rush the things and they're never as good as his. Pedro makes a great burger.

—So do you know when he's gonna be back?

—Back?

—Leo.

—He'll come tonight. Talk to you.

—Cool.

I stand there and eat my burger while he looks at me funny.

—You going to talk to them?

—Who?

—Them.

He points up the beach toward my bungalow. And for the first time I look that way and see the white police Bronco parked out front and the two guys in blue uniforms sitting on the porch. Sergeants Morales and Candito.

I drive over. They stand up and brush off the seats of their pants.

—Señor.—

—Buenos tardes, Sargentos.

I gesture toward the front door.

—Entrar?

—Si.

—Si, gracias.

I don't really want to invite them in, but it would be monumentally rude not to, especially seeing as I am perfectly innocent, have nothing to hide, and want only to help these men to do their job. I open the door, usher them into the cool shade inside, and we all stand there for a moment.

—Bebidos?

—Si.

—Si, gracias.

So I get us all lukewarm bottles of Jaritos from a cabinet and we all take a sip and Sergeant Candito looks at Sergeant Morales and tips his head in my direction and Sergeant Morales slaps his forehead.

—Si, si, claro.

And he pulls my passport out of his pocket and hands it to me. We all have a nice chat. It's a hard chat because there's no translator this time, but pidgin Spanish and pidgin English win out.

When we're all done they have assured me that all is well. They are so sorry they have inconvenienced me. I'm starting to relax a little, and Bud comes scampering out from under the bed.

Candito squats down.

—Ay, gato.

He pets Bud, then stands up.

—He is a nice cat for you?

—Yeah.

And I can't help but notice that Sergeant Candito now has a look in his eye as if he's just run into someone whose face he should know, but he can't quite remember why.

LEO COMES by after dark. He sits on my porch and sips Carta Blanca. I smoke and tell him exactly what I need. Leo listens, nods his head when I'm through.

—When?

—Tomorrow?

Leo shakes his head.

—No, man, too soon.

—Day after?

He squints, stares out at the water.

—Yeah, I think so.

—How much?

He shrugs.

—For me, nada. But something for Rolf, some other people . . .

—How much?

—Ten thousand U.S.

I go inside, come back out and hand him twenty thousand.

—And ten for you.

He looks at the money.

—I don't want that.

—Leo.

—Fuck you, I don't want it.

—Leo.

He peels off ten grand and tosses the rest back at me. I set it on the porch next to his knee.

—Leo, it's gonna be dangerous.

—Chinga! What do I fucking do for a living, maricon?

—More dangerous than that, it could get. People, the people who are looking for me might come around. You might have to hide for a little while if they do.

—Hide? Fucking!

He starts spewing Spanish, stuff about me and my mother and pigs and what I can do with my money and what he'd do to anyone who came around and thought they could make him hide. He runs out of steam after a couple minutes, drains the rest of his beer, starts to say something else, stops himself, and throws the empty bottle toward the water. We hear it thunk down in the sand.

I get up and walk over, pick it up and bring it back. I sit down and nudge the money closer to him with my toe.

—If they come. They'll be killers if they come, Leo. Take the money. I'm a pussy little girl and it will make me feel better if you take the money.

He snorts. I start talking in a high voice.

—Take the money, Leo. You can burn it later. Just let me see you take it. Make me feel better because I'm such a mujer.

He picks up the money and walks into the darkness.

—Be at my brother's at sunrise, day after tomorrow. And learn fucking Spanish, man. A mujer is a woman. A niña is a little girl.

WHEN PEDRO shows up the next morning I'm already at The Bucket, with the grill fired up and the coffeepot gurgling. I help him unload the ice and a couple cases of beer, then tell him to sit down. He sits on one of the swings.

I heat up some refried beans, throw a couple of the tortillas he brought from home on the grill, and fry two eggs. I smear the beans onto a plate, put the hot tortillas on top, then the eggs, then pour his wife's salsa over the whole thing. I put it in front of him and pour his coffee in my cup with lots of milk and sugar like he likes it. He looks at the plate of huevos rancheros, and then at me.

—I had breakfast two hours ago.

I SPENT close to a year sitting at Pedro's bar doing my drunken gringo act. He was pretty patient with me, I have to say. Some of that was because I was a great tipper, but we also hit it off from the start.

I had been in town for a couple weeks and spent most of the time in my room, growing facial hair, drinking, and lying low while news about me had a chance to die down. One night I lurched over to the main drag, Calle Cinco, and ended up getting my first tattoo: a heart wrapped in a banner that said MOM & DAD.

Afterward I started walking toward the darkness at the end of the street. That's where I found Pedro, working at a little patio restaurant with no one in it. I took a stool and he asked me what I wanted. There was a huge menu of drinks hanging behind the bar.

—Surprise me.

He fills the glass with ice, pours 151 over it and pineapple juice and orange juice and almond syrup and Coco Lopez and grenadine, shakes it, floats some dark rum on top, takes a very long straw from a box on the bar, cuts it in half and sticks both halves into the drink, and puts it in front of me on a little napkin. I pick it up, the napkin sticks to the bottom of the glass. I take a sip.

—Wow. That's good.

—Mai tai.

—No kidding. You know, I've never actually had one before.

I take another sip.

—This is great.

He points at the bandage on my shoulder.

—Tattoo?

—Yeah.

—What?

I set the drink down and peel up the bandage. He reads it.

—Mom and dad.

—I love my mom and dad.

—Bueno.

He lifts the sleeve of his shirt and shows me his shoulder: *MAMA y PAPA*.

—I love my mom and dad. Mi madre y mi padre. Mama does not like this. She say . . . uh . . . tattoo are for criminals. See.

He turns and lifts the other sleeve. There's a little homemade tattoo underneath, like the ones my buddies Wade and Steve gave themselves in high school. They'd wrap thread around the shaft of a sewing needle, then dip it in India ink. Ink would drip out of the thread down to the point of the needle while they poked their skin, making tiny anarchy As or spelling out OZZY. This one is a little vertical line, a triangle attached to the top half pointing to my right. He smiles.

—Mama, she beat my ass for this.

I turn my head, look at it again.

—What is it?

He laughs, points at the tattoo.

—P.

Points at himself.

—Pedro.

Ten months later, when nobody had found me and shot me and I had failed to drink myself to death, I started thinking about what might be involved in staying alive and staying hidden. I knew I was going to need some papers, a passport most of all. Pedro was the only person I trusted enough to ask for help. It turned out he trusted me too.

HE TAKES a couple bites of the eggs for politeness's sake, announces them fit, and tells me to eat the rest. I take the envelope from my back pocket, hand it to him, and start to eat. He opens the envelope and takes out the government leases and all the other legal documents regarding The Bucket and my bungalow.

—I went to the safety deposit box yesterday.

He's looking at the papers.

—No.

—I signed over both the leases to you.

Shaking his head.

—No.

—Pedro.

—No.

He goes behind the bar and starts banging things around.

—Pedro. If I ever make it back.

—Back. The policia gave you back the passport, yes?

—Yes.

—So no problema, you will come back.

I lift my bottle of seltzer from the bar and trace little lines through the ring of water it leaves behind.

—This is the old trouble, Pedro. My old trouble. The trouble you don't know about.

He stops banging things. I set my bottle down, look at him.

—Please. I was alone. Yo desamparado. Until you, I had no friends.

He looks at his feet. He picks up the papers, puts them neatly in the envelope and slips it into his pocket. Then he reaches out and puts his hand on the bar, palm up. I cover it with my own.

—Amigo.

He squeezes my hand.

—Eternamente, por siempre jamás.

—Forever and ever.

THE DAY-TRIPPERS clear out around four, and an hour later Pedro locks up. I take a couple swims, having to unclog my ears with the cigarettes after each. By the time the sun is down the local kids have finished their soccer game, the lovers I watch kissing retire to their *palapa*, and I have the beach to myself. I go into the bungalow, leaving the door and all the shutters open, light some candles, and start to pack.

Bud rouses himself from a nap and wanders over to see what's up. He keeps stuffing his head in the pack, getting in the way every time I try to put something inside.

—I know what you're thinking, but there's no room for you.

He meows as I push him aside so I can pack the bundle of protein bars I bought at the Chedraui.

—I know we did it last time, but that was then and this is now. Besides, this time I have a place for you to stay.

Now he's got the entire front half of his body stuck in there, rooting around. I pull him out and toss him on the floor.

—Cool it.

He hops back on the bed. I get everything stowed, close up the old army surplus pack, and put it next to the front door. I dig the money belt out from under my mattress, stick the John Carlyle papers inside along with my ID, and drape it over the pack. I close the front door, blow out all but one of the candles, and lie on the bed. Bud jumps down to the floor and walks to the other side of the room.

—You'll like it at Pedro's.

But he's not buying it. Bud is a bachelor cat who has only lived with bachelor men, first Russ and then me. Pedro's got the wife and three kids. Bottom line, Bud's gonna get chased around some and have his tail yanked a few times. Of course the option is for me to try and haul him to the U.S. and infinitely increase the odds of my getting caught.

—It's just not gonna work this time, guy.

I'm staring up at the ceiling, but I feel it when he jumps back onto the bed. He walks around me a couple times, then flops on my chest. I scratch his head, careful not to touch the scar, because he doesn't like that. He starts to purr.

Fuck. I'm gonna miss this cat.

THE NIGHTMARE that wakes me up is a new one. I'm at Paul's Bar the morning of the massacre. Instead of my old friends getting killed, it's people I know now. Timmy, Mercedes from the Pakmail, Leo, Rolf, the smiling Spanish girl. And I'm the one doing the killing, walking around the bar with a machine gun, murdering all the people. Until they are all dead, all except Pedro and two others. He's standing in front of the others, shielding them with his body. And I can see them, and it's my parents.

And I kill Pedro.

And aim the machine gun.

And I wake up.

A half hour later I'm crashing through the jungle, clutching Bud to my chest, with Sergeants Morales and Candito running after me.

THANK GOD for the swimming. Without the swimming I would have collapsed by now. Of course all that wonderful muscle tone isn't helping out with the searing burn in my lungs. Over thirty years without even trying a cigarette and I had to start. It was quitting the booze that did it. Drop one addiction and pick up another. Fucking idiot.

I trip over a tree root. Which is what I get for not paying attention to where I'm going.

I can't put my arms out to brace my fall without losing Bud, so I twist my body around and drop hard, the pack absorbing most of the impact. I start to get to my feet and hear Morales and Candito calling out to each other. They're a ways back there and they've stopped running. They're asking each other where I am. I get to my knees and peek out from behind my tree. But this being a jungle, I can't see more than a few feet.

What I need to do here is stay cool. Cut out all the crashing around and sneak my way to Pedro's. Bud twists out of my grasp and streaks off back toward the bungalow. Toward the cops.

There has to be, there simply *has* to be a statute of limitations on cat-sitting. I run after him. Almost immediately the sergeants hear me and they're yelling again and coming in my direction. I trip over another root.

And it catches me.

I start to shout, but Leo wraps a hand over my mouth. We make eye contact. I nod. He uncovers my mouth and hands Bud to me. I hear rustling as Morales and Candito creep by on either side of us, trying to zero in on me. The sound dies and Leo puts his mouth right against my ear.

—This way.

He's holding his arm straight out, pointing in the same direction the cops just went.

—Straight as possible, you'll come out by Pedro's.

—Cops.

—Shut up. Rolf will be there.

—What about.

—And hang on to the fucking cat.

He gets up and starts running loudly, and I hear the cops yell and take off after him. I head for Pedro's.

I POP out of the trees about twenty yards from Pedro's house, just off the highway. I can see the dune buggy parked out back and Rolf standing in the yard. I sprint over and Rolf catches me as I stumble the last few feet.

—Leo. Gasp. He. He. He. Gasp.

—He find you?

—Yeah. Gasp. He.

—Inside, dude.

We go through the screen door, he leads me to the kitchen.

—We saw them go past on the highway and head for the beach. Leo took off to warn you or whatever.

—He drew them off.

—Cool.

—No, we got to.

—Dude, we got to get you out of here is all we got to do. Leo's cool. Those guys will never find him in there.

In the kitchen the table is covered with food. Pedro is sipping coffee, listening to *ranchera* music. He clicks off the radio. His wife, who is usually on her way to town with the kids by now, is at the stove. She turns and gives me a tight-lipped smile.

—Buenos dias.

—Buenos dias, Ofelia.

She gestures to the table.

—Comer.

She's made a huge breakfast, a farewell. We're all supposed to sit at the table and have breakfast together, and I'm late. Rolf grabs a tortilla off the table, slaps some beans into it and takes a huge bite.

—Gracias, no, Ofi. We got to split. Andele muchachos big time.

I look at all the wonderful food and smile at her.

—Bonita, bonita. Muy bien. I'm so sorry. Gracias.

She nods.

Rolf is getting ready to grab something else off the table. She pushes him away and starts packing food in a plastic bag for us. Pedro puts down his cup and stands.

—Leo?

Rolf waves his hand.

—He's goose-chasing the cops, he'll be fine.

Pedro shakes his head. Ofelia finishes and hands me the bag of food.

—Gracias.

She puts her hands on my shoulders, pulls my face down close to her mestizo features, and kisses me on the cheek. Rolf grabs me and pulls me toward the door. Pedro follows us. We're halfway out when he puts a hand on my shoulder and points at Bud, still in my arms.

—Amigo.

—Right.

I hold Bud up so I can look at his face.

—OK, Buddy, time to go.

I hand him to Pedro. He curls up in his arms and starts purring. And that's that.

Pedro reaches into his pocket, takes something out, hands it to me, then turns and walks back into the house. Rolf hustles me to the buggy. I look back. Through the screen door I can see Pedro's three kids running into the room screaming.

—Ay, gato!

Good luck, cat.

Rolf fires up the buggy and guns it onto the highway as I take the holy medal Pedro gave me and loop it around my neck. Christopher, patron saint of travelers.

WE'RE HEADED down 184, the local highway that cuts across most of the peninsula. Rolf is driving with his knees, both hands in his lap, trying to eke flame from a Bic to light a joint in the roaring wind of the open buggy. He gets the doobie going and takes a hit.

—Voilà!

He offers it to me, I decline and he keeps at it, smoking it like a cigarette.

—Dude, check the bag, man, see if Ofi packed us any breakfast bread.

I dig one of the sugared rolls out of the bag and hand it to him.

—Thanks.

—So, Rolf.

—Yeah?

Crumbs fly from his lips, he's got the roll in one hand and the joint in the other as he pulls around a slow-moving pickup, passing it before a blind curve on the two-lane road.

—I have this thing about cars and speeding.

—Don't worry, dude, I'm a good driver.

—Right now you aren't inspiring much confidence, and seeing as how this jalopy has no seat belts, I was hoping you might slow the fuck down.

—Tranquilo, muchacho. No problem, man.

He decelerates.

—Thanks. So?

—Yeah?

—What's the plan?

—The plaaaaan. The plan is beautiful. You are going to love the plan.

—And?

—OK, it's total secret-agent style, the stuff I really love. None of that two-drunk-Cubans-in-a-boat shit. We are on our way to Campeche.

He draws out the last syllable: Campechaaaaaay.

—Actually, before Campeche, we'll pull off to this place called Bobola.

—What's there?

—Leo.

—Leo?

—Got to have Leo. He's the man who knows the people. If I try to deliver you? No go.

—Yeah, but last time I saw him he was getting chased by a couple cops.

—He'll get rid of the Federales and borrow Pedro's car. He's probably at their place right now digging into that food.

Nice thought.

—So where does Leo take us to?

—The Campeche airport. You afraid of flying, too?

—No.

—Good. I've seen this plane and you don't want to be afraid of flying. So this guy with the plane will fly you across the gulf to Veracruz. There, Pedro has a guy, an American with an excursion boat. He'll take you on, put together crew papers for you and everything, and take you back to his homeport.

—Which is?

—Corpus Christi, U.S.A., man. I know it sounds weird, but there's actually some pretty good surf in Texas. The general vibe in that state is all fucked up, but they have some decent waves.

Then he plugs a Tool tape into the deck, cranks the volume, and that's it for conversation.

The 184 wanders in and out of about a dozen tiny towns before it hits Ticul, where, Rolf says, we'll jump to the 261. Each town is peppered with speed bumps to keep the through traffic from blasting over the pedestrians as drivers try to get the hell to somewhere else, but this is a detail Rolf seems to have a habit of forgetting. Fortunately, as the day waxes and Rolf smokes more and more of the cheap Mexican brick-weed he's carrying, lead seems to drain from his foot. At Ticul we stop, gas up, and he drives the buggy into the middle of town, announcing that it's time for lunch and an early siesta.

—What about Leo?

—We aren't supposed to meet him for hours, man. The dude you're flying with, he doesn't like being airborne during the day. There's a great taco wagon here by the park. We can grab some snacks and take a nap on the lawn.

—Yeah, except that the cops are looking for me and sunbathing in the middle of town might not be the best thing right now.

—Dude, do you know how long it takes for a Mexican APB to go out? Let alone, man, to places like this. Chill. We'll grab a couple fish tacos and refrescos and find some shade.

He stops next to a tidy little park, gets out, and turns to face me.

—Besides, dude, if there's any trouble, I'm armed.

And he lifts the tail of his Spitfire Bighead T-shirt, revealing the butt of the pistol tucked in the waistband of his shorts.

—So no worries, man, let's eat.

And surprisingly enough, not only are the tacos great, but I do actually manage to drop off and take a nice little nap. Despite the stoned-

out-of-his-gourd, gnarly-brained surf jockey sleeping next to me with a
gun in his shorts.

THE SUN has crossed well past its zenith when Rolf shakes me awake.
—Dude, we totally overslept.

We're off the 184 now, heading south on 261. Rolf is laying off the
weed and has both hands on the wheel and both eyes on the road. And
I got to say: when he's paying attention, he *is* a pretty good driver. The
road turns west at Hopelchen and the low-hanging sun shoots into our
eyes. Rolf slips on a pair of Dragon Trap shades, a flame motif burning
down the arms. I put on my own cheap Ray-Ban Aviator knock-offs.

—We gonna make it?

—No problem, man. But there is a need for speed.

So he speeds.

A few miles outside of Campeche we turn south onto a one-lane
road. We bump along for a couple more miles, then roll into Bobola.
When I say this place looks like the modern equivalent of the town in
A Fistful of Dollars, I certainly don't mean to emphasize the word modern. We pass a handful of houses, then come into the square. It's a
classic: cobbled street circling a tiny park, lots of trees, and a big
church the Spanish left behind. There's a guy selling ices out of the
back of his pickup, and a couple kids buying. Nobody else. Rolf drives
us around the park, past the ice man and onto one of the dirt streets
that branches off of the square. He parks about a hundred yards up the
street.

—OK.

—OK?

—That's the place.

Across the street is a *tequilaria.*

—What now?

He looks around.

—Looks like Leo's not here yet, dude.

—So?

—Well, I know you're not a drinking man, but I could use one. Come on.

We cross the street and walk into the bar. It's dark inside and it takes a moment for our eyes to adjust from the afternoon sunlight outside. That's why it takes so long to realize that the two guys over by the bar, the only two guys in the place, are Sergeants Morales and Candito. That's also why it takes a moment more before we realize the pile of stuff on the floor next to them is actually Leo, who has very clearly had the shit beaten right out of him.

DESPITE WHAT many popular movies would have you think, the simple fact that Morales and Candito are Mexican does not make them stupider than shit. They have me: a somewhat mysterious and wealthy American involved in a somewhat mysterious death. And they have that odd little moment when Bud wandered out from under the bed and Candito gave me that funny look. Given the current level of digital technology, it probably wasn't too hard to poke around until he got rid of that nagging feeling that he had seen me *somewhere* before.

OBSERVATIONS: THE bar is empty except for the five of us, at a time of day when one would expect otherwise. Morales and Candito have parked their Bronco somewhere off the street where it cannot be seen. They have no backup; backup would have come crashing in by now. They have thrashed Leo and dragged him in here.

Hypothesis: They have cleared out the bar, chosen not to call in any other cops, and have Leo displayed here to communicate some message. What message? Well, one assumes it concerns funding their early retirement.

How do they know I have four million? They may very well not. But they know I have money, and I'm sure they want all of it.

*   *   *

THE GUN in Rolf's waistband is a revolver, a .32 or a .38, carrying five or six rounds. I'm guessing the pockets of his shorts aren't crammed with extra ammo, so if this turns into a shoot-out we're gonna be pretty well fucked.

Me, I'm all for bargaining. But first Rolf shoves me to the floor, yanks the gun from his shorts, and squeezes off two quick shots before he dives behind a table.

One of the bullets smashes into the bottles behind the bar and the other one smashes the bone in Morales's right thigh. I know this because I can see shards of it sticking out through his shredded uniform pants.

Rolf is huddled behind a table made out of an old tequila barrel. It looks sturdy and might actually stop or deflect some bullets. I knock over a card table with a thin sheet metal top emblazoned with a Sol advertisement, and hope nobody shoots any spitballs at me. I can hear Morales screaming high and shrill and Candito trying to quiet him.
—Tranquilo. Tranquilo. Tranquilo. Tranquilo.

The screams soften until there is just a constant, strangled keening coming from deep in Morales's throat. I peek out from behind my useless barricade. Candito, kneeling next to Morales, has taken off his belt and turned it into a tourniquet much like the one the macheted Cuban had. I look over at Rolf and see that he is starting to edge around his barrel, gun first.
—Rolf!

He ignores me, positioning himself to take a shot, but at the sound of my voice Candito stands, pulls his service piece, points it at Leo, and yells something in our direction. Rolf ducks back down.
—Fuck!

Candito yells again, but I still don't catch all of it. Rolf yells something back.
—What does he want?
—He wants me to throw out my gun, dude, what the fuck do you think he wants? Keep quiet next time, I almost had him.

Candito yells again.

—So throw your gun out.

—No fucking way.

—He's gonna kill Leo.

—Bullshit. That hick cop has never shot anyone in his life. He's pissing his pants right now. Besides, dude knows that if he kills Leo I'll fucking blast him.

—How does he know that?

—Because I told him.

Candito yells again and this time I get the word *dinero*. Bingo. Rolf looks over at me.

—He says he just wants the money.

—Yeah, that figures.

I open my shirt, lift my tank top up, rip the Velcro seal, and tug the money belt from around my waist. I take five grand and the John Carlyle ID and stuff them in my pockets.

—Tell him I'm gonna stand up.

—Dude, don't do that.

—Rolf, I'm hiding behind a beer can, I might as well stand up.

—No, dude, I mean don't give him your fucking money.

—Just tell him I'm standing up and not to shoot.

—OK, but I'm telling you we can get out of this, no problem.

He shouts at Candito and Candito shouts back.

—He says do it slowly. Hands up and all that.

—Right.

I hang the money belt over my shoulder, put my hands on my head, and slowly stand up. Morales is sprawled in a large pool of his own blood, still making that hurt animal noise, his right hand clutching the tourniquet, his left clawing and scratching at the floor. Candito is standing, blood stains on the knees of his pants, pointing his gun at Leo's head. Leo is still crumpled and motionless, unconscious for all I can tell. I take my right hand from my head and lift the money belt from my shoulder. Candito yells and I freeze.

—Rolf?

—Yeah?

—What was that?

—Just the usual. Don't fuck around with him or he'll fucking kill Leo and then you. That kind of stuff.

—OK.

I hold the money belt out in Candito's direction, nodding my head.

—Tranquilo, amigo.

The gun pointed at Leo's head is shaking, sweat is pouring down Candito's twitching face, and I realize that Rolf is right. This guy is scared pissless. I know the feeling.

—Tranquilo, OK?

I swing the money belt once and toss it to him. It lands neatly at his feet. He keeps the shaking gun pointed at Leo as he squats down. The fingers of his left hand fumble one of the compartments open and he pries out a thick sheaf of bills. His eyes flick to the money. He lets it and the belt fall into the edge of the puddle of Morales's blood, then he stands back up and starts screaming at me, the gun vibrating.

—What the fuck, Rolf?

—That's what *he* says, dude.

—What?

—He wants to know what that shit is, how much?

—It's about seventy-five thou.

Rolf looks at me.

—No shit?

—Yeah.

—Dude.

Candito yells at us. I take my right hand from my head and point at the money belt.

—Tranquilo, amigo. Setenta cinco mil.

He tilts his head, shakes it.

—Setenta cinco mil?

—Si.

Then he's screaming again, too fast for me to follow.

—Rolf?

Nothing.

—Rolf?

Nothing. I look at Rolf. He's staring at me.

—He says fuck your mother and fuck your seventy-five grand. He wants to know where the *real* money is.

—Tell him that's all there is and he can take it or leave it.

—What's he talking about?

—Fucked if I know. Just tell him that's all there is.

Rolf tells him, and Candito sprays curses and bends over to press the gun against Leo's head.

—He doesn't believe you, dude. He says give him the money or he'll shoot Leo.

I look at Leo heaped on the floor. I can't tell if he's breathing. And it's not like I can run out, call Tim, and have him ship the money back to me.

—Tell him there is no fucking way in heaven or earth that he is ever going to have more than what he has right now. That's all there is. Tell him if he leaves now, he can keep the money and probably still work it out so he keeps his job and keeps his partner alive. Tell him if he wants to shoot me he might as well do it because I'm about to walk over there and see if Leo is OK.

—Cool.

Rolf tells him. Candito looks from Leo to the money to me as I walk out from behind the table and start to cross the room toward him. Then he bends, scoops up the money belt, points the gun at me, and backs away shouting. I hold my hands out in front of me.

—Tranquilo.

—He says tranquilo yourself. He says he's gonna take the money and go get the doctor and when he gets back we should be the fuck out of here and if we hurt his partner he'll hunt us down and blah blah blah.

I stop walking and watch as Candito backs himself around the tiny bar to a doorway covered by a Virgin of Guadalupe curtain. He reaches behind himself and pulls the curtain aside, jabs the gun at me three times, emphasizing that I should not fucking follow him, then ducks through the doorway. I can hear his feet sprinting away on the gravel outside.

—Rolf.

He pops up from behind the barrel.

—Dude, that was tense.

I kneel next to Leo and roll him onto his back. His face is beaten and bloody. At least one of his teeth has been knocked out. I put my finger alongside his throat; his pulse is steady and strong. Rolf walks over and looks at his best friend.

—Motherfucker.

He looks at Morales where he's still sprawled on the floor, mewing, his eyes rolling in his head.

—Mother. Fucker.

He raises the revolver, shoots Morales in the face, and spits on his corpse.

—Rolf!

I'm staring at what used to be Morales's face.

—Rolf! What the fuck are you doing?

—You see what this dick did to Leo, dude?

—You don't just. You don't just. What the fuck?

—Dude! He fucked up my best friend.

I look at the lines tattooed on my forearm, and find I have nothing else to say.

—So what now?

—You take Leo in the buggy. There's only the one road in and out of town, so just cruise out to the highway, park, and I'll drive out in their truck after I take care of the other guy.

—Rolf.

—Hey! You hired the pros to get you out and shit got fucked up. That's cool, you paid, but now shit's got to be taken care of. These cops? They know who Leo is, where he lives. Get it? So untwist your panties and help me get him to the buggy, 'cause I got a pig to ambush.

And what do you say to that except *Yes, sir?*

LEO STAYS unconscious as we put him into the passenger seat of the buggy. I get behind the wheel and fire it up. Rolf slaps me on the shoulder. He's holding the revolver and has Morales's 9 mm dangling out of his hip pocket.

—Just turn north when you hit the highway and pull into the trees. I'll be there in a few.

He walks back into the bar. The town is dead silent, motionless except for one painfully skinny stray dog that limps across the park. I pull onto the road out of town. Behind me I might or might not hear gunshots. It's hard to tell over the roar of the buggy's engine.

Back on the 261, I pull into the trees where Rolf told me to. I get out, grab my pack, and hoist it onto my shoulders. It should be about twenty kilometers from here to Campeche. If I stay near the highway I can walk and be there in several hours. Or maybe I'll take a chance and stick my thumb out. If Morales and Candito were working alone no one will be looking for me. If not, they'll find me soon enough. I lick my fingers and rub a little blood from Leo's forehead, but there's nothing I can do for him. I check his pulse again, still strong, and put my face close to his.

—I'm sorry, my friend.

And it's time to get moving again before anyone else gets hurt.

I HITCH a ride with a family from Cancún that are on their way to Campeche to stay with relatives for Christmas. I sit in the back seat of their Jeep, between their two small sons. The boys are quiet for the first couple miles, but get over their shyness and are soon pointing at their own body parts and at things in the car, asking me to tell them what they are called in English.

—Ashtray. Headrest. Ankle. Gearshift. Eyebrow. Toenail. Booger.

They giggle after every word and try to repeat them back to me. Their parents sit quietly in the front seats, holding hands, seemingly happy just to have a break from entertaining the kids. They drop me off in the middle of the city and I take a cab to the airport.

Campeche is a state capital and a tourist destination; the airport has everything I need. I go to the departures board and find a flight. I call Aeromexico from a pay phone and get transferred to an English-speaking agent. She says I can't make a reservation without a credit card number, but assures me there is room on the flight and tells me how much it will cost. At the American Express counter I get about ten thousand pesos worth of traveler's checks.

I have to make a decision here about which identity to sign the checks with because that's who I'll be flying as. I'm about to give the guy at the counter the Carlyle passport when I remember that all it has is a three-year-old entry stamp and no visas. Not a problem with AmEx, but it will be a problem if anyone in a uniform needs to see it.

I give him the passport I've been using for the last two years. Of course there is a problem there as well. When Morales's and Candito's bodies turn up, the Federales will look into their recent cases and start asking questions. Soon, they will find that I have disappeared. After that they'll be looking for this identity. Of course if Rolf didn't get Candito, all of this is moot. Because Candito will be coming after me, the real me. And all this is just too confusing anyway; too many variables and too few options for a guy who needs to get the fuck out of Mexico. I sign the checks and walk over to the Aeromexico counter.

Buying a one-way ticket with cash is just as big a no-no in Mexico as it is in the States, the kind of tip-off that screams *SMUGGLER OR TERRORIST!* to any well-trained airline agent and has them buzzing security. That's why I'm using the traveler's checks and buying a round-trip ticket. It also helps that I'm flying nowhere near the border.

The airline man finds me an aisle seat on the flight and announces the total.

—Siete mil y cinco cien.

I sign a bunch of checks and slide them over along with my passport. He checks the signatures and prints up my ticket to Cabo.

THE FLIGHT gets in around one in the morning. I walk out of the air-port, get mobbed by cabbies, all trying to carry my pack for me, and climb into the closest hack. The driver asks me what bar I want to go to. I have him take me to a hotel instead, the Hyatt. I pay for my room for one night with more traveler's checks. It will make it easier for the *Federales* to track me this far, but I can live with that. I'll be dropping off the radar first thing in the morning.

In the brutally air-conditioned room I take a shower, flop on the bed naked, and smoke cigarettes. Soon the last of the adrenaline seeps from my body and I fall asleep. I wallow in utter blackness until four hours later when my wake-up call sends me jumping at the ceiling to dangle by my fingernails like a frightened cat.

Cat.

Shit.

I miss my cat.

CIVILIZATION ON the Baja, such as it is, clings either to the long ribbon of Highway 1 or to the coast, demonstrating two principles of survival: that life can be sustained either by water or by cars. It takes about two seconds of travel time beyond the edge of Cabo to feel that you are passing through one of the more forlorn wastes of the third world, which is apt, because you are. At the ABC terminal I pay pesos for the first bus going north. It will only get me as far as La Paz, but that's fine with me. I just want to get moving.

We roll up Highway 19 and I stare out the window at a landscape that puts me in mind of nuclear blasts. My brain turns on itself and I start thinking about all the things that can go wrong. It's a long list and it keeps me pretty busy for the three hours it takes to get to La Paz.

I HAVE an hour to kill. In the cantina across the street from the depot I'm able to buy a few packs of cigarettes; Marlboro Lights as they don't carry Benson & Hedges. The place is quiet, just a few other people waiting for the bus, and the mother and daughter team behind the counter. I get some coffee and blow smoke rings at the TV, where the news is playing. The sound is off, but I watch it anyway. So it's really impossible for me to miss the moment when photos of Sergeants

Morales and Candito are flashed on the screen with the caption my spinning brain can't translate except for the words *cimentar,* which I'm pretty sure means found, and *muertos,* which any asshole knows what it means.

BAJA HIGHWAY 1 is more a theory than an actual road, an impossibly long and narrow strip that connects Cabo with Tijuana. Upkeep on the highway is constant, but hopeless. The substructure of the roadway is sand or shale or crumbling coastal cliff face. Erosion has the upper hand here. Crews work endlessly to maintain this lifeline, but it's a losing battle and they know it. You can see it in their eyes when you pass them every hundred miles or so.

I have an aisle seat right up front where I can watch every oncoming vehicle that plows head-on toward us before veering to the side and scraping past. Hours of it have numbed me. All I can do now is twitch as the driver casually one-hands the steering wheel, balancing us on this rail of death as yet another semi slams by and rocks us in its slipstream. It's only about a hundred and fifty miles to Constitución, but by the time we get there I already feel like I've been on the bus for days. We have a half hour to stretch while passengers get on and off. If I time it right, I can smoke about ten cigarettes.

There is only one other white guy on the bus. We make brief eye contact and he lifts his hand-rolled smoke toward me. It's a joint. I shake my head and he turns and walks off a bit from the rest of the passengers to smoke. I wouldn't mind a little toke, but I need to avoid falling into any casual conversations with people who might be able to identify me later.

I smoke three cigarettes, grab a bottle of water and a couple pork tamales from a vendor, and get back on board. An hour later we start to climb the coastal mountains that run up the edge of the Golfo de California. That's where the ride starts to get really fucking scary. The 1 is still just as narrow and in the same state of disrepair, but now it twists and turns around safety-railless blind corners. The driver continues to steer with just the thumb and forefinger of his right hand. I am now seriously wishing I had smoked some of that joint. I get Steinbeck out of my pack and try not to look at the little memento mori altars that commemorate beloved victims of highway death every mile or two. I know exactly what it looks like when a body flies through a windshield and I don't need to be reminded.

THE BUS station at Santa Rosalia is just a counter in a bodega. We pull in well after dark. I stand in line for the bathroom inside, then go out to smoke. Right across the road from the station is a massive concrete breakwater. I walk out onto it a little ways to kill myself a little more. The guy with the joint comes up behind me.
—Hello.
He has a French accent.
—Hi.
—American?
—Yep.
He nods. He's got another joint, offers it to me.
—Thanks.
Not wanting to be a hero on the next leg of the trip, I take a big hit. He points at the joint.
—I could not do these long rides without it.
—Yeah, I could have used it on that last stretch.
I take one more hit and pass the joint back. He licks the tips of his fingers, pinches the cherry off, and drops the roach into his cigarette box. We start back toward the bus. He inhales the sea air deeply. There is a slight chill. I realize it is December and I am heading north for the first time in years. It will be strange to be cold.
—Do you have something to read on the bus?
I nod.
—Yeah, but I'm still reading it. I saw some books in the bodega.
We walk into the bodega together. The books are next to the cooler, mostly in Spanish, but there are a few tattered second-handers in En-

glish on the bottom shelf. I pull out a bottle of water from the cooler, grab a second one, show it to him.

—Want one?

—Yes, thank you.

I turn for the counter, catch something out of the corner of my eye, look again because I'm stoned and this can't be real. I grab a book from the rack and go pay for everything, my heart pounding. Frenchie was right there when I picked up the book. Did he see it?

He joins me outside and I give him his water. He doesn't look at me funny, just takes a sip.

—Thanks.

—Sure.

He holds up a beaten copy of *The Client*.

—The movie was crap, but I have never read any of his books. Maybe they're good?

—Don't count on it.

—What did you get?

—Oh, one of those true crime things. I'm a sucker for that shit.

The bus pulls back out. Most of the passengers are starting to settle toward sleep. I click on my overhead light and pull the book from my grocery bag. I hold it close to my body, like a poker hand. It's by a guy named Robert Cramer and it's called *The Man Who Got Away*. It is the unauthorized story of my life and crimes.

AT GUERRO Negro we cross over from Baja Sur to Baja Norte and soldiers come on board the bus. This is particularly bad timing as I've spent the last several stoned hours reading about the forces that warped me as a child and the role my parents played in turning me into a killer. By the time I realize what's going on, it's too late to hide this book, which features several photos of me, including the three-year-old booking shot on the cover.

One soldier stands at the front of the bus while another walks down the aisle. Behind me, he asks only one person for a passport. When a

French accent replies I know what to expect: this will be a passport check for gringos only. There are more soldiers outside, all armed with assault rifles. Are they looking for me or is this normal? Do they control border traffic like this all the time? If I give these guys the Carlyle passport there will be all kinds of questions about how I've been living illegally in their country for three years with no visa. If the search for Morales's and Candito's murderer has gone far enough the other passport will get me dragged off this bus by my ankles. And shit, which passport is in which pocket, anyway? Why did I get stoned?

The soldier behind me barks something and the French guy starts a stream of denials in Spanish. The soldier at the front of the bus raises his weapon and takes a step into the aisle. I close the book, tuck it between my thighs, and crane my head out into the aisle to see what's going on back there. It's pretty easy to figure out what the ruckus is about because the soldier is holding the French guy's open knapsack in one hand, and what looks like about a quarter kilo of weed in the other. They get the French guy off the bus and you can see by the looks on the soldiers' faces how delighted they are to be busting a white guy for a change. The last one has just climbed off and the driver is getting ready to close the door when the soldier steps back in and looks at me.

—Francés?

—No. American.

—Los Angeles?

I shake my head.

He narrows his eyes.

—San Diego?

I shake my head again, desperate not to be associated with either of these clearly undesirable locales.

—New York.

I move my hand toward my pocket, offering to get my ID for him. Hoping he won't want to see it.

He waves his hand at me, shakes his head.

—New York?

—Yeah.

—September eleven.

—Yeah.

He nods slowly, sadly, then smiles slightly and sticks up his thumb.

—Go Yankees.

I stick up my thumb.

—Yeah. Go Yankees.

He gets off the bus, and I make it to the can before I piss my pants.

THE FACTS of Robert Cramer's book were drawn from public records and exclusive interviews he conducted during the year of "exhaustive research" he spent writing *The Man Who Got Away*. He also refers to an episode of *America's Most Wanted* that seems to have featured me. The mind boggles.

The list of people he claims to have interviewed includes a couple childhood friends, an old neighbor, my fifth-grade teacher, my high-school counselor, my Little League coach (whose statements about my competitive nature Cramer makes great hay of), one of the surgeons who operated on my leg, two old girlfriends (who don't seem to have said anything too embarrassing), a few of my college professors, some former "regulars" from Paul's Bar (whose names I don't recognize), and the parents of Rich, the boy, my friend, who I killed when I crashed my car into a tree. Cramer quotes them as saying I showed no emotion at their son's funeral (true), never contacted them after (true), and had dragged him into a ring of juvenile housebreakers before his death (not so much true, as Rich was already a member of said "ring" when I fell in with him and my other delinquent friends, Steve and Wade).

Cramer dwells for some time on the "killer" competitive instinct my parents programmed into me as they sat on the bench at my baseball games with their "impossible to meet expectations arrayed about them." He consults a psychologist to diagnose the impact of my baseball accident and to attest to how it forced me to channel those instincts into other areas; thus my brief life of petty crime. He exposes my failed attempt to find a healthy outlet as evidenced by my six-year sojourn through college without receiving a degree. He charts my "loner" ways after my college girlfriend "abandoned" me in New York. And finally, he points to the eventual alcoholism that lit the fuse on all my inner rage and stifled need to win, to "beat others." And I am certain that if I had Robert Cramer in front of me right now, I would teach him all about beating others.

I AM standing at the top of Kukulcan. It is night and I am surrounded by all the people Cramer talked to for his book. They are lined up along the edge, their backs to the drop behind them. I push them one by one into the pitch darkness that surrounds the pyramid until I get to the end of the line, where I find my mom and dad.

I lurch awake with a slight cry. Still on the bus, still night. The book is open in my lap, facedown, the cover exposed. The old woman in the seat next to mine looks from the grainy black-and-white photo of my short-haired, clean-shaven former self and up to my shaggy, sweaty face. She gives me a sweet smile.

—Pesadilla?

Pesadilla. Nightmare. A word I actually know in Spanish. I nod, closing the book, tucking it into the pack beneath my seat.

—Si, pesadilla.

She smiles again, takes hold of my hand and squeezes it. Still holding it, she points into the darkness outside.

—Cataviña.

And out of the black desert around us, I see huge shapes looming in the light thrown by our headlamps. I've heard of this place. The Boulder Fields of Cataviña; miles and miles of boulders strewn singly or in mounds or in massive piles the size of small mountains. The boulders themselves range in size from cow to house, all dropped here by glaciers that carved the peninsula however many thousands of thousands of years before any of the people I've killed were ever born.

I fall asleep still holding the old woman's hand.

*　　*　　*

I WAKE to daylight just south of Ensenada. I look to my left and see the Pacific Ocean, the ocean I grew up with. The old woman is gone. About an hour and a half later we pull into the terminal in Tijuana where the Mexican bus lines end because, NAFTA aside, the teamsters don't want them in America.

Inside I find the Greyhound counter and buy the ticket that will take me over the border. I pay the bathroom attendant fifty *centavos* to get in the john and clean up a little. Then I go to the lunch counter, where I see the Raiders and Broncos playing on the TV and realize it's Sunday just before a score scrolls past at the bottom of the screen: DET 21 MIA 0 1Q.

BEFORE I get on the bus I find a trash barrel. I start by dumping Cramer's book, follow that with torn-up traveler's checks, the passport and ID I've been using for the last two years, and the Carlyle passport. That leaves me with Carlyle's driver's license, library card, gym card, and all the stuff you'd expect him to have in a wallet except credit cards.

I get on the bus. We drive a couple miles to the border and find ourselves stuck in a line of buses and cars, all streaming out of Mexico at the end of the weekend. The driver puts the bus in park and stands.

—It looks pretty bad out there today. It's up to you folks, but if I were you, I'd get out here, walk across the border, and catch one of the buses in the terminal on the U.S. side.

Most of the people on the bus decide this is sound advice. It is soon apparent that if I stay here I will no longer be just one of an anonymous crowd of passengers should an Immigration officer come on board. I grab my pack and walk off the bus. It's cool and I'm still dressed for the tropics. The sidewalk that leads to the border station is lined with vendor stalls. I see one selling long-sleeved T-shirts. I buy a white shirt with a Mexican flag on the front, Viva Mexico printed on the back. I look at the people around me, the Americans crossing back. Most are empty-handed or carry plastic shopping bags after spending the night getting drunk in TJ. I get a look at myself in a Corona mirror at one of the booths. I look like a vagabond who's been living here for years, which is only right, I suppose, but not the appearance I want to cultivate.

I kneel by the side of the walk and dig in my pack, making sure there's nothing in it with any of my names. I take out my Steinbeck and put it in one of the thigh pockets of my pants, then walk to a trash barrel and dump the pack. At another vendor's stall I buy a serape and an ashtray shaped like a sombrero. There's also a liquor store, where I get a bottle of mescal. I put on my sunglasses and walk into the border station.

The line is long but moves fast. The American officers thoroughly check the ID on anybody brown, but give just a quick eyeball for most of the white people. My turn at the front of the line comes.

—Nationality?

—U.S.

—ID.

I hand him Carlyle's driver's license, not knowing at all what will happen. *The Man Who Got Away* was published about a year after I left New York. Cramer says I disappeared virtually without a trace and that the NYPD and FBI assume I was either killed by rivals or fled the country. But that doesn't mean he was right about what the authorities really knew, or that they haven't put together more information since the book came out. For all I know, the name Carlyle being entered into an Immigration computer could open a trapdoor beneath my feet and send me dropping into a hole with Charlie Manson.

The Immigration officer looks at the license.

—Can you take off your sunglasses please, Mr. Carlyle?

—Sure, dude.

I push them up on my head.

—How long you been down?

—Friday.

He looks at the license again.

—From New York?

Fuck me.

—Naw, I lived out there for a while, but I came back after the economy tanked.

—Where's back?

—Fresno.

—You know this is expired?

—Yeah, dude, but I don't have a car anyway. I'm living with my folks right now. No work. Took the bus here.

I flash my Greyhound ticket.

—OK, but once it's expired, a license is no longer valid ID.

—Dude! No! Shit!

—It's OK, but get it renewed before you come back down.

—Yeah, right. Thanks, man.

He passes it back.

—Anything to declare?

I hold my shopping bag open.

—Some crap for my folks.

—OK. Have a nice day.

—Yeah, you too, dude.

I drop the sunglasses over my eyes, cross over onto American soil for the first time in three years, and see the camoed special forces types with black berets and automatic weapons. Well, that's new.

ACROSS THE border, I walk past the Greyhound terminal and follow the signs for the trolley to downtown San Diego. It costs two bucks and takes about forty-five minutes. Having just shown that Immigration officer my ticket, I have no intention of getting on another bus. I don't want to risk flashing the Carlyle ID anymore, so flying is out, and I don't have any credit cards to rent a car. What I do have is a little over four grand in cash.

As we enter the city we pass through a couple sketchy neighborhoods that look promising. I hop off at 12th and Market and stand on the corner in front of a liquor store. I see a couple coin-operated news racks across the street and step off the curb. I'm in the middle of the crosswalk when I register something I saw back on the corner. I stop, turn, take a step, and almost get sail-frogged by a heavily primered VW Westphalia. The bus swerves around me, missing by inches, and I get to the sidewalk and light up. Three years of Mexico have killed my traffic instincts.

I walk over to the little stucco house behind the liquor store and it's there in the driveway: a pale yellow 1968 BMW 1600 with a For Sale sign in the window and a sense of desperation in the air. I look back over my shoulder at the newspaper racks. Screw the *Auto Trader*. God knows how long that might take. I walk up to the front door and ring the bell. A little girl, maybe five years old, opens up and stands there behind the screen door. I smile.

—Hey, is your mom or dad home?

She slams the door in my face. I raise my hand to ring again, decide against it, and start for the street. I hear the door open behind me.

—What?

I turn. There's another girl there, this one about seventeen.

—Yeah, I wanted to know about the car. I asked your sister if your folks were home.

—Daughter.

—Right. She's a beautiful girl.

—Uh-huh.

—So. The car?

—What about it?

—It's for sale?

—Yeah.

—Is it yours?

—Yeah.

—How much you want for it?

—Five.

—Does it run?

—Yeah.

—Can we start it up?

She squints at me.

—You a process server?

—Uh, no.

—'Cause if I come out there and you try to stick some fucking piece of paper in my hand, I'm gonna take it and ram it up your ass.

—I am not a process server.

—I'll get the keys.

The car starts right up. She switches on the radio to show that it works, tells me the brakes need fluid, and asks if I want to take it around the block. I pop the hood, make sure the oil is full and not too black, quickly eyeball the plugs, fiddle with the carburetor for a second to even out the flow, and shake my head.

—No test drive, I'll take it as is, four hundred.

She turns the key, switching off the engine, and nods.

—OK, but I need a ride before you take it.

Christ.

—Where?

—'Bout a mile. I need to drop my daughter at her dad's place.

Last thing I need is this girl sitting in the car with me for a mile, and getting a good look at my face.

—Look, I'm sorry, but I really need to get rolling.

—C'mon, give us a ride. Otherwise I got to call the son of a bitch to come get her and he'll take all day coming over and I'll never get to work on time 'cause I got to take the bus now 'cause I'm selling you the car and I'm knocking a hundred off it for you anyway.

Oh, man.

—OK. I'll give you a ride, but let's get going.

—Thanks. My name's Leslie. Pink slip's inside.

The daughter is sitting on the floor in front of the tube watching MTV. A girl her mom's age is shoving her ass into the camera. Leslie points at a chair.

—Wait here.

She goes into a bedroom and I can see her take a box down off a shelf in the closet. I stand next to the chair and watch the girl watch TV. The video ends and she becomes aware of me.

—You like Britney?

—Not really.

—I used to like her, but now she's all dirty.

—Looks that way.

—You like Christina?

—Not really.

—My mom likes her.

—Who do you like?

—Eminem. Do you like him?

—Sometimes.

Her eyes are locked on the screen as she flips channels. Leslie walks back into the room, a massive black purse over her shoulder and a pink slip in her hand.

—Got the money?

I slip some bills out of my pocket and count out four hundred. She takes it and looks at the rest of the cash in my hands.

—You a dealer?

—No.

—Hn.

She hands me the pink slip, already signed, and I put it in my back pocket. She puts the cash in her purse and looks at her daughter.

—Cassidy, turn that off, we're gonna go to daddy's.

Cassidy switches off the TV, gets up, and walks out the front door without looking at her mom.

—She's a little pissed at me right now because I told her we had to get rid of the cable.

—Right.

I wait on the porch while she locks the door, twists the BMW key off the ring, and hands it to me. I point at the trunk.

—Anything you need to get out?

—Some tapes in the glove box, you can have 'em.

—OK.

Cassidy scrambles into the backseat, Leslie gets in front and looks over her shoulder.

—Put on your belt, honey.

Cassidy sighs loudly but buckles up and we do the same. I start the BMW and pull into the street. At the first stop sign I tread lightly on the brake pedal and roll halfway through the intersection before we stop. I pull us the rest of the way across and look at Leslie.

—Told you they needed fluid.

—No kidding.

—You want your money back?

—No. Which way?

She directs me through several blocks of run-down suburbia, brown lawns, peeling paint, overgrown tree roots pushing up slabs of sidewalk, until we pull into the driveway of another stucco job, this one with a rusted and empty boat trailer in the side yard. Leslie opens her door and sticks one foot out.

—Look, will ya do me a favor?

—Depends.

—I know I said I just needed a ride here, but will you wait a second in case he's not home and we need a ride to the bus stop? I would of called him, but the phone, ya know, like the cable.

Killing me, she's killing me.

—Just be fast, OK?

She nods sharply, gets out, and helps Cassidy from the backseat. I turn off the car and watch as they go up the walk. The front door opens before they can knock. A guy in his twenties, wearing sweatpants and a concert T with the sleeves ripped off, comes out. He sees me in the car and points.

—Who the fuck is that?

Oh no.

Leslie looks at me.

—That's the guy I just sold your fucking car to, you asshole.

Oh fucking no.

—See, fucker, I told you. I told you, pay your fucking support or I'd sell the fucking thing.

No more kindness to strangers. No more kindness to strangers. No more kindness to strangers.

Cassidy's dad sticks his finger in Leslie's face.

—You did not, you fucking bitch.

—Yes I did, I did.

She points at me.

—Go ask him. Go see, he has the fucking pink slip, you deadbeat piece of shit.

Cassidy walks past them and into the house with a shrug of her shoulders. *Been there, done that.*

The guy starts heading for me.

—You, cocksucker, get out of my fucking car.

Why do I keep landing in this shit? I mean, is shit just attracted to this fly or what? No matter. This particular shit is easy to get out of.

I start the car, drop it in reverse, zip out of the drive, and head back down the street the way we came in. Except, of course, I turn the wrong way out of the driveway and go straight into a cul-de-sac. Now I have to turn around and drive back past Cassidy's dad, who is standing in the middle of the street with a ball-peen hammer in his hand. Where the fuck did he get that?

I try to steer around him to the left, and he steps in front of the car; to the right, and he's there again. I think about just hitting the gas and going over him, but stop the car instead. He stands in front of the hood, hammer dangling at his side.

—I said out of the car.

Leslie has walked down to the bottom of the driveway.

—Stop being a dick, Danny. I sold him the car. You want to yell at someone, yell at me.

He keeps his eyes on me, but raises the hammer and points it in her direction.

—Get in the fucking house, bitch, I'll deal with you.

—Oh, fuck off, you're not my husband. Just 'cause ya knocked me up doesn't mean you can tell me what to do.

He turns to face her.

—Get in the fucking house before I kick your ass.

She shivers all over like she's cold.

—Ohhhh, I'm so fucking scared. You lay one fucking hand on me and you know my dad will come over here and kick your ass again.

Danny turns back to me, face boiling red.

—What the fuck are you still doing in my fucking car? I said get the fuck out!

—Leave him alone, Danny.

—SHUUUUUUT UUUUUUP!!!

He walks toward my door, hammer hefted.

He's smaller than me, but has one of those hard wiry builds. He could be dangerous. What say we play this one cool.

He grabs the door handle, yanks it open.

—Out.

—Easy.

I start to get out of the car. He grabs my hair, pulls me the rest of the way out.

—I said out, fuck.

He kicks me in the ass as he releases my hair and I stumble a couple steps.

Leslie is still on the curb.

—Knock it off, Danny.

He ignores her, focused on me now.

—She telling the truth? You got my pink slip?

—I got the pink slip.

—Let's have it.

—Look, man, I paid for the car.

—That ain't my problem. That bitch sold something ain't hers. You want your money back, talk to her.

Leslie takes a couple steps into the street.

—That's not fucking true and you know it. The judge gave me that car. It's mine.

—I. Don't. Give. A. Fuck. What. The. Judge. Said.

I raise a hand.

—Hey, whatever you guys have going on is.

—Give me my fucking pink slip right fucking now, asshole.

He's holding the hammer up at shoulder level, cocked and ready to swing.

—Give it to him, Danny.

—Kick his fucking aaaaaaaasss.

—Do it. Do it. Do it.

I look over at the porch of Danny's house. Three of his friends have come out to watch the party. They're all about his age, one with a shaved head, one with a ponytail, and one with a greasy mullet. I am now officially being hassled by the assholes who stole everybody's milk money.

Leslie turns to face them.

—Shut up, you dildos. This is none of your business.

The biggest of the three, or rather, the fattest of the three, he of the shaved head, gives her the finger.

—Fuck off, Leslie.

Danny jerks his head around.

—Hey! What did I fucking say about talking to her like that?

—She's being a bitch.

—I don't care what she's being, she's my kid's mom.

Leslie waves her hand toward them, done with the whole scene. She walks toward the car.

—Come on, mister, give me a ride to the bus, he's a fuckoff.

—Shutthefuckupshutthefuckupshutthefuckup!!!

Enough of this.

—Look, Danny.

He swings the hammer at me.

I MURDERED a man less than a week ago. I saw another man have his face blown literally off. That was . . . yesterday? One of my friends got beat half to death on account of me. I have four million dollars sitting at another friend's house in Las Vegas, sitting there waiting to attract killers or cops, whoever smells it first. I'm not sure anymore who may or may not be after me: the Russians, the Mexican police, the FBI, a bunch of fucking treasure hunters like Mickey. Whoever wants me or the money, all of them, can find out where my parents live whenever they want because Mom and Dad stayed put through all the killing, and the reporters, and the cops, stayed right in the house where I grew up. And I'm really, really fucking tired.

I actually hear the sound as I snap.

It sounds good.

Just like a bat hitting a ball.

I step inside Danny's swing. His forearm hits me in the shoulder and the hammer ends up slamming against my back. I hook him under the ribs, he folds in two. I grab the back of his head and bring my knee up into his face. He turns at the last moment so I don't break his nose. But I can fix that.

I have his head in the open car door and am ready to slam it on his face when I realize his friends are running into the street. I drop his head, scoop up the hammer from the asphalt, and swing it in a mad arc. They fall back, but stay in a tight group, and I dive at them, shoving the fat guy back into his two skinnier buddies. They stumble, Fat Guy falling on top of Mullet Head, and Ponytail Boy windmilling his arms to keep his balance. I start kicking at the heads of the two on the ground.

—Stop it! Stop it!

I turn, hammer raised. Leslie flinches back. I lower the hammer. Leslie sticks her finger in my face.

—What the fuck are you, some kind of maniac? Ya didn't have to beat the shit out of 'em, they're all a bunch of pussies anyway.

The two on the ground are curled into scared little balls, their knees drawn up, hands covering their heads. Ponytail Boy has run off into one of the houses in the cul-de-sac. I throw the hammer into some bushes. Danny is on his ass, leaning against the side of the car, holding his bleeding mouth.

—Danny.

He doesn't look up. Blood is trickling steadily from his mouth. I think he may have bit through his lip. I squat down in front of him. He looks up at me. His eyes narrow.

—Hey.

His hand comes away from his mouth and he points at me.

—Heeey.

—Get off my car, Danny.

He's still looking at me, tilting his head, squinting but not moving. I grab his legs and pull. He scoots on his butt to keep from tipping over. I drop his legs and get in the car. Leslie has followed me and squats down next to Danny.

—Stop being a dick to him, can't ya see he's hurt?

I close the door and start the car. I can feel a lump growing between my shoulder blades where the hammer tagged me. I shove the stick into first and pull away. In the mirror Danny is still sitting in the street, pointing after me. Leslie has one hand on his head and is giving me the finger with her other one.

I'm almost at the end of the block when a garage door back in the cul-de-sac swings up and Ponytail Boy comes screeching out in a jacked-up black Toyota pickup with monster tires.

Great. Pursuit.

I'VE BEEN lost in these tracts for about ten minutes now and nothing looks familiar. Or rather, everything looks familiar because it all looks exactly the same. Wait a sec. That's it. That's the liquor store where I got off the trolley. I stop the car, put it in reverse, and back up to the last intersection. There it is, just up the street. From there I can follow the trolley tracks back toward the I-5.

It only takes a few minutes to reach a major intersection, where I see signs for the highway. I'm almost at the on-ramp when I get a look at the gas gauge. Empty. I pull into the last-chance Shell and kill the engine.

I've got about four gallons in the tank when the black Toyota squeals to a stop at the intersection. Danny is in the front, Ponytail Boy behind the wheel, Leslie is squeezed between them, and Fat Guy and Mullet Head are in the back.

A big red Suburban is on the other side of the pumps from me, screening the BMW from the street. I duck down a little so they can't see me. When the light changes they'll go right past, and I can sneak out onto the freeway.

Then I see their turn signal flashing.

They're going to come in here.

The light changes. I pull the hose out, hang it up, and close the tank. Two cars make the turn before the Toyota. I reach into the car and hit the ignition, but stay standing so I can peer through the windows of the Suburban. The Toyota makes the turn and heads for the driveway behind me. I get in the car and ease it forward around the pumps and the Suburban, trying to keep it between me and Danny's crew as they pull into the station. If I time it right, I'll pop out on the other side of this behemoth, behind them, and be able to scoot away before they know I'm here.

I pull out from the cover of the Suburban. The Toyota is stopped right next to the driveway. Fat Guy has hopped out of the back and is asking what everybody wants from the store inside. They see me.

I hit the gas and squirt past them into the street. As I bounce over the curb, Fat Guy tries to climb back up on the truck, gets one leg in, and is dragged several yards before the truck stops and he is tossed to the pavement. I hit the intersection just as the light goes yellow and make for the on-ramp. I check the rearview, see the Toyota behind me jump the intersection as the light turns red, see it get snarled in a mess of squealing brakes and curses. I'm on the ramp, merging into traffic and on my way north.

I CAN tune in Westwood One on the old AM/FM in this piece of crap. They're broadcasting the Oakland vs. Denver game and I'm able to get updates on the Dolphins, which is as good as anything. Or, as it turns out, as bad as anything.

By the time the game ends, Miles Taylor's backup has stumbled to six yards rushing and three lost fumbles, two of which were taken back for touchdowns. Going into the game, Coach had not been overly concerned about his wounded secondary because Detroit has the worst passing attack in the NFL. He decided to load the line to stop Chester Dallas, their massive Pro Bowl fullback. Detroit focused completely on the air game, where they had three touchdowns and over three hundred yards at the half, while Coach kept eight in the box to stuff the nonexistent running game. DET 48, MIA 9 FINAL. Meanwhile, the Packers have decided this is the day to lose a December game at home for the first time since the Dark Ages, handing the Jets a one-game division lead over Miami. I turn off the radio and concentrate on not dying in this crappy car.

I manage to get it up and over the Grapevine. I gas up at an Exxon, buy a hot dog, a soda, and some Benson & Hedges in the convenience store, and get back on the road. About four more hours and I should be home.

The I-5 is the highway that the Baja 1 aspires to be: long, straight, impeccably maintained, and running through similarly featureless terrain. Endless rolling hills line the valley, all of them dirt brown year-round, except for a few brief moments in late fall and early spring. Orchards and cattle ranches offer an occasional break from the usual scenery, which consists of dead grass. There are the anomalous palm trees, the abandoned farm equipment, and the massive rest stops, but other than that, it's a long haul with nothing to look at but the other cars and the assortment of Oakland Raiders paraphernalia they sport.

With one hand I twist the cap off my water bottle and take a swig. I try to fiddle the cap back onto the bottle and it drops between my thighs. I feel around for it and my foot comes off the gas a little. The motor home behind me makes a move to pass me. I look down at my lap, find the cap, and put it back on the bottle as the motor home leaves the right lane and starts to slowly pass me on the left. Behind the motor home I see a black car coming on way too fast to stop. The motor home tries to get out of its way by ducking back into my lane. The huge RV veers at me, horn blaring. I push the brake, the motor home creeps farther into my lane. I stick my foot into the brake, the BMW skidding slightly as I try to steer onto the shoulder.

I drop back behind the motor home just as it swerves sharply into my lane and barely misses hacking off my front bumper. And now I see that the speeding black car has driven half onto the left shoulder to pass the motor home while it was passing me. I also see that the black car is not a black car at all, but a black Toyota pickup. Then I'm pulling to a stop on the side of the road, watching Danny and his friends as they speed up the highway. Fucking hell. What is this, *Deliverance*?

I LET Danny get farther up the road before I pull out. Around Coalinga I see a black pickup across the meridian, headed south. Could be them giving up, or driving back to scan the northbound traffic. I don't know.

It's after dark when I see my exit. By now my eyes keep dropping shut and I've lost most of the sense of forward motion; the road just seems to be reeling toward me as I stay in one place. I hit the blinkers and turn off.

God, I forgot what Christmas is like in the suburbs. It's still a couple weeks away, but lights are dribbling down from the eaves, reindeer are on the rooftops, forests of giant candy canes are growing from the lawns. We used to do that thing; drive around all the different neighborhoods looking at the lights. Christmas. I should have got them something. I park a few blocks away, rather than leaving a strange car in front of their house for the neighbors to see. Then I sit behind the wheel, trying to get my shit together. Maybe I should have called.

AS SOON as I knock on the door, the dogs start barking. The same dogs. I can hear her inside, coming into the hall, telling them to shush, and them not listening at all, just barking like crazy. A lock snaps open. They never used to lock the door, but I guess they've had reason enough the last few years. The door swings open just enough for her to look out and still keep it blocked with her body so that neither of the dogs can squirt out around her.

She looks at me.

Mom is a tiny woman. She likes to claim she's five foot two, but the truth is she's just a shade over five. At least she used to be. It's been several years and she looks a bit smaller now. And older. Much older. I did that to her. She looks at me, the guy on her porch with the deep tan, short beard, and long hair. She looks at the nose, crunched and bent, the extra twenty pounds of weight, the tattoos dribbling out the tugged-up sleeves of my shirt and down my forearms. There is no beat, no pause or halt, just instant recognition and the sudden escape of air from her mouth.

I push the door open, catch her as her knees give out beneath her. I hold her shaking body up and kick the door closed with the heel of my foot. She gasps for air and I give her a little squeeze and a shake and a huge gob of snot and phlegm flies out of her nose and plasters the front of my shirt and she starts to breathe again. I hold her tight and she shivers and sobs and pounds on my back and shoulders with her tiny fists and curses at me and tells me she loves me while the old dogs run around in circles, barking at me.

PART TWO

DECEMBER 11–14, 2003

Two Regular Season

Games Remaining

—Henry.

My name.

—Henry.

Hearing my name from my father's mouth almost starts me crying
again.

—Henry!

—Yeah, Dad.

—What the hell do you think you're doing?

What I'm doing is standing on the back patio, lighting a cigarette.

—I was just gonna have a smoke.

—When the hell did you start smoking?

—I don't know. Couple years ago.

I light up.

—Look at that, you have a great meal and now you're going to ruin it
by killing your taste buds and filling your lungs with that poison.

—OK, Dad.

—Look at the pack, it tells you right there.

—Got it, Dad.

I stub the smoke out in an empty flowerpot.

—They just about tell you that you have to be a suicidal idiot to smoke
the things and people keep smoking them.

I've been here for maybe two hours.

—It's out.

—And you, you wait over thirty years and *now* you start?

And already it's like I never left home at all.

—Dad, it's out. OK?

—Yeah, sorry. I just. I just don't want you to get hurt or anything.

He turns his head as tears start to well up in his eyes again. Well, almost like I never left home.

—I don't want to get hurt, Dad.

Mom opens the back door.

—Come inside, it's cold out.

THERE WERE steaks in the fridge. Dad grilled them for us, standing by the propane barbeque out on the cold patio, watching me through the windows as I helped Mom set the table.

He had been at the shop, working late just like he always did when I was a kid, unless I had a game. When he came home, Mom met him at the door. But she started crying before she could say anything. By the look he had on his face when I walked out of the kitchen, I think he was assuming the worst. One second he thinks his wife is trying to tell him their son is dead, and the next I'm standing in front of him.

After that there wasn't much to do except decide what everyone wanted for dinner.

NOW DAD and me come in and sit down at the kitchen table with Mom. She's sipping a glass of red wine and Dad is drinking some brandy he got from a bottle that was buried at the back of one of the cupboards over the sink. He pours himself another and looks at me.

—Sure you don't want one?

—No. I had a drinking thing there, Dad. In New York. I was drinking too much, so I had to stop.

—Yeah, we heard something about that.

Mom moves her hand so that it covers mine.

—People said a lot of things, Henry. We didn't know what to believe. Except about the killing. We knew they were wrong about that, we knew you couldn't kill anyone.

My left forearm is lying there on the table, the six hash marks exposed. I open my mouth, close it. Dad sets his glass down and covers my hand and Mom's with his own. He has big hands, nicked and cut and bruised from the shop, a thin rim of grease permanently tattooed under his fingernails.

—Why are you here, Hank?

Someone threatened to kill you and I came home to make sure it doesn't happen.

—There's just some more trouble, Dad, and I need to take care of it.

—But why, what did you do?

—I.

I helped a friend. I tried to protect people. I did everything I was supposed to and the only thing that worked was killing the people who were trying to kill me.

And then I took their money.

—Dad, I just tried to do the right thing.

He pours himself another drink. His fifth. I've never seen him drink this much before.

—So what now?

—I'm gonna take care of it.

—How?

—I'm gonna give these people what they want.

THEY GO to bed a short while later, and I page Tim. And wait. And then I page him again. And again. And again. And again. I page him ten times and he doesn't call back, and finally I'm just too tired to care.

AFTER MY leg was shattered and I couldn't play baseball anymore I took all my old trophies and plaques down, boxed them up, and stuck them in the attic. Sometime in the last three years Mom or Dad must have gotten those boxes down to look through them, because all the old trophies are in my old bedroom. My bed is still in there too. Other than that, it's a different room. Mom uses it for her sewing and cro-cheting and the several other crafts she's thrown herself into since she retired last year.

I lie in the too-small bed in the darkness and watch light from a street lamp glinting off of all the fake gold and silver. Outside, it's silent except for the occasional bark of a dog, quieter even than my beach in Mexico, where there is at least the sound of the surf.

On the nightstand is a small, framed picture of me. I'm sixteen, my hair is almost white from years under the California sun, my face is golden brown and unlined, and I'm wearing a cap from my high school team, the Tigers. I remember the day the photo was taken. I had pitched a shutout for the varsity squad, hit a homer, and had five RBI. I was six feet tall, a hundred and sixty pounds and still growing, work-ing out every day and eating anything I could get my hands on, trying to build muscle for the inevitable day when I would be a Major League player. To this day, it is the face I expect to see when I look in the mirror.

NORMALLY DAD would take the truck parked in the driveway to work, but today he fires up the tiny MGB in the garage. He hits the auto-matic opener, the door flips up, and he pulls into the street.

—Where did you park?

—Over on Traina.

There's been a lot of turnover on Dale Road in three years. A lot of people I used to know moved out during the year of constant attention from media, police, and sightseers that followed my adventures. But even the newcomers know who my parents are, know that they have a mass murderer for a son. I stay squished down in the footwell until we get a couple blocks away.

—A BMW 1600?

—Yeah.

—Oh, Hank, not this piece of crap?

I scoot up into the seat. Dad has stopped where my car is parked.

—Yeah.

—How much did you pay for that?

—Four.

—And you drove it from San Diego?

—Yeah.

—You're lucky you didn't kill yourself in that thing.

—It's not that bad.

—Like hell it isn't.

He sits behind the wheel of his perfectly restored 1962 British racing green MGB and stares in horror at my wreck.

—Well, let's get it over to the shop and out of sight.

I get out, start my car, and follow him over to Custom Specialty Motors.

CSM SERVICES and restores classic, exotic, and performance automobiles. Says so right on the sign. This is the business Dad dreamed of owning his whole life, the one he created and built over the last twenty years after he threw in the towel as hotshot mechanic for a series of high-end dealerships. His customers are mostly middle-aged men who finally have the money to buy the toys they craved in their youth, but who lack the mechanical aptitude to keep them running.

He unlocks the big rolling garage door and I drive into the shop. He pulls the MG in behind me, closes and locks the door, and switches on the overheads. Fluorescent light bounces off of some very expensive paint jobs. I get out of my crappy car and go look at a 1953 Corvette Roadster, cream with red interior.

—Wow.

—Look at this mess.

I look over my shoulder. Dad has the hood of the BMW up and is peering into the disordered engine compartment.

—Jeez, Hank, your plugs are filthy, there's corrosion on the battery cables, the gaskets on the carb are rotting, there's oil everywhere.

He grabs a socket wrench from one of the big rolling tool cabinets and starts pulling the plugs.

—Dad, you don't have to do that.

—There is no way you are driving this car anywhere without a complete tune-up.

—Dad.

—No way. Now, you go home and get out of sight.

He's right. His customers may not know how to change the oil on all this steel candy, but most are retired and they love to come around and get underfoot while Dad is working. He goes into the office and comes back with a CSM cap and windbreaker.

—Here.

I slip them on, get into the MGB, grab his sunglasses off the dash, and put those on as well.

He stands next to the car, not moving to open the door for me.

—Hey! Hey, we haven't talked about the Giants yet. Can you believe the season they had?

I know. I know they dominated the National League West, and won their first World Series since they moved to San Francisco. I didn't get to watch or listen to a single game, but I know.

—Yeah, I haven't seen much baseball, Dad.

—Oh.

—But maybe you can tell me about it later.

—Yeah, sure. At the house maybe.

He goes over to the door and pushes the big black button that rolls it up.

—Well, take it easy in that thing.

—No problem, Dad.

I drive home, this town's most infamous son, dressed as my father.

MOM WANTED to skip her volunteer day at the elementary school where she tutors special-ed kids. I told her it would be better if she and Dad did everything as normally as possible until I left. The specter of my departure made her start to cry again, but she went. Now I'm alone.

When the landlord cleared out my apartment in New York, he sent the stuff to my folks. Mom donated some things to Goodwill, but I'm able to find a couple boxes of my old clothes. The jeans and thermal top I pull on are snug, but they'll do while the clothes I was wearing go through the washer. In the meantime I page Tim some more and try to distract myself by watching *Monday Quarterback*.

The guys on TV are breaking down just how bad Miami is without Miles Taylor when the phone rings. I reach for it. Stop myself. I'll let the machine pick up. If it's Tim he'll let me know. The machine picks up and whoever is calling hangs up.

OK, not Tim.

The phone rings again. The machine picks up. The caller disconnects. Maybe it is Tim and he doesn't want to talk into the machine in case . . . In case what? God, who knows what that pothead could be thinking? The phone rings again. Christ! The machine picks up. The caller hangs up.

Jesus F. Christ.

The phone rings. It has to be Tim, who else would do this? The machine picks up. Caller hangs up.

Goddamn it, Timmy, you know I can't answer the fucking phone. Just talk to the machine, you burnout.

The phone rings.

Fuck. Fuck. Fuck. Fuck.

The machine picks up. The caller does not hang up.

—Mr. Thompson.

A voice I don't know, a caller for Mr. Thompson: my dad.

—Mr. Thompson? Are you there?

I stop holding my breath.

—Mr. *Henry* Thompson, please pick up.

Oh.

So yeah, turns out the call *is* for me after all.

MILL'S CAFÉ is the oldest restaurant in town. When I was in high school, Patterson was so small there wasn't anywhere else to go. Now there's a McDonald's and a Taco Bell and a Pizza Hut and God knows what else, all thanks to the Silicon Valley real-estate boom that sent people scurrying farther and farther east of San Francisco in search of affordable housing. We could have gone to one of those new places where all the employees are kids that I've never seen, but he wanted to try this place, where the waitress serving us is the same one who used to bring me burgers and Cokes after baseball games. I keep my shoulders slumped, Dad's sunglasses on my face, and try not to look around too much.

He takes another bite of his egg-white omelet and keeps talking.

—Honestly, it's easier to explain in terms of *political science* rather than *business.*

He pauses, gathers his thoughts.

—OK, OK, I got it, it's like this. When a country gets a nuclear weapon, the first thing they do is to test it. *Publicly.* They don't do this because they want to know if the weapon *works,* but because they want *everyone else* to know that it works. For a country, having nuclear weapons isn't so much about being *able* to blow up your enemies, it's about letting your enemies *know* that you can blow them up. You test your new A-bomb where it can be seen and heard so that you can be *sure* that your enemies know what's coming if they piss you off. Now Russians understand this kind of thinking because they pretty much invented it when they tested their first hydrogen bomb after the war. That's why *your* particular Russians never sent anyone to kill your parents. What would be the *point*? They kill your folks and it removes the biggest weapon from their arsenal and they don't get anything in return. What they wanted was for you to surface so that they could *threaten* to kill your parents unless you gave them back the *money.* Now, *after that,* they would have killed them, and then you of course.

A couple old-timers are at the counter reading the *Patterson Irrigator.* Other than that, it's just us. I'm drinking coffee, but I was only able to eat a bite of the English muffin I ordered. When he mentions my parents, that one bite of muffin flops over in my stomach.

—That was a sound strategy, and it was clear to me that it was one I should stick with. *Except* the part about killing your folks and you once the money is returned. That's just pure revenge. The *Russians* had their reasons for wanting revenge, but *I* could care less about what you did or who you killed. For me this is purely a *business* proposition, and revenge is a poor business strategy at best. If I get my money, that's all I care about. And I want no confusion about this: it is *my* money now. I paid for it.

He's just a few years older than me, and everything about him screams Manhattan. He's got one of those two-hundred-dollar haircuts that's engineered to look like he paid thirteen for it at Astor Place Hair, and the flecks of premature gray at his temples set off the titanium frames of the rectangular glasses he's wearing. His Levis look worn, but I'm certain they are a pair of phenomenally expensive historical replicas of a pair owned by some prospector in 1849. His feet are tucked into bright blue-and-yellow vintage Pumas, and over a designer T-shirt of some extra-clingy material that super-defines his razor-edged pecs he's sporting a black leather jacket of such ethereal smoothness that it almost feels like fur when I brush up against it. He's charming and affable, has bottle green eyes and a toothy Tom Cruise grin. I'd hate him even if he wasn't threatening my family.

—That's one of the things I need to be *certain* you understand. Whoever the money *might* have belonged to, and, believe me, I've done quite a bit of research on this, it is *mine* now. Sure, you could argue that ultimately it belongs to the depositors at the banks that the DuRantes robbed in the first place, but the insurance companies took care of those people long ago. After that, the most legitimate claim is the Russians, and for awhile they were committed to recouping, but after three years they pretty much gave up. They were ready to call it a day, write the money off, and kill your mom and dad out of principle. If you ever turned up later that would be great, but they were done looking. That's when I knew it was time for me to get involved. See, *what you do is,* you look at other businesses for assets you can pick up cheaply, especially from businesses that are struggling, and, believe me, the Russian mob is not what it once was. They had their heyday in the nineties. I mean, who didn't? But they're just not *cutting-edge* anymore,

not sharp, and the market wants you to be *sharp*. So I saw that they had
this great asset, which is essentially ownership of a four and a half million dollar IOU, *but* no real plan for collecting on it. See what I'm saying? Great asset, but they don't know how to make it work for them. *I
do*. So, what I do is, I go to a guy I know and I make an offer. I'll buy
your IOU for one hundred thousand dollars. Well, they balk of course,
but then, I give them the kicker: one hundred grand to secure the IOU,
which means that I become the sole agent licensed to pursue it, *and*, if
I recover the money, a guarantee that they'll receive ten percent of
whatever I recover, less the hundred they already have. But they keep
that hundred no matter what I get my hands on. Well, hell, at that
point they have nothing, so it becomes a no-brainer. And trust me,
when dealing with the Russian mob, a no-brainer is the only kind of
deal you can make. So they take the 100K, and take the guys who had
been looking for you and put them to work making money again. And I
put my plan into action.

The waitress brings the pot over again. He covers his cup with his
hand.

—No more for me, sweetheart, I'm about to float away. You want anything else?

I shake my head. He smiles up at her.

—Guess that's it, just the check when you have a sec.

—Got it right here, hon.

She scribbles on her pad, tears off the check, sets it on the table, and
walks back to the register.

He looks at the check.

—Unreal. You know how much that omelet would be in New York?

He takes out a twenty and drops it on the table. Leeann comes to
pick it up.

—Be right back with your change.

—It's good like that, sweetie.

—Thanks.

—It OK if we hang out here just a little?

—Sure, long as you like.

She leaves. He smiles after her.

—Sweet lady. Where was I?

—Assets.

—Right. So now I have this asset, this *IOU*, but, and here's the rub, no way to collect. Well, I've already spent a hundred thousand on this project, I'm not about to sink more capital into sending a bunch of headhunters out to find you. So what *do* I do? Do you know what I did?

—You had my parents' house staked out until I came home.

—No. Because I had looked into that, and do you know what I found out? Stakeouts, a *real stakeout* in a suburban neighborhood, that is both constant and imperceptible, is very difficult and expensive. So that's not it. Any other guesses?

—No.

—OK, here it is, this was my multimillion-dollar idea: I paid one of your parents' *neighbors* to watch the house and call me when you turned up. Brilliant, right? I mean, not to blow my own horn, but this is a recurring expense of five hundred dollars a month with a possible, if not likely, return in the *millions*.

There's no smoking in Mill's, there's no smoking anywhere in California these days, so I've been fiddling with an unlit cigarette for about half an hour. I snap the filter off and break the rest into little quarter-inch pieces.

—Which neighbor?

—Hey now, that would be telling.

WE SIT in his rental car in front of my parents' house. I look at the other houses on the street and watch for someone peeking from behind a curtain or over a fence, someone advertising their guilt. No luck. The car is a nonsmoker, which should really come as no surprise. He hands me a cell phone and a recharge cable.

—We could do this *a lot* of ways. I could have someone sit in the house with your mom and dad while you go and get the money or arrange to have it sent from wherever it is. I mean, assuming it's not here. It's not here, is it?

—No.

—I figured not. The thing is, that's not my *style* of business. I really *prefer* to manage in a hands-off kind of way. Keep my distance until my presence is *required*. What I want to do is back off. Let you get the money together and give me a call when you have it. That phone has my number programmed into it, and I'm talking about my *personal* number here, so please don't go giving it out. Just to be clear, there will be *people* here, employees of mine, and they will be *watching* your mom and dad. And I'm not talking about neighbors this time, I mean *professionals*. Understand? I do need an answer on this, Hank. Understand?

—Yeah.

—If my employees see your parents try to leave town, etc? Well, to return to my metaphor, if they leave, they can no longer be detonated, and they are no longer of value to me. I need them here where they can be *watched*, where I can get to them in case you fail to bring me my money. So if my employees see any indication that your parents are trying to leave or to seek shelter, I'll have no choice but to *detonate* my "weapon." You understand all of this?

—Yes.

—Good. So, you go get the money in what we will simply call a *reasonable* amount of time, and call me. After that, you pay off your IOU and I disassemble my arms, so to speak.

He sticks out his hand.

—Deal?

I look at his soft, well-manicured hand.

—What's your name?

—Jeez, did I do that again? Sorry. I'm *Dylan*, Dylan Lane.

His hand is still sticking out.

—Dylan?

—Yes?

—Keep my parents safe.

—Trust me, that's in *my* best interest, too. And hey, I won't even bring up the police, because they would be in *no one's* best interest.

I shake his hand, it's almost as soft as his jacket, and he drives off.

I stand on the curb and imagine all the things I could do to make myself dead. I remember all the drunken times in Mexico that I thought about trying to swim to Cozumel, knowing that I would drown long before I got there. And I never did it. I sobered up and stayed alive long enough to kill a man who threatened my folks. And then I ran home to protect them. And by doing those things I have put their lives at greater risk than they ever were before.

Looks like it's a good thing Dad is tuning up the BMW, because I can't wait around here any longer for Timmy's call.

But I do have something I'd like to do before I go.

—SO, MOM, how have the neighbors been, any of them come around?

She looks up from the pasta Dad made for dinner.

—Pat and Charley used to check in on us, that first year, when it was especially hard. But, then they moved last year to . . . Oh, where did they go?

Dad is over at the stove, serving himself seconds from the big pot.

—Vacaville.

—Vacaville, they moved to Vacaville.

Anyone else, what about the new people?

—I don't know, Henry, they know about us, but I don't think. It's not the kind of thing that comes up in conversation. A couple of my friends at the school, they ask, if we've heard anything, if we know how you are. But.

She sighs. Little Dog wanders into the kitchen and starts snuffling at her feet.

—Oh, get away from there. You know you're not supposed to be in here.

But she scratches Little Dog behind the ear. Dad sits back down at the table and gently kicks at Little Dog.

—Don't encourage her.

Now Big Dog comes over to see if any treats are being handed out. Dad shrugs his shoulders in surrender.

—See, now they're both in here.

He turns to me.

—We try to keep them out at meals, but your mom.

—Now don't start that, you feed them from the table all the time.

—I? I feed them?

As he says this, he's sneaking a scrap of bolognese from his plate and slipping it to Big Dog. Mom slaps his shoulder.

—See, see, there, now you have to give some to both of them.

—See what? I didn't do anything.

And he tosses a bit of meat to Little Dog. Mom throws her hands up in the air.

—You, you encourage them and.

Dad's laughing now.

—I don't encourage anything, you're seeing things. See, Hank, your mom is seeing things.

He leans over and kisses her on the cheek. She shoves him away.

—Pest.

—You like it.

—I do not.

He leans over to me and stage whispers.

—She likes it.

I shove my linguine around the plate and think about Dylan Lane threatening these people.

—But no one else asks about me?

Mom stops playing with the dogs and goes back to her dinner. Dad sets his fork down.

—We don't talk about you, Hank. We don't talk about you to anyone. We don't talk about you with each other anymore. We had to stop.

He picks up his fork and takes a bite and chews it hard. Mom looks up at me, tears floating in her eyes.

—It hurt too much, Henry. We. And there was nothing to talk about. We didn't know anything.

I smile at her, at my dad.

—It's OK, I understand.

We all eat for a minute. Mom wipes some sauce from her lips.

—Wade calls sometimes.

—Wade?

—Your friend from high school.

—I know. Last I heard he was in San Jose.

—Yes, he moved there, and then a few years ago. You remember his mom died so young?

—Yeah.

—Well, his father passed a few years ago and Wade moved back here with his family. They're living in his old house.

—Right around the block?

—Uh-huh. And he was so sweet right after all the trouble. He came over, and I hadn't seen him since I don't know when, and he's such a grown-up I didn't recognize him. And then we didn't hear from him for awhile and then I ran into him at the market and he started stopping by every now and then to see how we are, if we need anything, if we've heard anything.

Wade, my old housebreaking partner, the guy who liked to go into houses where people were still at home and awake. He always was a sneaky fucker.

BIG DOG and Little Dog sleep upstairs with Mom and Dad and, both being half-deaf and half-senile, they don't raise a fuss as I slip out the back door. I walk over to the fence and boost myself over into the yard behind ours. I edge along the fence until I get to the next fence down, and boost over again. If I'm remembering this right, it should be the third house down after this one. I hop another fence.

Dog.

It's a big fucker. It runs up to me out of the darkness, skids to a stop a foot away, and starts barking like hell. I sprint to the next fence; halfway there I get clotheslined by a clothesline. Who has a clothesline anymore? I scramble to my feet, the dog barking at my heels, run to the fence, and vault over into the next yard.

Dog.

It's a terrier. The first dog is still on the other side of the fence going apeshit. All the other dogs on the block are starting to join in. The terrier yaps at me as I make for the next fence, then it leaps forward, bites at my ankles, and gets a mouthful of my pants cuff. I hop across the yard, trying to shake it loose, but the little ratter has a good grip and isn't letting go. I make it to the fence and a light pops on inside the house. I cock my afflicted leg back, kick out with all my might, and hear the cuff tear. The terrier flies off and I jump the fence before he can scramble back at me.

I fall into some bushes. I can hear the terrier raising hell and bouncing off the fence as he tries to get through it to kill me. The porch light comes on in the terrier's yard. I hear a sliding glass door open and then a woman's voice.

—Digby! Digby, shut up. Shut up! Come here and shut up.

And so on. I lie in the dirt while she collects Digby and takes him inside, and then wait while the other dogs on the block settle down. By the time I crawl out of the bushes to see if I'm in the right yard, the night's chill has gone through the thin CSM jacket I'm wearing, straight into my bones, and the front of my jeans are soaked through from the damp earth. There's plenty of light spilling into the backyard from the street lamp and the Christmas lights strung across the front of the house. I'm in the right place. The paint job is different and the yard has been relandscaped, but I recognize the house and the big redwood deck.

I can't see any lights on in the house. I squint and scan the roofline, looking for one of those motion-detector security lights. No sign. I scuttle to the side of the house where I remember the side door to the garage being. I edge past a stacked cord of firewood. No helpful warning sticker left by an alarm company on the door. None of the alarm tape you would expect to see on the window in the door if it had been rigged. I put my hand on the knob, twist it slowly. Someone jams a gun into the back of my neck.

—Don't you even breathe, fucker.

I don't.

—Open the door.

I do.

—Now crawl inside. Stay on your hands and knees.

I do. The barrel of the gun stays pressed against my neck and I hear the door close behind us, then the lights come on.

—Turn around.

I shuffle around on my hands and knees, and look up at Wade and the huge revolver he's pointing at me.

His brow furrows. Air hisses out between his teeth.

—Hank?

He lowers the gun.

—Your mom and dad are really worried about you.

And that's how I know he's not the one who sold me out to Dylan.

THE GARAGE is stocked with a particularly large supply of suburban toys: a couple of Jet Skis; a small powerboat on a trailer; two golf bags stuffed in a corner; a massive tool bench running down one side, with every imaginable power tool displayed on the peg wall behind it; snow skis laid out on the rafters; two Honda motocrossers, a massive 420 and a matching 125; and five mountain bikes dangling from overhead hooks.

—Beer?

—I don't drink.

—Why not?

Because I got drunk and forgot something one time and a bunch of people died.

—It was bad for me.

—Soda?

—Sure.

Wade gets off the stool he's sitting on and opens the garage fridge.

—Sprite or Coke?

—Sprite.

He tucks the Colt Anaconda into his armpit and grabs a can of Sprite and a bottle of Miller High Life. He hands me the can, twists the cap off his beer, tosses it into a waste can under the workbench, and takes a drink. Then he digs a key from the pocket of his Carhartt jacket, opens a drawer on the bench, takes the gun from his armpit, and drops it inside.

—Stacy would shit if she knew I had that thing, but I always keep it locked up.

I get a good look at the chambers in the cylinder before he closes and locks the drawer.

—It's not loaded.

He looks at me like I'm an asshole.

—With three kids in the house? No, it's not fucking loaded.

I open my Sprite, take a sip, and huddle a little closer to the space heater he fired up for me. I point at the side door.

—How did you?

—I was out here sneaking a cig before going up. Stace won't let me smoke in the house. I heard all that barking, switched off the light to take a peek, and saw someone hop the fence. Went out and hid behind the woodpile. Stupid shit, should have called the cops, but I was pissed.

He fingers a gouge in the surface of the workbench, looks at me.

—You any warmer?

—Yeah.

—Good, let's take a walk, I don't want you in here if Stace wakes up.

WE STROLL around the block, our faces illuminated by streetlamps and the colored lights flashing on the rooflines of the houses. Wade left his smokes back in the garage and has to bum one of mine.

—Benson & Hedges?

—Uh-huh.

—Kind of an old lady cigarette. How'd you get started on those?

—Long story.

We pause while I light his cigarette, continue. Walking past houses I remember from my childhood. We stand in front of one with a particularly elaborate display: a mini Santa's Village built on the lawn and spilling onto the driveway.

Wade looks down, sees something, bends, and picks up a pigeon feather. He tucks it into the zippered breast pocket of his jacket, sees the look on my face.

—I use them for work.

—What for?

—Marbling paint. You dip them in your dark color and run them over the base color while it's still wet. Have to be real gentle, but you get a great effect. I save them in a little box.

He points at the display.

—Remember stealing Christmas lights?

—Yeah.

—What were we thinking?

—God knows.

We start walking again.

—What were you doing in my backyard, Hank?

WADE HILLER was the toughest guy I knew. The lead burnout in school. The kid in PE class who never dressed out. The guy with the mouth on him, who never wanted anyone else to have the last word. Corkscrew hair past his shoulders, thick arms and chest from hours of bench presses in his dad's garage, a box of Marlboro Reds always rolled up in the sleeve of his T-shirt. He grew up around the block from me, went to all the same schools, but it wasn't until I broke my leg that we had anything to do with each other. Jocks and burnouts: do not mix.

I couldn't participate in PE and ended up sitting around with Wade and his pals Steve and Rich. And it turned out they were OK guys. Steve was really fucking smart, Rich was as mellow a person as I'd ever met. And Wade. High-strung, quickly violent, but just exciting and fun to be around. And then they got me into the whole burglary thing and me and Wade got busted, and I thought it was time for me to forget my new friends. Last I heard about Wade, he was well on his way to spending his life hanging out in Santa Rita County Jail.

I sit on the back bumper of one of his three trucks. Each of them with the words HILLER INTERIOR CONTRACTING painted on the side. Wade comes back out of the garage, a fresh beer in his hand.

—It's cold, let's get in.

He unlocks the truck and we climb into the cab. He hasn't said much since I told him I thought he might have been spying on my folks for someone trying to find me. He sips at the beer.

—You know, I didn't graduate from our school. I was way short on credits, had to go over to the continuation school where your mom worked. This would have been the year after you went off to college. She tell you about that?

—I guess I heard about it.

—She was great to me. I was a real fuckup. You know. She took me seriously, didn't just write me off as a lost cause. And that was after we got arrested together. I figured she'd blame that shit on me, but she never even brought it up. I would never have graduated without her.

Mom always had a soft spot for the troublemakers, that's why she took the job as principal at the continuation school in the first place.

—And after I graduated she was the one who convinced me to take some classes over at Modesto City. My dad did OK with me, but after my mom died.

I'm digging another smoke out of the pack and he reaches over and takes one for himself. I pass him my matches and he lights up.

—I'm gonna reek when I go in. Stace is gonna shit.

—Will she be worried where you are?

—I have insomnia, she's used to me taking walks late. Besides, she sleeps like a rock.

We smoke.

—Yeah, Dad was a great guy, but he drank a lot after Mom died.

I remember raiding his dad's booze after school. The handle-bottles of Jack Daniels, cases of Coors stacked in the garage.

—I remember that. Not your mom.

—Yeah she was gone before we were hanging out.

—Your dad drinking.

—He wasn't mean or anything.

—I know.

—Just wasn't there.

His dad, passed out on the couch by midday on the weekends.

—Yeah.

—Didn't have much left over for me. Anyway. For a couple years, after I moved to San Jose, when I'd come home to visit him, I'd stop by the school to see your mom. She ever tell you that?

—No.

—Well, I did. And she was always encouraging me, always happy for me. Even when I got Stace pregnant and she was only eighteen and I was nineteen and we weren't married yet. She sent us a card and a baby gift.

—I didn't know about that.

—A little teddy bear.

—Yeah, that's Mom.

—She kind of saved me, made a real difference in my life. I have my contractor's license, my own business, been married for fourteen years. I have three great kids. Honestly, I don't think I would have any of that if not for your mom.

He opens the window and flicks his butt out.

—So when that stuff happened in New York with you, I knew two things. I knew I'd do just about anything for your mom, and I knew there was no way that woman raised a killer. And I would have believed that even if I didn't know you myself.

Wade takes the last swallow of his beer.

—So what did you think you were gonna do, coming over here in the middle of the night?

Kill you.

I finish my own smoke and toss it.

—I don't know. I was pissed. Beat you up. Maybe.

He grunts.

—What now?

—I need to get out of town, take care of something.

He nods. .

—I'd help, but. I have Stace and the kids to. I can't.

—I understand.

—Maybe there's something. Something small?

—Don't suppose you know anyone in Vegas, someone could help me find someone else? Someone lost or hiding.

He laughs a little.

—You know, you know who's in Vegas? Remember T?

T? Oh shit, T.

—The dealer we scored off? The spaz?

—Yeah.

—I thought he got three-striked and put away.

—No, no way. He had two convictions and was on parole when they busted him the third time. Somehow his lawyer got him bail, and he jumped it. Went to Vegas.

—I don't know, man, he was such a . . .

—Such a fuckup?

—Yeah.

—Well, I guess that's why we all got along.

I laugh.

—Yeah.

—You know what? He sends me, you'll love this, he sends me Christmas cards, every year.

—No way.

—Yeah, complete, the guy is *wanted* here, and he sends me Christmas cards complete with a return address.

We're both laughing.

—I just got this year's, like, yesterday. Want me to go get it?

He puts his hand on the door.

—No, no, I don't think T is the guy I need for this.

—No, you should see, you should see this, it's a riot.

He's really laughing now, and I can't help but join in.

—Yeah, OK, OK, I want to see it.

—Hang on.

He opens the door and steps out just as the black Toyota pickup squeals around the corner and plows into the front of the truck, sending Wade flying to crash against the front of his house.

I OPEN my eyes. Where am I? I've been in an accident. I was driving my Mustang and something happened and. Oh, God. I think I killed Rich. Oh, God.

I'm lying on my back, looking up at the stars. I'm not in the Mustang. It's not then, it's now. I'm lying on my back in a driveway looking up at the stars. I've been in another accident. I'm lying next to a huge, long-bed pickup with the driver's door hanging open. There's a black pickup that looks like it tried to occupy the same parking space as the long-bed. Bad call. I must have been thrown out of the long-bed when . . . When what?

My head is lodged in a cone of silence. I shake it and the sounds start to penetrate: dogs barking, car alarms set off by the crash, someone crying. Someone crying. I should see if I can help. I move my arms: check. I move my legs: check. Here goes. I roll onto my stomach and get myself up on my hands and knees. I won't say it feels good, but nothing screams too loudly. OK, let's go for broke: I stand up. My head does a little spin and tumble, the world spins the opposite way, trying to catch up, they crash together, and everything stops moving around. Safe to say I have some dings and bruises, but I'm better off than the guy with the mullet who's lodged in the windshield of the long-bed. Mullet. When was the last time I saw someone with a mullet? Oh, right. The puzzle pieces in my head fall back together into the shape of my brain.

Fat Guy and Mullet Head must have been riding in the truck bed. Mullet Head is jammed into an indentation in the long-bed's windshield that is shaped exactly like his body. Fat Guy is sprawled on the hood of the Toyota, just now propping himself up on his elbows to look around. Ponytail Boy is behind the wheel, trying to get his door open, but it looks like both of his arms are broken so he's not doing a very good job of it. Leslie is the one who's crying, except it's more like screaming. She looks OK (has her seat belt on and everything), but she's clutching something limp and dollish. Her door is hanging open. As I walk over, I hear a rustling sound, and turn to see a pair of feet sticking out of a bush, which tells me where Danny is.

I reach into the truck cab. Leslie stops screaming, lets me take Cassidy out of her arms and sits there holding herself, rocking back and forth.

I lay Cassidy on the pavement. There's blood covering her face, and her long, honey hair is stuck in it. I take off the CSM jacket and wipe at the blood with the cotton lining. There's a gash in her forehead where it must have slapped the dash. It's bloody like all head wounds, but not too big. I press the jacket against her head and feel her pulse. Good, her pulse is good, her chest is rising and falling regularly, there's no blood coming from her mouth, and none of her limbs are obviously broken. She was probably sleeping in her mom's lap, her body limp and relaxed for the crash. That's good.

—Leslie.

She's staring at her daughter. Lights have come on in the houses on the street, people are standing on their porches in nightclothes.

—Leslie!

She looks at me.

—Come here and help.

She unbuckles and climbs down out of the truck.

—Take this.

I put her hand on top of the jacket over her daughter's forehead.

—Just hold it here, keep pressure on it.

Patterson doesn't have its own police force; it's served by the Stanislaus County Sheriff's Department. Last I knew they had two cars working the whole west side of the county. With a bit of luck, they'll have to send one from Newman. The nearest hospital and ambulance service is in Turlock. So the siren that raises up now is probably the fire department.

I take my hand off of Leslie's. She looks from her daughter's face to mine.

—I think she's OK. Just keep the pressure on and someone will be here real fast.

She nods.

—I have to go.

I walk up the driveway to Wade. His body is a tangled jumble. I touch his face, pocked with acne scars, the crazed hair clipped short and thinning. Oh shit, Wade.

—Wade?

I turn my head at the voice. A woman my age is standing at the top of the drive. She's wearing flannel boxers, a too-large jacket she must have grabbed on her way out the door, and little booty socks on her feet. Her face is pillow-creased and her short dark hair is severely bed-headed. I recognize her from high school. Stacy Wilder. Wow, Wade hooked up with Stacy "The Wild One" Wilder. Way to go, buddy.

—Wade?

I stand up. Point at him.

—He.

And Danny shoots me in the back.

IT'S THE back of my leg, really.

My left leg flies out from underneath me and I fall on my back. Beyond the sound of the shot echoing in my ears, I hear doors slamming shut up and down the street as the rubberneckers dive back inside. The siren is coming closer.

—Got you, fucker.

I tilt my head and see Danny behind me.

—Got you good, wanted man.

Wanted man? Now how in hell does he know that? He takes a step closer. He's bleeding from his mouth. Something to my left moves. I look and see a boy coming up behind Stacy, where she stands frozen, staring at Wade.

The boy is about thirteen, has Wade's hair and flat nose. He's wearing a San Jose Sharks jersey and carrying a hockey stick. He's sees me and Danny. And then he sees his dad. His eyes go big and his mouth opens. I lift a hand.

—Stacy.

She looks from her husband to me. Danny nudges my head with his sneaker.

—Shut up.

I point at the boy.

—Stacy, get your boy inside.

Her eyes move from me to Wade, to me again, to Danny's cheap Korean Glock knockoff. She turns, finds her gaping boy there, grabs him, and pulls him toward the front door.

—Shut the fuck up.

He's right over me now. Perspective has him flipped upside down.

Upside down.

That's a good idea.

—Danny, shouldn't you be taking care of your daughter?

He turns his head to look over his shoulder and I reach up, grab his ankles, and pull his feet out from under him. The gun goes off and a bullet pokes a hole in the garage door. Danny hits the ground flat on his back, makes a woofing noise, and the gun jars out of his hand and skips down the driveway. I stand up, take a step to go after the gun, and my left leg folds under me.

Oh yeah, I'm shot.

Danny rolls onto his stomach and is crawling for the gun before I can try to stand again. I look at my leg. It's bleeding, but it looks like it's just the obligatory flesh wound, a shallow gash on the side of my thigh. Ready for the pain this time, I get to my feet and start limping around the side of Wade's house, running from Danny and his shitty gun and the siren that is now very close.

The gate is unlatched from when Wade and I came out for our walk.

I swing it open and pull it closed behind me, hearing the latch click as it locks. I limp toward the woodpile.

—Freeze, fucker.

Danny is climbing over the gate, gun waving in my general direction. He slips at the top of the fence, lands roughly on his side, and the gun goes off again, splintering firewood. I dive through the side door into the dark garage, close it and lock it, and limp toward the workbench.

I grab the drawer and yank. It's locked. Well, of course it's locked, you watched him lock it, asshole. There's a crowbar mounted on the pegboard over the bench. I shove it into the crack between the drawer and the benchtop and heave. Grinding and a small snapping noise, but the drawer holds. Danny is banging on the door. I can see him framed there in the window. The siren sounds like it's right up the street. I heave again, the drawer flies open, off its tracks and onto the floor. Danny presses his face against the glass, trying to see through the darkness inside.

—Open up, fucker. Fucking open up!

I grab the gun, flip the empty cylinder open, and squat painfully, digging through the mess that fell from the drawer, looking for ammo. Nothing.

Danny hits the window with a piece of firewood and it shatters.

I stand, and right there at eye level, on a shelf above the bench, is a black plastic box with MAGNUM written across the top in big red letters. I grab the box, pop the lid, and a handful of feathers flutters out.

Wade Hiller on the subject of pigeon feathers: "I save them in a little box."

The siren screams close and stops right out front. For a moment a red and blue light pulses through the hole Danny shot in the garage door. Then he turns on the overheads and everything goes bright.

I flip the empty cylinder closed and turn. Danny squints at me and I squint back. He's raising his gun. I bring up the .357 he has no idea I'm holding, and point it at his face. His eyes turn into Frisbees. He freezes, his gun hand wavering.

Before he can decide to shoot me, I do what Jimmy Cagney would do, and throw my empty gun at him.

AT SIXTEEN, my fastball was in the mid-eighties and frequently grazed ninety. I used to stand in the backyard and throw pitch after pitch from the mound Dad and I had made, through the tire he had hung from the limb of a tree exactly sixty feet and six inches away, Major League distance. Once, with a bunch of teammates watching and egging me on, I threw a hundred and four in a row, right through the center. All fastballs. My shoulder blew up like a pumpkin and Dad was pissed at me for risking my arm, but the kids talked about it for weeks, and it made me feel so cool.

A BASEBALL weighs about five ounces. The gun in my hand feels like it's two or three pounds. Fortunately, Danny isn't sixty and a half feet away. More like eight. The Anaconda clocks him in the forehead and he goes down.

I can hear voices outside yelling. I walk over to Danny. He's out. I stuff the Anaconda in my jeans and grab his pistol. There's blood all over his face from the mouth wound and a new cut I've opened on his forehead.

Over a black leather jacket, he's wearing a blue-jean vest covered in patches: Insane Clown Posse, Slipknot, Godflesh, etc. The jacket has fallen open; underneath is a bloodstained concert T-shirt, the same one he had on the other day.

Except it's not a concert shirt.

I tug his jacket open the rest of the way and expose the big *America's Most Wanted* logo. I remember Robert Cramer mentioning my episode of that show in his book, and the expression on Danny's face when I looked him in the eye after I beat him up, and the way he pointed at me.

Danny knows who I am.

Which means his friends know who I am.

Which means, just as soon as the cops get here, they'll be telling them that I'm alive and in town.

Glass crunches under a shoe. The firefighter standing in the door is a woman around twenty-five, she's carrying a big EMT kit. She sees me, sees the gun. Freezes.

Too late, Henry. Too late to do anything now but run.

I tilt my head toward the street.

—The sheriffs out there yet?

She licks her lips.

—Not yet.

—How long?

—Couple minutes maybe.

I point at my leg.

—I need you to wrap this up. Quick.

She doesn't move.

—It's OK, you're gonna be OK, I just need you to do your job.

She nods, walks over, kneels, and opens her kit. I reach down, grab the edges of the hole in my pant leg, and rip so she can get to the wound. She tears open a sterile pack and starts wiping blood away. I whine a little and grit my teeth. She stops and looks up at me.

—It's OK, just hurry.

She looks at the wound.

—It needs stitches.

—Just bandage it, for Christ sake.

She starts wrapping my leg, going over the wound, and around the pant leg.

—The guy outside, next to the garage?

She's concentrating on her work.

—Yeah?

—He alive?

—I don't know, my partner's on him. One of the neighbors said someone in the garage might be hurt. I came in here.

The wrap is done.

—Got any penicillin in there?

—Yeah.

—Better give me a shot.

She pulls out an ampoule, rips it out of its pack, and stabs me in the leg. I can hear another siren. The sheriffs. Time to go.

—Thanks.

I point at Danny.

—Why don't you work on him and we'll skip all the lying-on-the-floor-and-counting-to-a-hundred crap.

—OK.

She turns to Danny and takes his pulse. I open the door to the house.

STACY WAS a year behind me and Wade. She was a real good girl; honor roll, student government, extracurricular this and that. She was also the hottest chick in school. Being a star jock at school, I crossed paths with her brainy-but-popular crowd. I remember flirting with her once, not really trying to get anywhere except in the way teenage boys are always trying to get somewhere. But I didn't try that hard. I didn't have to try hard with any of the other chicks, so why bother with one who wanted me to work for it? What I thought. Wade's crew of burnouts wouldn't have crossed paths with her clique, wouldn't have even had classes together, let alone social interaction. But I remember being baked with him in PE and watching her run track with the girls and him saying that if he could nail any chick in school she'd be the one. Man, I'd love to hear the story of how they hooked up in the first place. But Wade can't tell me, and I can't ask Stacy because she's too busy right now beating me with her son's hockey stick.

I STEP inside, close the door, and get one upside the head. I take a couple more weak blows before I get a grip on the stick and rip it out of her hands, and she comes at my face with her fingernails. I get my forearm in front of my face and shove her off as I run toward the back of the house. She keeps after me, beating on my back. I duck into the kitchen. Down the hall I catch a glimpse of her kids; the boy I saw before, another a few years younger, and a tiny little girl who's going to grow up to look like her mom.

Stacy shoves me hard and I stumble into the kitchen as she runs toward her children.

—Get upstairs! Get to your rooms!

And that's the last I see of her, herding the kids upstairs, away from the scary man. I head for the patio door at the back of the kitchen. Stop. There's a pile of mail on the kitchen table. I flip through until I find what I want, and cram it in my back pocket. I go out the back, close the door behind me, and pause for a moment, staring back into the house. The Christmas tree and decorations, the Nativity scene, the mess of kids' toys. Then the sheriff's car sirens up in front of the house.

THEY'RE UP. With all the noise, how could they not be up? I come over the fence into the backyard, see the lights on inside, walk to the side of the house, and dump the guns over the gate into a bush in the front yard. I won't carry a gun into my mother's house. When I open the back door and come in limping, Mom starts to cry.

—Henry. Henry.

—It's OK, I'm OK.

She's shaking her head.

—Something woke us up, a crash and then, then, then.

She can't talk, she's crying too hard. Dad holds her.

—It sounded like guns out there, Hank.

I'm turning off the lights.

—I'm going to go away.

Mom buries her face in Dad's chest. It sounds like she's saying no over and over, but I'm not sure.

—The police are gonna know I'm here. I have to.

Dad is shaking his head.

—We can talk to the police, Hank, it's time to stop this. It's time to fix this.

—Dad.

—We can, we know people here, we can fix this and you can stop.

—Dad, listen.

He grabs me by the shoulders and looks into my eyes.

—You listen, son. Enough of this. It's time for you to stop running from this trouble and do something about it.

I've never said no to my father, always done what he told me to do. I look back into his eyes.

—I killed people.

Whatever was going to come out of his mouth freezes in there, and dies.

—Some of the people they said I killed. I killed them. I'm a killer.

I go upstairs to my old room. I grab my money and the clothes I washed earlier and the phone Dylan gave me and I go back down. Dad is at the foot of the stairs, Mom next to him. Dad reaches for my hand as I come down, I pull it back.

—I need the keys to the shop.

He points at the table next to the front door. I grab the keys. I feel Mom's hand on my back.

—Henry, oh my poor baby. Oh, baby.

She wraps her arms around me, and I feel Dad grab us both in his big arms and squeeze us together, trying to compress us into the one flesh we once were. But we are no longer. I am different. I pull myself free.

—Don't try to protect me anymore. It's not. I'm not worth it. Just.

Mom tries to hug me again, I look at Dad, he stops her.

—The police will be coming, tonight I think. You can't lie about hiding me. Tell them you tried to get me to give up and I ran. It's the truth. Tell the truth.

I reach for the doorknob. Stop. Turn and grab Mom and kiss her cheek.

—I love you, Mom. I won't be back. I'm sorry. I love you, Dad.

I open the door and the dogs come barking down the stairs. Blow up the world and they won't notice, fuck with the front door and they go berserk. I step outside. Over the barking dogs I hear Mom.

—We love you, Henry, no matter what.

I pull the door closed, and I'm running again.

THE SHOP is in the middle of town, about a ten-minute walk. I can't move very fast with my leg, but I know a shortcut. I dig the guns out of the bushes, huddle there for a second as a van drives past on the street, then walk up to the corner, take a right, and climb a short chain-link fence. It's not easy with one leg to work with, but I make do. On the other side, I sit down on the edge of the dry culvert, push off, and slide to the bottom. I hit bottom and get a shock of pain up my left leg.

I'm lucky it's been a dry winter so far; there are only a couple inches of water down here. I splash through the darkness for a couple hundred yards till I get to the spot where steps are carved into the south wall of the culvert. They're steep, like Kulkukan. I shake that vision from my head. No time for that.

At the top some kids have clipped a hole in the chain-link. I squeeze through and pop up under the bleachers of Patterson High's football field. I weave through the lattice of struts, come out from the west end of the stands, cross the track that circles the football field, cross the field itself, and stop. Right in front of me are the baseball diamonds. I trot as quickly as I can between the diamonds, glancing at the spot where I broke my leg and U-turned my life.

Get over it, Henry.

The campus is pretty much like it was back in my day. I cross the quad with the big red *P* painted in the middle. This is where we used to grab unsuspecting freshmen and dump them facedown in trash cans for showing insufficient Tiger Pride, and then I'm on the street in front of the school looking at downtown Patterson in all its after-midnight glory.

CSM is tucked between a John Deere dealership and a U-Haul. I unlock the office door, go in, close it behind me, head into the shop, and flick on the lights. And there's my car, wheels removed, up on jack stands. Right where Dad left it so he could start replacing the brake pads first thing in the morning. Thanks, Dad. Then the alarm goes off because I didn't enter the code within thirty seconds of opening the door.

DANNY WAS wearing an *America's Most Wanted* shirt, which means he's a fan, which means he recognized me when I beat him up, because, according to *The Man Who Got Away*, I have my very own episode of *America's Most Wanted*. Even a dildo like him could hop online and do enough research to find out where my parents live and come here looking for me. He probably thinks catching me will earn him a reward and make him some kind of hero. And it would, it would.

The sheriff and his deputies know who my folks are. They know Mom because they frequently dealt with her students at the continuation school and, after my shit went down, they spent a fair amount of time staked out in front of the house, helping to deal with the media and such. Danny or Leslie or one of their cronies are going to pop out with my name. How long till that happens? How long after that till one of the deputies remembers how close my folks live to Wade? How long till they get a report on the alarm at CSM and remember my dad owns it? How long will it take for these podunk cops to connect the dots and really be after me? And how long after that before the state cops and the FBI are involved?

Leslie is hysterical. Danny was unconscious when I last saw him. Ponytail Boy had two broken limbs and is probably in shock. Mullet Head? He didn't look like he'd be talking to anyone soon. Fat Guy. Will he talk? Will he say, "Yeah, we spun up here after a wanted murderer instead of calling the cops because he beat up my friend and we crashed our truck here and . . ."? He'll keep his mouth shut. That's what he'll do. That's what he has to do for me to have a chance.

*   *   *

I'M PULLING tarps off of cars while the alarm continues to ring, calling to deputies who are otherwise engaged. The '53 'Vette is way too visible. Likewise the '73 Jaguar XLS. The 1970 Mercedes 280 SL has no engine. The '50 Studebaker Commander is buried at the back of the row. But the '85 Monte Carlo SS is just right. I grab the keys from the rack on the wall and hit the ignition. Nothing. Of course, because no one has driven it lately and the battery is dead. I wheel the charger over, pop the hood, and stare at the big block 502; 450 horses and over 500 lbs of torque. I hook up the charger.

While the car is juicing I go back in the office and dig around the shelves until I find a greasy road atlas. I limp back toward the shop and trip over something. A box of CSM jackets, each one wrapped in plastic. My jacket! The jacket that Leslie had pressed to her daughter's forehead. That's the kind of clue that will get the cops here in a hurry.

I try the key again and the Monte Carlo rumbles to life, almost as loud as the alarm. I disconnect the charger, drop the hood, and hit the button to roll up the garage door. It's almost one in the morning. Outside, the heavy San Joaquin fog is starting to muffle the valley. I ease between the other cars, hoping that Dad's insurance is up-to-date. I stop the car just outside, go back, reach in, and hit the button, dropping the door. No reason to invite trouble. I'm behind the wheel, seat belt on. I take a right out of the drive directly onto Highway 33, and gun the engine, popping from first to second to third. The fucker is so loud I don't hear the siren of the sheriff's car until it bursts off of Poppy Avenue, right in front of me.

My left foot jacks the clutch while my right heel-toes the brake and the gas. I crank the wheel over. The rear of the Monte Carlo whips out and around and keeps whipping. Instead of pulling a nice neat one-eighty, I doughnut all the way around and end in a dead stop. The sheriff's car swerves around me and streaks into the CSM driveway, out for bigger fish than a late-night joyrider like me. Cool. I pop into first and roll. The sheriff backs out of the driveway, pivots, and comes after me.

I hit it, heading west, straight toward . . . Newman and the sheriff's headquarters. Not cool. Let's try that one-eighty again.

Clutch, heel-toe, crank wheel (not too much this time), come off the brake, into the gas, clutch coming out straight into second gear, rear wheels catching, sheriff's car whirling into view through the windshield, jolting forward, teasing wheel to right as sheriff brakes and jerks left, correcting wheel for fishtail, left rear quarter panel banging sheriff's left rear quarter panel as we pass, correcting again, and blasting back north on 33. Just like Jim fucking Rockford. The sheriff's car gets turned around and is on me with full sirens and lights as I brake hard, take a right off of 33, and ease over the train tracks onto Las Palmas.

EAST LAS Palmas Avenue shoots northeast out of the center of Patterson and straight into ranch country until it bends due east and becomes West Main Avenue around the almond orchards, then turns into West Main Street as it passes through Hatch, and finally crosses the 99 just outside Turlock. It's a fifteen-mile shot all the way out, but the first mile and a quarter is the tricky part, the stretch where the avenue is lined with huge palm trees, one every ten yards. You hit 100 mph there? The trees look like a wall. When I was a kid, we'd drag here when we thought we could get away with it. Right before getting into your car, you always said the same thing to your opponent: "Don't fuck up."

The Monte Carlo was clearly put together with an eye toward on-track drag racing, but it's currently geared for street use. That slows down the acceleration a bit, taking your 0-60 sprint time from a flat six seconds to something around seven. Ho-hum. I lead-foot the pedal to the floor.

The dual carbs make a huge sucking sound as they fly wide open, the rear end bites down hard, smoke spews out from under the tires as I leave fifteen-foot twin stripes. The animal under the hood screams and I explode forward, the cop lost in the cloud of wheel-smoke behind me. I'm still in third when the speedometer hits 100.

I am not prepared to control something like this. No one is prepared to control something like this. I'm just trying to keep straight. If I waver I'll lose traction and spin into the wall of massive palm trees flipping by on either side. I ease off the gas. The needle peaks at 110 and starts to drop. I want to check the rearview for the sheriff, but don't dare move my eyes from the road. The last of the trees blinks away behind me and an ounce of tension leaves my shoulders. The sign in front of me announces that my lane must merge left due to road construction.

I take my foot off the gas and tap the brake. It works just fine. I scrub a couple mph off, down to about 90. There's the lane shift. I tap again, again, blip the steering wheel left. Too much, I'm headed for the center divider. Tap, blip right to keep from slamming the divider, and shoot into the left lane too sharply. Orange traffic cones hammer off my right fender, and rocket, wheeling into the sky. I keep my feet off all pedals as the Monte Carlo scrapes past the five-hundred-yard gouge on my right where the tarmac has been carved away. I'm down to 70 by the time the road widens back out. I hear the siren behind me again.

The sheriff's car is entering the construction lane. What the fuck am I doing? This isn't a monster, it's a car. I get back on the gas, pop into fourth, and the engine rumbles happily back up to 80. The last of the streetlights disappear behind me as our chase clears the town line. I see the next sign, the one that warns about the sharp turn up ahead that you should take at 30 mph.

It starts as a bend, swooping to the right between a fallow strawberry field and a windbreak of trees. I tap, tap, tap and get down to about 65 for the bend. Rubber screeches, but the tires stay firm on the road. Then I hit the hard angle of the turn. I can take it. This huge mother will stay on the road. I know it will.

There's a little bump. It startles me, and I jerk the wheel a fraction to the left, overcorrect to the right, and the rear end slips and starts to carry me toward the trees. I dart the wheel into the skid, feel the tires grab, take it right, into the angle of the curve, lose traction again. And the road takes control.

The rear end spins around, I spin around, the trees reel in front of me, traveling from right to left a foot from the hood of the car, and disappear. Something crunches and jerks the car and bounces it back to the center of the road, spinning in the opposite direction now. I keep my hands clear of the wheel as it flings itself around, not wanting to break a wrist by trying to control it. I see the trees again, traveling left to right this time and much farther away. The car falls out from underneath me as it skitters off the road, then it jumps up to catch me, crashing into the field, still spinning, plowing the field into a storm of dust that screens me from the world as the Monte finally grinds to a halt.

In all the skidding and screeching and crashing, the radio has clicked on. I loll on rubber muscles, unable to move. My brain is a flat horizonless plain. I can sense, but not make sense of the siren screaming close by and the red and blue lights fluorescing the dust cloud outside the windows. Closer by, I recognize a voice. Yeah, that's The Warrior, the late night DJ for 104.1. The Hawk. I loved that station when I was a kid. The siren stops, and through the blue and red haze, a shape starts to emerge. The deputy opens my door and points his gun at me. The Warrior stops talking and a song comes on the radio. Thin Lizzy. "The Boys Are Back in Town."

THE DEPUTY seems to have been trained well. I mean, sure, maybe he should have ordered me out of the car before he ran over here and opened the door, but other than that I'd say he's doing a pretty good job for a kid whose most serious calls are probably knife fights at local roadhouse bars.

He takes one look at my limp body and knows not to move me. Thank you. He talks to me, tells me to put my hands on the wheel where he can see them, but my hands seem way too far away to really have anything to do with me, so I just leave them in my lap. He talks some more and I don't move some more so he keeps the gun pointed at me as he reaches in and pats me down for weapons. I have none because both Danny's pistol and Wade's revolver have banged around the inside of the car and are on the floor somewhere. I'm just grate-

ful neither of them hit me in the head. Wait a second. Did one
hit me in the head? I concentrate on how my head feels. It feels
bad. Maybe one of the guns hit me on the head. Not that I really care.
About anything.

Now he circles around to the passenger-side door. It grinds open.
He looks in the glove compartment, finds nothing, feels under the
seat and comes up with the pistol. He tucks that in his belt, folds
the front seat down, and checks out the backseat. When he comes
back to me, I can see he now has the revolver as well. Good for him.
He asks me again if I can move and takes my immobility as an answer.
Now, just for good measure, he tells me *not* to move, that he's gonna go
call for backup and an ambulance, and he disappears into the dust
cloud.

The Monte Carlo's engine ticks. The dust is fading now and I can
see an outline of the deputy standing next to his car, watching me
while he talks on his radio. My eyelids start to flutter and droop. I force
them back open. Concussion. I most certainly have a concussion and
need to stay awake. My eyes close. I hear an engine buzz up the road
and stop, a couple doors opening and closing. Voices.

—You OK? Need help?

—Just stay up there on the road.

—What?

—Don't walk in the tracks there.

—I said, do you need help?

—Stay out of the wheel marks!

—What?

—Just get back up on the road.

—Sorry, just trying to help.

—Get out of the tracks and get back up on the road.

—Yeah, sorry. Dude.

And a pop.

And another pop.

And another.

And feet scrunching through the dirt. And hands unbuckling my seat belt and pulling me from the car as a new song comes on the radio. Led Zeppelin: "When the Levee Breaks." Now this is rock 'n' roll. But I just can't stay awake to enjoy it. So I don't.

—WAKE HIM up.

—Huh?

—Don't let him sleep.

Someone is shaking me.

—No go.

—Slap him.

SLAP!

—Dude, not so hard, just a little smack.

Smack.

—He's out, dude.

—Try some water.

My head is tilted. Something is in my mouth, filling it.

—Choke! Cough! Choke!

—On his face, on his face!

—Dude, you come back here and try.

My eyes open.

—No, wait, he's awake.

I'm on my back. Lights swirl above me. I'm moving. No, I'm on my back inside something that's moving.

—You OK?

Something dark looms over me. Someone.

—Sid, take the wheel.

The someone disappears. I hear shuffling.

—Got the wheel?

—Yeah.

The moving thing lurches, then straightens out. Someone new looms.

—You OK?

There's that question. Am I OK? Well, honestly, that's just a little too deep for me to handle. So I don't handle it.

—Are you hurt?

That's much less ambiguous, I can handle that one.

—Yeah.

—Where?

Also an easy one.

—All over.

A little laugh. Wait, do I know that laugh?

—Where ya headed, where do we take you?

Jesus, that's a mind-bender. I'm headed . . . home? No, that's not right. I was already home and that didn't work out. I close my eyes and see a sunny place next to the ocean. That's nice. That's where I want to go.

—OPEN YOUR eyes, dude, got to stay awake.

I open my eyes. Where am I?

—I want to go to the beach.

Whew, that just about took it all out of me. I close my eyes.

—WAKE UP.

Water splashes my face. I open my eyes. I'm moving. Someone is looming. What am I doing? I'm moving. Moving? Oh right, I was going somewhere. It was real important.

—Are we there?

—Where, dude?

Well, how do I know? Oh, wait, I do know!

—Vegas.

—Vegas?

—Are we?

—Is that where?

—Vegas.

Mom and Dad snapshot into my brain, fade, disappear. A Polaroid developed in reverse. I try to sit up.

—Vegas, I have to get to Vegas.

Someone pushes me back down.

—It's cool, dude, we're on our way. Sid.

—Yeah?

—Head for Vegas.

I close my eyes. Someone shakes me, but it's too late, I'm chasing myself down a long dark tunnel, away from all the things I know are waiting to hurt me when I finally wake up.

If I wake up.

—I'M TELLIN' ya, dude, they ain't shit without Taylor. We ain't getting any help.

—Yeah, but.

—No "yeah, but" about it, dude.

—They're at home.

—They're choke artists. Everyone knows you never take the Dolphins in December.

My mouth is gunky and my throat is a dry rasp, but I still manage to get in my two cents.

—He's right.

Silence.

—Was that him?

—Get some water.

Footsteps. Water running. Footsteps.

Water splashes my face. It feels good.

—You in there, dude?

More water. I open my eyes, see someone I know.

—Hey, Rolf.

—How you feeling, dude?

He's sitting on the edge of the bed I'm lying on. I turn my head to look at the room. My eyes aren't focused yet, but I don't really need them. Motel. Cheap. Anywhere. I turn back to Rolf.

—Let me have some of that water.

The blurry guy behind him hands him a plastic cup and Rolf holds it to my lips and I guzzle it down.

—More.

Rolf gives the cup back to the blurry guy and he leaves and I hear water running in a sink.

—Where are we?

—The Downtown Motel.

—Where?

—The Downtown Motel.

—*Where?*

—Oh, Barstow.

Barstow. Have I ever heard anything positive about Barstow? No. Just a town in the desert that sounds like a good place to dump a dead body. The blurry guy comes back with more water. He comes into focus as I drink it. Younger than me and Rolf. A short, bleached Mohawk; a bare torso of lean, flat muscle; a small, blue Ocean Pacific logo tattooed over his left breast, just where it would be if he was wearing one of their shirts.

I pass the empty cup back.

—Thanks.

He takes the cup, grinning.

—No prob, dude.

Rolf points at him.

—This is Sid. Sid, this is my friend, Henry Thompson.

—Cool, right, I know. Cool to meet you, dude.

He sticks out his hand. I manage to lift mine off the bed and shake. Rolf reaches in his pocket, takes out some money, and hands it to Sid.

—Why don't you run over to the IHOP and grab a grilled cheese for Henry? I'll take a chef salad.

—Cool.

He backs away, eyes locked on me, then turns suddenly, unlocks the door, and dashes out. Rolf smiles at me.

—I think he has a crush on you.

I try to push myself up in the bed and get hit with a sack of cramps and aches. Rolf helps to get me sitting and puts an extra pillow behind my back.

—So, Rolf?

—Yeah.

—Funny seeing you here.

—Yeah.

—What's it about?

He digs in the back pocket of his shorts, pulls out a piece of paper, unfolds it, and hands it to me.

—It's about this.

I take the paper. It's a photocopy of my NYPD wanted poster, the Spanish language version. It has blood on it.

CANDITO HAD the wanted poster in his pocket. Rolf found it when he was looking for the Bronco keys so he could meet me and Leo back at the highway. But he had to kill Candito first.

—Dude, was that nasty. I was thinking bushwhack: get back in the tequilaria and hide behind the bar and blast him when he came back in. No go. You took off and I went in and he was just coming in through the back door with the town medico. Old guy, fat, with a big old mostacho. The real deal, right out of a Sergio Leone flick. I come through the door and the Federale goes for his gun and I raise my hands and start babbling about how I dropped the car keys and I just need to get them and I'll be gone and, dude, just be cool. He tells the doc to get to work on the other cop, the one without a face, right?

I'm sitting on the side of the bed now, drinking more water. My head feels like it's been cut off and stuck on a pike. I keep having little moments where I suddenly get dizzy and my vision blurs. It's a safe bet that I have a mid-level concussion. Which would explain why I don't remember much after I got in the Monte Carlo. A chase. A crash. A cop. The back of Rolf's bus. This room.

—The Federale covers me while I walk over to that table I was hiding behind. I point at the floor and go all, *Hey, there's my keys,* and I duck down like I'm grabbing my keys just as the doc walks around the bar and sees the dead cop.

Dead cop. A deputy was calling for help on his radio, and then I heard gunshots, and then Rolf and Sid were pulling me out of my car. Dead cop.

—So now the doc is telling the Federale that he can't do anything for his friend and the Federale is all, Que? Que? Que? So that's it, the jig's up. I pop up to do one of those gangsta moves with the dead cop's piece in one hand and my revolver in the other and, dude, there's the doc and the Federale standing over the dead guy, I'm totally forgotten. I pull the trigger on that cheap cop gun and it goes off and jams right away. So now, dude, the live cop is drawing a bead on me and I got just three round in *my* piece and the one shot I got off hit the doc in the gut and he's lying on his side on the floor scooting around in a circle like one of the Three Stooges with a hot rivet in his pants. No shit.

My head spins some more and I lie back with my knees bent over the edge of the bed, feet on the floor.

—You OK, dude?

I keep my eyes closed and wave my hand.

—You sure?

I breathe deeply a few times.

—Yeah.

—OK. So, the Federale is bringing up his piece and I have this moment where I blank. I, seriously, I panic. It's like surfing. I'm all over a wave and then it just surges and becomes like something else, like a beast, and I realize I'm totally in over my head and I'm just gonna get wiped out if I don't hold my shit, but it's too late, just taking the time to think makes it too late and next thing I know I'm plowed because what's happened is, I've totally panicked. Choked in the clutch. And that's what I did. The Federale is taking aim and I got my gun up and ready, and I freeze 'cause I don't know if I should blast my three bullets and, if I miss, hope he misses so I'll have time to duck and un-jam the cop piece, or duck without shooting before he has me in his sights, and by then it's too late to do anything, dude, 'cause he's pulling the trigger and I'm gonna get plowed. And then the doc freaking out on the floor kicks him in the back of the leg and he falls down and I shoot him.

I open my eyes. Nope, the world is still blurry and out of focus.

—Dude, it was one of those freaky moments where everything just works out for you. He's still alive, so I have to put another one in him before I come out from cover, but then that's it. All over.

All over.

—What about the doctor?

—Oh, dude, bummer. That was fucked up, but the way it worked out for me, I kind of figure it was meant to happen. I mean, I wanted to thank the guy and all, but there he is, gutshot. I got him flipped over and shot him in the back of the head. Total drag. So, then I go looking for the Bronco keys and find the wanted poster, and you know what's really weird, dude?

—No.

—Like a year ago, I saw the Henry Thompson *America's Most Wanted.*

There it is again.

—And I totally thought he looked like you, but it just seems too far-fetched, right? So that was that. But the second I looked at the poster? *Bang!* Just like that I got it. Then I motored out to the highway and found Leo, and you were gone. That sealed the deal.

—How is Leo?

—OK, last I saw. I took him back to Pedro's and he was awake and could talk a little. Said the Federales caught him in the jungle and beat it out of him about where I was taking you. He felt real bad about that. Anyway, Pedro called Doc Sanchez and I took off. Looked like a good time to return to the States for a vacation. Also, I wanted to look you up.

—Why?

Not that I need to ask.

—Dude, way I figure it, I'm owed some money. Leo may be one of those cats who will do anything for a friend. But me? I like to get paid.

And there is no fucking way that if I'd known who you were I would have helped out for the standard fee. I mean, if I'd known I was gonna have to kill three guys, I probably would have said, like, double. But now? Shit. Way I figure, I know you have money 'cause you gave the Federales 70 Gs and they thought you should have more.

Something occurs to me.

—What happened to the seventy?

—Shit, dude, I got it.

He pulls up his shirt and I see my money belt wrapped around his stomach. Bloodstained just like the wanted poster. He drops the shirt.

—But, dude, that's besides the point. I mean, that's like salvage and has nothing to do with you owing me for services rendered.

I open my eyes. The world has stopped spinning and has come back into focus. Money.

—How much?

—Well, I'm willing to listen to an offer, dude.

—Hundred thousand?

—Shit, dude, if you can rattle off 100 Gs just like that, you can probably do two.

—Yeah, I probably can.

—Dude! How much do you have?

—A lot.

—OK, OK, that's cool, I'm not greedy. Two! Two is cool. But hey, that only stands as long as things don't get any harder, OK?

—Yeah.

I sit back up and my stomach lurches. More concussion symptoms.

—Rolf?

—Dude?

—Did you kill a deputy after I crashed?

—Yeah. Didn't know what else to do there.

I stand up and stumble. Rolf catches me.

—Easy.

I clamp my mouth shut and point at the bathroom and he helps me to the toilet. He stands in the open door as I spill my guts. The water I drank comes up, and then it's dry heaves. I finish and slump on the floor. Dry heaves suck. Dry? Didn't I just eat with Mom and Dad?

—How long have I been out?

—Almost twenty-four hours, dude.

Shit, oh shit.

—Phone! Phone! Did I have a cell phone?

—Yeah.

—I need it right now.

MOM AND Dad are in police custody, and Dylan wants to explain to me why he's not happy about it..

—Is this how you do business, Hank? Because if it *is*, if this is what I have to look forward to, I may just have to back out of this deal right now.

I'm sitting on the bathroom floor talking on the cell phone Dylan gave me. Sid has come back from the IHOP and is sitting out in the room, eating a stack of banana pancakes. Rolf is standing next to the open door so he can listen in.

—I had some trouble.

—Is that what you call trouble, Hank? Because if it *is* . . .

He breathes deeply.

—OK, this isn't doing either of us any good. It does nobody *any* good for me to lose my temper. What we need to do here is evaluate the situation. Our problem is that as long as your parents are with the police, my employees cannot reach them. I can see where this might give you comfort, but what you need to remember is that it also removes my *leverage* with you. Which increases my legal and economic *exposure*. Which makes me nervous and more inclined to take aggressive *action* once your parents are released. Now, why don't you tell me what happened and we'll come up with some strategies to fix *our* problem?

How much to tell him?

—I went to see a friend. These guys I scrapped with in San Diego showed up. I think they figured out who I am and were looking for some reward money or something.

—I know that, Hank, I can get that information from the *TV* at this point. They most certainly do know who you are, and now the police and the FBI and the *national media* know that you are still alive and at large.

Oh, God.

—We can solve this, Hank, we can. Where are you now?

—I'm on my way to get the money.

—Where? The police said they found your car, so *where* are you?

I look at Rolf looking at me, listening to my end of the conversation.

—I got out of town, Dylan, that's all you need.

—Hank! Hank, are *you* now telling *me* what *I* need to know? Because if you are. . . . If *you* are trying to tell *me* what *I* need to know, then *I* have to tell *you* that *you* are very much mistaken. The police have not charged your parents and even if they *do,* it seems unlikely that they will have any trouble making bail, seeing as they are such pillars of the community. Trust me Hank, they will not be *safely* in police custody for long. Now, I would rather not do so, but if I do not have some *assurances* soon I will be forced to secure my leverage at the earliest possible opportunity, Hank. I will be forced to take *custody* of your parents until our business is concluded one way or another.

I close my eyes.

Mom and Dad.

I open my eyes.

—Dylan, I'm out of Patterson. I'm on the road and undercover and on my way to get the money. All you need to do is sit tight and I will take care of everything. I have some experience in this, after all.

He's quiet for a moment.

—That's a good point, Hank. Very well put. Experience is *invaluable* when the rubber hits the road. OK. OK. This is me, this is my weakness. I try to micromanage. You just can't do that and expect your people to do their job properly. But now, now I do need to establish a timeline. I was willing to work without a clock before this, *but now* . . . we need some targets.

—Like what?

—It's . . . eight forty-seven PM, Tuesday night. Let's call it nine PM. I want my money in *five days.* And, so there is no confusion, that means in my hands no later than nine PM this coming Sunday. *Understood?*

—Yes.

—And, I'm sorry to ask for this, but I'll also want progress reports. That means at least one call every twenty-four hours. *Understood?*

—Yes.

—OK. Well, that looks like it. Hank, I want to thank you for being patient while I blew off steam and I want to thank you for your problem-solving skills. *Thank you.*

—Sure.

—*And* . . . I'll talk to you tomorrow.

He hangs up. Rolf points at the phone.

—Dude?

—This guy is keeping an eye on my folks for me. I owe him some money for it.

He nods his head.

—Money.

—Yeah.

—There gonna be enough for both of us?

—Yeah, there'll be enough.

But there isn't. Dylan wants it all, and Rolf will want it all, too, when he finds out how much there is. The difference is that Dylan has Mom and Dad. Rolf just has Henry Thompson, and I don't care much what happens to him.

I get myself to my feet. I wobble and Rolf puts a hand on my arm.

—What now?

What now? I could try calling Tim again. But who's fooling who here? Something's gone wrong in Vegas and Tim is not going to be returning my calls. So what now?

I point into the room where Sid is watching the Winter X Games.

—TV.

The story isn't getting full-blown, nonstop coverage, but CNN has given it a title: *Henry Thompson: The Return.* I am a sequel.

When we tune in, they're showing tape shot earlier in the day in front of Wade's house. The two trucks are being untangled, yellow tape is strung everywhere, sheriff's deputies and State Police and guys in dark suits are walking around. I catch a glimpse of a chalk outline at the base of the garage door. They cut to more tape from the strawberry field off of Las Palmas: the wrecked Monte Carlo, a sheriff's car parked next to it, cops combing the ground for evidence. Cut to an earlier shot at the same scene: a covered body on a gurney being loaded into the back of an ambulance. On the bottom of the screen, a name: Deputy Theodore T. Fischer.

Sid points at the screen.

—That's him, that's him.

Rolf puts his hand up, hushing him.

—Cool it.

—Dude, that's my guy.

I look at him.

—You shot the deputy?

—Yeah. My first.

—Your first?

—My first kill.

He's staring at the screen, eyes sparkling. I give Rolf a look. He shrugs. *Kids these days.* Great, Sid the Junior Psycho is stoked because he just earned his Murder Merit Badge.

More tape: the outside of Emanuel Medical Center in Turlock, three ambulances unloading, and the back of a head between two state cops. Danny. The reporter is listing names and injuries and legal statuses.

Hector Barnes (aka Fat Guy): lacerations, abrasions, contusions; in good condition. "No charges as yet." Kenneth Pitlanske (aka Ponytail Boy): abrasions, contusions, multiple fractures; in stable condition. "No charges as yet." Willis Doniker (aka Mullet Head): DOA. Uniden-

tified female eighteen (aka Leslie): abrasions, contusions; released
from hospital. "In police custody." Daniel Lester (aka Danny): facial
lacerations, contusions, abrasions; released from hospital. "In police
custody." Unidentified female minor, six (aka Cassidy): facial lacera-
tion, minor concussion; in fair condition. Wade Hiller: DOA.

And more tape: the front of my home, cops, Mom and Dad being led
to a sheriff's car by two deputies, reporters shouting and shoving cam-
eras into the air to get a shot. They're in custody, uncharged, but being
questioned.

The punch line comes last, a statement from the San Joaquin
County Sheriff taped a few hours ago.

—We are still investigating the incidents in Patterson that occurred
early this morning, but we do have some information. Um, there have
been three deaths, two in an apparent automobile collision and the
other a shooting. Deputies responding to the collision were informed
that shots had been fired at that location and, and, wait, I'm sorry, and
T. T., uh, Deputy Fischer was responding to that call when he was redi-
rected to an alarm call that we had reason to believe might be, uh, con-
nected with the earlier, uh, earlier call. The collision and shots fired.
He, uh, gave pursuit. He gave pursuit to a vehicle fleeing the scene of
the alarm call, and the suspect vehicle, uh, crashed, and while the
deputy was, we believe at this point, that while the deputy was appre-
hending the suspect in the, uh, suspect vehicle, another vehicle ar-
rived at the scene and one or more people shot T. T., shot Deputy
Fischer at that time and fled with the suspect, the first suspect. Uh.
Just give me a . . .

He turns from the microphones and wipes at his tearing eyes.

—Um, at this time, we believe that the suspect that fled, the second
scene, the alarm call? We believe that suspect had already fled the
scene of the collision and shots fired and that, we have eyewitness tes-
timony at this time that this suspect is Henry Thompson, the suspect
wanted for several murders in New York, uh, three years ago.

There is a great deal of hubbub from the reporters. Sheriff Reyes, a
man clearly out of his depth, raises his hands for silence.

—I'm not, we're not going to answer any questions, no questions. We do have, we do have some pictures we want to show and a number for information that we want to give out.

Reyes holds up a sheet of paper and the camera zooms in on it. It's my booking photo from New York.

—This is a photo of Henry Thompson as he looked three years ago. Based on our, uh, witness, this is what we think Henry Thompson may look like now.

He holds up the other paper. It's a sketch based on the photo, a few pounds and years added, along with more hair and a beard.

—We have copies for the press and the number is there at the bottom and we'd like you to run that number at the bottom, the bottom of the TV screen. And, this man is armed and very, very dangerous and we, as I said, we do believe at this stage that he has at least one accomplice and.

I turn it off. Sid jumps off the bed.

—Cool! Cool! Dude, is this what it was like in New York, is this what it was like?

—Yeah, this is pretty much what it was like.

—Cool!

He starts jumping around the room, punching the air. I turn away. Rolf picks up the remains of the grilled cheese I took three bites of, and tosses it in the trash.

—Sorry 'bout your folks, that's harsh.

I don't answer. Instead I point at Sid. He's standing in front of the bathroom mirror, unaware of us, doing his best *Taxi Driver*.

—You talkin' ta me?

I shake my head.

—What the hell, Rolf?

Rolf shrugs.

—Yeah, he's a handful.

Sid catches us looking at him and points at me.

—Well, I don't see anyone else here, so you must be talkin' ta me.

He laughs, quick-draws pistol-fingers, and shoots them at me.

—You the man! You. The. Man.

Then he closes the bathroom door and we can hear him pissing. Rolf laughs.

—And like I said, dude, he kind of has a crush on you.

I want to leave right away, but Sid insists that we sweep the room to leave the fewest possible clues.

—Dudes, I can tell you right now, the cops are all over your mom and dad's neighborhood asking about suspicious vehicles and shit. And someone always sees something. Sooner or later, someone's gonna say something about my camper being parked on the street. They're gonna look into it, and dudes on the block are gonna be all, *nope not mine*. Next, they lift a tire track from the field where I kacked that deputy.

He's going around the room with the liner from one of the waste-baskets, filling it with every scrap of trash he can find, along with strands of my hair that were on the pillow and any other bodily effluvia laying about.

—Where we get lucky, dudes, is that I have some custom Pirellis on my ride. So the tracks won't really point at the funky '72 Westy people saw around your folk's place. 'Course, that only plays if we didn't leave a track in a oil puddle in front of their house or something. Which is why I'm doing this shit, 'cause if the cops start telling people to keep their eyes peeled for my ride, the guy up at the desk might remember it. Next thing ya know, this room is wrapped in plastic, vacuum-sealed, and they're running swabs over the rim of the toilet looking for our DNA.

Rolf and me help him clean up.

SID HAS a copy of *The Man Who Got Away* that he wants me to sign. It's in a milk crate full of true crime books in one of the cabinets in his Westphalia.

The Westphalia rings a bell somewhere in my scrambled brain.

—Rolf, how did you find me?

Turns out Rolf, not being wanted by the police, flew back to the States on a commercial flight, took a bet that I'd try to cross at the busiest port of entry on the border, and started hanging out in T.J. And he found me. Motherfucker actually saw me walk out of the border station, jumped into Sid's Westphalia, followed me into San Diego, where they almost ran me over, and then tracked me up the I-5. And can you believe that shit?

—Can you believe that shit, dude?

No.

—I mean, I hopped online at the airport before I flew out of Cancún. Got all kinds of stuff about you, like where your folks live and all. You being a novice at border hopping and probably headed for Cali, I figured T.J. was a no-brainer. But the stakeout at the border? That was Sid.

Rolf is driving, Sid is in the passenger seat and I'm on the bench-seat behind them. Sid raises his hand.

—The stakeout was mine.

—Yeah, 'cause I was all about heading for Patterson and looking for you there, 'cause there was no way I figured we'd spot you coming across.

—And I was all, *Dude, what if he doesn't go to see his rents? Then what?*

—Turns out we were both right.

—Yeah, but come on, give me props.

Sid holds out his fist and Rolf punches it lightly.

—Props.

The lighter on the dash pops out, Rolf hands it to me. I light the cigarette I'm holding, hand the lighter back, and he clicks it back into its slot.

—Then we just kind of hung back to see what was up.

Sid turns to face me.

—We didn't want to freak you out, and Rolf was all, *Dude, we need to wait till he makes a move for whatever ducats he has stashed.*

—We drove by the house every hour or so. Hung out at the Mickey D's by the highway and then parked up the street after dark.

—We had the beds down and our bags out when we heard that crash, and then the shots. I was all, *Hit it!*

—Took us a couple turns to find the scene. By then the fire department was there, so we cruised by and went around the block to your folks' place.

—And, dude, there you are, comin' out the front door. Like, total kismet.

—We lost you when you hopped the fence, but we had seen you take your car to the garage, so we went there.

—And there you are blastin' away from that cop. Damn! Wicked!

—So we followed.

—And I took care of that deputy dog and here we is. More props.

He sticks out his fist and Rolf props him. He offers his fist to me. I look at it.

In the cabinet with the true crime books, Sid also has some of the most rancid and violent porn I have ever seen, a stack of *Soldier of Fortune* back issues, the boxed *Faces of Death* DVD set, and some other shit that makes me suspect central casting called and requested a potential serial killer. He's waiting, his fist held out for props. I give him props. Now is not the time to get squeamish. I just have to make sure to kill him before he can hurt anyone else. That should be easy. Look at how much more experience I have at it than him.

IT'S ABOUT a hundred and fifty miles through the Mojave to Vegas. Even at the Westphalia's putt-putt top speed, we should be able to do it in three hours. After that? We go to Tim's, I pay off Rolf, and he and Sid disappear. I take the rest to Dylan, and he accepts it even though it's a bit light. I walk into a police station and turn myself in, and my folks stop getting hassled. And I begin what will end up being years and years of trials and appeals and . . .

But it won't work out like that. It will never work out like that.

For now I focus on getting a step closer to the money, and keep smoking cigarette after cigarette because they seem to help just slightly with the massive headache I've had since Rolf and Sid started talking football.

They're both San Diego Charger fans and are looking for help this week from my precious Fins. Rolf is still behind the wheel, Sid is in the living space of the van, stripping and stuffing all his clothes into a plastic garbage bag.

—Dude, if they can just beat the Raiders, and we take the Broncos, we clinch the AFC West. That's all I'm asking for, one win.

As he drives, Rolf is taking hits off a sneak-a-toke that's camouflaged to look like a stubby cigarette.

—Ain't gonna happen, dude. And you shouldn't be thinking like that anyway. It's so negative. Our destiny is in our own hands: win the last two games and take the West. Don't be looking for help from other teams, especially not the Fish, and, dude, not without Miles. Without Miles they're rank.

I keep my eyes closed and pinch the bridge of my nose, which also seems to help a bit with the pain.

—Actually, Sid, he's right. The Dolphins have a long history of choking in December. Win your own division and let me worry about mine. I mean, after we lose this week, we have to go to New York and get really humiliated by the Jets to finish the season.

—Dude, losing to the Jets sucks.

—Yes, it does.

Sid climbs back up front. He's changed into bright red hemp jeans tucked into fringed moccasin boots, and a short-sleeved, blue Lycra rash guard.

—Your turn.

—Right.

I climb around him into the back and start taking off my tattered clothes. I'm still in the thermal top and ragged jeans I had on at Wade's. The clothes I cleaned at Mom and Dad's got left in the Monte Carlo. Now Sid wants us all to change and bury the stuff we're wearing so we don't "leave a chain of physical evidence." I drop my dirty clothes into the plastic bag.

The bandage the EMT put on my leg is expert and still holding firm. It has a large red stain on it. The wound throbs in time with my heart-beat, but it's a much more manageable pain than the rods of agony that shoot through my concussed head. There's not much I can do about that right now. The only real treatment for a concussion is rest, and that's not an option.

I look through Sid's duffel bag and cabinets for something to wear, but, at five nine and about a buck sixty, Sid is five inches shorter than me and forty pounds lighter.

—None of this is gonna fit.

—It's all baggy shit, try it on.

I end up decked out in a pair of drawstring pants that just go over my waist, the cuffs dropping to the middle of my calves, and one of those hooded surf tops with the kangaroo pocket in front. There's no way his shoes are gonna work for me, so I stick with the trail sneakers I put on way back at the bungalow.

I stop, pull my Levis out of the bag, and go through the pockets. Nothing.

—Rolf?

—Dude?

—Do you have my cash and stuff?

—Yeah, sorry, man, kind of went through your pockets while you were out. Look in the zipper pouch on my day pack under the sink.

I open the sink cabinet and take out Rolf's red, white, and blue day pack. In the pouch I find the cash, the Carlyle ID, and the Christmas card I took from Wade's kitchen table. I also find the Anaconda and Danny's pistol. I stuff the card and money in my pocket. I look at the ID. I don't recall the border guard making any record of my name when I crossed, but with my face all over the TV who knows what he'll re-member. I dump the useless ID in the garbage bag and leave the guns in Rolf's pack.

—You're up, Rolf.

He scoots out of the driver's seat and Sid scoots in under him, a smooth and practiced move. He comes back and I sit on the floor while he strips naked except for the money belt. Up front, Sid slips System of a Down into the stereo and cranks it up.

Rolf dumps his clothes and finds Sid's black leather pants.

—Haven't worn a pair of these since I moved to Mexico.

He's Sid's height, but a couple pounds heavier. He has to lie on his back, kick his way into the pants, and suck in his stomach to button them.

—Sweet.

He shrugs on a yellow long-sleeved T-shirt with black stripes running down the arms, and gets his feet into a pair of Red Wing work boots.

—Kinda metalish for my taste, but fuck it, we're incognito, right?

I don't say anything, just tilt my head toward Sid. Rolf looks over his shoulder toward the front of the van. Sid is singing along to "Chop Suey!" Rolf looks back at me.

—What's up, dude?

—Where did you get him?

—He's the kid brother of this chick I used to hook up with in San Diego. Couple years ago he came to Mexico on a surf trip and looked me up. We stayed in touch. I needed a ride and some help here, so I called him.

—You know he's a psycho.

—Dude. I knew he could get pretty violent. I mean, his pop kicked him and his sister around pretty fuckin' hard, so that's like his socialization, right?

I don't say anything. He licks his lips, nods.

—OK. Yeah, dude, I know. He's psycho. Why do you think I brought him along?

—What?

—Dude, no way I'm gonna go bustin' a cap in any more people. I most especially don't intend to be doin' it now that I am north of the border. That would be unwise. But there may be killin' to be done.

—So you brought Sid.

—So I brought Sid. Killin' time is hard time. And, if we get caught? Hard time is *not* in my plans. Sid can take that heat.

I don't say anything to the man in front of me, the man I used to go fishing with in Mexico.

—Dudes!

Rolf looks over the seat into the front of the bus.

—What's up?

—We need gas. Baker's right up here. I'm gonna pull off. And, dudes, we can check out the World's Tallest Thermometer.

I stay in the back and look at Rolf's day pack and think about the guns in it.

SID PULLS off the I-5 onto Baker Boulevard, into the heart and soul of Baker. That heart and soul is an expanse of tarmac that hosts the Mad Greek, the "Original" Bun Boy, the Country Store ("the Luckiest Lotto Dealer in California"), and the Will's Fargo, Bun Boy, and Arne's Royal Hawaiian motels. All have a great view of the thermometer. Then again, all of Baker has a view of the hundred-and-thirty-four-foot ther-mometer.

—Sid?

—Dude?

—Isn't this stop playing against the plan to keep moving?

—Dude, we need gas. Oh, man, check it out!

He's pointing at the thermometer.

—I'm gonna get a picture.

He grabs a disposable camera from the glove box and jumps out of the VW. We watch as he runs to the base of the thermometer, stands with his back to it, holds the camera at waist level, pointing it up at himself, and clicks a picture. Then he runs back and jumps in.

—That is gonna be rad.

He pulls the bus under the brightly lighted awning of a Shell station.

—Uh, dudes, I could kinda use some gas money.

Rolf pats his pockets, ignoring the seventy-five grand wrapped around his middle.

—Yeah, dude, I'm kinda tapped too.

I reach in my pocket. After buying the BMW, I have just under four thousand left. I take five hundred off the roll and hold the cash out to Sid.

—For travel expenses.

—Dude, you sure?

—Yeah.

—You are so cool. Thanks, dude.

He hops out to fill that tank and climbs back in a couple minutes later.

—Dude in the station says we got to have a strawberry shake at that Mad Greek place. How 'bout it? My treat, seein' as I'm flush.

He parks at the far end of the lot, away from the lights, and goes in for the shakes. I get out and stand, stretching my cramped limbs and trying to walk the stiffness out of the wound in my left thigh. My head is still goofy. If I turn it too quickly everything blurs and I have to wait for all the ghost images to catch up with the real world. But my stomach has settled and I'm looking forward to my shake.

Sid comes back. I slide the side door of the bus open, sit on the floor with my feet hanging out, and sip my shake. Rolf stays in the front seat, sucking hard on his straw. Sid is pacing back and forth in front of me, drinking his shake and trying not to look like he's watching me, but he is.

I don't want to look at him. I don't want to talk to him. But I need him to like me. I need it to be harder for him to kill me, if it comes to that. When it comes to that.

—Sid, why don't you sit down?

—That's cool, dude, I'm OK.

—You're making me a little nervous, have a seat.

He shrugs and sits next to me, leaving as much room as possible between us. He kicks his feet against the tarmac, takes a sip, and lifts his shake.

—Good, huh?

—Yeah.

—Yeah.

There's a loud gurgling slurp as Rolf hits the bottom of his shake. He climbs out of the bus and points at the Mad Greek.

—I'm gonna piss, dudes. Then we roll.

Sid bobs his head.

—Dude, yeah, we, like, still have to find a spot to bury the clothes and shit. I mean, that's cool right, Hank? That's the way to do it?

—Yeah, sure.

Rolf walks toward the restaurant. Sid watches him disappear inside. He sucks some shake into his straw, pulls the straw from the waxed paper cup, and shoots a stream of shake onto the ground. He looks at me out of the corner of his eye.

—It's OK, dude.

—What's that?

—If you think I'm a freak. Like the story of my life. Whatever.

He leans forward and puts his elbows on his knees, fills his straw with shake again, and starts Pollocking little abstracts on the ground between his feet.

—I don't think you're a freak, Sid. I just don't know what you're doing here.

He shrugs.

—I don't know.

—Is it the money?

Thinking about his cabinet of fetishes, knowing already it is not about the money for this guy. He shakes his head, hard.

—No, dude, I don't want your money, man. I mean, like, I like money. I'm not that big a freak, but.

He takes another sip of his shake, then pulls the top off and dumps the rest of it on the ground, obliterating his design.

—What, Sid?

He crumples up the cup, throws it in some bushes alongside the parking lot, stands up and faces me.

—I don't want your money, dude. I want to be a part of something. I just, like. Like, when Rolf told me he needed help finding someone, and there was cashish in it, I was all, *Totally, I'm in.* But then, when I found out it was you? Dude! I was, like, all, *No way!* I'm . . . I *am* such a freak, and I've never done anything. I mean, if I told you, if I told you just how fucked up, how stupid my life is, *dude,* you just wouldn't fucking believe. But you? You're this totally famous dude! You've done so much with your life. When I found out Rolf knew you and all, I just wanted, I just wanted to meet you and. I just wanted to help out, do my part and be a part of something for once. Be a part of something important, dude. Like when, dude, when I shot that cop? That was, that was, it was so ir-fucking-revocable. That was real. I was all, *This is me now doing this and I can't take it back.* And I totally felt it. In the moment. More than anything I've ever done in my life. More than fucking or getting high or holding up a gas station or even catching a monster wave, dude. I mean, I've been *dreaming* about a feeling that real my whole life. And I got to feel that because of you.

He kicks at nothing, hard.

Dude! I'm sorry. I'm not trying to freak you out, but I am like such a fan and I just think you are so cool and I can't change that, you know? And this is just such an amazing experience for me. Shaaaw! I am such a geek.

He stands there in front of me, staring at the ground, too embarrassed to look up. Behind him, through the windows of the Mad Greek, I can see Rolf coming out of the bathroom.

I can do this.

Mom and Dad.

I can do this.

—Actually, man.

Sid looks up a little.

—Actually. I think that's pretty cool, Sid.

A smile cracks across his face.

—Dude?

—I think it's pretty cool that you want to be a part of something, that you have ambition. And, you know, I've never had a fan before.

He comes over and sits back down, close to me this time.

—Never had a fan? Oh, dude, you have no idea! Online? There are, like, sites just for you, just for people to chat about you. Like, never had a fan? Uh-uh. Huge fan base, dude.

Rolf exits the restaurant.

—That's cool, maybe you can show me sometime.

—Dude!

—Let's chill for now. Rolf's gonna give us both a hard time if he hears this shit. Call us fags.

—No worries, dude.

He looks from my face to where Rolf is approaching, and back at me.

—But, dude, you know I'm totally not.

—What?

—A fag.

Rolf walks up and stands in front of us. Sid spurts out a nervous laugh. Rolf looks at him.

—What?

Sid shakes his head.

—Nothing, dude.

He laughs again.

—Dude, what up?

Still laughing, Sid nods, waves his hand, climbs into the bus, gets behind the wheel, and starts the engine. Rolf leans close to me.

—Dude, I like the little dude, but he *is* kinda freaky, ain't he?

THERE'S A checkpoint at the state line. The lights appear on the horizon and we figure what it must be before we get there. Sid slows down, but keeps driving toward it. Rolf climbs in the back, pulls the foam pad off of the bench/bed at the back of the bus. There's a shallow depression underneath and the underside of the pad has been carved out to create extra storage space. Rolf grabs the sleeping bags currently occupying this space and tosses them on the floor.

—Dude, can you fit in here?

I peek in the cramped space.

—Uh, maybe I should just stay up here, put on a hat and.

—They have your picture, dude.

—They're not looking for three guys in a.

—You been listening to Sid? We don't know *what* they're looking for.

Sid is nodding.

—Dude is right. If they're looking for a Westy, we're fucked no matter what. Otherwise, *you're* the wanted man.

Rolf tosses the guns from his day pack into the stash space.

—Even if they search us, there's a good chance they won't find you in there.

—Let's just turn around.

The lights are bright now. Sid's shaking his head.

—Too late for that, dude. They see us flip a bitch here and we'll have to pull a *Smokey and the Bandit* in this thing. No way.

Rolf is holding the pad up.

—In, dude.

—Maaan.

—Dude, who's the professional people smuggler?

I climb in, kick the guns to the bottom of the space, and try to make myself flat. Rolf stuffs a couple sweatshirts around my head.

—What the hell are those for?

—In case a cop decides to sit on you.

—Oh, fuck you, man.

He laughs and drops the pad.

I'M NOT claustrophobic, but I do a pretty good impersonation of someone who is. It's not so much small places that I'm afraid of as being restrained. I wasn't born with this fear, it's just that it reminds me of being gagged with a dirty sock, pinned to a bed, and tortured. That is something I have experience with, and I don't expect to be getting over it. Ever. I looked it up once. There's no name for my specific association, but there's something called merinthophobia: the fear of being bound or tied. Being packed into a shallow depression and having a foam pad stuffed on top of you may not count as binding or tying, but it will do in a pinch. So I think skinny thoughts, try not to breathe too much, and eke what oxygen I can through the foam.

I HEAR the engine vibrating right under me and the squeak of the brakes as we stop. There are some sounds that might be voices, and then the bus is moving again, pulling forward. Fuckin' A, that wasn't too bad. We're through.

The bus swings to the right, stops, and the engine cuts out.

My heart starts trying to slam a hole in my chest. I suck air, oxygenating my blood like a diver, knowing what's coming.

The weight in the bus shifts. I hear two bangs: Sid and Rolf climbing out and slamming the doors. A gliding shiver, another bang, another lurch of the bus: the side door being pulled open and a cop climbing in. I stop breathing.

One. Two. Three. Four.

I'm counting. That's a bad idea. Counting will just make me think about how long I'm holding my breath. I should think about something else. Calm thoughts. The beach. I picture my place at the beach. Palm trees waving, waves lapping. One wave. Two waves. Three waves.

Stop it.

Voices now.

—Mumble mumble in that cabinet?

Has to be a cop.

—Mumble here.

Rolf.

How close are they if I can tell what they're saying? One foot? Two feet? Three feet? Stop it!

—In that bag mumble?

—Mumble laundry mumble mumble.

—Under mumble there mumble?

Under? Under what? The rug? Are these guys looking for a fugitive or just hassling Rolf and Sid? Under? Fuck! The bench/bed is the top of a low cabinet.

—Mumble look mumble in there?

—Sure, dude.

Fuck you, Rolf.

I can hear it, I can feel it: the cop kneeling on the floor inches from me, popping open the cabinet doors, shining his flashlight inside, digging around right under me, trying to find something that will make his evening more interesting.

He's digging and digging. One. Two. Three. I need to breathe. I have to move. I can't be held down like this. I shift a quarter inch to the left and something pokes me in the side. Pictures in my head: being forced facedown on my bed, a man sitting on my legs, pulling out surgical staples, digging holes in my back. One. Two. Three. Stop! Please stop!

I feel pressure on top of the pad. Two hands on my stomach as the cop uses the bed to push himself up. All the remaining air is forced from my lungs.

—Thanks mumble.

And I open my mouth wide and suck and gasp.

Out! I need out!

—No mumble worries.

I shove the pad off. It flops silently to the floor as the door slides shut and bangs tight behind the exiting officer. Rolf glances back at me as he climbs in the front seat and we drive away from the roadblock. The highway patrol cops wave us on.

Up front, Rolf and Sid slap hands and laugh while I hyperventilate and ask myself just what the fuck I think I'm doing with these two. When you get right down to it, are these guys anything but a pile of dead bodies waiting to happen?

We go around a bend, and the guns Rolf stashed in the hole with me slide across the wood and bang against my knee.

BETWEEN JEAN and Sloan, about twenty miles outside Vegas, Sid has Rolf pull a couple dozen yards off the highway, takes the garbage bag full of our clothes and a fold-up camping shovel, and gets out of the bus. Rolf sits in the driver's seat. I sit behind him on the bench seat. We watch Sid, illuminated by one of those multipurpose emergency lights, as he digs his hole. The Westphalia screens the light from the drivers on the highway. I climb into the front passenger seat, roll down a window, and stick my head out to look up at the stars. Nothing, clouds. Rolf has put in an Allman Brothers tape. I pull my head back in and light a smoke and listen to "Melissa."

—Rolf?

—Yeah?

He's focused on his lap, where he has several roaches and scraps of shake spread out on a back issue of *Rolling Stone*. This is the last of his stash, he's rolling a couple joints to get him through until he can score some more in Vegas.

—What about Leo and Pedro?

—Dude?

—Do you think they knew who I was? Who I am?

—Who knows what they know, dude? Those guys, are like the. That thing they have in the desert?

—What?

—The thing that doesn't talk? Napoleon's soldiers shot the nose off of it?

—The Sphinx?

—Yeah, dude, Pedro and Leo are like the Sphinx, who knows what they know?

He has half the grass scooped onto the cardboard flap of a pack of Zig-Zags. He dumps it into a creased rolling paper he's holding in his other hand. I check on Sid: still digging.

—Think they'll get hassled much? Over me?

—Hard to say, dude. Figure those Federales were working on their own, but sooner or later some dude that's been at The Bucket's gonna see your pic on TV and remember you. Then who knows what goes down?

I finish my smoke, toss it out the window, and reach in the kangaroo pocket of my pullover for another. My hand slides across cold steel. I feel the cigarette box, take it out, and look inside: three left. I light one and keep the box in my hand.

Rolf is right. My photo is on cable news along with the sketch. That means it will be seen all over the world. A Mexican cop will remember me from Chichén Itzá, or somebody from the beach will see it and call the police. Sooner or later they'll find the connection between the sergeants and me.

—Will they hook Leo to the dead Federales?

The joint is rolled, he's scraping the rest of the grass together to make a second.

—Nah, I don't see why they would, dude. I mean, dude, you're Henry Thompson. After they trace your movements around and talk to people and investigate you for that Russian guy's death? They'll finger you for the Federales, and the doctor, too. Why make it harder than it has to be?

Once again, other people's dead bodies piling up in my account.

—Sorry 'bout that, by the way. Not the way I planned it, dude. But whatever.

—Yeah. Whatever.

He has the second scoop of grass resting in a paper, and holds it while he presses a fingertip onto little flakes still on the magazine cover and flicks them into the unrolled joint. I drag off my cigarette.

—Dude, you need to, like chill out now. Leo and Pedro are total survivors. Their shit might get messed with, but it's not like they'll do any time or anything.

He rolls the second joint, tucks it behind his right ear, pulls the first one from behind his left ear, puts it in his mouth, and lights it.

—Want to mellow out?

—I'll pass.

He tokes the joint and reads *Rolling Stone* by the light of his Bic. Sid has tossed the bag in the hole and is filling it in. I take a last drag, flick my butt out the window. I slip the cigarette box back in my pocket, and fill my hand.

—So, Rolf, what am I doing with you guys?

He's still looking at the magazine.

—Dude?

—I mean, why should I stay with you?

He turns his head to look at me and sees Danny's pistol in my hand, pointed at him.

—I mean, what is it you're threatening me with?

Rolf starts to straighten up.

—Just stay the fuck where you are.

—Dude, this is so uncool, we have a deal.

—Screw you. I am so sick of that line. I've had deals with people like you, and they always get fucked up, and I always end up *getting* fucked.

—This is such a bad call, dude.

—Why? Tell me why? You can't go to the cops. You can't threaten my parents, because you can't go anywhere near that town. The only thing you can do is kill me or hurt me, so why shouldn't I just get away from you?

—Oh, dude! *Threaten your parents?* Like I would do that. That's ill.

—Is that supposed to make me feel better? Is that supposed to reassure me? *Oh, don't worry, dude, I would never, like, hurt your folks. That shit is, like, totally out of bounds, duuuuuuude.*

—Dude, you need to chill.

—Get out of the bus, Rolf.

—Dude.

—GETOUTOFTHEFUCKINGBUS!!!

Something changes outside. My eyes flick to the right. Sid's light is off. I can't see him. I can't see where Sid is.

Rolf moves. He yanks the door handle and pushes backward, falling out of the bus.

My finger jerks on the trigger as Rolf, still in the line of fire, is dropping to the sand. Nothing happens. There is a thump as Rolf lands on the ground, out of view.

I look at the pistol. The safety is on.

The front passenger door opens right behind me. Sid! I fling myself to the floor between the front seats, twisting to land on my back, thumb groping for the safety. I land hard and my head whaps the driver's seat and my vision rolls a couple times like a TV with the vertical hold out. Sid climbs into the passenger seat I've vacated, the stubby camping shovel in his right hand.

—Dude!

My thumb clicks the safety. I'm waving the pistol up and down like a conductor's baton, trying to track Sid as he flips up my eyeballs over and over.

—Chill.

I pull the trigger and a bullet whangs through the roof of the bus, followed immediately by three or four more. Danny, the incredible asshole, has set the trigger weight at an insanely high sensitivity, and the pistol jumps in my hand, the recoil of each round triggering the next. The blips in my vision roll around once more, and stop as Sid pushes back, tumbling out the door like Rolf did. Time to go.

I crane my head around and reach for the steering wheel to pull myself up, and am just in time to see Rolf's arm stretched through the open driver's door, his hand snatching the keys from the ignition.

—No!

I grab at the keys, snag the cuff of his yellow shirt, and press the barrel of the gun against his wrist.

—I'll blow your fucking hand off, Rolf. Drop the fucking keys.

The bus rocks. Sid again. I turn, bringing the gun around. Rolf pulls free, Sid brings the flat of his shovel down on my right foot and ducks back out of sight before I can get off another shot. This is not working. My little plan of kicking Rolf out of the bus and driving off is not working. I stay low and edge back until I hit the bench seat. The throbbing in my head and left thigh has been joined by one in my right foot.

I peek left and right through the open front doors. No sign of either of them.

—Rolf!

—Dude?

He's still outside the driver's side.

—Toss the keys in and then I want you both to walk over in front of the bus where I can see you.

—Dude, no fucking way.

—Rolf, I am going to come out there and just shoot you guys. Now throw in the keys and get where I can see you.

—Dude, you know we have a gun, right?

Uh?

—Like, Sid had to shoot that deputy with something, right, dude?

My stomach drops.

—Bullshit. Why didn't he just shoot me?

—Dude, because I don't want to.

Sid, still on the passenger side.

—Bullshit.

BANG!

I duck.

—That wasn't *at* you, dude. Just to, like, prove it, you know.

Bad plan, Hank, very bad plan.

—So, dude, toss your piece out and we'll all chill and get back with the program.

I get on my hands and knees and crawl around the bench seat, into the back of the bus. I find the Anaconda where I stashed it under a loose flap of carpet, and stick it in the pocket of my pullover.

—Dude?

I edge up onto the bed where I hid earlier, staying flat so I can't be seen through the windows. I grab the handle that opens the rear window, push the little button at its center, and twist.

—Dude?

Is he a little closer? I shout.

—I need to think!

I push the window and it lifts up and out.

Sid calls.

—Brah, don't do this, man, don't fuck this up. You know, you so know how important this is to me. I'm all, I'm all . . . *please*, dude.

I let go of the window and springs draw it open. I lever myself up

and over the window's lip, roll out, and drop to the ground. The landing jars my squishy brain and blackness strobes at the edge of my vision, then recedes. I crawl the first few feet, the sand dragging at my
clumsy limbs, then get into a low crouch, stumbling away from the
bus, trying to keep it between me and them.

—DUUUUUDE!

I hear them behind me, climbing into the bus. I drop flat on the
ground, worming around so I'm facing the VW. I hold the pistol out,
line up the sights with the open rear window of the bus. Rolf's dreadlocked head appears in the window. I have a shot. I drop the sights and
pull the trigger. The bullet dimples the body of the bus and Rolf disappears.

—Dude! No good, man.

—You guys fuck off right now. It's over.

—Dude. It is not over.

—Rolf, I got more than a few rounds left. You want to rush me? Wait
me out till daylight when anyone can see us? It's over. Take the bus and
get going.

—We had a fucking deal.

—Not anymore.

Silence. Then the front doors shut and the bus's engine starts. The
running lights blip on, the bus moves forward a couple feet, stops, and
the passenger door opens. Sid steps out.

I draw a bead on him.

—Get back in, Sid.

He walks to the back of the bus.

—I'm gonna shoot, Sid.

He stops, stands there, bathed in red from the taillights.

—This is wrong, Henry. We should all be, like, working together. We
can do things together. It's no good being alone, dude.

—Get back in the bus or I'm gonna shoot you.

—Dude, so ill.

He turns and shuffles back through the sand, head hung low. He's
climbing back into the bus.

—Sid!

—Dude?

—Try not to hurt any more people. It's wrong.

—Whatever.

He gets in and slams his door. The bus heads for the highway. At the edge of the blacktop it pauses, the headlights come on, a blinker blinks, signaling a merge onto the empty road, and the Westphalia pulls away, the sound of the Allman Brothers spilling from the open back window. "Whipping Post" trailing into the distance.

I stand there, alone in the desert with two guns.

JUST TWENTY miles to Vegas, and I may not be able to make it.

Walking through loose sand in the dark with a gunshot wound in your left leg, a swelling right ankle, and a concussion, is an ordeal. Thirty minutes into the hike I'm exhausted and I've smoked my last two cigarettes. I stumble into an embankment, falling into loose rock, and jarring my head. Again. I wait a moment for my vision to clear.

I remember Russ, remember dragging him around, his head getting knocked over and over after I had already smacked it with a baseball bat. The way his speech started to slur, the way he silently died. I need to stop falling down.

I crawl up the short embankment, and grab onto a steel rail. I've tripped over the tracks of the Union Pacific.

I pick my way over the tracks and down the opposite embankment and find a two-lane local road. I look in both directions. The road is long and straight and has a culvert running parallel to it. I walk along the edge of the road, making better time, the aches in my foot and leg easing a bit. I pass a road sign. I'm on the County 6 East, six miles from Sloan. Great. Sloan. Not that I know what I'll do when I get there.

I'm getting cold. I stuff my hands into the front pocket of the pullover along with the two cold hunks of steel. Then I hear a sound building behind me and look over my shoulder. No headlights, but it sounds like a diesel is back there. I edge down into the culvert and lie on my stomach. I can feel a vibration going through the ground. Oh. I flip over and see the headlight of the locomotive coming up the track. Train. I could hop a train. Do these tracks run into Vegas? Where else would they be going out here?

It's hard to tell how far away the train is, but it must be pretty close for me to feel its vibrations. And it doesn't look like it's going all that fast. I climb out of the culvert, hustle as best I can to the tracks, and crouch there. Yeah, this should work. The light gets brighter. The train gets bigger and louder, taking its time, chugging closer. Bigger. Louder. Closer. Bigger. Bigger. Uh. A multiton, yellow and black monster of steel slams past at sixty, buffeting me in its diesel cloud, shaking the earth like a quake and leaving me clutching the rocks on the rail bed, in awe at my utter stupidity. I get to my feet, still shaking, and watch the train disappear in the night. Well, that was an interesting way to almost kill myself.

A mile later I come to a place called Erie, find the same train sitting on the siding, creep up to a car loaded with Nissans, and climb on. Sometimes, even I get lucky.

THE TRAIN pulls out five minutes later and I spend the next half hour huddled between the nose of one Pathfinder and the rear of another, and try to expose the least possible amount of my flesh to the wind of our passage. When I feel the landscape open up around me in the darkness, and the deafening thunder of the train rolls out across the desert, I stick my head out. Up ahead I can see the apocalyptic glow of Las Vegas, the spear of light from the top of the Luxor shooting into the underside of the cloud cover.

Soon, we are passing through the kind of gritty neighborhoods you expect to find bordering a rail line. I see street signs like Blue Diamond Road, West Warm Springs Road, West Sunset Road. None of them are on the very short list of Vegas place names I have in my head, most of which have been culled from *Viva Las Vegas* and the one trip I took out here when I was in college. Then it's there, The Strip, a couple blocks off to the right. I can't see much, but, even ten years after my only visit, I know that's the place.

We pull into the Vegas rail yard. The train is slowing now, but not much. Doesn't matter, I have to get off before I find myself in a locked yard patrolled by Union Pacific security.

The train can't be moving faster than twenty as it pulls in to the yard and I fling myself from the edge of the railcar. I hit, bounce, flop to the ground, and roll over and over in the rocks, praying that the loaded guns in my pocket don't go off. They don't.

I sprawl on my back, watching the strange oyster glow of the sky swim around, wishing desperately that I could stay here until someone comes along from UP maintenance to scoop me up with a shovel and toss me into the bed of a truck with the rest of the rail-kill. But I have things to do. I creak to my feet, and limp away from the tracks and around the corner of the wall that surrounds the yard. The signs at the corner tell me I'm at East Charleston and Commerce Street. I close my eyes and collect my thoughts one by one and stack them up where I can look at them.

I need to get the money to keep Mom and Dad safe. I gave the money to Tim. Tim has gone missing. But I do know Tim's address. Hey! I know Tim's address! It hasn't been beaned out of my brain. I can go to Tim's and . . . do something! Great! OK. I need a map. I walk into the middle of the empty intersection and look up and down the streets, and see, several blocks away on Commerce, the bright sign of an ampm.

I LOOK like shit. I do not need to see myself to know this, but I take a look in the wing mirror of a parked car just to be sure. I have a cut over my right eye, sticky with clotted blood, my hair is matted with sand and soot, my clothes are torn and filthy, and my hands are scraped and black with the greasy dirt of the train. Wait a minute, what am I worried about? An ampm? In this neighborhood? I am far from the worst case they've ever seen in there. Hell, they've probably had worse tonight alone.

I walk into a land of fluorescent light and Muzak Christmas carols. The pimply kid behind the counter looks up from his comic book. He looks at me hard. Maybe I look even worse than I thought. Oh, fuck, Hank, you don't care what you look like, you care about people recognizing you. How did I forget that? Oh, yeah, brain hurt bad. The zitty kid is still looking at me.

—Yeah?

I gape at him.

—You can't use the bathroom. For customers only.

I don't need the bathroom. I need. Oh, crap, what do I need? I look around the store. What did I want? No clue. I reach in my pocket and feel around. Guns: two. Check. Cigarettes: none. Check. Cigarettes! I need cigarettes. I take the empty Benson & Hedges box from my pocket, walk to the counter, and show it to the kid. He finishes the page he's reading, puts down his comic, and looks at the crushed box.

—Benson & Hedges?

I hold up two fingers, and he reaches up to the rack above the counter, grabs two packs.

—Seven even.

I hand him a hundred. He takes it and holds it up to the light, then rings in the sale. I take my smokes and the change and he picks up his comic.

Cool, I've achieved something. He lowers his comic a bit and looks at me still standing there.

—What?

Huh?

—You need something else, hombre?

Uh?

—Yes? No?

I shrug.

—So get lost then.

Lost! I look around the store again, and see the maps on the magazine rack. I grab one of Vegas and hand it to the kid. He slaps his comic down on the counter.

—Fucking A. Three ninety-five.

I walk out of the store, map in one hand, cigarettes in the other, and get blinded by the headlights of a car as it pulls up to the pumps. I head for the light cast by a street lamp, and sit down on the curb. I open the map and run down the lists of street names, looking for Commerce. I find it and trace it until it runs into the intersection with West California where the gas station sits. OK, this is a start, I know where I am. I smudge some grease from my finger onto the spot so I won't lose it. Now, what is Tim's address? Shit! I had it before. I know where Tim lives, and his address is? Oh, fuck me!

I'm cold and tired and lost and I've had enough and I want, I want, I want to call home. I've got a phone. But I can't call home. I can't do that to them.

Sitting still isn't good. It's too easy to feel the pain. Pain spiking my head, throbbing in my thigh, and scratching at a hundred nicks and bruises. My head drops forward, my arms flop at my sides, the map held limply. I'm in bad shape. I know I'm in bad shape. I gotta get out of here, I gotta get up off the ground and go somewhere and get some sleep. I'll be so much better if I can just get some sleep, give my brain a chance to shut down. Where? Where am I gonna go? What am I gonna do?

I dig a cigarette out of one of my fresh packs.

Where are my matches? I paw through my pockets looking for a match. Where are my goddamn matches? I empty everything from my pockets except for the guns, and dump it all on the cement between my legs. Map, cell phone, charger, cigarettes, Christmas card, empty matchbook, a crumpled pile of hundreds and twenties, a spill of change. Headlights blast me from behind and a car horn jolts me to my feet. I spin, the car from the pumps is a few feet from me, its horn blaring. The silhouette of a head emerges from the driver's window.

—Get the fuck out of the way!

I look around. I'm right in the middle of the entrance to the station. The driver honks again, loud and long. I hold up a hand, palm out toward the car, bend down to pick up my stuff, and step out of the way as the car moves forward. It's a taxi. The driver looks at me as he eases past, shakes his head in disgust. I stand there with my hands full of junk. Map, cell, charger, smokes, Christmas card, money.

Christmas card!

The cabby taps his brakes, halting for a moment as a bus drives past. I run up to his open window and stick the red Christmas envelope inside.

—Here, I need to go here.

He ducks back from me and pushes my hand away.

—Fuck off!

I have my head and right shoulder stuck in the window. He tries to shake me loose, and I stumble alongside the crawling cab. I shove the envelope in his face.

—Here!

He's looking less pissed and more scared now as he slaps at his armrest, trying to roll up his window, but only succeeding in locking and unlocking the doors over and over. I get my other hand inside the window and shake a handful of cash at him. The taxi stops moving.

—A hundred bucks. I'll give you a hundred.

He looks at the envelope I'm sticking in his face.

—That address is in California.

What? Oh, Christ.

—The other one, the return.

His eyes move to the return address and then to the money in my other hand.

—Two hundred.

—Two hundred.

I peel off two hundreds and hand them to him along with the card in its envelope, then I pull open the back door and flop across the seat.

—You puke or piss or anything back there and it's gonna cost you another hundred.

The taxi starts to move. I close my eyes.

*   *   *

I OPEN my eyes.

Fuck me; oh fuck me, what am I doing? I look around. Taxi. Got it, I remember. I scooch up in the seat. The cabby is looking at me in the rearview.

—Too much tonight, buddy?

Way too much.

—Yeah.

He stops at a red light.

—In town for the rodeo?

Rodeo?

—Uh.

—Only guys I see as messed up as you are cowboys. You a cowboy?

I laugh.

—Yeah, yeah, I'm a cowboy.

—I figured. Couldn't pay me enough. Crazy shit.

—Yeah, crazy-shit cowboy, that's me.

He's looking at me again in the mirror.

—It's about a ten-minute ride. Go ahead and take a nap. I'll wake you.

A nap. That sounds good. I close my eyes.

SOMEONE IS pulling on me. I open my eyes.

—OK, buddy, here we are.

The cabby is tugging me out of the back of his cab. I jerk free and get out, almost fall, and he catches me.

—I got ya.

He's leading me toward a rust-streaked, white and turquoise trailer. We're in a trailer park. He helps me up the steps to a small porch and plops me onto a beat-up couch, setting off an eruption of dust. I cough. He points at the trailer.

—OK, this is the place. Don't look like anyone's home.

He's whispering.

—How can ya tell?

—I knocked.

He's still whispering.

—Just lie down.

He pushes on my shoulder. I lie back on the couch and close my eyes.

—Here's your Christmas card back.

Still whispering. I feel his hand shoving the card deep in my hip pocket. His hand grasping.

I grab his wrist and lurch up from the couch. He takes a step back, my hand locked on his wrist, his hand still deep in my pocket. I jerk it out and it comes free; the card and a litter of my cash dropping from his fingers. He yanks his hand away. Both of us standing now, he sees just how big I am, how big he is not. I take another step toward him. His eyes are huge. He's appalled at what he's tried to do: roll a crazed drunk.

—Easy, buddy.

But I don't want to be easy. I've been easy, now I want to be hard. Instead, I trip over my own feet and fall onto the porch. The cabby seizes the moment, runs to his taxi, and speeds away toward the entrance of the trailer park.

I lower my head. The Astro Turf that covers the porch scruffs against my ear. I look across the flat plain of the porch at my scattered money, and the Christmas card a few inches from my face. I grab the card and roll onto my back. I take the card from its envelope and hold it up to catch the light from one of the lamps that illuminate the park.

It's a homemade job, worked up on Photoshop or something. It's a still from *A Charlie Brown Christmas,* the part where Lucy is flirting with Schroeder, bent over his piano trying to get him to play "Jingle Bells." The still has been altered. Charlie Brown is standing next to his director's chair shouting "Action" into his megaphone. Schroeder is playing the piano, he's naked except for blinders and a red ball-gag. Snoopy is dancing on the piano in front of Lucy, his big dog dick stuck in her mouth. The caption reads "EUGH! DOG GERMS." Inside is another altered still that features Charlie and Lucy engaged in an act of coprophilia with the caption "Of all the Charlie Browns, you're the Charlie Browniest." Charlie's face has been removed from this one and T has superimposed his own.

Fucking T.

I close my eyes.

PART THREE

DECEMBER 14-17, 2003

Still Two Regular Season

Games Remaining

T was a quiet kid in junior high, one of the Dungeons and Dragons crowd that kept their heads down, trying to draw as little attention as possible. In the summer following eighth grade, his mom died, eaten from the inside by stomach cancer. He showed up the first day of freshman year with a brand new mohawk, safety pins in his ears, and a Clash shirt with the sleeves ripped off. The only punk in a school full of jocks, cowboys, and lowriders, he spent the next couple months getting gang-tackled and having his face stuffed in a toilet every time he turned a corner. Until he bit off Sean Baylor's earlobe. After that, everybody decided the risks of beating on the school freak outweighed the pleasures.

The only group that would have anything to do with him were the burnouts, and that was only after he started selling off his mother's leftover pain medication. Then Wade's mom died, and he and T started hanging out. By the time I came around, T was a regular in stoner circles. He was the guy that could get his hands on good weed, acid, speed, mushrooms, and coke from time to time. But that didn't make him any less freaky.

Going to T's house to score an eighth was a roll of the dice. He might be zonked in front of his Apple II playing *Zork*, or he might be in the backyard, shirtless and frenzied, the Dead Kennedys screaming from the house stereo, bench-pressing a board with cinder blocks balanced on either end until veins bulged over his scrawny torso like swollen night crawlers.

We didn't talk much. He was just too strange for me to handle, and

I was just the crippled jock tagging along with his pal Wade. He was the only guy in school who actually gave me a bad time about my injury. *Hey, superstar, how's the leg? Hey, superstar, race ya to the corner. Hey, superstar, that joint ain't a talkin' stick, pass it over here. My bad, I'll come get it, you need to stay off your feet.*

Last time I saw T was at graduation. He had spent four years smoking, sniffing, and eating anything he could lay his hands on, alienating virtually every member of the student body, faculty, and administration, and he graduated with an effortless 3.9. Someone told me he had scholarship offers from the computer departments at Berkeley and Stanford. Instead, he did a quarter at Modesto Junior College, started dealing crank, and ended up taking a jolt in county, and later another for the state.

—EASY, HITLER.

I wake up shivering.

—Easy, Hitler.

Why is it cold in the Yucatán? Because it's not the Yucatán maybe? Ass. Hole. Something growls.

—Shush, Hitler.

I open my eyes, and see a dog as big as a truck. It's growling and showing me all of its teeth. It's wearing a collar, but no leash. I tilt my head and look up. Elvis Presley is standing behind the dog. He's about five eight, wearing pegged black Levis, black engineer boots, and a black leather vest over a white T-shirt, is beanpole skinny, and has sideburns down to his jaw and an oily black pompadour.

—Who the fuck are you and why are you on my fucking porch?

What am I doing on his porch? I start to sit up.

—Don't fucking move or Hitler's gonna eat your face.

I don't want my face eaten by anyone, let alone Hitler. I stick out my hand to ward off any face eating and Elvis grabs the Christmas card that I'm clutching. He opens it.

—What the fuck?

He looks from the card to me, and does the best double take I've ever seen in real life.

—Holy shit! Holy piss, shit, motherfucker, tits. Fuckshit. Holy fuckshit, fucking Christ. Fuck me. Fuck me. Fuck me.

—Nice to see you too, T.

He picks up all the money, drags me to my feet, hauls me into the trailer, and dumps me on a couch in only slightly better repair than the one on the porch.

—Still havin' trouble walkin', huh, superstar?

He takes the two guns from my pocket. The dog stands in front of me, teeth still bared, assuring that I stay put. No problems there. I close my eyes.

—WAKE UP, superstar.

I open my eyes. T is sitting on the coffee table in front of me, his left hand resting on top of the dog's head. The dog is an English Mastiff, a light-coated two-hundred-pounder with a sad face. T snaps open a Zippo with an American flag sticker on its side, and holds the flame to the Marlboro Red in his mouth. I stop staring at the dog and reach in my own pocket for a smoke. The dog twitches.

—Hitler, no!

The dog eases back. Comprehension finally dawns.

—Hitler is the dog.

T nods.

—Hitler is the dog.

I take my empty hand from my empty pocket. I've lost my cigarettes somewhere. I point at T's pack.

—Can I have one of those?

He nods, hands me a smoke, and lights it for me.

—Didn't think superstars like you were supposed to smoke.

I take a huge drag.

—Yeah, things change.

He laughs.

—Shit yeah, they do. Shit. Yeah. I mean, check this out. Me and you, we never had much to say to each other, and yet here we are chatting. How's that for change? Or how 'bout this? Last time I saw you, you were this kind of fallen, small-town golden child and I was a wigged-out school freak. And now? Wow. I may not have come far, but look at you. Now you're a full-blown success story, an American celebrity. Must feel great to have all that thought-to-be-lost promise come to fruition. Yeah! Gotta admire a guy with that kind of drive. Can't get to the top the way you planned, so just go out and blaze a new trail up there. Bang, bang, bang. I tell you, man, everybody back home is real impressed at what you've done with your life. Especially, you know who is especially impressed? Wade. Oh, I'm sorry, that should have been past tense, shouldn't it?

There are burn scars up and down T's forearms. The smaller ones are dots the size of M&Ms, the largest are lines almost exactly the length of a cigarette from tip, to the top of the filter. T's favorite game in high school was Cigarette Chicken. Two players press their fore-arms together and drop a lit cigarette lengthwise into the crease where their arms meet. First one to pull his arm away loses. I never partici-pated. From the fresh pink of some of the scars, it looks like T is still an avid player.

—I didn't kill Wade.

He stubs his cigarette out in an ashtray made from an old cylinder head.

—No shit, numbnuts, no one said you did. Seems pretty fucking clear to anyone who can watch TV that that punk Danny Lester was to blame for that shit. One look at that guy on the tube and you just know he's the biggest dick ever. A lying sack of shit, he is. But fuck, who cares, right? Wade is dead all the same, which believe me when I say I think is pretty fucked up, seeing as he was just one of the only people I gave a shit about in the whole world. And now here I come home from a late night of work and find you nodded out on my porch in a pile of money with the Christmas card I sent him in your hand. Which has to beg the question: What the fuck is your fugitive ass doing here, try-ing to fuck up my already legally fragile situation?

I open my mouth, close it. Open it again.

—I.

I take in his bouncing knee and the way he's furiously scratching Hitler between the eyes, and I realize for the first time that he's thoroughly speeded up. He opens his red, jiggly eyes wide as they will go.

—Come on, man, enlighten me.

—OK, I. See. How much? Do you know much about New York? Or?

Oh, Jesus, there is no way I can do this now.

—T, I don't think I can really.

I open my hands, my jaw slacks helplessly.

—I don't even know where to.

—Right. Right. It's late and you've clearly had a rough night and would like to get some rest. We can take care of that.

He opens his cigarette box, digs his index finger inside, and pulls out a little white tablet.

—Take this.

—Oh, T, no, that's such a bad idea right now.

He balances the pill on the tip of his index finger and holds it in front of my mouth.

—Don't be a pussy, superstar, this is a fucking diet pill. I deal harder stuff to the kids at UNLV so they can cram for their finals. Eat it.

He presses it onto my lips.

—C'mon. Here's the train, open the damn tunnel.

I haven't popped a pill since my freshman year of college. But I don't have the will or the energy to argue with a speed freak right now; especially not one with a monster dog at his beck. I open my mouth. He drops the pill inside, and it sits bitterly on the tip of my tongue. I dry swallow it down. T smiles.

—OK, spill.

And I do. I start talking, and soon enough, I couldn't shut up if I wanted to. And I don't want to. My thoughts crystallize into a lattice of narrative logic and I want nothing but to share it with T. I tell him the whole story, with illustrations and examples drawn from film, literature, popular music, and Greek philosophy, with sidebars on the topics of media politics, Superman vs. Batman, and Schrödinger's Cat, with references to our shared history and revelations about a secret and mutual admiration, I tell him the whole story in every detail. I have never told the whole story before, not even Tim knows all the things I'm spilling to T.

And now I sit exhausted and sleepless, sucking on my twentieth or thirtieth cigarette of the day, and looking out the window at the sky getting ready to go a brilliant desert blue. And I feel better. I feel better having told the story and having someone else know everything. No matter what else, I feel better.

T goes into the kitchen and comes back with a small brown pill bottle. He shakes three pills into his hand, pops two in his mouth, and offers me one.

—No, no way. I'm never gonna sleep again as it is.

He shakes his head.

—It's a 'lude.

I look at it. I don't want to take it. I remember what it's like to go on a speed jag, pills to get up, pills to get down. I don't want to take it. But I know in my heart I'll never sleep without it, and I need sleep now, more than anything in this world I need sleep. I drop it in my mouth.

T nods.

—C'mon.

He starts down the hall. I get up and follow him, and Hitler follows me. T stands in an open doorway at the end of the hall.

—Spare room.

I look inside. There's a worktable, a computer, masses of paper, and jumbled piles of disks. The walls are covered in thumbtacked rock and anime posters. In one corner is a foam pad covered by a dingy sheet and a rumpled blanket. T jerks his thumb toward the other end of the trailer.

—I'll be in the master suite. Holler if you need anything.

I stumble to the pad. It's the most comfortable bed I've ever been in, so soft and mushy, just like my skeleton is soft and mushy. Whoa. Here comes the 'lude. T flicks off the light.

—Night.

—Night, T.

He turns to go.

—Hey, T?

—Yeah?

—What now?

He is an angular silhouette in the doorway.

—My dad died.

—Sorry, I didn't know.

—Cancer got him last year. Just like my mom.

—Sorry.

—Being an orphan sucks. That's what I'll miss about Wade, knowing there's a guy who knows how I feel.

—Yeah.

His silhouette shifts, he looks down the hall.

—So we're gonna find your buddy and your money and save your mom and dad from the bad guys. OK?

—Yeah. Thanks.

He disappears down the hall, followed by his huge dog. I close my eyes.

—Superstar?

I keep my eyes closed.

—Yeah?

—It's kind of cool you came to me for help.

—Didn't have no one else.

I hear him laugh.

—Yeah, well, it'd have to be something like that, wouldn't it?

I WAKE up to the sound of Hank Williams singing "Mind Your Own Business." My body is impossibly stiff and sore. The good news is that the needle-sharp pains, nausea, and confusion of the concussion seem to have receded. The bad news is that they have been replaced by a post-speed hangover made up of blunt trauma, general anxiety, and global-sized guilt pangs.

I make it to the bathroom and look inside. T is standing in front of the mirror, combing globs of Murray's Superior Hair Dressing Pomade into his hair, crafting it into a high pomp. He turns to face me and spreads his arms wide, smiling.

—Morning, superstar! Ready to take a bite out of life?

He slaps me on the arm and I flinch.

—Hell, you need a pick-me-up.

—I need a shower.

He turns back to the mirror and flicks the comb through his hair a couple more times.

—Well, it's all yours, but I'm telling you what you need, and what you need is a pick-me-up.

—Uh-uh.

—Suit yerself.

I step out of the way as he heads for the kitchen.

—There's something wrong with my water heater, so turn the cold on all the way and don't touch the hot. Otherwise, you'll burn your hide off.

I close the door, turn on the shower, and peel Sid's filthy clothes from my body. My right ankle is puffy and bruised, but I can move it. Steam is already pouring from the shower. I stick my hand in to test the water and just about sear the flesh from my fingers. I wait another minute and climb over the side of the tub. It's way too hot, but I can take it. I let the water run over me, sluicing off the grime and sweat of the last couple days. The water soaks the crusty bandage on my left thigh and I strip it away. The wound has mostly scabbed over, but a slight ooze of blood is leaking out from a crack at the edge. I scrub my body hard with the bar of Lava from the scummy shower caddy. Slowly, tension eases from my muscles and the pain in my head recedes, but the anxiety and the guilt stay right where they are.

I get out, find some Band-Aids under the sink, and stick a couple over my wound. I wipe steam from the mirror and look at myself. The cut over my left eye is closed up. I have bruises on my shoulders and ribs and a big one across my chest where the Monte Carlo's seat belt caught me during the wipeout. My hands and knees are scraped up from all the falling down I've been doing.

I look at the tattoos. They start on my left forearm, run up to my shoulder, across my chest, and down to my right wrist. When Dad saw them he made the same sound he made when he saw me light a cigarette. Mom kind of liked them. She touched the one that says Mom and Dad, shook her head at the naked pinup on my right bicep. Tears leaked from her eyes when she saw the banner on my chest with Yvonne written on it. I hold up my left arm and look at the hash marks. Still one short; got to get Mickey on there.

I carry the trashed clothes to the kitchen, a towel around my waist. T is drinking a beer and eating a Hostess Fruit Pie.

—Want one?

My stomach is tight and empty, but I don't feel hungry.

—Pass.

OK, but there ain't much else.

—I'll manage.

He scarfs the last bit of crust and gooey cherry filling and washes it down with the dregs of his Bud. I hold up the clothes.

—Any place I can dump these?

He takes them from me.

—I'll take care of 'em.

Hitler wanders in from T's bedroom and growls at me. T comes around the counter to me.

—Here, we gotta take care of this.

He wraps his arms around me.

—T?

—Hitler needs to see you're a friend.

—Oh.

We stand there like that for a minute, T embracing my half-naked body, Hitler sniffing around us as T whispers to him, calling him a good dog, telling him I'm a friend. Hank Williams singing "I'll Never Get Out of This World Alive." And even in this context, it feels so good to be held.

T lets go of me, takes a step back, and Hitler comes over and licks my hand.

—That should keep him from eating your balls.

—Come again?

—He's a rape dog.

—Come again?

—He's an attack dog. I had him trained by these guys in Colorado who specialize in dogs for victims of rape, women who have some serious fears based on fucked-up personal experience. So he's trained to go for an attacker's balls or neck. Whatever's closest.

Hitler sniffs my crotch.

—OK, I'm gonna head out to work for a couple hours and then I'm gonna pick up some clothes for you. A disguise. How 'bout that? Later we'll go find your guy's place. There's a robe in my room. Help yourself to whatever else you find. I'm gonna take some of this money for the clothes, OK?

He scoops up a handful of money from the pile on the coffee table. He opens the door, turns, and looks at me.

—You sure about that pick-me-up, man? You look like shit.

I stand wounded in his living room, my bare toes flexing in the greasy fibers of his carpet. I look around at the beat-up couch, the brick-and-plywood coffee table, the milk crates stuffed with vinyl and paperbacks, the stacks of porn videos surrounding the TV. I think about being alone in this room for the next several hours, watching the few bits of my life that I have left, the few I kept because I thought I could control them, spinning away from me the way the blood spun off of Mickey's head as he bounced down the stone steps.

I think about what an ideal place this is for a suicide.

—Yeah, maybe you better give me something.

He gives me a Xanax, and gets Hitler into his Chrysler 5th Avenue. I stand in the open door in his robe as he pulls out.

—T, wait.

He puts on the brakes.

—Yeah?

—I thought you were dealing?

—Sure.

—So what's the job?

—I DJ the morning shift at a strip club on Fremont. It's fun and the girls are great customers. See ya in a couple hours.

He drives off, Hitler sitting up in the seat next to him. I stand in the door and look out at the sharp blue sky over the trailer park.

AMERICA IS in love with my parents. Eighty-six percent "support" them and a whopping ninety-three percent "feel sorry" for them. This according to a poll on CNN.com.

Other than a written statement read by their court-appointed attorney, they have refused to speak with the media. *We are so sorry for the losses suffered by the families of Deputy Fischer, Willis Doniker, and our friend, Wade Hiller. We don't understand what has happened. All we know is that we love our son and we want him to come home and turn himself in so that we can help him.* Their stoicism, combined with their blue collar–suburban appeal, have "endeared" them to the American public. This, according to one of CNN's media/legal experts.

I've already seen the tape of them being escorted from the court building in Modesto and being loaded into the unmarked car that took them to a hotel. They can't go home because the house is still sealed, being picked over by the FBI. They look tired and old and confused and lost. Not even the Xanax can make this bearable. So I don't bear it.

I switch on ESPN.

The NFL wrap-up is starting on the six PM *SportsCenter*. The Dolphins coach is talking about how disappointed he was in his team's effort against Detroit. But, he's telling everyone in South Beach there's no need to panic just because the Jets beat Green Bay and moved into first in the division. The Fins still control their own destiny because they play the Jets on the last day of the season. Get a win against Oakland this weekend and against the Jets the following weekend and the division is ours. I am not reassured.

Miles Taylor is doubtful for Sunday, and Coach is babbling about passing more. This, despite the fact that he has a noodle-armed quarterback whose one great ability is to hand a football to Miles. Add to this the Raiders' top-ranked secondary, and I have yet another reason for wishing Coach would stop breathing air that other people could be using.

I hear a car scrunch up through the gravel. I look at the clock on top of the TV. Over six hours have drifted by since T left. The back door opens and Hitler explodes into the trailer. He freezes when he sees me, growls once, remembers we've met, and hurls himself into my lap. I wince as he puts a paw on the bullet wound in my thigh, and manage to shove him back to the floor, but not before my hands are coated in drool. T walks in behind the dog, his arms loaded with shopping bags and a big cardboard box. He dumps all of it on the floor.

—Here.

He walks back out the door and the dog runs after him. I look through the bags: 501s, a black cowboy shirt with white piping and pearl snap buttons, and a pair of black Tony Llama boots. I pick up the box and set it on my lap. T comes back in, a case of Bud balanced on either shoulder. I open the box and pull out the black Stetson within. T turns from where he's set the beer on the counter and smiles.

—How 'bout that? I almost went with brown, but then I thought, you're a bad guy, why fight it?

I turn the hat in my hands.

—T, I thought you were gonna get me a disguise. Something to make me *less* conspicuous.

He takes the hat from my hands and sets it on my head.

—Rodeo week in Vegas, man. No one is gonna look twice at you in that stuff.

Rodeo. I've heard that before.

—Rodeo?

—The NFR, man. National Finals Ro-day-o. Ten days of broncs and bulls, man. Big business for me, that's why I was out so late last night. I tell ya, those cowboys are bigger speed freaks than the strippers. I'm making bank over at the Mack Center and hanging around the Frontier.

—Rodeo. Got it.

I get up, walk to the bathroom and look at myself in the mirror. The hat covers my hair and the brim leaves my face in deep shadows. T may be on to something.

I walk back out to the living room. T is in the kitchenette tossing beers into the fridge with freakish precision and speed. He looks over his shoulder at me.

—Well?

I sit back on the couch.

—Yeah, it works.

—Shit yeah right it works.

He takes a last beer from one of the cases, tosses it high in the air, hops to his feet, kicks the fridge door closed, and catches the beer.

—Ye-haw!

He grins at me, waxy skin sheened with speed-sweat, eyes popping and dark ringed. Jesus, did he sleep at all? He cracks the beer open and guzzles half of it. Then he hunts through the pile of shopping bags and grabs one with something heavy sagging the bottom.

—Got these for you, too.

He upends the bag and the contents bang onto the coffee table. Two boxes.

9 mm.

.44 Magnum.

T STARTED going gray in high school, so he's been dyeing his hair since he was twenty. He uses a set of clippers to shave my beard, leaving a long drooping cowboy 'stache down to my chin, and sideburns to my earlobes. I wash my hair and he combs in the same black dye he uses himself, then does the moustache, burns, and my eyebrows. He speed-raps the whole time, giving me a rundown on his life in Vegas, a detailed Godzilla filmography, and his top-ten porn-star list.

I rinse and wash and dry and go in to the spare room and put on my cowboy gear: BVDs, Levis, wife-beater, clean white socks, pointy-toed boots, pearl snap shirt, black leather belt with a big silver buckle, and the hat. It all fits. I step out of the room and T takes a long look at me.

—Bad. Ass. You're like Sam Elliot and Greg Allman's secret love child.

I look in the mirror. Badass.

I'VE REMEMBERED Tim's address. It's a wonder what a little sleep and medication will do for a concussion. We park in front of a stucco four-plex on King's Way, me and T up front and Hitler in the back. T kills the engine and the headlights.

—This is it.

I look up and down the block. It's a street full of driveways that lead into apartment complexes. Only Tim's building and a couple others front the street itself. I look at T.

—Kind of early. Maybe we should come back later, when people are asleep.

T shrugs.

—It's a 24/7 town, man. Doesn't really matter what time it is. But the good news is, people pretty much mind their own business.

—OK, OK. You, uh . . .

—Wait here?

—Yeah. You wait here and . . .

—Honk if someone shows?

—Yeah, that's good.

—Yeah. That Xanax still cooking? You seem a little out of it. You want something to give you an edge?

No, no more pills.

—No, no, I'm cool. I mean, I'm mellow. I'm just not exactly sure what to do. Can you, if I can't get in, can you pick the lock?

T looks at me sideways.

—Shit, man, I'm a dealer, not a thief.

I don't want to bring the guns. I don't want to bring them, but I know

I should. So I split the difference. I leave them in the plastic grocery bag with the ammo, tucked under the passenger seat of T's car. I feel safer without them.

Tim's apartment is #4, upper right corner. I climb the stairs and ring the doorbell. I ring it again. And one last time. There's a kitchen window. I push on it and it slides open, unlocked. Great, Timmy. I look up and down the empty street, and boost myself through the window.

I land on the kitchen counter, my hat tumbles to the floor, and I slide after it. I get to my feet and turn on the lights. The kitchen has one of those pass-through counters that opens on to a small living room. The living room has a sliding glass door that opens on a tiny balcony. There are two bar stools at the pass-through. The place looks pre-furnished, lots of black leather bachelor stuff that is not Tim's style at all. But he's been at work here. The walls are covered in jazz and blues posters. And there's a brand-new stereo, the box full of foam packing still sitting next to it. It's one of those hunks of Japanese engineering that only an audiophile like Tim would buy. I walk down a short hall to a large bedroom. The bed matches the living room furniture. More posters here, a nice boom box, more CDs, an orange iMac on a desk, and a beeper and a huge bong on the nightstand.

There's a knock at the door. Shit. Concerned neighbor? Girlfriend? Russian mafia? Why did I leave the guns in the car? I sneak up to the door and press my eye to the peephole. T is on the landing. I open the door and he comes in, followed by Hitler.

—What? Is someone here?

—No.

—What's that matter?

—I couldn't sit out there, I'm way too jacked-up, man. I was about to fucking vibrate to death.

—Jesus, T. You're the lookout. I mean, fuck.

—You were right, superstar, you don't need anything to give you an edge.

—Yeah, I'm on edge. And, Jesus, what about the dog? What if it starts barking?

He rubs the top of Hitler's head.

—Hitler don't bark. Ever. Only time this dog makes noise is when it farts.

—Great. Look, just, just see if you can find anything out here or in the kitchen. I'll be in the bedroom.

I head down the hallway.

—And what am I looking for?

—A really big box full of money.

It doesn't take long. I don't find the money or any indication that Tim was kidnapped or killed. The place is a mess, but that's just Tim.

T is on his knees in the kitchen, his head stuck in the cabinet below the sink. I kick the sole of his shoe.

—Anything?

He pulls his head out.

—This.

He tugs a blue day pack from the cabinet and unzips it, revealing about twenty small, colored plastic boxes. This is Tim's dealing stash. Each box is stuffed with hydro-grade buds of varying quality. The color of the box indicates the content's price. Hitler sticks his nose into the pile of boxes and shoves them around.

T shakes his head.

—I don't know your boy, but speaking as a dealer? I generally take it as a bad sign when a professional disappears without his stash.

T FINDS a couple bottles of Tullamore Dew in one of the cabinets and breaks the seal on one of them. I get a glass of water from the tap and flop on the couch. T takes a slug from the bottle of whiskey and starts flipping through Tim's CDs. Hitler rolls around on his back.

—So you think he ripped you off?

I stare at the wall.

—Could be.

—Think maybe the Russians found him?

—Could be.

—What now?

I look at the clock on the VCR. It's almost nine.

—I need to make a call.

I take the cell from my pocket. T sits on the floor with his back against the wall, empties Tim's day pack in his lap, and starts looking at the little boxes.

—Dylan?

—Yeah.

—What ya gonna tell him?

I don't know, so I just dial the number. It rings once.

—I thought we agreed to updates every *twenty-four hours.*

—Hi, Dylan.

—Did we not *agree* to that?

—Yes, and it's not quite twenty-four.

—That's cutting it very fine, Hank, very fine indeed.

—Sorry.

—No, no, *you're* right. We said every twenty-four hours from nine PM pacific. *You're* right. So what have you got for me?

—Not much.

—OK, well, that's fair, but this is *supposed* to be a progress report so why don't you tell me what *progress* you've made.

—Well, I haven't been captured.

—OK, sarcasm aside, that *is* progress. What about my money, Hank? Any progress there?

T is trying to juggle three of the little colored boxes from Tim's stash.

—I haven't been captured.

Pause.

—Yes, we covered that.

Pause.

—You haven't asked about your parents, Hank.

Pause.

—How are my parents?

—Have you been watching the *news*?

—Yes.

—Then you may have seen that they were released from custody and taken to an undisclosed location.

—Yes.

—Well, you'll be happy to know that they are staying at the Days Inn at the Los Banos rest stop. I'm told by my employees that the security at a Days Inn is somewhat lax, and shouldn't present any difficulties for them. You understand?

—Yes.

—Good. So, have you made any progress on my money?

T drops the boxes, gets up, and walks back to Tim's bedroom.

—Yes.

—Good. Tell me, please.

T comes back down the hall carrying Tim's bong.

—I am lying low while I ascertain if my position here is tenable.

T looks at me and crosses his eyes. I listen to Dylan.

—Good. And?

—I expect to make contact with my "banker" in the next twenty-four hours.

T is shaking his head. He cracks open one of the little bud boxes and starts filling the bong.

—And?

—Within twenty-four hours of that, I expect to receive your money and have it in your hands shortly thereafter.

T puts his lips to the top of the bong, holds the flame of his lighter over the bowl, and rips.

—*Good.* That's good. See, this is the kind of clarity I'm looking for. Like I told you, Hank, I'm a control freak. The more *information* I have, the more in *control* I feel. And that makes me more *comfortable*. None of this is about you or your abilities, it's about my personal weaknesses. And I want you to know how much I appreciate you dealing with them so well.

—Sure.

—*And* . . . I guess that's it?

—It is.

—*OK,* I'll expect to hear from you in the next twenty-four, and look forward to seeing you in the next forty-eight to seventy-two.

—Yes.

—*Well* . . . good-bye.

He hangs up. T exhales and starts hacking.

—What? Hack! What the fuck was that? Hack! Bullshit?

—That was the kind of bullshit he wants to hear.

—Fuckin'A. Hack! What a prick he must be.

I nod, and lie back on the carpet. T comes over and stands there looking down at me, bong in one hand and one of the pot boxes in the other.

—What now?

I stare at the ceiling. What now? Fucked if I know. Why can't someone just tell me what to do for a change? Why can't someone tell me how to stop all of this?

—T, I get it that you're not a criminal mastermind or anything.

—Thanks, asshole.

—But do you know how to get information? About people?

He smiles.

—Shit, yeah. No problem.

T SITS in front of Tim's iMac. I sit on the foot of the bed and look over his shoulder as he scrolls through the Google results for "Dylan Lane."

—There's a shitload here, man. Guy's got a record

—What for?

T clicks around.

—SEC violations.

—What?

He clicks on the heading.

—Looks like he was investigated for insider trading and some other shit.

I shake my head.

—I don't think that's him.

He clicks a couple times and a photo starts to resolve on the screen.

—This your boy?

I look at the pic. It's Dylan. He's a few years younger, standing in a big, partitioned office space, surrounded by a group of very young and geeky-looking men and women.

—Yeah, that's him.

T clicks through a series of articles from the New York papers.

—So dickhead here was some kind of financial whiz kid in the stock market. Kind of a flavor of the week broker in the early nineties, but then he got busted for manipulations and shit and disappeared for a couple years. Didn't do jail time, of course. Fuckos like that never go to jail. Then he pops back up just in time for the fattest part of the Internet boom. He got money from somewhere to get a start-up rolling in Silicon Alley. Well, he was the flavor of the week again, and his company is a big fucking hit, and then the market folded. No criminal charges this time, but he disappears again, except for some gossip column shit about him. Stuff like, "Dylan Lane was MIA for fashion week, but several of his *comrade* investors were in attendance in hopes of giving a bear hug to the former dot-com darling." And more of the same. Innuendo about him being a shady character, but no details. Any help?

I flop back on the bed.

—It explains why he talks like an asshole.

T spins the chair around to face me.

—So?

—What?

—*What now?*

—What now? I'm fucked, that's what now. I don't know how to find Tim. I can't go to the cops without risking Mom and Dad. I don't have anything to use to cut a deal with Dylan. I have a few days till Sunday to do something, and I don't know what the fuck to do. You know this town. How do I find Tim?

T shrugs.

—Fucked if I know.

I stare at the ceiling. My heart is jumping and sweat is starting to break out all over my body. I know what this is. It's panic. A scream has been living in my gut for years, and now it wants out. I don't have any moves left to keep it down and the Xanax has worn off and it's going to come out.

T sits next to me on the bed and puts a hand on my shoulder.

—You OK?

I shake my head side to side. The scream is in my chest now. Climbing.

He digs in his pocket and pulls out a pill.

—Here.

I look at it. I don't want any more drugs. I want to feel this. I deserve to feel this. But I can't afford to feel it right now. I can't scream now. If I start now I'll never stop. It's in my throat.

T presses the pill against my lips.

—It's Percocet. It'll chill you out.

I remember the Percs my doctor gave me after my leg broke, the ones I shared with Wade and Rich and Steve. They killed the pain and made the world balloon off and bob at the end of a string.

I let the pill into my mouth and swallow. It chases the scream back down into my belly, and, almost instantly, long before it can possibly be taking effect, I feel better.

—I don't know what to do, T.

He picks something up from the floor and hands it to me. It's one of Tim's pot boxes.

—I think I know someone who can help us.

T DRIVES us to the North Strip. We park the car, leave Hitler inside, and walk down Fremont Street. A few blocks of Fremont have been converted to a pedestrian mall and covered by a canopy about two stories high, its underside lined with lights. Christmas carols are blaring from a PA system as the lights flash, creating a variety of holiday-themed images that flicker across the canopy. A crowd of tourists fills the mall, their heads dropped back to gape at the spectacle as candy canes, Christmas trees, stockings, and Santa and his reindeer all twinkle overhead. T nudges me and points ahead.

—It gets better inside.

In front of us is a strip club; a huge neon cowgirl in white boots, a bikini, and a cowboy hat hangs above the door. A long line of cowboys waits underneath her to get in.

—No way, T.

He looks at me.

—What?

—We can't go in there.

—Why not?

—Way too many people.

—So what? They're all drunk and they're all dressed like you.

—No.

He reaches inside his jacket, takes out a pair of big black Wayfarer sunglasses, and puts them on my face.

—There. Now you look even more like every other rube in town.

I take the sunglasses off and start to head back to the car. He grabs me.

—Look, man, this place is my office, right? I kick back to the house and they give me the franchise in there to deal speed to the strippers.

—So?

—I have the speed franchise. Someone else handles all the pot.

He shows me the little plastic box Tim's pot came packaged in.

—And last time I checked, it came in these.

I put the sunglasses back on.

WE JUMP the line. The bouncer gives T a hug and we're inside. On one side of the bar is a long runway with a pole every few feet. Each pole is being worked by a G-stringed former aerobics instructor who realized she could make ten times as much money by taking her clothes off. Screaming cowboys waving dollar bills in the air fill every square inch of floor space. On the other side of the bar is a row of smaller stages. Each has a single pole and a dancer. Banquettes line the walls, occupied by a rail of cowboys being lap danced in the shadows. At the back of the club is a separate room, Champagne Lounge spelled out in pink neon above the door. Flecks of red and green light spray from a Christmas-colored disco ball and bounce off the mirrored walls that have been flocked with fake snow. T puts his mouth next to my ear so I can hear him over the Divinyls' "I Touch Myself."

—Merry Christmas.

The bartender comes over, a woman with dark skin and a pile of curly black hair. She's in a red tube top and jeans cut so low you can see her hipbones sticking up over the waistband. Anywhere else, she'd have all eyes locked on her. Here, she is seriously overdressed.

—Hey, T, what's up?

T points at me.

This guy's my friend. Keep an eye on him, OK?

She shrugs.

—Sure.

T puts his mouth next to my ear again.

—You hang here, I'm gonna go set something up with the pot franchise.

He squeezes into the mob of denim. I turn back to the bar just as the bartender sets a beer in front of me.

—First one's on me.

—Ya know, I don't.

But she's already gone to take care of the service bar.

I look at the beer.

The Percocet has smoothed the edges of the pain in my leg and ankle. The scream is still there, but has been drawn away into the distance where I can contemplate it without feeling it. I like this. I like feeling like this. Feeling so little.

I look around the club. When was the last time I was around so many people, all crammed together, music blaring, that smell of beer and sweat soaked into the floor and the upholstery? Years.

I look at the beer.

I slide my finger through the drops of condensation on its side. Drinking this beer would be a bad idea.

Something soft and smooth presses against my back. Hot breath hits my ear.

—Can I have some of that, cowboy?

I turn and look at the stripper standing behind me. Her face is inches from mine. Too much makeup, too much hairspray. I look at her hand, set lightly on my thigh. A woman's hand touching me. I take in her body in its translucent sheath of pink Lycra. Breasts patently fake, booth-perfect tan, ass and legs stair-machined to some ultimate balance of muscle tone and body fat. She leans into me, reaching for the beer, and her superhero breasts graze my upper arm. She holds up the beer in front of my face.

—You mind?

I shake my head and she takes a long sip, then hands me the bottle. She's so close.

—Thanks. Dancing makes me thirsty. *Hot and thirsty.*

I look at one of the solo stages. A stripper has one knee cocked around the pole and is spinning like an ice skater.

—I guess it would.

—What about you? Dancing make you *hot?*

She's so close. She's silly and fake, but she's so close. And I don't feel the panic, the visions that grabbed me when I scared the smiling Spanish girl on the beach.

She scratches a fingernail against the nape of my neck.

—You wanna dance with me?

I remember my last time with a woman. I was still drunk. Once I stopped drinking, I started thinking. That was it for women and me. I don't say anything.

She smiles, mock sadly.

—Your loss, cowboy.

She turns and starts to leave, her hand slipping from my thigh. I grab her wrist. She turns to face me.

—Is that a yes?

I nod.

—Well, come on then.

She takes my hand and starts to pull me from the bar.

—Hang on.

She stops.

I shouldn't be doing this, I shouldn't be doing any of this. I know that.

I put the beer to my lips, turn the bottle upside down, and empty it.

—OK, let's go.

And she leads me to the banquettes in the darkness against the far wall. She sits me down and the dress slides off. Wearing only a G-string and high heels, she takes my hat from my head and waves it in the air and rides my lap slowly, while "Sweet Emotion" plays.

I FEEL great. Honestly, I can't remember the last time I felt this good, this great. It makes me wonder why I haven't had a drink in so long. I mean, it's been at least five minutes since I had my last beer.

—Hey, yo, 'nother Bud down here.

The bartender nods in my direction as she sets a couple drinks on a cocktail waitress's tray.

—Comin' up.

A guy with a buzz cut, wearing tight Levis and a PBR Tour T-shirt, shoves into the space next to my stool.

—Sorry, been tryin' ta get myself a beer for 'bout a half hour.

I smile.

—Hell, no problem.

The bartender comes over with my beer and sets it in front of me.

—Eight bucks.

I pull out a twenty and hand it to her and point at the guy in the PBR shirt.

—Here, get this guy one too and keep the change.

She takes the money and looks at the guy.

—What ya having, cowboy?

—Burt Light.

She slides open a cooler, pulls out a bottle of Coors Light, yanks an opener from the back pocket of her low-rider jeans, pops the cap, and puts the beer on the bar.

—Thanks, fellas.

Me and the PBR guy watch her ass as she walks back to the service bar to take care of another cocktail waitress. PBR shakes his head.

—Damn. That was one of the sexiest things I've ever seen.

A dancer in a formfitting green slip dress presses herself up against PBR's back. Her hand slithers through his buzzed hair.

—Cowboy, if that's the sexiest thing you've ever seen, you need a dance with me.

PBR looks her up and down.

—Honey, you are damn right about that.

—Well c'mon, Hoss, I'll give you the rest of this song and all of the next.

She walks away with him trailing behind like a dazed child. He looks back at me.

—See, ya 'round, pal. Thanks for the Burt Light.

He hoists his beer in the air. I stand up on the foot rail of my stool to keep him in sight.

—Hey, why ya call them that?

But he's gone.

—That's what they call them in Oklahoma. 'Cause Burt Reynolds drinks Coors.

The bartender with the lowriders is in front of me. She places a Coors Light on the bar.

—Burt Light.

She places a Coors Original next to it.

—Burt Heavy.

I pull out another twenty.

—I'll take one of each.

She pops both tops, puts the beers next to my almost full Bud, takes the twenty, and looks at the three beers.

—Got some catching up to do.

—Baby, I've been resting up for this.

A hand lands on my shoulder and I slip off my stool. T catches me.

—Whoa!

—T! T, where ya been? This place is great! I'm having a great time.

I guzzle beer and some of it slops onto my shirtfront. T grins.

—I thought you weren't drinking.

—Who me? No, you have me confused with some limp-dick, pussy motherfucker who doesn't know what's good for him.

—Well, what ain't good for you is drinking while you're on Percocet. You're lucky you can stay on that stool at all.

—Stay on the stool? Stay on the stool! That's the least of what I can do.

I start climbing up to stand on the stool and T pulls me back down.

—C'mon, King Kong, let's get you back in your head.

He's tugging me from the bar.

—Wait a sec, wait a sec.

I grab at my beer, but it's not where it looks like it is and I knock it over.

—Aww, fuck man, look what ya made me do ta Burt.

My head bobs around on the end of my neck. Colored lights whirl through the air, cowboys and pole-dancing beauties orbit irregularly around me. The sweat covering my body goes cold-hot-cold-hot.

T leads me into the john. We walk past the condom machine and the line of occupied urinals, to the second of three stalls. We both squeeze in and he closes the door. I lean against the partition and start to slide down. T grabs me and sets me on the toilet seat. He takes a fold of magazine paper about half the size of a matchbook from his vest pocket, leans over me, and shakes its contents onto the back of the toilet tank. A tiny heap of rough yellowish crystals. He gets out his lighter and presses it flat against the pile and rocks it firmly side to side, the crystals making little crunching noises as he pulverizes them into powder. He lifts the lighter away and licks some dust that is clinging to its side. Finally, with an old Kinko's copy card from his wallet, he shapes the brown powder into two fat lines, gets out a twenty, rolls it into a tight cylinder, and hands it to me.

—Batter up.

I look at the twin lines of crank.

—I don't think I'm up to that, T.

—Hank, this is your doctor speaking. We have people to talk to, things to do, and you're about set to go all gape-mouthed and drooly on me. You need to wake up and get your head back in the game, superstar, and this is what's gonna get you there.

What is he talking about? People to talk to? Man, I just want to relax at the bar. I look again at the crank. But hey! I seem to remember being able to drink like a maniac on this shit. I stick the rolled bill in my nose, place the other end against one of the lines, and inhale.

It burns. It burns like a motherfucker. Like a hot razor blade being dragged down my nasal passage to the top of my esophagus, where it stops and a bitter, mucousy poison drips down the back of my throat. I rip my face away from the line and tilt it back and press the heel of my palm against my nostril.

—Fuck me!

T laughs. He grabs the bill, neatly whiffs half of the other line into his right nostril, half into the left, and hands the bill back to me.

—Clean your plate.

The burn has crept up behind my right eyeball. I look down at the half line left on the toilet tank. I do the remainder into my left nostril and it feels like scrubbing ground glass into an acid burn.

—Jesus! Jesus fuck!

T runs his finger over the specks of crank left on the tank, licks it clean, and does the same with the residue on the inside of his twenty.

—C'mon. Let's go see my friend.

He leads me out of the bathroom, and I'm already starting to think he was right about the crank because things are really starting to fall into place and make sense to me, who I am, why I'm here, what I'm doing, how, in an amazing way the shit I'm in has given my life purpose and meaning; I mean, here I am, a man with a mission, a real mission, how many people can say the same, I mean, for the first time I can remember, I know exactly who I am, where I am, and what I'm doing.

I'm Henry Thompson.

I'm in a strip club.

And I'm trying to save my parents' lives.

SHE'S A big girl, probably five ten in her bare feet, but well over that with her fuck-me stripper heels on. She's all tits and ass and pale white skin, her black hair clipped in a Betty Page. There are Vargas-style pin-ups tattooed on both of her shoulders and a row of emerald-green, quarter-sized stars trace the edge of her collarbone above the bustline of her black vinyl minidress.

—This is Sandy Candy. Give her three hundred dollars.

The Champagne Lounge is a small, very dark room set off from the main club. I'm half-blind in here, what with the sunglasses still on my face, but I make out big padded chairs, small cocktail tables, and a handful of cowboys getting some serious full-contact lap dances from their strippers.

—Why?

—Because it costs three hundred dollars to be in the Champagne Lounge.

I peel three bills off my depleted bankroll and hand them to Sandy.

—Sandy, what do I get for three hundred?

She tucks the bills into a miniature Hello Kitty! lunch box she's carrying.

—Tonight, you get to talk to me while I get off my feet.

—That's some expensive talk.

—I'm known for my conversation.

T takes the little plastic pot box from his pocket and puts it on the table.

—We're looking for a guy.

She picks up the box and shakes her head.

—Fucking Timmy.

I lean forward.

—Yeah, fucking Timmy, that's the guy.

* * *

SHE WORKS for the same guy as Timmy.

—What the hell is your name anyway?

My name? I open my mouth. Nothing comes out.

—Wade.

I look at T. He keeps his eyes on Sandy.

—His name is Wade.

Sandy nods.

—OK, *Wade,* here's the deal. Like I told you, I work for the same guy as Timmy, guy named Terry. What we do, the delivery guys, we show up at work, which is this small warehouse over in Paradise. We don't all come in together, we have different times. Staggered. Like, I used to see this therapist because I used to be bulimic because I had all these food issues because when I was a baby my mom didn't want to mess with feeding me so she tied my bottle to the side of the crib like a hamster bottle so I could feed myself, so because of that I saw this therapist and she would stagger the patients so you didn't have to run into anyone if you didn't want anyone to know that you were coming to see her. I didn't care myself, but some of them were freaky about it. Like, I came in early once and this lady was coming out of the office and saw me in the waiting room and the therapist had to come out and ask me to turn my back while this woman left. Weird. So, Terry, the boss, he does the same thing so that not all the delivery guys know each other, which is the way some of them want it in case someone gets busted. But me, I'm pretty mellow, and so is Tim. So we run into each other over there a couple times and find out that we're both cool. So sometimes if I came up short on my stash, I might call Timmy and he'd front me so I could take care of my customers. He's cool like that. So, the point is, we never all come in at once to get our stuff. But!

She holds her hands up like she's about to deliver a dual karate chop. She's a big hand-talker, Sandy is.

—But! This one day I show up and everybody is there. All the delivery guys are in there, the ones I know and the ones I don't know. Terry, the boss, he's not even really a boss, he's just a dealer who pays us a commission to make these deliveries, but we call him a boss. But Terry, he's been making us all stay until everybody is there, except Tim. And that's when he asks if anyone has seen him around. And it looked to me like Terry did it that way so he could watch everyone all together when he asked, to see if anyone *looked* at each other, like they maybe *knew* something they weren't telling. But no one did. And that's pretty much it.

She peels her lips away from her teeth and grinds her molars.

—Shit, T, this is serious stuff.

I shake my head.

—So, wait, but where's Tim?

—Hell if I know.

—That's, that's all you?

—For now. I tried to get ahold of Terry, you know, see if anything had popped up, but he ain't around. I can try him in the morning, I mean after the sun comes up. But.

She shrugs.

—But, what was the last time someone saw him?

She slaps her forehead.

—Oh, shit. Right. Well, maybe Saturday because Tim always takes Sunday off and Monday was when he was missing, but that's not what I was gonna. This other guy! I forgot to tell you.

—What other?

—Hang oooooon. OK, this other guy was in there, in the office I guess, this morning, when I went in for my pickup, and I heard him talking to Terry a little, and I think I heard him say Tim's name, and then he left.

—Who was he?

—Well! At first, I thought the guy was a cop collecting a payoff because he was in a suit, but then when the guy left I heard him say good-bye and he can't have been a cop, because of he had a Russian accent.

My heart jackhammers. I could say it's just the speed. But I'd be lying.

*   *   *

I WALK out of the stall. At the sink, I splash water on my face and inhale, sucking it into my nose to ease the chemical burn from the bump I just did. I look in the mirror and there I am: Stetson pulled low, sunglasses still on, skin waxy and drawn under my Mexico tan, jaw muscles flexing as I grind my teeth. I turn off the sink and walk out of the bathroom, water still dripping from my moustache.

Coming out of the tiled calm of the bathroom, I am hit by the ceaseless wave of slots racket. Gding-gding-gding, punctuated by the occasional mechanical cry, "Wheel of Fortune!" or the chang-chang of a nickel machine paying out. My heart leaps arhythmically in my chest, trying to match time with the din. I freeze.

Where am I? I stand in place and turn in a slow circle and look around the Western-themed casino. I see a sign. Sam's Town Gambling Hall. Oh, right. Sam's Town. This is the place Sandy wanted to hang while . . . While? We're waiting for something. For . . .

—Where have you been, baby?

Sandy grabs me from behind and wraps her arms around me, I rotate within her grasp, feeling our bodies slide against each other, and put my hands on her hips.

—Got me.

She smiles, puts a finger on the bridge of my sunglasses and pushes them down. She looks at my eyes.

—Oh, baby, you are tweaked aren't you?

—Got me.

She laughs.

—Well, hand it over, it's mama's turn.

I dig in my pocket for the bindle T gave me and pass it to her. She points at the tables.

—T's right over there.

And she walks toward the bathrooms. I turn and find T at a ten-dollar craps table.

—T, what are we doing here, man?

He tosses a chip onto the table.

—All the hards, heavy on the eight.

I stand next to him at the table, watching the multicolored chips dance across the green felt, shuttled by the croupiers. I put my hand on his sleeve.

—I mean, this is bad, I shouldn't be out.

The roller tosses the dice. A croupier calls them.

—Seven! Craps!

T's chips are raked from the table. He looks at me.

—We're waiting for the call.

—What call?

He shakes his head.

—The call, man. Her boss is gonna call with some more skinny on your boy Tim.

—Right, the call.

Sandy crashes into us, giggling and grabbing at our arms to keep from falling on the floor. We catch her and get her steady on her feet. She gives us both a kiss on the cheek.

—OK, who's buying the next round?

SANDY'S BOSS still hasn't called.

We're in T's car; the three of us squeezed together, Sandy in the middle, her arms draped across our shoulders. She wants to party some more.

—I got a couple bottles of Veuve at my apartment. I got them, this regular of mine is a liquor salesman and he's always bringing me stuff, and I have these amazing bottles of champagne. So, so we take the party back to my place and we can smoke some grass, and what I love is to sprinkle a little meth over the weed and base it that way, and we'll open the bottles and maybe I'll do a little dance. Put on a little shoooow for you boys for being so niiiice to me.

I lean against the door and look through the window at the bluish tinge lining the edge of the valley. I look at Sandy. Her pale skin is almost glowing it's so bloodless, her mascara has run, giving her raccoon eyes, and a smear of red lipstick is slashed from the right corner of her mouth. T is leaning forward, bony finger wrapped tight around the wheel, chewing on the butt of a Marlboro, eyes bugging at the road ahead. I shake my head.

—I'm done.

Sandy slaps my thigh.

—Doooone? C'mon, Wade, I'm talking about a party here, special prizes and giveaways and.

—I'm done.

She crawls into my lap.

—Baby, don't be a party pooper.

I am not a pooper. I mean, I don't even know what I'm doing here. There's a Russian looking for Tim. What the fuck am I doing here? What the fuck am I doing? I need some sleep. I need to get this shit cleaned out of my system and get some sleep and.

Sandy is nuzzling my neck.

—C'mon over and just hang out. You can lie down if you want and then you can join the party later. C'mon. My guy'll call soon and.

I push her off.

—No. T, we got to go home.

He keeps his eyes locked on the road.

—Fuck, man, I ain't got to do nothin'. You want to go home, cool, but I'm gonna party with Sandy.

Sandy screams and turns around and grabs T, making the car swerve.

—See, Wade, T knows how to make a girl happy.

T UNLOCKS the trailer door.

—I'll be back in a few hours.

He hands me the key and jerks his thumb toward the car, where Sandy is waiting.

—Sure you don't want in?

I shake my head.

—No. I need to sleep.

—OK. Percs are in the medicine cabinet, that'll put you down.

—No, I'm too fucked-up, doing stupid shit.

—What're you supposed to be doing, man? We'll talk to Sandy's dealer later, see if he knows anything. Other than that? Pain sucks, so kill it.

He's right, pain does suck. I have been killing it and I like killing it. It's so easy. I worked so hard for so many years to control myself, to keep everything in balance, but it's so much easier to just take a pill. Easier and better. But I'm starting to fuck up. And I can't do that.

—Call me when you hear from her boss.

He shakes his head.

—I don't have a phone in the trailer.

I take Dylan's cell out of my pocket, turn it on, and its number flashes on the screen. T finds a pen in his jacket and writes the number on his hand. Sandy sticks her head out the car window.

—Hey, T, leave the dog here, I don't want it crapping on my rug.

He walks toward the car.

—Sorry, baby, he's not the kind of dog you leave at home with company.

He gets in the car and they drive off.

I'm alone.

The speed is crashing hard and I'm starting to feel all the booze I drank tonight. I'm going to be in very bad shape very soon. I open the door, step inside.

The TV is on.

I start to turn and run, but someone trips me and I fall onto the porch and I'm dragged back into the trailer. Someone sits on my back. I struggle.

—Chill, dude.

ROLF IS pissed, so he beats me up a little.

Sid sits on the couch and watches.

Rolf drags me to my feet, makes sure I see the gun Sid is holding, and punches me in the gut. I fall back on the floor and he kicks me a few times in the back and the legs, then he gets down on his knees, straddling my body, and pummels my arms and torso as I try to cover my face. And then he's done.

He slaps the side of my head and stands up.

—You keep acting like I'm a tool, Hank. Not telling me and Leo who you really are, so we can't do our job the right way. Then that shit in the desert? Dude. That was bogus beyond belief. But then, dude, you come *here*, to the address that was on that *Christmas card*? After you totally know that I *saw* the thing? I mean, do you think I smoked away all my short-term memory? Oh, and, dude, by the way, where the fuck is my money?

—Rolf, I have no clue.

He picks up a book from T's coffee table.

—You ever read this, dude?

It's Sid's copy of *The Man Who Got Away*. I nod.

—Skimmed it.

—Yeah, well, let me read you my favorite part.

He flips to a dog-eared page near the end.

—*And what was it all about? The blood and the killing? The murder of innocents? The chaos that reigned in Gotham for two days as Henry Thompson rampaged through the streets? With no survivors or witnesses left to tell the tale, we can only surmise. But were there no witnesses? What of the bodies of Edward and Paris DuRante, later identified as the duo behind a string of daring Midwest bank robberies? What of the investigations into Lieutenant Detective Roman's dealings in the underworld and the revelations of his ties to organized crime? What of the scale of the carnage in Paul's Bar? What might inspire such bloodshed? And, finally, what of Thompson's utter and complete disappearance? What could facilitate such an escape? All these mute witnesses point to one thing: money. A great deal of money. Rumors on the street suggest that the long hours of fear that clutched The City That Never Sleeps were the product of the powerful lust for profit that rules the small minds of brutal men. The illgotten gains of the DuRante's, estimated by some to be well over ten million dollars, were no doubt the treasure sought by the darker figures of this tale. Their error was to have swept Thompson into the storm of their greed, never knowing the beast that lurked inside his secret heart.*

He holds the book out to me. I take it from him, look at the page, close it, and hand it back.

—It's only about four million really.

Rolf jumps to his feet.

—Four million! Dude. OK! OK, we need to get organized. That guy you were with, Elvis? When's he comin' back?

—He said a few hours.

—Cool. So no hurry.

He looks at Sid, who's still motionless on the couch.

—Sid, did you hear that? Four mil?

Sid shrugs, keeps his mouth shut, his eyes on the TV screen. Rolf waves a hand like he's done with him and kneels next to me.

—Now, dude, all fucking around aside, where is the money?

What was my life like before the money? Was it a good life? Was it interesting? Did I live it well? Was I useful to other people? Was I happy? I don't really remember anymore because I've heard the question Rolf is asking far too many times.

—I don't have it, man.

—Look, dude, I understand. Four mil is a lot of money. I get it how you don't want to let on and all. And look, I'm not, we had a deal for 200 K and you broke it. So yeah, I want more, but I'm not greedy. I'm not some asshole who wants to clear you out. I want half. So it's like this simple question of *How valuable is your life?* Almost anybody would kill for two mil. And almost anybody would pay two mil to keep from getting killed. So tell me where the money is and you get two, and I get two, and everybody goes their own way. Flipside is, dude, no one gets nothing and we kill you.

Sid points at the TV.

—It's on again.

Rolf looks at the screen

—Shit!

I catch a quick glimpse of nighttime video footage. A bunch of SWAT guys surrounding a vehicle pinned in the spotlight of a hovering chopper. Rolf switches the set off.

I look at him and smile.

—Man, that looked just like Sid's Westphalia. You guys really need that money now, don't you?

—Shut up.

—You may have wanted it before, but, man, you need it now. Have they shown Sid's driver's license photo yet?

—Shut up, dude.

—'Cause that'll be next. They'll find out who that thing is registered to, and his photo will be all over the place. After that? They start looking into his known associates. Did anybody see you when you hooked up in San Diego? Any of your old buds?

—Shut the fuck up, dude!

—Or what? Look at me, I'm a fucking mess. Go ahead, beat on me some more.

He clenches his fists and shakes them.

—Just tell me where the money is, dude.

—*Duuuude,* I told you, I don't know where the money is.

He talks between gritted teeth.

—Tell. Me. Where. The. Money. Is.

—In. My. Ass.

He puts his hands on my neck, holds them there, shaking. Sid is leaning forward on the couch, watching closely. I could die here. This is another time that I could die. But I don't. Rolf takes his hand away, walks to the couch, and kicks it five times, then sits down.

—Dude, just tell me where.

—Rolf. I don't know.

I get myself off the floor.

—But someone else does.

I tell them the truth. Sort of. I tell them about Timmy and how I have a *great* lead on him. I tell them all I have to do is wait for a call that will tell me where he is, and then we can go get the money.

I don't tell them about Dylan. If they find out about him, they'll know there is no way in hell I will ever let them near the money that can save my parents' lives.

And the story I tell them gives me time. Time for all of us to sit on the couch and watch TV and wait for a call that may never come, while I try to figure how to get them out of here before T comes home and chaos ensues.

My phone rings.

—WHO IS it, dude?

—I don't know.

—Well, is it your connection or whatever?

—I don't know.

Rolf grabs the phone and looks at the screen.

—Where's your caller ID?

I take the phone back.

—I don't think it has that.

—You bought a phone and didn't get caller ID? Dude, ID is key.

The phone rings for the fifth time. What if it's Dylan? I don't want to talk to Dylan in front of these guys. It rings again.

—Well, answer it, dude.

I hit the green button.

—Hello?

—Wade?

My stomach lurches. Then I get it.

—Hey, Sandy, what happened to the party?

—Party? Oh, yeah, baby, we got it goin' on. But. Hey, hey, baby, good news. I, we came back to my place, and there was a message from my boss, Terry.

—Yeah?

—He says he knows something.

—Yeah?

—Yeah.

—OK, well?

—Well, yeah, but, baby, he wants some money and says he won't. You know?

—Wait. Does he know where Tim? Hey, is T there, can I talk to?

—He's indisposed, baby, in the john. But my guy.

—Right, your guy. How much?

—Just five. He said a grand, but I told him you were nice so I got him to go five.

—Thanks.

—Sure. So, he says the money, he wants to get the money and then he'll tell you.

—He knows where Tim is?

—I think. He said he has some info on him, so I think so, yeah.

—So when?

—Um, he's gonna come over in like an hour? Is that? Over here? Can you?

—Yeah, I'm just not sure how I'm.

That's when I hear a noise in the background. A noise I now realize has been there through this whole call.

—Uh, you know, Sandy, I don't have a car or.

—Well.

—So it'll take me awhile and I'm still pretty fucked-up, so later would be good.

—Well, he's really.

—So have T call and tell me what time.

I hang up. She'll get me a later meet. But it won't be T who calls. I'm sure of these things because of the way I could hear Hitler barking in the background. Hitler, who never makes a noise except for a fart, barking mad and angry through the whole call.

T's in trouble.

And I'm being set up.

I look at Rolf and Sid, waiting for me to tell them what the deal is. And I realize that being set up may be just what I need right now.

SID STILL hasn't said a word to me. He sits as far from me as possible, his arms and legs crossed. I sit on the couch between the two of them and Rolf tells me what they've been up to.

He tells me how, after I left them, they drove down to Vegas. How they found T's trailer and realized there was no way to stake it out without being seen by everyone in the trailer park. He tells me how Sid decided it was time to ditch the bus. How they left it on the roof level of a parking garage at one of the malls in Paradise, Sid hot-wired a car a few blocks away, and they got a room at the Super 8 just up Boulder Highway from the trailer park. How they came back here after the sun went down last night and parked across from the park entrance until they saw T's car leave. How they followed us, and how it wasn't until we came back out of the apartment and they saw me take off my hat that they figured out that I was the cowboy.

Rolf nudges me.

—Cool 'stache, by the way.

I nod and look at the TV. My folks were moved back home from the motel last night. The reporters are staked out there now. The lawn is trampled and there's a lot of empty paper coffee cups and McDonalds bags in the gutter. The reporters are milling around while a group of twenty or thirty gawkers stands behind a barrier on the sidewalk and snaps pictures. A sheriff's car is in the driveway and a deputy is standing on the porch in front of the door. The camera zooms in suddenly as a curtain is pulled away from one of the upstairs windows, but the curtain drops back into place without anyone being revealed. That you, Mom? Dad? I'm sorry. I'm so.

I shake my head. Rolf continues.

—Anyways, when you guys came out with nothin', we followed you over to that strip club. And, dude, what was that about?

—We needed to talk to someone.

—You took your time. We waited awhile, then I was like, *let's just blow back to the trailer and search it.* I figured if the money wasn't here we could wait for you and Elvis and jump you. And, dude? Was I relieved when he didn't come in with that big fucking dog. Hey, here it is again.

He points at the TV. It's the footage of the SWATs again.

The bus is isolated on the roof of the garage, centered in the jiggling helicopter spot. The team edges up, assault weapons ready, and cracks the sliding door.

Rolf talks over the footage.

—At first, we were hidden and waiting for you guys. Then it just took forever, so we turned on the set and watched this happen live around one AM. Dude, was that freaky.

One AM, when I was in a casino, the last place on earth you'll ever get news of what's going on outside.

The morning briefing from Sheriff Reyes comes on and Rolf unmutes the TV.

—The van, the bus, was seen in the vicinity of the collision and shooting on Nicastro Road in the twenty-four hours before, before that, those, incidents. Also, tracks we believe are from this vehicle were recovered and matched. That is, they match tracks found at the scene of the shooting of Deputy Fischer. So, and all this makes us believe that the suspect Henry Thompson and his, his, accomplices may have fled in this vehicle. We put out, with the help of the FBI, we put out a BOLO alert, a "Be On the Look Out" yesterday afternoon. Last night we received word that the vehicle had been found by officers of the Las Vegas Metro Police Department. And the focus, the focus of the investigation is, we don't really have much to do with it anymore, and this will be, I'll only be briefing on the case as it pertains to the crimes committed in our jurisdiction. The hunt for Henry Thompson and his suspected accomplices will be, is being . . . this is Special Agent Willis Tate and he'll be briefing, answering questions about the, the hunt.

Sheriff Reyes steps aside and a man in his forties steps up to the mikes. He has a slight potbelly and a shiny bald bullet head and wears steel-rimmed glasses and a government suit. He opens his mouth to talk and Rolf mutes the sound.

—This guy. He started showing up last night. Up. Tight. Reyes is cool, like he's your favorite shop teacher or a mellow uncle. He makes me feel safe. But, dude, this guy makes me feel oppressed, you know? Like, knowing he's running around with his cronies makes me feel like I'm not even a citizen in this country.

Special Agent Tate speaks into the microphones. He makes a gesture toward Reyes, nods his head, and then turns back to the reporters and starts to read from a prepared document.

I point at the TV.

—We should be listening to this.

Rolf waves his hand.

—Dude, he's just all, blah blah blah, jurisdiction, blah, good work of local authorities, blah, nobody panic 'cause I'm in charge now, blah.

Tate indicates a video monitor behind him and the camera zooms in on it. The image is fuzzy; a TV image of a TV image of a bad photo, but it's still easy to recognize Sid in his driver's license picture.

SID STARES at the picture of himself on the TV. After a few moments, they pull back to the shot of Tate talking at the podium, then cut back to the studio, then to a graphic showing an outline of Nevada with a se-ries of concentric circles centered on Las Vegas. Something swirls up out of the dot that represents Vegas. It resolves into my NYC booking photo and is followed by another swirl that becomes Sid's photo. Then letters are smashed down below them one by one, as if by a giant, red-inked typewriter: WANTED. And cut to an antacid commercial.

I look at Sid. He looks at me. And nods his head, like some suspicion he has long held has at last been proven true.

Rolf stands up.

—And on that note, dudes, I'll be using the can.

He heads off down the hall.

Sid and I sit next to each other, the TV still on, silently trying to sell us things. He reaches across me for the remote, picks it up, and turns the TV off.

He pulls his gun from his waistband. It's an older model Colt .45, a Gold Cup target pistol. It's a good gun, accurate and powerful, not the kind of thing you get off the street, but a tool you buy because you know its quality. He sets it on the coffee table and stares at the floor, elbows on knees, head hanging.

—I thought about what you said, about killing people being wrong. And, dude, it's not like I don't know that. I know people are, like, all sa-cred and life is a special thing. A gift? It doesn't have to be from God or anything, it can just be that life is this gift from the universe and it's special because, as far as we know, there isn't any more of it, so it's really, really rare. And what you do with your life? What you *do* with this gift, dude, that, like, totally makes you who you are. I really believe that. But. I don't think that makes killing people wrong? 'Cause if our lives are gifts, are special, then all lives are, whether it's a bug or a cow or whatever, and we kill them all the time. So death and killing is just a part of life, a part of the universe whether God made it, or whatever, it's just this natural thing. And some things, dude? Some animals? They kill, that's what they do, and it just makes them what they are? And people? We're just animals. So why shouldn't some of us be killers? Why can't that be just what makes some of us who we are? So I really kind of think you may not be right, and killing people isn't "wrong." It's just a thing some people do.

I look at the gun. I could make a grab for it. Grab the gun while Sid is listless, his eyes on the floor. I'll have to shoot Sid. Grab the gun, shoot Sid in the top of his head, run down the hall, and shoot Rolf while he's still trying to get his pants up from around his ankles. I know what it looks like when people get shot, what it feels like to shoot them. I have experience with sudden violence. And violence is like anything else, the more you do it, the more you get used to it. And the better you are at it. I could make the grab and kill them both. But I don't. Because I think I'm gonna need them.

Also, I'm afraid of Sid.

ROLF IS just coming out of the john when the phone rings again. He runs down the hall and stands in the middle of the living room. Sid picks up his gun and tucks it back in his pants. I flip the phone open and look at the clock. It's about forty-five minutes since the first call.

—Wade?

—Hey, Sandy.

—Hey, hey look.

—Where's T?

—Oh, baby, he passed out. You really should have come over.

I think about T while I listen to her light a cigarette. I try to imagine him passing out with anything but an elephant tranquilizer stuck in his neck. Not likely. Sandy exhales.

—You still could, you know, come over and party.

I light my own cigarette and say nothing. Her voice drops to a whisper.

—How's that sound, a little private party?

I take a drag and jet smoke from my nostrils. Rolf has joined Sid on the couch. They sit there watching me as I pace back and forth across the tiny living room.

—What happened to your boss, that guy Terry?

—He, you know, I told him you wanted to meet later so he's not coming by for awhile. So what about it?

—Weeell, you know I want to, but I still don't have any wheels.

There's a pause and a rustle, like maybe she's covering the mouthpiece.

—I could come and get you.

I keep my mouth shut, listening. I can still hear Hitler's nonstop barking. I flick some ash onto the carpet.

—You know what, baby, that's great, but I still think it's a bad call. I'm so wasted I'd probably just conk out right next to T. What time is your guy gonna show?

—Uh, well.

Another muffled rustle.

—Around twelve.

I bend over and stub my cigarette out in T's overflowing ashtray.

—No, that's still too early. I really need to crash.

—I, well, baby that's up to you, but I don't think he.

—No problem, I want to talk to the guy, but if we can't do it later.

—No. I. When? I can probably.

—Just, you know, a little after six, maybe.

—OK, I'll need to.

—Hey, what's your address, anyway?

—Um, I.

I snap my fingers at Rolf and make little writing gestures in the air. He digs through the back issues of *Mojo* and *Hustler* that are piled on the coffee table and finds a ballpoint.

—What was that, Sandy?

—Um, 262 Jewel Avenue.

—262 Jewel Ave. Got it.

I watch as Rolf writes the address in the whiteness of a naked thigh on one of the magazine's covers.

—But, Wade, I should really talk to.

—No problem, I'll be there right around six and Terry will either be there or he won't.

Rolf is holding up his hand trying to get my attention.

—Gotta go, baby.

—OK, I'll. I'll call after I talk to Terry and.

—I'm gonna turn my phone off to get some sleep. I'll just see you at six.

Rolf is waving his arms now. I turn off the phone. Rolf stands up.

—Dude, the Chargers game is on tonight.

—So?

—Dude, it's a ESPN game. A Thursday night game, it starts at six.

—Rolf, believe me when I tell you, I know how you feel, but it's about having priorities right now.

—Yeah, I know. I know I'm being lame, but, dude, I really wanted to see that game.

—It won't take long. We'll see the second half.

I'm out of cigarettes again. I remember T getting a pack of smokes from the fridge. I head for the kitchen. Rolf sits back down.

—You don't think this chick and her guy are gonna freak when you show up with two extra dudes? 'Cause you know you ain't going over there without us.

I open the freezer and pull a pack out of one of the three cartons inside. I remember Wade's dad used to do that, keep his cigarettes in the freezer so they'd stay fresh longer. I wonder if that's where T got it. From Wade's dad. Wade. Did you keep your cigarettes in the fridge in

your garage? Did you buy cartons and store them there and sneak out
to smoke late at night? Did Stacy ever come out with you to have a couple drags and sip a beer? Shit, Wade, oh shit.

—Dude.

I come back from where I was, close the freezer door, and open the
pack of Marlboros.

—Sorry. Fazed out for a second. I think I need some food and some
sleep.

—Sure, but answer the question?

—What?

—Why didn't you tell her you were bringing a couple extra dudes?

I light my fresh, cold cig and draw chilled smoke into my lungs.

—What's the point? If I tell her I'm bringing guests, she'll say no way.
And, like you said, you aren't gonna let me go over there alone. We just
show up? What are they gonna do? The guy's gonna want his five bills,
so he'll have to talk. And if he doesn't want to talk, there are three of us
there and he won't want to piss us off. Either way he'll end up telling
us where Tim is.

Rolf looks at the clock on the VCR; it's not even eight AM yet.

—We got some time to kill, dude.

—I'm gonna crash, you guys kill it however you want.

I GO to the room down the hall, take off my clothes, and lie back on
the foam pad. I'm desperate for sleep, but I need to think first.

I think about our meet with Sandy at the strip club. After we talked
she put the call in to her boss, this Terry guy. She said she left a message, that he'd call back. But she could have talked to him, told him
there were guys looking for Tim. And he could have told her what to
do: string us along, keep us out waiting for a call, keep us drinking and
blowing crank. And then she just about begged us to come and party at
her place. And she told T she didn't want him to bring Hitler.

Someone was waiting at her house when she got home with T. At
least two guys who work for Terry. Or maybe two Russian gangsters

reneging on their deal with Dylan and coming after me for the money. Take your pick.

So I'll go over to Sandy's and walk into whatever trap is waiting for me, because she's still the only lead I have on Timmy. But I'll bring Sid and Rolf with me.

Whoever's waiting over there won't be ready for Rolf and Sid. Nobody is ready for Rolf and Sid. I just need to be ready, ready to grab T when the shooting starts.

I close my eyes.

The chemicals in my body are still fighting a pitched battle. My heart leaps and starts like a faulty engine.

I open my eyes.

They feel dry, almost cracked. My tongue is swollen and rough and my whole mouth is seared from inhaling smoke. I'll never be able to sleep.

I close my eyes.

And am swallowed whole by jungle, darkness, and nightmares.

I JOLT awake, covered in sweat. The scream sitting at the back of my mouth. I bite it and swallow it back down.

Sid is sitting on the edge of the foam pad, holding my arm. He's changed into a pair of T's black Levis and a pink bowling shirt with the name Al embroidered over the breast pocket. He releases my arm.

—Sorry to wake you, dude. You were totally having a nightmare.

I pull the blanket up to cover my body. He looks at me.

—You OK now?

I nod. He gets up. I tilt my chin at him.

—Nice threads.

He looks down at himself and tugs at the loose waist of the jeans.

—Yeah. They're a little big. Anyway, dude's taste is not mine, but I need some kind of disguise, I guess. I got some shades in my pack and a bandana I can like tie like a do-rag?

I nod.

He points at my cowboy hat sitting on the edge of T's desk.

—I get the cowboy thing, dude. I didn't when we saw you, but then I saw all the other cowboys at the strip club and remembered the signs for the rodeo. Good call.

—Not my idea.

—Good one, anyway.

The sun is shining brightly through the hall window.

—What time is it? Can I catch a few more Zs?

—It's early, but you better get up, dude. We have some shit to figure out.

I nod. He steps to the door, stops, looks back at me.

—I know what that's like, dude, nightmares. If you ever want to talk, or.

He shrugs once. And leaves the room.

Sid was so high-strung when I met him at the motel in Barstow that I assumed that was what he was like. I was wrong. This is the real Sid; shy, pensive, glum. He was up at the motel because of what had happened in the strawberry field. He was up from killing Deputy Fischer. But the high has worn off. He'll be wanting that high again. Soon.

I get up and dress.

WE HAVE a new car.

I peek out the living room window and see one of the most fabulously nondescript automobiles ever manufactured. I turn to Rolf.

—Chevy Cavalier?

—I know, dude, but it's not like I was looking for style. I needed something easy to rob.

—Where'd you get it?

—I hopped one of those CAT buses and rode over to UNLV. Got it out of the parking lot.

—Gas?

—Dude, I'm not a fucking amateur. I stopped by a Shell and filled it up and checked the oil and shit.

—What happened to the car you boosted last night?

Sid looks up from the TV. As promised, he has tied a red and white bandana over his head and is wearing chrome-finish sunglasses that fit his face tightly, like a pair of welding goggles.

—The cops will be looking at stolen car reports from anywhere near where we dumped the Westy. That thing is no good for us.

—Where is it?

Sid looks away, embarrassed.

—About a half mile up the road. At the Super 8 we checked in to.

I stare at him.

—A half mile?

—Dude, I know.

—A half fucking mile?

Rolf puts his hands up palm out.

—Dudes, chill. Even if they find it.

—*When* they find that car they're gonna wrap up this whole area. We have to go.

Sid points to Rolf.

—Told you, dude.

—Dude! You said it'd be cool.

—Well, you were all, *We can't walk too far.* So, I was, like, *OK, we can leave it at the motel, but we don't want to be around it too long,* and you were all, *No prob, we'll scoop up Hank and be outy.* So, yeah, I said it was cool to be here for a little while, but dude, not this long.

They grab their day packs while I collect the cell phone and my hat and put on my boots. Rolf goes out and starts the Cavalier. Sid and I wait inside for him to beep, telling us the coast is clear. The car horn sounds, and Sid starts to open the door. I put a hand on his shoulder.

—Hang on.

I run back to the spare room and find the map I bought at the ampm. I head back to the front door, but stop at the bathroom. My head feels like badly scrambled eggs. As much as I need to clean it out and get it straight, I also need to be mellow and clear for the next hour. I open the medicine cabinet and get out the Percs. I try to shake one onto the palm of my hand, but a whole pile tumbles out. I put one in my mouth, start to drop the others back into the bottle, and shove them in my pocket instead. T may be in bad shape. He may need them. That's what I tell myself.

SID AND I pile into the car, me in the back and Sid up front. Rolf pulls away from T's trailer and stops at the exit from the park. Sid and Rolf look left. Down the highway I can see the Super 8 sign, sticking up above the telephone poles. Rolf elbows Sid.

—See, dude, no problem.

—Whatever.

—Well, where to?

Where to? It's just after two PM. I slept for almost six hours. Might as well get started.

—Got that address?

Rolf pulls the scrap of Hustler cover from the tight pocket of his leather pants.

—262 Jewel.

I uncrumple the map and spread it on my lap. I point to the right.

—That way.

—Dude, I thought we weren't supposed to show till six?

I check our route on the map. Jewel Avenue is just a few miles away. Ten minutes at most.

—No problem. She kept saying the sooner the better. And this way, we'll be done in time for kickoff.

Rolf flicks his turn signal and takes the right.

SANDY LIVES in a pink stucco tract house with a roof of fake ceramic tiles. There's a tidy little lawn out front with a sprinkler waving water over it. A red Miata with a dented back end is parked in the driveway. T's Chrysler and a black Land Cruiser are at the curb. Rolf drives past, flips a U-turn, and parks across the street. We sit there, the engine running, and Rolf adjusts the rearview mirror so he can see me without turning around.

—Dude, remember all that shit about me not being a tool?

I poke at one of the bruises on my torso.

—Yeah.

—Just for the record, I know something is fucked-up here.

I can see only his eyes in the mirror, staring at mine. I shrug.

—OK.

He turns around.

—What I'm saying, dude, is, let's not fuck around here. For everybody's spiritual and physical well-being. Is there anything going on in there we need to know about?

I look at the house, then back at him.

—I don't know what you want me to say, man. You were there when I took the calls. Far as I know, Sandy took my buddy T home with her, he passed out, she got the call from her guy, and now we're here. Are they gonna be displeased I brought friends? Sure as shit they are. Do I think it's gonna be trouble? No. Could the whole thing be a setup? Shit, man, anything can be a setup. Should we be on our toes? Well, it always pays to be prudent, right? That's all I can say. If it's not good enough, we can drive out of here and wait for her to call again and set up something else. But I'd just as soon get this done.

He looks me over, turns back around, and looks at Sid. Sid nods. Rolf reaches under the dash and untangles the two red wires twisted together there, and the engine dies.

—OK. But, dude, if it's fucked in there? Sooner or later we're just gonna get sick of your shit and kill you, money or no.

He opens his door and gets out. Sid tucks his pistol into the rolled waistband of his too-loose jeans, drops the tail of his shirt over it, and we get out and follow Rolf.

From the porch we can hear Hitler barking somewhere inside the house.

Rolf taps me.

—That your buddy's dog?

—I guess.

—What's he pissed about?

—Nothing, he always barks.

I face Sid and Rolf.

—All paranoia aside, guys, let's remember these are just some mellow potheads. Try to be mellow too, OK?

Rolf shrugs.

—Hey, dude, they be mellow, we be mellow.

Sid adjusts the pistol in his waistband.

—Whatever.

I ring the bell.

Hitler's barking gets louder. I wait a minute, ring again, and hear what sounds like someone shouting at Hitler to shut up. We wait another minute, then Rolf nudges me.

—Ring again, dude.

—Hang on, they're probably sleeping or fucking or something.

Or getting ready to jump us.

—Just ring.

He reaches past me and pushes the button three times in a row and Hitler gets even louder.

—Hang on! Who is it?

Sandy's voice, right on the other side of the door.

—Sandy! It's me, Wade.

Barking.

—Hey, baby, what's up?

—I'm here. Open up.

Barking.

The door opens a crack and Sandy's face is framed in the five-inch gap.

—Hey, hey, Wade.

—Hey, I got my shit together a little early and thought I'd come by.

—Yeah, uh.

She's looking past me to Rolf and Sid.

—Sorry, these are my buddies. They gave me a lift over. Is your guy around, or?

—Uh, uh, yeah, he's here, but.

She looks back into the house and then at us.

—He's here, but your buddies, they should. Can they wait in their car? He's in the kitchen and won't come out till they leave.

—Yeah, sure, but they're totally cool. Also.

I hook my thumb at Sid.

—He needs to use the can.

She bites her lip.

—Wade, this is pretty uncool. I mean you know.

—Yeah, but T knows these guys. They're cool. Go get him, he knows these guys are cool.

—Yeah, but T, T is still out, and.

—Jesus, what did you guys?

—We just came back and smoked out and he went down.

—Is he?

—He's cool, he's OK, but he's out.

—Cool, OK, but just let us in so he can use the can and then they'll leave and we can talk. Be cool and let the guy take a leak.

—Uh.

Another glance over her shoulder.

—Uh, OK, OK, that's cool. OK. Just, all of you can come in, that's cool.

She pulls the door open. I step inside. The house is dark. All the curtains are drawn. I pull my shades down my nose a bit so I can peek over them. Rolf and Sid come inside. Rolf nods at Sandy.

—Hey.

She half smiles at him.

—Hi.

Sid doesn't say anything. Sandy closes the door. She points straight ahead.

—You guys can kick it in the living room. The bathroom is just to the left.

I stay where I am.

—What's up with Hitler?

Sandy is wearing only a shorty kimono, her legs and feet bare. All her makeup is gone, her hair mussed, face flushed. I can see now how young she is; no more than twenty. She draws the kimono tighter, hiding the stars on her chest.

—He, he freaked a little and chased my cat, so I made T put him in the master bathroom.

—Hunh.

I walk into the living room. Sandy touches Sid's arm. Sid just stares at her. She tries a smile.

—Bathroom's down there.

Sid looks down the hallway, the open door of a bathroom visible at its end. A closed door on its right, Hitler's barking coming from behind it. He looks at me.

—Well, go on, man.

He looks at Rolf, then turns and walks into the bathroom and closes the door, his movements as stiff and unnatural as a robot. But he's not afraid. He's excited; charged with violence.

I look around the living room. Electric blue velvet couch against the left wall, matching love seat against the right, a deco coffee table between them, wood floors partially covered by a fake Moroccan rug, fireplace in the far wall, entertainment center next to it, two floor lamps with colored scarves draped over them. On the walls, framed movie posters for *I Want to Live* and Betty Page's *Variatease,* along with a print of Klimt's *The Kiss*. Billie Holiday is singing "Good Morning Heartache" on the stereo. Sandy is clearly going for a 1940s Hollywood-starlet bungalow kind of thing.

She goes to the coffee table and finds her pack of Camel Ultra Lights among a jumble of binge trash. Two overflowing ashtrays, a mirror smeared with white residue, crumpled squares of magazine paper, three empty Veuve bottles, a colored pot box like the ones we found at Tim's, a loaded bong, and three Bic lighters. She drags hard on her cigarette.

—So you get some rest?

There's a doorway covered by a beaded curtain next to the love seat. I'm guessing that's the kitchen. Terry is in there, listening. I light one of my own smokes and bob my head up and down.

—Oh, yeah, I'm good to go. But, man, was I wasted.

—Yeah, me too.

I drop a spent match into one of the ashtrays and point at all the gear.

—Not too much to keep going.

—Yeah, yeah, well, me and T got started and then he, you know, and the guy, my boss, Terry, came around so we.

—Kept the party going.

—Yeah, yeah, but yeah, I'm ready to crash.

The toilet flushes and Sid comes back into the room. Sandy jams her smoke out in an ashtray and starts for the front door. I sit on the couch, Rolf drops down next to me, and Sid moves over by the fireplace. Sandy stops.

—So, you guys need to, like, go wait in the car now.

—They're gonna stay here, OK?

She crosses her arms and shakes her head.

—Motherfucker.

—It's cool, Sandy.

—Fucking, what is this, Wade?

—It's cool, baby. These guys are just helping me find Tim and they need to hear what your guy has to say.

—This is so uncool and you know it is.

—Baby, the guy, he wanted a grand, right?

I take my money out of my pocket. After T shopped for me, after paying Sandy last night, and after partying my ass off, I'm down to about fourteen hundred. I count off a thousand.

—Tell him he can have it. All he has to do is walk out here and talk to us.

She looks at the money.

—This is wrong, this is so.

—Baby, take the money and go talk to the guy.

The index and middle fingers of her right hand are scissoring against each other and she's shaking her head.

—Please. Don't.

I push the money to the edge of the coffee table.

—I'm sorry, baby. But this is the way it's gonna be. These guys have to stay. So take the money and go talk to your guy and make him understand. Take the money, baby.

She rubs her forehead.

—Shit.

She steps to the table, scoops up the money, and pushes through the curtain, the strings of beads swinging and clicking behind her.

She's afraid.

And she should be.

We are violent men.

TERRY'S BEEN spending a lot of time in the gym and the tanning salon. I can tell because of the way his tailored black slacks stretch to cover his thighs, and because his light blue silk shirt with the white French cuffs and collar is hanging open so we can all look at his washboard stomach. He's completed the look with high-gloss blond hair, sculpted straight back from his forehead, black loafers with no socks, and a Rolex. Terry may be a pot dealer, but he clearly has higher aspirations.

He sashays into the room, his arm draped over Sandy's shoulder, the tips of his fingers dipped inside her kimono, grazing the top of her left breast. He reclines with Sandy on the love seat across from us.

—Get me a smoke, babe.

She leans forward, gets one of the Newports from the coffee table, hands it to him, and lights it.

—Thanks.

He puts his arm back around her and draws her close until her head is on his shoulder. He looks at Sid by the fireplace and then at me.

—You Wade?

—Yeah.

—I'm Terry.

He waves his cig in Sid's direction.

—Want to tell your friend there to sit down?

—Why?

—Because he's making me a little uptight and if he doesn't sit I'm gonna walk out of the room and you can fuck off.

Sid doesn't move, but Rolf looks at me.

—Dude.

I put my hand on his thigh.

—It's cool.

Terry points his cleft chin at Rolf.

—He gotta problem?

—It's cool.

Rolf rolls his eyes, but keeps his mouth shut. I point at the end of the couch. Sid takes three tightrope-walker steps and sits down.

—Better?

Terry nods.

—Oh, yeah, love it.

Sandy has half her face buried in his shoulder. I can see tears on the other half. Her left hand is clenched in a fist, balling the material of Terry's shirt. Whatever's coming is coming soon.

—Hey, Sandy.

She jumps at the sound of my voice.

—Yeah?

—You got any coffee or anything in the kitchen you could make for us?

Her lips stretch in a tiny smile.

—Uh, yeah, yeah I could.

She starts to lean forward to get off the love seat, but Terry keeps his arm around her, holding her in place.

—She's cool here. You guys won't be around long enough for coffee.

Sandy crouches back into his embrace and hides her face again, closing her eyes this time. Hitler is still barking, somewhere on the other side of the wall right behind me. Barking and barking and barking. Terry smokes and says nothing, a dicky smile on his face. I pull another of T's cigarettes out of the box in my breast pocket.

—So, Terry, what's up?

He raises his eyebrows.

—With me?

I put the cigarette in my mouth.

—Yeah.

He shrugs, the smile still on his face.

—Not much, just hanging out mostly.

Rolf slaps my leg with the back of his hand.

—Dude!

—It's cool.

I start to light my cigarette, and realize that I am already holding a lit one. I flick my eyes up at Terry and watch the smile spread wider on his face.

—Hate it when I do that, don't you?

I keep my mouth shut, light the new smoke, and stub the other one out in one of the ashtrays already crammed with butts. Camel Ultra Light butts. Newport butts. Pall Mall butts. Lots of Pall Mall butts. Hitler's barking gets louder.

I look from the ashtray to Terry. He nods.

I start to move, but the sound of a shotgun being cocked to my right stops me. Terry takes a drag from his cigarette and blows a smoke ring.

—So whatsay we all be cool now and just wait for the Russian?

TERRY'S GOONS are a couple of clowns that smoke Pall Malls.

Both wear Professional Rodeo Cowboy Association T-shirts with the word CLOWN spelled out in Western-style lettering. The one with the Remington shotgun has set his outfit off with an NFR 2003 cap, while the guy with the weird little rifle is wearing a camo-patterned cap. NFR stands a few feet away, across the coffee table, covering us with his twenty gauge while the other one pats us down.

He starts with me, holding his gun in his right hand while he feels me up with his left. I look at his gun again. What the . . . ?

—Is that a crossbow?

He runs his hand over my pockets and pulls out my phone and the last of my money, and puts everything on the table.

—Fuckin' A right it is, boy. So don't you go movin' round or I'll put a bolt through your eyeball.

I stay still. He stands back and takes a long look at me.

—He's clean, but I can't figure out what he's s'posed ta be.

He points the crossbow at my face. I flinch away from it. He laughs.

—Ya s'posed ta be a cowboy? That it, you a cowboy?

He turns to face the guy with the shotgun.

—Hey, Ron, fella thinks he's a cowboy.

He knocks the hat off my head and the sunglasses from my face.

—Shit, ya ain't no cowboy.

Camo Hat finishes with me. He moves on to Rolf and looks at his dreads.

—An' who the fuck you s'posed to be, Snoop Doggy Daaaaaawg?

He laughs and puts his hand on Rolf's shoulder. Rolf slaps it away.

—Uh-uh, dude.

Camo Hat guy stiffens and brings his weapon up in both hands. Ron shifts so he can blast Rolf with the shotgun without hitting his pal. Rolf puts his hand down. Camo Hat leans in and presses the crossbow against Rolf's forehead.

I lean away, not knowing how much blood might spray if he shoots that thing.

—Don' you fuck around with me, boy. This is a two-hundred-pound Exomag. I pull this trigger an' this bolt's gonna jump at three hundred and thirty feet per second. Know what that is in real numbers, boy? That's over two hundred miles an hour. It'll go clean through your skull and inta the next room and stick the guy in there.

Guy in there. Now I know where T is.

Terry flicks his cigarette. It bounces off the back of Camo Hat's neck and Camo jumps.

—Hey! Don't fuck around like that when I'm holding a weapon.

Terry waves his hand.

—Yeah, sure. How about this, Dale: you shut your mouth and just do your job and check them out.

Dale grunts, turns back to Rolf and starts to pat him down. Terry points at me.

—Wade.

—Yeah?

—What's the score?

—The score?

—What's the fucking score?

—I don't.

—Hey! Hey! Hey!

He lights a fresh smoke and points it at me.

—Think about it.

—Wh?

—Hey! Think about what you are going to say. What's the score?

I think about it.

—I don't know what the hell you're talking about.

He gets up and shrugs his open shirt onto the floor. I don't think he's quite five seven, but he's made up for it with the weights. His skin is strained over muscles so sharply cut I can see the fibers and veins scrawled all over his torso. He looks like he'd pop if I stuck him with a pin.

—It's like this, Wade. I'm a team player. I go along, help out the team. Somebody needs to get hurt, they get hurt. But I like to know what the score is. Couple days ago, they tell me a Russian guy is coming around for Tim. No problem, I play. Problem is, nobody tells me the score. They don't tell me that Tim isn't supposed to know someone is coming for him, so I tell him not to go anywhere for a couple days, and what happens? He takes off. Tim goes missing. I try to find him. I play. Then the big bad Russian comes to town, and I don't have Tim, and suddenly my bosses want to rip me new assholes. And all of this, why? Because I didn't know the score. Now Sandy calls me, tells me a guy is looking for Tim. I play, I call the Russian. But I still don't know the score. And I want to know it, before the Russian gets here. Because I don't want any new assholes. So I ask again, what's the score? And you're gonna tell me or I'm gonna come over there and give you some free dental work.

Sandy jumps off the couch.

—Stop it!

Terry looks at her.

—Shut it.

—Fuck you. This is my house and I don't want any more of this in my house. Just get out of my house.

He punches her. He balls his hand into a fist and punches her in the mouth and she drops to her knees, blood pouring from her lips.

Dale turns to watch, but Ron keeps us covered with the shotgun.

Terry grabs her by her hair and yanks her to her feet.

—I said, shut it.

Blood is running down her chin and spattering her kimono. Terry lets go of her hair and she runs up the hall and I hear a door open and slam shut. Terry shakes his head.

—Chick wants to make some money, but thinks it should be easy, thinks nobody should get hurt.

I exhale. Because *I* know the score now. These clowns may be OK at roughing people up, but that's their limit. That twenty gauge is a small-game weapon. And a crossbow? Not what a pro is likely to carry. As for Terry, Terry's not a killer; he's a girl puncher. There are only three killers in this room, and we're all sitting on the couch. I can chill this out and put myself back in the driver's seat and all it's gonna take is a little talk. I open my mouth.

Hitler stops barking.

We all look.

T is slumped against the wall in the hallway. His eyes are glazed, only half open. His face is swollen and bruised and dry blood is crusted around his nostrils and lips, fingers of it dribbled down his neck. Hitler is standing next to him, teeth bared, straining forward, an invisible force holding him at bay.

Dale swings his crossbow around and aims it at Hitler.

—Control your animal, fucker!

T slumps farther. Hitler edges forward.

—Control that fuckin' thing, boy!

Ron's mouth is shut, his shotgun still centered on the couch. I slowly raise my hand.

—Everybody just take it easy. No one has to get hurt if we all just take it easy.

Sandy emerges from the hall behind T.

—T! No, T.

Terry shakes his head.

—Stupid bitch.

T lifts his left hand, from which a pair of handcuffs dangle, and points at Terry.

—Hitler! Auschwitz!

Hitler launches himself at Terry.

I put my feet on the coffee table and shove it.

Dale fires his crossbow.

It sounds like someone striking a steel wall with a plastic plank. The bolt hits Hitler in midair, passes so quickly through his left hind leg that it looks like a magic trick, and plunges into T's calf, pinning him to the wall. The coffee table hits Terry and Ron in the shins just as Ron pulls his trigger. He stumbles, the barrel of the Remington jerks up, and a load of birdshot blasts a hole in the wall just over Rolf's head. Terry falls flat on his back, his head slamming against the floor, and he gets a perfect view as Hitler soars over him and crashes into the love seat.

Sid pops up from the couch, his hand flying to his gun just as it slips down into the leg of his baggy jeans. Rolf grabs one of the sofa cushions and flings it at Ron as he swings his gun back in our direction, pumping another shell into the chamber. Ron ducks and Rolf jumps across the table at him.

Terry rolls and squirms around as Hitler scrambles back at him. Terry lunges backward and strikes the coffee table, and that's all the running away he gets to do. Hitler latches on to the closest target. Terry starts to scream like a dying rabbit.

Sid's gun slides down his pants leg, out the cuff, and clunks to the floor, and Dale swings his crossbow at him like a pickax. Sid leans back, the crossbow whistles past his face, Dale is dragged off balance, and Sid grabs the back of his neck and pushes him down to the ground.

Rolf has grabbed the barrel of the Remington and is lurching around the room with Ron as they struggle for control of the weapon. Blood is gushing out from between Hitler's locked jaws as he jerks his head from side to side. I'm almost grateful for Terry's screams, for keeping me from hearing the tearing sounds.

I grab my money and phone and step over to T. He's out cold, keeled over on the floor, the fletched shaft of the bolt sticking out of his leg. I grab hold, and yank. The bolt doesn't budge. It's gone through his leg and the Sheetrock of the wall and sunk itself deep in a 2x4 stud. I look over my shoulder.

Rolf has forced the barrel of the shotgun into the air and grabbed Ron's throat with his free hand. Ron is still holding the butt, his finger on the trigger, but has his other hand on Rolf's throat. They swing around in a circle a couple times, and then Ron pulls the trigger, blowing a hole in the ceiling, and Rolf yelps and lets go of the gun. Sid is kneeling on Dale's back; he's grabbed one of the Veuve bottles and has it raised in the air. I turn my head, but hear the sound as the thick glass shatters against the back of Dale's skull.

I try to get a grip on the arrow, but it's too slick with T's blood. I wrench at it anyway and my hand slides off and I end up tugging it to the side, opening the wound farther. T groans, but stays unconscious.

I need to get out of here.

Terry has stopped screaming. I look. Rolf is bent over, his arms wrapped around Ron's waist in a bear hug while Ron brings the butt of the gun down on his back, trying to break the hold. Sid is rising, dropping the jagged, bloody neck of the champagne bottle as he reaches for one of the two others. Dale is motionless on the floor, shards of glass sticking out of his scalp and neck. Hitler is looking at me. He has released Terry and is standing on his chest looking at me as I try to free T.

I stand up. Hitler takes a step toward me, gingerly placing his wounded leg down, and then lifting it into the air and holding it there. I take a step away from T, and Hitler takes a step closer.

Ron has beaten Rolf down to his knees, but Rolf refuses to let go. Too late, Ron realizes someone is coming at him from the side, and Sid's bottle arcs toward him before he can bring the shotgun around. The bottle splinters against his face, the gun goes off, one of the silk-covered lamps explodes, Hitler flinches and blinks, and I turn and run.

The door next to the bathroom is open. I lunge through it, spin, see Hitler running at me, and slam the door closed just as he crashes into it. The force of two two-hundred-pound bodies colliding sends us both hurtling backward. I hit a wall and watch him scrabble on the bare wood floor of the hall and come back at me. I kick the door and it bangs closed and latches as he piles into it, cracking the lower half, and starts trying to dig through it.

I turn and get only a glimpse of a big brass bed with a leather jacket draped on one of the posts and bloodstains on the sheets. I tear across the room to where Sandy is climbing out the window with an Adidas bag around her shoulders. She's crying and trying to pull the bag loose from where it's gotten caught on the window lock, and doesn't know I'm in the room until I yank the bag's strap free and shove her out the window to fall a few feet into the flower garden outside. I get one foot on the sill, then dive back into the room, grab the jacket from the bed-post, and jump out the window.

Sandy is still picking herself up. I hook the bag strap and start drag-ging her after me as I head for the path that runs to the front of the house. Sandy screams and tries to pull free. I wrench her to me, wrap my left arm around her neck, and lock my hand over her mouth. She struggles and scratches at my arm and I give her a hard shake, still pulling her along.

—Sandy. Stop it. You'll die if you don't stop. You'll die.

She stops, but I keep her in the headlock, my hand over her mouth. We round the side of the house and start down the short path to the gate that opens onto the driveway. I stop at the back door and peek through a gap in the curtains.

It's awful.

Dale is still immobile, unconscious or dead. Ron is on his back, rolling from side to side, his face covered with both hands, blood streaming from between his fingers. Terry is still alive and has some-how gotten himself flipped over, inching himself toward the front door, leaving a snail-trail of blood in his wake.

Sid has recovered his .45 and is standing over Ron, watching him writhe. He starts to raise his foot. Rolf has Ron's shotgun and is point-ing it up the hallway. T has come to and is holding his hand in the air, out toward Rolf, warding him off. Hitler is barking in the hall.

I start to look away, but I'm too late and I see it all. Sid's foot coming down on Ron's face. Rolf pulling the trigger. The blast that was deafen-ing in the small room is just a muffled pop out here.

Hitler stops barking and T screams and struggles to pull his leg free of the arrow holding him prisoner. That's all I can take.

I haul Sandy to the gate and look over it. Nothing. A quiet street, everyone at work or inside resting up for a late shift. I push the gate open and start down the drive toward T's Chrysler, holding his jacket collar in my teeth, feeling at the pockets until I find the keys. I walk around the car, open the driver's side door, and shove Sandy inside, pushing her ahead of me into the passenger seat. She pulls the door handle and tries to climb out. I grab at her and get a handful of hair, pull her in, and get the door closed. I let go of her hair.

—They're killing people in there, the guys I came with are killing peo-ple. We have to go. You have to go with me.

She doesn't move, so I go to stick the key in the ignition and miss. I try again and miss again and grab hold of my shaking right hand with my shaking left hand and manage to guide the key home. I start the car, over-revving, and drop the gearshift into drive as the front door of Sandy's house flies open and Sid and Rolf run out.

Sandy screams and I jam my foot down. The tires spin and smoke and we fishtail away from the curb as they run to the sidewalk. I straighten the car out and we're in the middle of the street, speeding away. I look back and see Sid pointing his gun at us and Rolf grabbing him and pulling him back up toward the house before he can shoot.

And we turn the corner and drive away, the trail of blood behind me stretched longer still.

WHEN I was a kid and I'd do something stupid, Dad would sit me down and ask me, "What were you thinking?" I'd shrug and say, "I dunno." He'd nod and put a hand on my shoulder and say, "You weren't thinking, were you?" And I'd say, "No, I wasn't." He'd tell me he knew I wasn't thinking, because he knew I was a smart kid and if I stopped and thought things through, I'd do the smart thing. All I had to do was stop and think and I'd do the smart thing. Always.

How am I doing now, Dad?

I DRIVE us back to Boulder Highway, take a left, drive up the road, and pull into the first parking lot I see: The Boulder Station Hotel. I park the Chrysler near the other cars in the lot, leave the engine running, and reach under Sandy's seat. The plastic bag snags on something and I give it a yank and it tears and the guns and the boxes of ammo spill out onto the floor next to Sandy's feet. She gives a little shriek at the sight of the guns and pulls her feet up onto her seat as if the footwell were full of spiders. I flip the cylinder open on the Anaconda, pop open the box of Magnum shells, and start to load the revolver. My hands are still shaking, it's hard to get the rounds in their chambers, but I manage. I close the cylinder and turn around in my seat and look out at the highway through the back window. I give it a couple minutes and see no sign of Rolf and Sid chasing us. I turn around.

Oh, my God. Oh please, Jesus. I close my eyes and see Terry crawling, trailing blood. Oh, Jesus, what have I done? I open my eyes and see the gun in my hand and raise it and press the barrel against my forehead.

—Jesus, oh, Jesus. Make it stop, please make it stop.

—Nonononononono.

Sandy is pressed against the passenger door, still in her kimono, blood still trickling from her mouth, staring at me, as I'm getting ready to kill myself. I pull the gun away from my head and drop it in the back-seat.

—It's OK.

—Nonono.

—It's OK, Sandy. It's over. It's OK.

I touch her. She closes her eyes.

—Sandy.

She whines.

—Sandy.

She opens one eye, like a kid who's watching a horror movie and doesn't want to see too much of the scary stuff.

—I'm not gonna hurt you.

I reach in my pocket and take out a pill.

—Take this. It'll help.

—I TOLD you, Terry's my boss, my dealer. And kind of my manager.

Oh, Christ.

—Your pimp, Sandy?

—No! My *manager*.

We're still in the parking lot at Boulder Station, but the Perc has Sandy mellowed out. She's in the backseat changing into clothes from her bag.

—I'm not a total cliché, Wade. He, he knows people at the big casinos, and I want to dance in a show, and he was helping me. He got me an audition at Bally's for *Jubilee!* But they didn't like my tattoos and I didn't get the job. I'm tall enough and I have the tits and ass and I can dance, but once they get a look at my tattoos they say no go, and it costs a hundred times as much to get the things taken off as it does to have them put on. Fuckin' tattoos.

She climbs into the front seat, now dressed in faded blue jeans, black Doc Martens, and a black AC/DC tank top.

—What else is Terry into, baby? What else does he do?

She wipes her eyes.

—Mostly he deals. He works for some people, I don't know. The people he gets his grass from. And sometimes he does other stuff for them, like collections and stuff.

—What about the Russians? Do they know who I am? Do you know who I am?

She looks at me sideways.

—You're Wade?

I let it go.

—Why was Terry there with those clowns?

—Because I called him.

—When?

—After we talked at the club, before I asked for a lift. I called Terry and told him you were looking for Timmy, and he told me to get you guys good and fucked-up and get you to come back to my house. But. But. But. You didn't come, and I went back with T anyway and I told him to leave the dog in the car, but he wouldn't, and then I said to put him in the garage, but he wouldn't, but he locked him in the bathroom in my room, in the master bedroom and then I got him to lie on the bed and handcuffed him to the frame like I was gonna strip for him, and then Terry came in and started asking T about Timmy, why he was looking for Timmy and who you were and why you were looking for Timmy, and T didn't know anything, and Terry, he had those hicks with him, and they started beating on T. And. And. And. I *like* T. I didn't want him to get hurt. And. And. And.

She's gasping for breath.

—Easy, take it easy.

She rubs the heels of her hands into her eyes.

—Terry made me call you to try and get you to come over, but you wouldn't, and that pissed him off, and he was also pissed because T and the dog wouldn't shut up and the dog wouldn't stop barking and he couldn't do anything about the dog, but T was carrying a bunch of ludes and Terry forced a few down T's throat and that knocked him out. And then. And then? And then we didn't expect you until six or so and Terry had those fucking guys with him and he had been, he met them at Circus Circus and was supposed to set them up with a couple hookers and when he got the call from me he asked if they wanted to make a couple bucks instead and they had gotten wiped out at the craps table so they went out to their truck and got that gun and that bow thing and Terry drove them over in his Cruiser and we had to wait for you and they were bored and wanted to leave and they thought I was a hooker and wanted Terry to make something happen for them and they kept grabbing at me and Terry made me give them all of T's crank and my Veuve and then you just showed up. And? And?

She runs a hand through her hair.

—God, I love Percs. Got any more?

—Later. What happened when we showed up?

—Nothing. Oh, except Terry got pissed again, but he's always getting pissed and flexing his muscles like he invented them. I mean, he's mostly an OK guy, but he was really bad today because nothing was working the way he wanted it to and that's like one of his big things, bitching about how things don't work the way they're supposed to. Also? He has those guys there to show off in front of and he was doing crank and he's already high-strung from the 'roids so that wasn't a great idea and then you show up and I look out the peephole and you have those guys and he was all *Nothing works the way it's supposed to,* and then he told me to only let you in, but you brought those guys and . . .

She shrugs. *That was that.*

—Besides, I think he's scared of the Russian.

Who isn't?

—What about the Russian? What do you know?

—Nothing. Except Terry's bosses told him to help out finding Timmy, so he called *him,* the Russian, after I called about you, and *he* told Terry to get ahold of you, and Terry called *him* from my place to say you'd be there around six, and then after you showed up early, he called *him* again to say you were there. I think. But that's all I know.

I look at her.

She doesn't know anything. She doesn't even know who I am. And if she did? All she could tell anyone is that I'm in Vegas. And it seems that everyone already knows that. I reach across her and unlock her door.

—You can go.

Her jaw drops.

—And do what? Go home? I'm not going back to that place. And who knows who'll find me if I go to the club? So fuck you, Wade. You kidnapped me and you are fucking stuck with me. You're the pro, you're the one who knows what you're doing, so I'm sticking with you until those psychos you let in my house are out of the picture.

She puts on her seat belt.

—So what now?

She's right. If Rolf and Sid get their hands on her there's no telling . . . The carnage at her house strobes through my head. The carnage I brought there. I don't want to imagine what they would do to her. But I do. Sandy is my problem now.

I start the car.

—We need a hideout.

She stretches.

—Oooh yeah, I could get behind some sleep.

—Where?

She yawns.

—I know a place.

THE ROOM at the El Cortez has cable. I sprawl sleepless on my bed and watch the Chargers and Broncos go at it.

The teams of the AFC West have been unstoppable this season. Coming into this week, the Raiders and Chargers are locked with unreal 13-1 records and both have clinched at least a Wild Card. Each has lost a game to the other and has an identical division record, but San Diego has a slight edge in their conference record. That's why Rolf and Sid are so eager to have my Fins top the Raiders on Sunday. If the Raiders lose and the Chargers win, San Diego will clinch the division championship.

Of more concern to me are the Broncos. At 11-3 they still have an outside shot at the West, but only if they beat San Diego and Miami beats Oakland. Even if they lose the last two games, Denver is primed for the remaining Wild Card spot. I desperately need them to lose tonight to keep that Wild Card door open for the Fins, because the 11-3 Jets are playing miserable Detroit this week. So if Denver wins and New York beats Detroit and Miami loses, NY will lock up the AFC East division title and Miami will miss the playoffs entirely. Again.

All of these playoff contortions are yet another reason why I hate football, and hate myself even more for having been sucked into caring about it. I hate the NFL for creating Wild Cards, and I hate it even more for having spread that madness to baseball. It used to all be so easy, the best team in each division plays in the postseason. Now? Chaos. Don't get me started.

The game kicks off.

Denver has the top passing offense in the NFL and San Diego has the top rushing offense. It should be a good, close game. Sure enough, the Broncs pick the Charger's secondary to pieces, and the Chargers roll over the Bronc's defensive line. By halftime it's SD 21, DEN 24. Then it gets weird.

The Broncs put up another field goal in the third quarter to stretch the lead to six, but their nine-time Pro Bowl kicker comes off the field limping and word quickly hits the broadcast booth that he has torn his hamstring. The Chargers score another rushing TD and take a one-point lead. Late in the fourth, the Broncs QB gets chased out of the pocket and turns a busted play into a thirty-five-yard score, but his knee gets hammered as he crosses the goal line and he is carted off. His rookie backup, who has taken three snaps all season, will have to come in when they get the ball back.

The Denver defense holds SD down, all the kid QB has to do is pick up one first down and then he can kneel out the game. I'm banging my head into my pillow, willing the Chargers' defense to do something. On first and ten, the rookie bobbles the handoff, tries to pick up the ball instead of falling on it, and the ball is scooped up by a Charger linebacker, who takes it all the way home. With SD back on top by one, less than two minutes on the clock, no time-outs remaining for either team and the kid QB pinned at his own seven yard line by a monster kickoff, I'm starting to celebrate a little. Then San Diego goes into a prevent defense and the kid starts throwing to the middle of the field and manages to put his team on the Chargers' thirty-five before spiking the ball with three seconds left. The kicking team comes on.

If this was the Broncs' kicker, I'd be worried. That guy's been slamming fifty-yard field goals in the thin air of Mile High Stadium for the last decade. But it's his backup, the punter. He sets up for the kick, and the rookie QB kneels behind the line to take the snap and hold the ball for him. And nobody on the San Diego special teams unit notices that the Broncs' starting tight end has checked in on the right end of his line.

It's ugly.

The ball is snapped directly to the punter, who rolls right as the rookie QB rolls left and the tight end releases his defender and runs upfield. The punter is pancaked, but not before a wobbly duck flops out of his hand, hangs in the air, and lands in the arms of the rookie, who is still behind the line of scrimmage. A Charger defender is running behind the tight end by now, grabbing on the back of his jersey, trying desperately to yank him down and stop him, perfectly willing to take the penalty in order to end this madness. The rookie sets up and launches the ball across the field just as he is speared in the chest and goes down. It is one of the most beautiful passes in the history of the NFL. It spirals as tightly as a drill bit and drops into the arms of the tight end just as the San Diego player behind him gives a heave that drags him to the turf. As he falls, the tight end stretches the ball forward, and breaks the plane of the goal line.

SD 35 DEN 40 FINAL.

SANDY TOLD me she knows the front desk guy at the El Cortez Hotel and Casino.

She sometimes works a hustle on guys she picks up at the club. She brings them to the El Cortez, gets a room, and starts to get frisky. Then Terry busts in like the jealous boyfriend and the mark empties his wallet to keep from having his ass kicked. The guy at the desk gets a cut, so he's happy to take cash for our room and keep his mouth shut. I try to give her the last of my money, but she doesn't need it. She grabbed her stripper/dealer stash on her way out the back window at her house, a clutch of rubber-banded cash rolls. Be prepared.

She goes in alone and comes out with a key. I drop my guns in her bag and lock up the car. We walk through the lobby together, my face buried in her neck; just another couple in romantic Las Vegas.

Upstairs, I stay in the room and she goes back down for a couple things from the drugstore and gift shop off the lobby. When she comes back she has cigarettes, shampoo, soap, deodorant, four Hershey bars, Band-Aids, Ben-Gay, a couple cheeseburgers from Careful Kitty's Café, and a few airline bottles of vodka.

She showers while I eat my burger, and comes back into the room in red panties that say Friday across the ass, the AC/DC tank, and a towel wrapped around her hair. I go into the bathroom and strip out of my clothes. The jeans have a dark, crusty spot where my thigh has been leaking blood. I take the Band-Aids off my thigh and the makeshift bandage from my ankle and get into the shower. Fear and violence make you sweat. I stink of fear and violence.

Out of the shower, I use the vodka. Sandy said they didn't have rubbing alcohol in the gift shop, this was the best she could do. I pour it over the bullet wound in my thigh and rub it into my various cuts and scrapes. I use several large Band-Aids to hold the wound closed, and cover all my lesser injuries, then I rub Ben-Gay into my sore muscles. There's a bottle of vodka left. I could drink it. I pour it down the drain. I think about flushing the seventeen Percs I have left, but don't have the willpower. They make me feel numb, and I may want to feel that way again. Soon. I pull on my dirty BVDs, my jeans, and my tank top, and go back into the room.

Sandy is trying to eat her burger. She says the Percs took her appetite. She's starting to cry again, tears running down her face as she chews, and then she's gagging and running into the bathroom, where I hear her vomiting.

When she comes back she asks for another Perc and I give it to her. She's done. She's had too much today and can't fight off the things in her head anymore. She takes the pill, crawls onto one of the full-size beds and falls instantly to sleep.

I turn off all the lights, draw the curtains and shades so that the room is nearly black, and lie on top of the bedspread of my own bed. The clock radio on the nightstand glows 4:46 PM. I close my eyes. And I am instantly wired and restless. I lie on the bed with my eyes closed, praying desperately for a sleep that seems to be creeping further and further away, until, over an hour later, I finally give in and turn on the game.

And when that is over and sleep is still no closer, I surrender again to weakness, take two Percs, and return to the jungle.

I AM back at Chichén Itzá, on top of Kukulkan. It is night. I'm alone, looking out at the darkness, the jungle black against the slightly lighter sky. I hear someone behind me and I turn. It's Willie Mays, dressed in San Francisco Giants' home whites. I smile.

—Say hey, Willie.

He smiles back at me.

—Say hey, kid.

He has a bat in his right hand, the barrel resting casually against his shoulder, and he's tossing a ball up and down with his left. I point at myself.

—You won't remember, but we met when I was a kid. I did a Giants fantasy camp and you visited one day and gave a hitting clinic.

—Sure, I remember you. You had a cap with Dodgers Suck written on the bottom of the bill.

—That is so cool that you remember. You signed a ball for me that I still have. Or, I don't have it, 'cause it was in my apartment when I got into some trouble a few years ago. So now it's maybe at my folks' place or maybe the super or a cop or someone stole it. I don't know.

—I heard about that, that trouble you were in. How'd that turn out?

—Don't know, it's still happening.

—What's that about, kid? What's all this trouble about? Kid like you in all this trouble.

—I wish I could tell you.

—What are you thinking out there, doing all that stuff?

—I dunno.

—I do. You're *not* thinking, that's the problem. Smart kid like you, if you just think things through, you'll always do the smart thing.

—Ya think so?

—I know so.

—Thanks.

—Kid with skills like yours. Yeah, I remember you, eight years old and I could tell you were a pro soon as I saw you. You could have been the greatest Giant ever.

He winks.

—Or the second greatest, anyway.

—Nobody will ever be greater than you, Willie.

—Weeeell.

—Nobody.

—Nice of you to say that, kid. Look, let me give you some advice.

—Sure.

Someone taps me on the shoulder. Willie tucks his ball away and gets into his hitting stance.

—It's about your swing.

Another tap. I turn. It's Mickey, wearing a Dodgers cap and holding up a ball and a Sharpie.

—Excuse me, Mr. Mays.

I frown at him.

—Wait your turn.

I look back at Willie. He's stroking the bat through an imaginary strike zone.

—And keeping your balance back like this.

Tap.

—Mr. Maaaaaays!

I turn.

—Look, you're not even a Giants fan, so wait your turn.

I turn to Willie, who is putting the bat back on his shoulder.

—If you do all that, you'll bring your average up at least ten points.

—But.

TAP!

—Williiiiiiieeeeee!

I spin.

—Wait! Your! Turn!

And I shove Mickey. And he stumbles back. And he balances at the edge. One foot raised. Arms waving. Ball and pen still clutched. And then he falls.

All.

The.

Way.

Down.

Willie and I stand there, looking down into the darkness. He shakes his head.

—See what I'm saying, kid? You didn't think about that at all, did you?

—HEY, HEY, baby, you OK?

I open my eyes. A pretty girl is sitting on the side of my bed. She has long black hair with sharp straight bangs, an amazing body, and is wearing very little. I come back from the jungle and remember her name.

—Hey, Sandy.

—Nightmare?

—Uh-huh.

My eyes don't want to stay open, they keep sliding me into darkness. Sandy's are doing the same.

—Me too. I love Percs, but they fuck with your dreams.

I drag my eyes open.

—My dreams are always fucked.

She scratches her head.

—Can I get in with you?

—Sure.

I hold the covers up and she gets in and spoons her back against my front. She smells good.

—You smell good.

—Thanks.

She yawns. I yawn. She reaches a hand out to the radio.

—Can I put on some music?

My eyes are closed again.

—Sure.

I hear stations flip by and then a DJ for UNLV radio talking and then Nick Drake sings "Place to Be." Sandy sighs.

—I love this song.

My eyes are closed again.

—Yeah.

—Wade?

I'm almost asleep again, but the name of my dead friend brings me back.

—Yeah?

—What did you see when you looked in my house? When we were running away?

Bad things.

—Nothing, really.

—What do you think happened to T?

Bad things.

—I think they killed him.

—Your friends?

—They're not my friends, but yeah.

Her breathing is getting deep.

—Sandy?

—Umhunh?

—Why did you let T go? Why did you unlock his cuffs?

—I told you, I like T. I was getting ready to go out the window and I wanted him to go too. But he didn't.

No, he didn't. He tried to help me instead. She twists her head around to look at me.

—What about us? Will those guys try to find us?

Hadn't thought of that. Yeah, they'll try to find me. What else do they have now? And Sandy? She's a witness. Sid will want her.

—They might.

She reaches back, finds my hand, and pulls it around her like an extra blanket.

—So then we have to stick together.

I count the people who have been hurt or been killed because they've stuck with me. Like counting backward from ten when you're on an operating table, I am asleep before the pain starts.

I wake up and find Sandy sitting at the bottom of my bed, eating French toast from a room-service tray. I pull back the covers. Sandy looks at me over her shoulder. She chews and swallows the food in her mouth.

—Morning, Henry.

The tube is on, but Sandy isn't watching MTV.

THEY FOUND Sid and Rolf's hot car at the Super 8. The clerk identified Sid and was able to give a good description of Rolf. So they have a sketch of him now. There's a decent chance someone who knew him in San Diego or Mexico will see it and identify him.

There's also some footage of Danny standing with one of the lawyers from O.J.'s defense team, but I make Sandy change the channel before I have to hear them say anything. Sandy is taking it all pretty well.

—It's just a relief more than anything else. Like when you know you've seen an actor in a movie before, but can't figure who he is. Or the name of a song you can't remember? How annoying is that? I mean, I knew you had to be wanted for something. But I was like, who is this guy? I saw something on the news about something happening in California a couple days ago, but I had no idea you were supposed to be *here*. Weird. And now I'm thinking I almost hope those assholes that killed T and Terry find us, 'cause I got you on my side.

At first I thought she was so wired because she got some good sleep, but then I realized she had found the last three bindles of crank in T's jacket. I watch as she dips the tip of her cigarette into the yellowish powder and then lights up, giving herself a little freebase hit on her first drag.

—Wheeew, that's good. Sure you don't want some?

—No.

My body is still trying to wring out the last of the poisons I've been dumping in it, but at least I got some real sleep. I have that stupid feeling you get when you sleep too much. I look at the clock. 9:27. Shit, I slept almost twelve hours. I go to the curtains and pull them open. It's dark out. Sandy laughs.

—Yeah, can you believe that? Nothing like Percs to knock you out.

I look at the clock again. 9:27 PM. It's Friday night. I've slept for twenty-four hours. Again.

—Where's my phone?

Sandy shrugs.

Where's my phone? Where's my fucking phone? The TV. I turn the volume back up, but it's Larry King now. They'll cut in, right? If something has happened to Mom and Dad, they'll cut in. Phone! It's not in my pockets. I didn't leave it on the nightstand.

—Is this it?

Sandy's standing in the bathroom door with the phone. I left it in there when I cleaned up. I grab it from her and turn it on. It powers up and chirps and the LED screen shows that I have eleven messages. Fuck. I don't even know how to get messages off this thing. I flick to the phone book and find the only number in there, Dylan's number. The phone rings and I jump and it falls to the floor.

—Fuck.

Sandy reaches for it and I knock her hand away.

—Don't touch that!

She holds her hands in the air.

—Excuse fucking me.

I pick up the phone, take it in the bathroom, and close the door. It rings a third time and I push the green button.

—It's me. I'm here. I'm sorry, I.

—Dude, that you? Don't you ever check your messages? Hey, I got someone here wants to talk to you.

I listen while Rolf passes the phone off.

—Hank? They killed Hitler. They killed my dog.

I COULD let him die. I could tell Rolf and Sid to fuck off. They have no idea where I am. I could just let them kill T, and their part in all this would be over. I mean, who is T? Just a guy I barely knew in high school. Just a crazed speed freak with a death wish anyway. Just a guy who wanted to help me protect my parents for no reason other than he misses his own.

Shit.

And anyway.

Tim is gone.

My friend took the money and he's gone. That's clear now. And my choices are gone with him. The ship is sinking and it's time to get as many people off as possible.

I lie again.

I tell Sid and Rolf I know where the money is. I tell them I got Sandy to tell me where Tim is and I found him and he told me where the money is. They want to know where he is now. I tell them something they'll believe, I tell them I killed him.

They want to meet where the money is, but I tell them no chance. I tell them we'll meet someplace public, they'll let T go, and I'll take them to the money. They like that idea because it means they get the money *and* me. We decide to do it at the hotel. They're calling from a pay phone outside a supermarket. Sandy gives them directions and the name of the guy at the front desk. He'll set them up with a room, and then they'll call us and we'll do the swap.

After I get off the phone Sandy goes down to the front desk to pay for the extra day on our room and to tell her guy that some friends of hers will be coming in.

I make my call.

—Who the hell are *Rolf* and *Sid,* Henry, and why are they leaving you messages?

It should have been obvious, I guess. He gave me the phone after all, so of course he has the code to retrieve all the messages Rolf and Sid left for me.

—More to the point, what are they doing talking about *my money*?

—Take it easy, Dylan.

—Don't. Don't even start, Henry. I have been *very* patient with you, treated you like a professional, and where has it gotten us? You blow off the deadlines for *two* progress reports, and when I investigate your absence I discover you have been receiving calls from people who seem to be trying to make a deal for *my money*. And who are these people? No, don't answer that because I think I know. Sid, I gather, would be the Sidney Cain the authorities are looking for, and Rolf is most likely the nameless gentleman whose sketch is now being circulated. Are these your allies, Henry? Are these the kind of subcontractors you have employed? If so, and I am *certain* that it *is* so, I can only call your judgment *questionable*. No, pardon me, I am being sarcastic, let me be more blunt. You're fucked-up! You are completely fucked-up and you are pushing me and your parents very close to the fucking edge!

—I have the money, Dylan.

—Where?

—Here.

—*Here* being Las Vegas, if I am to believe the news reports?

—That's right.

—Well it is *Friday night,* Henry. Don't you think you should be rushing my money to me?

—I can't.

—*Why not?*

—Because my picture is on the TV, Dylan, and I can't really travel much.

—What do you propose?

—Come and get it.

I give him the address where I plan to be and hang up.

I try to make myself see this ending with my parents still alive.

I snort two fat lines of crank to give me an edge, and eat a Perc to keep from feeling anything.

All I have to do now is kill everybody.

ROLF CALLS my cell from their room and tells me the number. I tuck the Anaconda and the 9 mm in my pants and give Sandy the keys to the Chrysler and tell her to wait here for fifteen minutes and then leave if I'm not back.

—Where?

—A lawyer, go to a lawyer and tell your story.

—And then what?

—You didn't do anything. If they're any good, they'll get you out of trouble and sell your story to Fox. So just find a good lawyer.

I open the door to go to Rolf and Sid's room.

The problem is, Sandy didn't tell her guy at the desk not to give Rolf and Sid our room number, which is why Sid is standing right outside our door, shoving his .45 in my face and forcing me back into the room.

SID STILL isn't talking to me. I open my mouth to say something, and he shakes his head, and I close it. He looks disappointed in me.

He takes my guns and makes Sandy and me lie side by side on the floor in the little space between the beds. He sits in the room's only chair and watches us. Sandy is shaking. I put a hand on the back of her head.

I should have sent her to the car right after she came back up from the desk, but she took forever to get her shit together and get dressed. I should have known they'd have something planned. That's me, three steps behind, as usual. There's a tap on the door. Rolf. Pissed again.

He grabs me by my hair and drags me out from between the beds. Sandy whimpers and clutches at me, but Rolf yanks me free and she wriggles under one of the beds. I get to my hands and knees, crawling as he leads me around the room by my hair.

—Dude, you are so fucking lame.

—Cool it, Rolf.

—Did you just tell me to cool it?

He pulls my head back so he can see my face.

—You still think I'm a tool, don't you, dude?

He slaps me.

—You think I'm a tool, and that makes you think you can get away with this lame shit.

SLAP!

—Think you can ditch us?

SLAP!

SLAP!

—Stop it, Rolf.

—What?

Gritting my teeth.

—Just stop, man. Be cool.

—Oh, I'm being cool, dude.

SLAP!

—Be cool. Let's go to your room and cut T loose and then we'll get the money and.

SLAP!

—The money, dude? Dude, you really do think I'm a tool.

SLAP!

—*Yeah, man, you come here with T and I'll take you to the money.* How many times do you think you can tell the same fucking lie, dude? You're so like the boy who cried money. You tool.

SLAP!

—Well, news flash, dude: I'm not here for the money, I'm here for you. I mean, fuck that wild goose. Your friend and the cash are gone, any asshole can see that.

SLAP!

—But you, dude? I can go two ways with you. I can use you to cut a deal with the cops. Or, dude, I chop your fucking head off for a souvenir and just run back to Mexico with the 75 K I already got. Once I'm back in Margaritaville, no one can find me. So who's the tool now?

SLAP!

—Huh? Who's the tool now, dude?

Rolf taps his finger hard between my eyes.

—Tool. Tool. Tool. Tool. Tool.

And his head explodes.

Sid gets off the chair, a whiff of smoke drifting from the barrel of his gun. I don't move. I can't. My face is pressed against the carpet, I can see Sandy under the bed. Frozen like me.

Sid takes a couple steps. He puts his foot on Rolf's shoulder and shoves him onto his back. I can see the little hole punched though Rolf's left eyebrow, and the big hole in the top of his head. The blood is pumping out, which means his heart must still be beating, which means he's still alive. But I guess I knew that already because of the way his mouth is opening and closing, like a fish drowning on dry land.

Sid grabs a pillow from the bed. He places it over Rolf's face, pushes the gun deep into it, and pulls the trigger. He takes the pillow away, looks at the hole where Rolf's upper lip used to meet his nose, then looks at the bloodstain on the back of the pillow. He drops the pillow back on Rolf's face and looks at me.

—Dude, you still got your buddy's car?

I nod. He points at Sandy.

—Get the girl, dude, we gotta get out of here.

I coax Sandy out from under the bed and she huddles against the wall, staring at Sid. He opens the door. I remember something.

—Hang on, Sid.

I go to Rolf's corpse, lift his shirt, and tear off the money belt.

—We may need this.

Sid nods.

—Yeah, dude, good thinking.

THE EL Cortez is a very cheap hotel; the walls are about as thin as you would expect. Sid did a good job deadening the sound of the second shot with that pillow, but the first one was more than loud enough. When we step into the hallway, every door on the floor slams shut simultaneously as our nosy neighbors duck back inside. Sid walks us down the hall to the fire stairs. He stays behind us, his gun in his hand, my guns in Sandy's Adidas bag draped over his shoulder.

The fire alarm sounds as soon as we open the door to the stairs. We're on the eighth floor; by the time we hit the fifth, a few people have started joining us on the stairs. I think about making a move in the confusion, but it will only get people hurt. Besides, I want to stay with Sandy. I want to get her out of this if I can.

We exit onto the Sixth Street sidewalk, into the middle of a crowd that has been evacuated from the casino. We walk through the mass of fixed-income seniors and hard-core lowball gamblers that inhabit the Cortez, and turn onto Fremont Street, past the main entrance to the hotel. Just as we make it onto the tarmac of the parking lot, I see two beefy security guards escorting a blue-haired woman in a nightdress. She sees us and points. One of our neighbors from the eighth floor. One of the guards lifts his walkie-talkie to his lips while the other one undoes the brass button on his blue blazer and starts to trot after us.

—Halt!

We walk around the corner of the wall that surrounds the parking lot. Sid tells us to stop. He turns and flattens against the wall. The security guard comes around the corner. Sid shoots him in the ear. Sandy screams and tries to run, but I grab her, knowing that he will shoot her down if I don't. He takes us to the Cavalier and opens the trunk. T is inside. His wrists and ankles are bound with wire, and a gag is stuffed in his mouth. There's more blood on his face than before, and a red-soaked pillowcase is wrapped around his calf where the crossbow bolt hit him. But he's conscious. When the lid pops open he lunges weakly at Sid, who brushes him off.

—Get him out of there.

I reach into the trunk, wrap my arms around him, boost him on to my shoulder in a fireman's carry and start walking to the Chrysler. Sirens are approaching. Sid makes Sandy open the trunk of the Chrysler. There's an old blanket inside, probably Hitler's. I lay T on top of it. His left eye is swollen shut and his right has blood in it, but he's looking at me, seeing me. The gag is made out of duct tape sealed across something stuffed in his mouth. His nose is swollen and clogged with blood. He's slowly suffocating. I look at Sid.

—I'm taking his gag off.

I rip the tape away before he can stop me, but he doesn't seem to care. He watches me, studying my moves. I pry a blood-slimed piece of cloth from T's mouth. He chokes and grabs my hand and hisses.

—Save me.

Sid pushes Sandy at the trunk.

—Her too.

She tries to take a step back, shaking her head from side to side, her hair flailing the air. I pull her to me and slip my arm under her legs, lifting her as if to take her across a threshold, and deposit her next to T. Her eyes are huge. She's trying to say something; another scream will burst from her mouth in a moment. I slam the lid closed, muffling her cry and cutting off T's guttural pleas.

Sid hands me the keys and we get in, me behind the wheel, him beside me, holding his gun. We pull out of the lot, away from the El Cortez, as emergency vehicles arrive. I catch a glimpse of the other security guard kneeling next to his dead partner, and then we are back on the Boulder Highway.

Sid wants a hideout.

—Dude, twenty-four hours of cruising around in that Cavalier? Talk about ill shit. Don't want to be on the road in a stolen car, don't want to risk trying to steal a new one. Don't want to park too long in one place and have people being all, *Hey, what's with the two dudes sitting around in that car for so long?* So cruise, park, call you, leave another message, cruise some more. And talk about golden tickets? Finding your cell number written on T's hand? Huge. I mean, dude, that's the only reason he's alive. I mean, if we didn't have a way of talking to you and threatening to kill him? What would be the point, right? So it all worked out. But if I don't get to sit still for a few hours, I'm gonna freak. Also, dude, like you probably noticed this by now, but I totally reek.

He's on a killing high again.

Feeling real.

And he wants to take a shower.

I take him to T's trailer.

I SLOW down as we get closer, and point at the Super 8 up the road.

—You seen any news?

—Naw, dude, told you: drive, park, call, drive some more.

—They found that car you stole.

—Yeah?

He points at the entrance to the trailer park.

—Think they found this place?

I shrug.

—Might have, if someone from the Super 8 saw you guys come over here. You want a place to rest, this is the best I can do.

—OK, dude, it's cool. Let's do it.

He hefts his gun.

—But, dude, if there are cops? It's, like, blaze of glory time.

I can tell he's into the idea. But there aren't any cops.

HE WON'T let T and Sandy out of the trunk. That's OK with me. It means they're out of the way.

Inside, we flip on the TV. The local stations are covering the parking-lot killing at the Cortez. They don't know about Rolf yet. Soon, someone will see the dreadlocks on Rolf's corpse and realize he's the guy in the police sketch going around, and then CNN will pick up the story.

Sid makes me come into the bathroom with him. I sit on the toilet. The crank I sniffed at the hotel is peaking. My knee is bouncing up and down while I grind my jaw. He stands in front of the door and starts to strip, his gun on the edge of the sink right next to him.

—That was hairy back at that chick's house, dude. Seriously, I didn't know what the play was gonna be, but when your dude showed up with his huge dog? That was whack. What kind of dog was that?

—English Mastiff.

—Dude, that was a big dog.

—Sid?

He puts his right foot up on the sink.

—Dude?

Why did you kill Rolf?

He starts to unlace his moccasin.

—Dude.

He pulls off the moccasin, switches feet, and starts to unlace the other one.

—He was being a dick.

He pulls off the other moc and stands there, looking at it and fiddling with the laces.

—He was, you know, pretty cool to me and my sis when I was a kid. And it was cool when I visited him in Mexico that time. And I thought it was awesome when he showed up and asked me for help. But. Shaaaw! All he was about was getting paid and getting high. And I started remembering things? Like, how, when he was hooking up with my sis, how he used to like to pick on me and be all Mr. Cool, like he *always* knew *everything*. And. And nothing was, like, *real* to him. Like, he wanted to kill you, right? After. After you left us in the desert, all he could talk about was how we'd find you and then get your money and then *I* was supposed to kill you? But. Dude. I. I didn't want to. I mean. Dude, I was pretty, I don't know, hurt by that, you splitting. But I understood. And even after you blew us off again and Rolf was all,

OK, *that's it, his ass is dead and fuckity-fuck-fuck-fuck,* and all. Even then? I kind of had an idea of what you're about and why you had to leave us.

He strips off his pants. Standing there in his Fruit of the Looms, looking like the skinny kid he is.

—I mean, it's like. I meant what I said before, about being a fan. And. More than that? A, like, a admirer? And I also felt like I understood, because you're like, all about *survival,* and I get that. Like, you're all, *Whatever I have to do to stay alive I'll do it and fuck everybody else.* And that makes total sense to me, and what Rolf was about didn't. Make sense. And I didn't want to kill you. Because. Because it seemed like being with you was real and honest, and being with Rolf was a lie. And I just want to lead a real life and do real things that affect people and change things. And then. Dude. While we were driving around? He was treating me like I did something wrong. He was all, *Where were you and why didn't you shoot him and what's wrong with you?* And at the hotel back there? He was, he was being such a dick. He was doing shit just like my dad used to do to me. Picking. Asking questions that he *so* already knew the answer to. Like to make himself feel big. And it totally doesn't matter what you say because he's gonna beat the shit out of you no matter what. I know all about that game and. And.

He rubs his eyes.

—And, I guess, I just realized that Rolf was full of shit, and you're not. So I shot him.

He pulls off his underwear.

—Sit on your hands.

I sit on my hands. He picks up the gun and pulls the bath curtain open and steps onto the mat between the toilet and the edge of the tub. Still facing me he reaches back and twists the hot water knob. The pipes wheeze and gurgle and spit a jet of scalding water onto his arm, shoulder, and neck.

He flinches away from the water, turning his head, and I kick him above the knee. His feet skid on the bath mat and he tumbles into the tub, clunking his head on the tile and falling into the stream of boiling water.

—Fuck! Fuuuuck!

He still has the gun. He's flopped in the tub sideways, his legs hanging out over the rim, blood starting to well from the cut on his forehead where he smacked it. He's trying to draw a bead on me and get out of the way of the scorching water. His skin is already turning bright red.

I drop from the toilet seat onto the floor as he pulls the trigger, exploding the toilet tank. He kicks at me as I reach through the billowing steam and grab hold of his gun hand. The long sleeves of my shirt give me a moment's protection, and then the water has soaked through and is burning my arms, droplets splashing onto my face and eyes as I try to grip his slippery, naked skin.

He's flailing at me with his feet, kicking me in the ribs as I lean over the edge of the tub, one hand holding his wrist and the other peeling his finger back from the trigger, bending it. He's slapping at the hot water knob with his free hand, trying to turn it off, but he twists it the wrong way and it pounds down on us, scalding the side of my face. His finger snaps and I bend it until it's pressed flat against the back of his hand. He lands a kick on the side of my head that sends me falling backward into the cold toilet water pooling on the floor.

The sudden cold makes me feel just how bad my burns are and I scream. Sid's mouth is wide open, but a whistling rush of air is the only sound coming out. He pulls his legs into the tub and gets them underneath his body and starts to stand up. The water is still crashing on him and he's twisting the knob with his left hand. I reach back into the tub and grab one of his legs. He points his gun at me, but his broken trigger finger dangles uselessly. The stream of water fades to a dribble and I yank on his leg and he falls back into the tub, swinging the gun at me on the way down and cracking me in the skull.

The world flips.

The world rights itself.

The gun has bounced out of Sid's hand and landed in a puddle of steaming water at the hair-clogged drain. Sid paws at it with his lobster-red left hand and shoves his mauled right hand in my face, trying to hold me at bay. His broken finger slips into my open mouth and I bite it. He screeches and slaps his left hand against my right ear, setting off an explosion of pain. I swing my right arm up in an arc, wrapping around his left arm, bring it down, and squeeze my elbow into my side, pinning his arm in my armpit. He's on his back now writhing in two inches of seething water. His right hand is squirting blood into my mouth, the other is trapped, and his legs are useless inside the tub. I punch him in the face with my left fist, and throw myself on top of him in the tub.

He's pinned beneath me. He pulls hard on his left arm and it starts to slip free. The flesh at the break in his finger is starting to tear between my teeth. I wrap my left hand around his throat and let his left arm free and he grabs my lower lip and pulls down, trying to free his other hand from my jaws. I reach beyond his head into the puddle of hot water and wrap my fingers around the butt of his pistol. Too late, he realizes what is happening and grabs at my right arm. I lean all my weight into my left arm, squashing his throat. His mouth flies open and I shove the gun inside of it until I feel the tip of the barrel hit the back of his throat and he starts to gag on it.

I pull the trigger. Water drains from the new hole in the bottom of the tub.

WHEN I open the trunk Sandy hits me in the arm with the lug wrench. I take it from her and we get T into the back seat. I give the keys to Sandy and she gets behind the wheel and drives us to Tim's apartment.

The only place left to hide.

SANDY PLAYS nurse. She gets us inside, puts T in Tim's bed, fills the tub with cold water, and cuts the clothing from my body with a scissors from Tim's desk. Once I'm in the tub, she empties all the ice trays into it.

My right arm and hand are raw and red and dotted with white blisters. My knees are also scalded, but not as bad. I know the right side of my face and neck are bad, but I can feel the pain, so the tissue damage can't be too deep. My vision is speckled with black dots and I don't remember what happened right after I shot a hole in the back of Sid's mouth. I try to remember some details and the black dots blur into a single huge dot and I find myself choking on ice water. Sandy pulls me up, out of the tub before I drown. I get up and stand on the linoleum floor while she blots my skin dry as gently as she can. I think it's a safe bet that Sid aggravated my concussion when he smacked me with his gun.

There's no burn cream in Tim's bathroom, but there is a bottle of aloe. We smear that over my scalded skin. There's nothing to use as a burn bandage except some Saran Wrap from the kitchen. Sandy carefully wraps it around my knees, arm, shoulder, and neck. My face and hand will have to go without. She drapes a sheet around me like a toga and helps me into Tim's room and I sit on the edge of the bed. T's awake.

—My dog.

—I'm sorry, T.

—My fucking dog.

—I know.

—Gonna kill the fuckers.

Too late.

Sandy has already stripped him and wrapped a towel around his calf. It's still bleeding. My hands are shaking from the speed and I don't think I could hold a needle in my burned right hand anyway. And I could just black out again at any moment. Sandy shakes her head when I ask if she thinks she can sew him up. We have to stop the bleeding.

I give T two Percs and he goes out. I tell Sandy to try and clean up his face and I go in to the kitchen. I want two Percs. Really, I want all the Percs in the world, but I'll have to live with the one I took back at El Cortez. In the kitchen I find a serving spoon. I turn one of the stove's gas burners to high and set the handle of the spoon in the flame and go back to the room with a whiskey bottle. We unwrap T's leg and bathe it in Tullamore Dew and I have Sandy hold a clean towel around it while I go for the spoon. I hold it, the glowing handle sticking out of a wet rag, and press it into one end of the hole in T's calf. He jerks and I tell Sandy to hold the leg tighter and she gags at the sound and the smell and then it's over. Then we do it again, cauterizing the other end of the hole, as well.

That's all I can do for my friend. There's a murdered body at his home and his car was seen speeding away from the scene of another murder and soon the cops will be after him, and when they catch him they will send his ass back to California and lock it up for the rest of his life.

So he has to go now.

SANDY DRESSES T in a pair of Tim's shorts and a Les Paul Live at the Iridium sweatshirt. I find a pair of overalls that touch as little of my burned skin as possible.

T comes to as we slide him into the backseat of the Chrysler.

—What the fuck?

—Hey, T.

—What the fuck?

—Yeah, I got that.

Sandy gets behind the wheel and buckles herself in. I sit in the passenger seat, but don't close the door. T focuses his good eye on me.

—You look all fucked-up, superstar.

—It's going around.

—I wanna go home.

—I'm sorry, T, you can't.

—Fuck you.

—I'm sorry about your dog, T.

—Said, fuck you.

—Thanks for helping me. I.

I shake my head, unable to finish. He reaches out a hand, puts it on my arm, and closes his eye.

—Fuck. You.

His hand slides off and he's asleep again.

I close the door and go stand next to Sandy's open window.

—You sure?

She runs a finger around the steering wheel and nods.

—Yeah. My fault he's all fucked-up, anyway.

—OK. Just find a place out of the way, over the state line where the cops won't look for him. Arizona, not California.

—I'll find someplace safe.

—And get rid of the car as soon as.

—I will.

I show her the money belt, now stained with the blood of three men.

—Take what you need and give the rest to him.

—What about you?

—I don't need money anymore.

I hand her the belt.

—Once he's safe from the cops, go find a lawyer for yourself. You'll be fine if you.

A car comes down the street and I duck to avoid the headlights as it passes. She points at Tim's apartment.

—Get back inside.

—Yeah.

I touch her shoulder with my left hand. She brushes it off and starts the car and turns on the headlights and pulls away from the curb. And just like early yesterday morning, T and Sandy are driving away, leaving me alone. I watch until they turn the corner, and then go up-stairs.

I GAVE Sandy some of the Percs to feed to T for his pain. I sit on Tim's couch and spread the ten Percs I kept on the coffee table, right next to the Anaconda and Danny's 9 mm.

IT'S GOING to be easy.

Doing this is going to be so easy.

*   *   *

DYLAN WILL come here to this address. He'll come himself because he won't trust anyone else to get his money. He may bring muscle, but he'll come. I don't care about muscle. I just need Dylan here.

At first I wanted him here so I could threaten him and force him to make a call, make him tell his men to back off. And then I could kill him. But that's not the smart thing to do. I've finally figured out the smart thing. The smart thing is for me to die.

But I need him here for it to work. I need him to see my corpse with his own eyes. He'll get the message. It's over. The money is lost and it's over. He'll call in his dogs and leave Mom and Dad alone. Killing people costs a lot of money and it involves risk. Dylan is an asshole, but he's also a businessman. After all, who's gonna drop a nuclear bomb on their enemy when the enemy is already dead?

This is the smart thing. I've thought about it, and I'm sure.

I could use a gun, but I don't have the guts. Funny that. So I swallow the Percs one by one, washing them down with Tim's Tullamore Dew.

It's nice, not having to worry anymore. Not having to worry about staying in control, about keeping it all together, about what to do next. I can just take these pills and they'll do all the worrying for me. I love you Mom and Dad. But I don't want to hurt people anymore.

—HOLA?

—Pedro, it's me.

Silence.

—Pedro?

—Si?

—Have you seen the news, do you know?

—Si. I know.

—I should have told you.

Silence.

—How's Leo?

—He will be OK.

—The police?

—We will be OK.

—OK.

  Silence.

—How's Bud? Is he?

—The cat is fine. The hijos love the cat.

—Good.

  I hear a voice in the background, Ofelia. Pedro covers the mouth-piece and says something to her and then comes back on.

—I must go.

—Yeah, I'm sorry.

—No problema.

—Good-bye, Pedro.

—Via con Dios. Henry.

  I hang up. My hand goes to my neck, but I've lost the holy medal he gave me. Where? Doesn't matter. Not likely that any saints are going to be looking out for me these days.

  I probably shouldn't have made that call. But it was the closest I could get to calling home. I look at the clock. How long since I took the pills? How much longer will it take? My eyes drift shut. I open them. Not long.

  I flick on the TV to pass the time. I flip past CNN and ESPN. Cartoon Network is doing a twenty-four-hour marathon of Christmas shows. I settle in to watch.

  I black out.

I'M SITTING on Tim's couch. The TV is on. It's a cartoon. *A Charlie Brown Christmas.* It's the part where Linus stands on the stage and the spotlight turns on and he explains the meaning of Christmas. My favorite part.

—Hank.

  I turn my head. Tim is sitting next to me on the edge of the couch.

—Hey, Timmy.

—Thank God, man. I wasn't sure you would ever wake up.

I point at the TV.

—Let's watch this.

—OK.

We watch Linus finish his speech and then a commercial comes on. I turn back to Tim.

—Where ya been, Timmy?

—New York.

—No kidding. How's the old neighborhood?

He shrugs.

—The same. You know.

—Yeah.

He reaches out a hand to touch me, but doesn't.

—Hank, you look pretty messed up.

—Well, yeah.

—Maybe we should do something.

—Sure.

—And I think I should get you out of here.

—Sure.

He stands up. I hold up my finger.

—Hang on just a sec, I got something for you.

I reach out my burned right hand and pick up the Anaconda. He takes a step back.

—Hank.

The revolver feels like it's on fire. I point it at his stomach.

—Don't worry, Timmy. This is gonna hurt me a lot more than it's gonna hurt you.

And it does hurt. The huge weapon bucks in my hand and the pain flares up my arm. But it probably hurts him more.

A LOUD noise wakes me up.

I'm sitting on Tim's couch. The TV is on. It's a cartoon. *A Charlie*

Brown Christmas. It's the part where Charlie tries to decorate his piti-
ful tree and it collapses and he thinks he's killed it, but then his friends
come and make it beautiful. It's the end.

—Hank.

I look at the floor. Tim is sprawled there, a huge hole in his stomach,
his hands pressed over it, trying to keep the blood inside, but it's
spilling everywhere. Something is hurting my hand. I look. I'm holding
Wade's Anaconda. I drop it.

—Timmy?

—Oh shit. Oh shit, Hank.

Nonononono.

I slide to the floor.

—Timmy.

—What? Hank? What?

—Oh. Oh. OK, we can. I can.

—Hank. I did.

—What?

—I did what you told me. I did.

—It's OK, man, just be.

—I went. Ohgodohgodohgod. This guy from, from New York was, I
heard this guy was coming. A Russian. Hank, there's a Russian.

—I know. Shhhh. I know.

—And I did what you said. And I. You told me if anyone came to. You
told me.

—I did. I know. It's OK.

I'm pressing my hands into the wound, but there's too much of it to
cover.

—You told me to get out if anyone came, and I did, I took the money
and I.

—Of course you did, you're a good friend, Timmy, I knew you'd.

—And my beeper. Ohshiiiiit. I'm such a idiot. You were gonna call my
beeper. But.

—It's OK.

—No.

—OK.

—I'm a idiot and I forgot the, I forgot my beeper.

Tears are pouring out of his eyes, his teeth and tongue and lips are sheened with blood.

—And the news, I saw it, I saw they said you were here in Vegas and.

He breathes a couple times.

—It's starting not to hurt as much, Hank.

—Good, that's good.

—You were in Vegas and, but I didn't know how to find you or call you.

He winces and blood wells up out of his mouth and over his chin. He spits.

—I came back. I came here. I thought. And you were here, Hank, and it was all OK.

—I know. You did what I told you. That's all, Timmy, you just did what I told you.

—And, Hank. The money, it's OK.

—No.

—The money is OK.

—Don't, I don't wanna.

—No, it's OK.

—I don't wanna know, I don't wanna.

He's nodding his head up and down, still talking, but there's no air coming out of his throat anymore. Only blood. He tries to talk through the blood, tries to say words made out of blood, but there's too much of it.

I COVER Tim with a blanket.

I WILL be the last one to die.

And could it have ever ended any other way?

For the last time, I close my eyes.

*   *   *

I OPEN my eyes.

Something is in my mouth, stuck all the way to the back of my throat. I picture the barrel of Sid's .45 stuck deep in his mouth, him gagging on the steel. I throw up. Someone pulls my head forward so I puke between my legs, and then the thing is back in my mouth and I puke again. And one more time. I fall back onto the couch, gasping.

—Here.

A glass of water. I spill some in my mouth and swish it around and spit.

—Drink it.

I take a swallow and cough.

—I feel terrible.

—Yes, I would imagine that to be the case.

A voice I don't know. A Russian voice. I look up.

He's in his fifties, close-cropped salt-and-pepper hair and beard, an expensive-looking gray suit. He's wiping the finger he shoved down my throat on a silk handkerchief. He points at Tim's body.

—Did he tell you where the money is?

—No.

—Hm.

He leans over and looks at my pile of vomit.

—How many pills did you swallow?

—Ten.

He covers his finger with the handkerchief and sifts through the mess.

—Yes, they are all here. That is good.

My guns aren't on the coffee table anymore. I look around the room.

—I've hidden them.

—Kill me.

He drops the handkerchief so that it covers the vomit.

—And waste my efforts? No.

—I need to die.

—No, Henry, you need to live. It is very important that you live.

—Who are you?

—David Dolokhov. I am Mikhail Dolokhov's uncle.

—I don't know.

Oh, fuck. I close my eyes.

—Mickey.

—Yes. I am Mickey's uncle. His father's brother.

DYLAN IS a liar.

—Dylan Lane is a liar, Henry. He is a debtor and a welsher and a liar and he does not do the things he promises he will do for his partners.

I'm sitting on one of the barstools in front of the kitchen counter. David Dolokhov is making coffee and toast.

—When Dylan needed money for his start-up, he went to the usual places. He went to California, to Sand Hill Road where the venture capitalists are, and asked them for money. But they did not give it to him. So he went to the banks. But he had problems with the SEC and his credit was bad. So he went to his family and friends. But they had given him money before and he had lost all of it. So he came to us. And we gave him the money. And with our money, he was able to attract more money, because money loves money. And at first, we were very happy. His company had an IPO. Very exciting. The stock. The stock, it topped at one sixty-four and one half! We were very happy. But Dylan? He is a greedy man. He is bound by laws of the SEC that prevent him from selling his shares just then, and he is greedy. Rather than using his new leverage to finance a loan to pay us back, what does he do? He uses the leverage to invest in commodities. A long story short, he trades on margin and the market craters and his margins are called and his personal fortune is destroyed. And his company's own stock becomes valueless. And when we encourage him to sell off the company's assets to repay our money? There are no assets. The company has been a shell game all along. So now, Dylan Lane is in the shit.

The coffeemaker beeps and he picks up the pot. He pours two cups and hands one to me. I lift it with my unburned left hand and bring it to my lips and sip, feeling the heat radiate into the burns on the right side of my face.

—So now Dylan hustles. He hustles this and he hustles that and he makes just enough as a hustler of this and that to make his interest payments. But he has dreams of being a big man again, and he is always looking for an opportunity to make enough money to pay us back. And then he hears the story of Henry Thompson and the four-and-a-half million dollars. And he comes to me with a proposal. He will, as he says, *Buy the debt*. But with what I ask? He still has no money. He will buy it, he says, on credit, and pay it off along with his own debt when he has the money.

The toast pops up. He butters it and cuts the slices diagonally and puts them on a plate in front of me.

—Eat.

I take a small bite and chew. It hurts.

—I ask Dylan his plan to get the money and he tells me that he has a man who will watch your parents and tell him if you appear. Well, this is bullshit. This is a bullshit plan. And I tell him no. And he leaves. And then nothing. Until a year passes. And my nephew is killed in Mexico.

He wipes the kitchen counter clean, tops off his own coffee, then comes around the counter to my side and sits on the other stool.

—My nephew, Henry. My nephew was an asshole. But his mother, the woman I swore to my brother I would care for, she loved him very much. And so I personally go to Mexico to discover what has happened. I arrive in Mexico last week, on Thursday. I go to Chichén Itzá and see where my nephew died, and find out that when he fell, a man was with him on the pyramid. I go to the police and talk to the two men who have investigated the death, and they show me a photograph they have taken of you.

He widens his eyes and spreads his hands open. *Shock*.

—A coincidence! But not so much perhaps. I suspect my asshole nephew was in some way seeking to extort the money from you. I whisper in the ears of the policemen. I tell them a tale of treasure, and I promise them a share if they will arrest you and bring you to me. And they try. And you disappear.

He hangs his head and shakes it. *Such sadness*.

—But all is not lost. Because, Henry, because I know you have a friend. I know, we know, that someone helped you in New York, and we believe it is this same man who has recently moved to Las Vegas. I make phone calls. I call people we know from business and find out where this man is, and I make arrangements to meet him. You are running, Henry. Where will you run to, but to a friend? Or to family? I remember Dylan's man who lives on your parents' street. I look in my memory and I find the man's name and I call him and offer him money to "keep his eyes peeled." And I learn something. He tells me that Dylan has already paid him to watch. For a year Dylan has paid him. Dylan had asked for permission to pursue the money, and he had been denied, but he has paid the man anyway. Greedy. Liar. So I pay the man more money, and he does not tell Dylan that I know of this betrayal. And now, I fly to Las Vegas myself. And two things happen. Your friend in Las Vegas disappears, and the man in California calls me. He has seen you.

He holds his coffee cup up in a toast.

—And I tell him to call Dylan. Because, Henry, because you are a dangerous man. You have killed other dangerous men. There will be risks in dealing with you. I will let Dylan take those risks, and if he gets the money, I will take it from him. Because he is not a dangerous man.

—He has men.

—No. He does not.

I tear a corner off of a piece of toast.

—He is a liar, Henry. He will have told you that he has dangerous men, but he neither has the money to hire such men, nor the knowledge of where to find such specialists to do the things he will have threatened. To kill your mother and father at a whim. It is hard to kill people, Henry. The men who do it well are rare and prized. You should know that.

I push the plate of toast away. David Dolokhov pushes it back in front of me.

—Eat.

I take another painful bite.

—And now there is a great deal of farce, a great deal of following and losing and trailing. And new crazy men arriving to kill. And confusion. But when you run from California, I stay in Las Vegas to be near the home of your friend, where I think you may run to. And you do. I was here, Henry, watching when you came with your new friend and the large hound. I watched, and I realized something. You were searching.

He points an index finger at the ceiling. *Eureka!*

—You do not have the money. It is your friend all along. He has had the money, and now that you have come for it, he has run away so to keep it. And now I will watch what you do and you will find him for me. But that is not altogether correct, is it?

—No.

I tell him about sending Tim the money. He shakes his head again.

—And he took it to hide it from us?

—Yeah.

—And he came back for you, into the teeth of danger.

—Yeah.

—And you killed him.

—Yeah.

He nods. *This is the way these things happen.*

—He was a good friend.

—Yeah.

—But he did not tell you where the money is? Do not answer. Why else would you kill yourself? Or try. And what luck! I had lost you, Henry. I lost you almost as soon as I had found you. I fell asleep in my car outside of the Sam's Town casino. And when I awoke? You were gone. I did not know where to look. But I still had Dylan. If you found the money, you would take it to him, and, so, good enough. And then a phone call from a man named Terry, an unreliable man. But I go to him anyway. And what do I find? Mayhem. Bloodshed. Grotesque.

He closes his eyes. *That such things should be.*

He opens his eyes.

—And so what now am I to do? Nothing. I can only wait and hope that you will contact Dylan and he will lead me to you. But! If I must wait, I will wait here, outside this building, and see perhaps if your friend makes a return. And last night. *You* come. With a woman and your friend with the hound, and you are hurt. And there is news on the radio of violence, and I know you have been in it. And I wait until you are alone. But still you are a dangerous man, and so I call for help. And while I wait, I see your friend appear! And he goes inside. And I wait, thinking that this will be it, the money is near and you will lead me to it, but no one comes out. A man arrives. My dangerous man. We come in here.

He turns on the stool and looks at Tim's body. *And we find this.*

—My dangerous man takes your guns and goes outside. And I?

He leans toward me.

—I save your life, Henry. To find out where the money is. And you do not know where the money is. But I tell you this story. Why, Henry? Why are you still alive if you do not know where the money is?

I look at Tim's corpse. Blood has soaked through the blanket that I used to cover him. Why am I still alive? Why has God not come out of his heaven to destroy me?

—I don't know.

He smiles. His teeth are perfect.

—You are alive because you are a dangerous man. And I have uses for dangerous men.

DYLAN SHOWS a little later.

He knocks on the door and I tell him to come in and he comes in and he looks like shit. He's wearing the same outfit as when I first saw him, but it's rumpled and he's unshaven and has dark rings under his eyes. But he's excited too. He's been living on stress and fear, hoping that this gamble will pay off. And now it's payoff time.

It's dark outside. I've left only one light on and moved the coffee table over the bloodstain where Tim's body was. Dylan stands in the open doorway, looking at me. He licks his lips and points back outside.

—I have someone with me, Hank.

Liar.

I nod.

He takes a step into the apartment.

—Anyway, I *know* it's not necessary to tell you that, I'm just making a point.

He closes the door. I wave him into the living room. He's nervous about coming farther inside. But he's greedy, so he does.

—Well, Hank. *You* look a little worse for wear.

I nod. He nods back.

—*So.* Shall we?

I point at the cardboard box next to Tim's stereo. He walks over to the box and opens it and sees the big chunks of Styrofoam inside. I pull the Anaconda from between the sofa cushions and point it at him.

Dylan raises a finger as if to make a final point.

—*Your parents,* Hank, think of *your parents.*

I do.

I love you, Mom and Dad.

And I prove it.

DAVID DOLOKHOV'S dangerous man comes out of the bathroom and takes the gun from me and tosses it on Dylan's body. He takes my arm and leads me to the door and down the stairs and up the block to a silver Lexus. I get in the front passenger seat. The dangerous man nods at David Dolokhov, who sits in the driver's seat, and then walks away. Dolokhov starts the car and drives down the street.

—My daughter wants a nose job. She is sixteen and she wants a nose job. Why? There is nothing wrong with her nose. She has my nose. Is there anything wrong with my nose?

I look at his flat and crooked nose, and shake my head. He smiles.

—Of course there is not. For me, this is a perfect nose. But for my daughter? She has a point. And I love her. So for Christmas, I will get her the best nose money can buy.

He stops at an intersection, looks both ways, and turns left.

—I tell you this to warn you, Henry. Because the truth is, the man who will work on you? The man who will change your face? I would not let this man near my daughter's nose.

THE NEXT day Miami gets pummeled by Oakland. The final score is too embarrassing to believe. But in the late game, I get to watch Detroit run back the first kickoff of sudden-death overtime for a game-winning TD over the Jets. And that's fun. So next week the Dolphins and the Jets will square off in a winner-takes-all game for the division.

The motel is in Henderson, I think. The room is big. It has to be for the pieces of rented hospital equipment to fit. The doctor comes and looks at my face and says we should wait until the burns heal, but Dolokhov says we need to hurry. So the doctor gives me something to make me sleep.

I sleep.

EPILOGUE

DECEMBER 25, 2003

Final Day of the

Regular Season

t's Christmas Sunday.

I am not home.

The doctor stops by to look at my bandaged face. He nods a few times and makes a joke about not being able to unwrap me yet, and then he leaves.

My face feels swollen and hot, but I have a button in one hand that I can push when the pain is too much. I push it quite a bit. In my other hand, I have the remote control for the TV. I use it to see things. I have been seeing things all week.

I see a computer graphic, a map with the faces of dead people, and a series of lines tracing their deaths to me.

I see my friends in Mexico. Pedro on his front porch, shaking his head and denying that he ever knew me. He looks OK and I'm happy to see that, but it also makes me sad because it reminds me that I will never swim again in the Caribbean and have to sit on my porch afterward with cigarettes in my ears. And, behind Pedro, I think I see one of his children in the background playing with a cat. And that makes me smile. It hurts to smile, so I stop.

I see Leslie and Cassidy being interviewed, and someone asking Cassidy if she was scared of me, and her saying that I seemed nice. I liked you too, Cassidy.

I see Danny explaining how he felt it was his duty to pursue me when he realized who I was. Telling the story of how he trailed me north on the I-5 and lost me and went home and found my parents' address online. He starts to talk about how he had "patrolled" their neighborhood and saw me with Wade and attempted to "apprehend" me. His lawyer shuts him up before he can say any more.

I see the funeral of Sheriff's Deputy T.T. Fischer.

I see Wade's widow, Stacy, with her kids. They are all crying, the kids. Stacy is cursing me and saying that if she had known what a monster I would turn out to be, she would have killed me when we were in school together. Her kids are beautiful. You have beautiful kids, Wade.

I see Rolf's body being removed from the El Cortez.

Sid's body at the trailer.

Dylan's body taken from Tim's apartment.

Timmy.

So many bodies.

I see the APB they put out on T's car, and the California booking photo of him that they put up on the screen. I see the discovery of the "Death House," aka Sandy's house. But I don't see T or Sandy. Stay low, guys. Stay low.

And I see Mom and Dad on their porch, begging me to please come home and turn myself in. And the TV shows them over and over, and every time I see them, I push the painkilling button and everything goes away.

I also see David Dolokhov's dangerous man. He stays with me in an adjoining room, and I watch him all the time. I watch him to see what a dangerous man is like.

This one is medium tall and has a potbelly and very little hair. He's a bit over forty and wears those cheap reading glasses you get at drugstores. When he talks, which is never very often, he has a Slavic accent, but it's very different from Dolokhov's. He also drinks a lot of beer without seeming to ever get drunk and, based on the tunes I hear coming out of his room, he's a big R&B fan. He did me a favor and picked up a copy of *East of Eden* for me. I lost the one I had in Mexico and never got to finish it. Of course, I'm too doped-up to read, but it was a nice thing for him to do.

He comes into my room now and hooks up a new bag to the IV needle stuck in my arm. Sucking on a straw hurts and I can't chew at all, so I'm getting fed through a tube for now. I'm also not allowed to smoke, but as long as I have the button in my right hand, that doesn't bother me much. Maybe I'll quit.

When the dangerous man is done, he gestures, asking silently if I'm OK. I give him a little thumbs-up and he nods. I can't tell if he's quiet by nature or if he's simply gotten into the spirit of my own silence. He goes back to his room, leaving the connecting door open, and turns on the radio.

I watch him because I want to know what a dangerous man is like. Because that is what I am becoming. That is what I will be. That is my deal with David Dolokhov.

I will be his new dangerous man. And for my services, I will be paid. David Dolokhov will pay me with the lives of my mother and father.

So, as it turns out, I will not buy their lives with dollars.

I will buy them with violence.

"Purple Rain" starts to play in the next room. I flip away from the news. Tired of it. A week without a new dead body and they're running out of things to say.

The Dolphins-Jets game is on. But I don't watch it. I'm not a hunted man anymore. I'm a found man. I don't have to hide myself any longer. So screw football. Pitchers and catchers report in eight weeks.

I turn off the TV, and hit the pain button.

ACKNOWLEDGMENTS

My gratitude to Simon Lipskar, Mark Tavani, and Maura Teitelbaum for professional support and friendship.

Thanks to Dr. Cybele Fishman, who generously gave her time to discuss the dos and don'ts of impromptu plastic surgery.

Virginia Smith continues as my first reader, trusted critic, and wife. I have no words to thank her.

CHARLIE HUSTON's previous novel, *Caught Stealing*, was the first in a trilogy about Hank Thompson. He lives in Manhattan with his wife, the actress Virginia Louise Smith.